John Connolly was born in Dublin in 1968. His debut – EVERY DEAD THING – swiftly launched him right into the front rank of thriller writers, and all his subsequent novels have been *Sunday Times* bestsellers. BOOKS TO DIE FOR, which he edited with Declan Burke, was the winner of the 2013 Anthony, Agatha and Macavity awards for Best Non-Fiction work. He is the first non-American writer to win the US Shamus award and the first Irish writer to win an Edgar award. www.johnconnollybooks.com

Praise for THE UNQUIET:

'This man's so good, it's terrifying . . . a quieter, subtler, more reflective way of scaring us into shivering wrecks . . . His gift for instilling terror is undimmed . . . Connolly operates in the terrain between unease and horror and does so without resorting to hysteria. He writes about evil lyrically, with biblical fervour. At times he approaches the spiritual and the super-natural without falling into the abyss of total impossibility.'

Marcel Berlins, *The Times*

'Connolly handles the unspeakable with consummate ease.'

Daily Mirror

'Originality in story and style is what makes Connolly stand out from the thriller pack. *The Unquiet* is plotted and paced not to break your neck, like those of his rivals in the business, but to efficiently crush every bone in your body.'

Daily Sport

'John Connolly draws their shady presence into his rich, southern Gothic style which assumes evil to be an omnipresent, corrosi Parker seeks truth and discovers pain. . *Unquiet* a thril *agazine*

'Connolly's greatest skill lies in his descriptions of the bad guys . . . The description of their crimes are where Connolly is at his chilling best, and it is his attention to detail that makes them so terrifying and so believable.'

Sunday Business Post, Dublin

'Connolly writes convincingly of thugs, criminals and the supernatural, and Parker is a classic character who walks straight and tall like someone from the old west, and the reader knows all will be well once he arrives in town. *The Unquiet* just won't let you put it down as the plot careers across the pages like a runaway train. Excellent!'

Mark Timlin, *Independent on Sunday*

'Eerie, cozy, seductive. He has a way of moving in and out of tender and violent, of warm and cold, like I haven't seen before . . . He describes and writes like a poet. Each paragraph ends with a trail of magic dust behind it – the details are so rich, vivid, nothing is left out.'

Mark Kozelek
(of Red House Painters/Sun Kil Moon)
Mojo Magazine

Also by John Connolly

The Charlie Parker Stories
Every Dead Thing
Dark Hollow
The Killing Kind
The White Road
The Reflecting Eye (Novella in the Nocturnes Collection)
The Black Angel
The Unquiet
The Lovers
The Whisperers
The Burning Soul
The Wrath of Angels
The Wolf in Winter

Other Works
Bad Men
The Book of Lost Things

Short Stories
Nocturnes
The Wanderer in Unknown Realms (eBook)

The Samuel Johnson Stories (For Young Adults)
The Gates
Hell's Bells
The Creeps

The Chronicles of the Invaders (*For Young Adults*)
Conquest (*with Jennifer Ridyard*)
Empire (*with Jennifer Ridyard*)

Non-Fiction (as editor, with Declan Burke)
Books to Die For: The World's Greatest Mystery Writers on the
World's Greatest Mystery Novels

JOHN CONNOLLY

THE UNQUIET

HODDER

First published in Great Britain in 2007 by Hodder & Stoughton
An Hachette UK company

This paperback edition published in 2015

5

A CIP catalogue record for this title is available from the British Library

ISBN 978 1 444 70474 7

Printed and bound by Clays Ltd, St Ives plc

Typeset in Plantin Light by Palimpsest Book Production Ltd, Falkirk, Stirlingshire

Hodder & Stoughton policy is to use papers that are natural,
renewable and recyclable products and made from wood grown in
sustainable forests. The logging and manufacturing processes are expected
to conform to the environmental regulations of the country of origin.

Hodder & Stoughton Ltd
338 Euston Road
London NW1 3BH

www.hodder.co.uk

For Emily Bestler, with much affection,
and with thanks for persevering with me.

Acknowledgements

Grateful acknowledgement is made for permission to reprint from the following copyrighted works:

When in Rome by Nickel Creek: 'When in Rome' written by Chris Thyle © 2005 Mad German Music (ASCAP) and Queen's Counsel Music (ASCAP). All rights reserved. Used by permission.

'John Wayne Gacy Jr.'. Written by Sufjan Stevens. Appears courtesy of New Jerusalem Music Publishing.

Extract from *The Hollow Men* © T. S. Eliot. Taken from the book Collected Poems 1909–1962 by T. S. Eliot, used by permission of Faber & Faber, United Kingdom on behalf of the T. S. Eliot Estate.

Excerpt from *Skunk Hour* from COLLECTED POEMS by Robert Lowell, copyright © 2003 by Harriet Lowell and Sheridan Lowell. Reprinted by permission of Farrar, Straus and Giroux, LLC.

Extract from *Dirge* by Stevie Smith. Used by permission of the Executors of James MacGibbon Estate.

Extract from the poem *Buffalo Bill's* is reprinted from COMPLETE POEMS 1904–1962 by E. E. Cummings, edited by George J. Firmage, by permission of W.W. Norton & Company. Copyright © 1991 by the Trustees for the E. E. Cummings Trust and George James Firmage.

INTRODUCTION

I'm often asked if I plan out my novels before I begin writing them, as I think it's generally assumed that mystery novels resemble clockwork mechanisms, requiring meticulous design if they are to function properly. But, as in any genre of writing, there are as many approaches to the form as there are individual writers. Among mystery writers, the two most extreme examples I can name are Jeffery Deaver and James Lee Burke.

Deaver is a meticulous planner, constructing outlines that may be fifty or sixty thousand words long, with the twists and turns carefully tested in advance to ensure that the book runs true. Burke, on the other hand, will finish a novel on Thursday, and on Friday will sit down at his desk, type the words 'Chapter One' and wait to see what emerges. Burke believes that the book is already in there – or out there – somewhere, and if he sits at his desk and puts in the hours, it will find its way on to the page.

I suspect that pretty much every other writer falls somewhere between those two extreme poles, and I'm closer to the Burke end of the scale than the Deaver. I tend to know how a book will open, and I may have an idea of one or two incidents that will occur somewhere down the line, but the end remains murky at best. In that sense, my experience of writing the first draft is not dissimilar to the reader's experience of reading the finished book: it's a process of discovery, with the nature of the book slowly revealing itself as it progresses.

Occasionally, though, something will land in a writer's lap that either causes a reconsideration of the direction of the book, or influences its construction in an entirely unanticipated way. This is what happened when I was mulling over *The Unquiet*. I knew that, after *The Black Angel*, which was epic in scope, I wanted to write a book that was more subdued, and restricted itself to the state of Maine. (I find that each novel I write is a reaction to the one that went before it, so a very fast-paced book is likely to be followed by one that takes its time, or a book with a significant level of violence and action will probably spawn a successor in which the violence is minimal.) I had also decided that *The Unquiet* would deal with the subject of child abuse, but would do so in the subtlest of ways. I wanted no explicit details, for I did not intend to leave myself open to accusations of exploitation. Actually, my interest lay more in those who have to deal with the abused and their abusers, in the difficulties presented by such cases and the effects on the men and women who investigate them.

So the book was percolating away in my mind, probably as I was working on the edits for *The Book of Lost Things*, when I chanced upon an exhibition at the Center for Maine History in Portland. It contained, as I recall, items from a private collection of Maine folk art and general artifacts, and resembled the contents of a junkyard, or someone's attic. Among them were some of the possessions of a man named Dave 'The Guesser' Glovsky (1909-1997), of whom I had not heard until that moment. Dave the Guesser operated a booth at the Palace Playland at Old Orchard Beach in Maine from 1949 until the 1990s, at which, for a dollar a time, he would guess a punter's weight, or occupation, or make of car. He kept a weighing scales in his booth so that the accuracy of his guesses could be checked – assuming someone was willing to have his or her weight publicly broadcast to an amused crowd on a sunny day – and there is even a photograph of him guessing Louis Armstrong's weight when Satchmo played Old Orchard Beach in the 1950s. He remained married to the same woman, Blanche, for 66 years, and attributed his enduring good health to an absence of worries. 'Worries,' he once warned his son-in-law, Art Hale, 'will kill you.'

And suddenly I had the opening of *The Unquiet*: Dave the Guesser, standing on the boardwalk at Old Orchard Beach, realizing that his time is drawing to a close, and being approached by a man who invites Dave to guess his occupation. Except Dave doesn't want to guess it, doesn't want to speak it aloud, because he can smell blood on this man, and knows that he's looking at a killer.

As with real crime cases, I'm naturally reluctant to use actual individuals in my books, or certainly not without their permission. Dave the Guesser had been dead for five or six years by that point, and I briefly considered creating a character based upon him, but then I thought that it would be terribly unfair to steal aspects of this man's identity when he was, by all accounts, such a singular individual. Instead I hoped that his appearance at the start of the book might stand as a tribute to him, and I was gratified at the number of people that contacted me to say they remembered him, and was even happier to correct those who assumed he was my invention.

So the opening of this book is one of two elements in it to which readers often refer. The other is the presence of a character called the Collector.

One subject of particular interest to my readers (along with issues like the planning of books, and the possibly warped nature of my imagination) is where my villains come from, and to that I really have no answer. They are creatures of the id, and I'm usually as surprised as anyone when they appear fully formed on the page, and often already in possession of a name. Apparently my unconscious is always busy, even when I'm not.

After delivering the fourth Parker novel, *The White Road*, to my publishers in 2001, I decided that I was going to take some time to write a standalone book, *Bad Men*, and a collection of short stories, which became *Nocturnes*. But by the time I had finished most of the *Nocturnes* stories, I was itching to return to Charlie Parker, and so I added a Parker novella entitled 'The Reflecting Eye' to the anthology. I felt that it fitted in with the general tone of *Nocturnes* because it was a haunted house tale, but I began writing – in the manner described earlier – with only the image of a rundown old house that had once belonged to a notorious child-killer.

Then out of the shadows stepped a man in a dark suit and a once-white shirt, his fingers stained with nicotine, hell-bent – and I use the word advisedly – on gaining access to the house, and whatever had secured itself inside. This was the Collector. His entrance wasn't planned, and I had no intention of including such a figure in the story when I started it. He was simply there, waiting for the right moment to make his presence felt, and he took over the tale. He has since become a crucial figure in the Parker mythology: a being of possibly supernatural origin, an instrument of punishment and vengeance for a god who, in the words of a song by the group Low featured on the CD that came with early copies of the book, needs 'a murderer/ Someone to do your dirty work'.

So I wish I'd invented the Collector, but I didn't. He is entirely his own creation. After 'The Reflecting Eye' he found his way into other books, and *The Unquiet* is the first of them.

I

Where can a dead man go?
A question with an answer only dead men know.

Nickel Creek, *When in Rome*

Prologue

This world is full of broken things: broken hearts and broken promises, broken people. This world, too, is a fragile construct, a honeycomb place where the past leaches into the present, where the weight of blood guilt and old sins causes lives to collapse and forces children to lie with the remains of their fathers in the tangled ruins of the aftermath.

I am broken, and I have broken in return. Now I wonder how much hurt can be visited upon others before the universe takes action, before some outside force decides that enough has been endured. I once thought that it was a question of balance, but I no longer believe this. I think that what I have done was out of all proportion to what was done to me, but that is the nature of revenge. It escalates. It cannot be controlled. One hurt invites another, on and on until the original injury is all but forgotten in the chaos of what follows.

I was a revenger once. I will be one no more.

But this world is full of broken things.

Old Orchard Beach, Maine, 1986

The Guesser removed the fold of bills from his pocket, licked his thumb, and discreetly counted the day's takings. The sun was setting, shedding itself in shards of burning red like blood and fire on the water. There were still people moving along the boardwalk, sipping sodas and eating hot buttered popcorn, while distant figures strolled along the beach, some hand in hand with another and some alone. The weather had altered in recent days, the evening temperature dropping noticeably and a sharp wind, a herald of a greater change to come, toying with the grains of sand as dusk descended, and the visitors no longer lingered as they once did. The Guesser felt his time there drawing to a close, for if they would not pause then he could not work, and if he could not work then he was no longer the Guesser. He would just be a small old man standing before a rickety assemblage of signs and scales, trinkets and baubles, without an audience to witness their display, his skills might as well not exist. The tourists had begun to thin, and soon this place would hold no appeal for the Guesser and his fellows: the hucksters, the nickel-a-ride merchants, the carnies, and the flimflam men. They would be forced to depart for more rewarding climes, or hole up for the winter to live on the summer's earnings.

The Guesser could taste the sea and the sand upon his skin, salty and life-affirming. He never failed to notice it, even after all these years. The sea gave him his living, for it drew the crowds to it and the Guesser was waiting for them when they came, but his affinity for it ran deeper than the money that it brought him. No, he recognized something of his own essence in it, in the taste of his sweat that was an echo of his own distant

origin and the origin of all things, for he believed that a man
who did not understand the lure of the sea was a man who
was lost to himself.

His thumb flipped expertly through the bills, his lips moving
slightly as he ran the count in his head. When he was done, he
added the sum to his running total, then compared it with his
earnings from the same time last year. He was down, just as
last year had been down from the year before, and that year
less than its predecessor in turn. People were more cynical now,
and they and their children were less inclined to stand before
a strange little man and his primitive-looking sideshow. He had
to work ever harder to earn even less, although not so little that
he was about to consider giving up his chosen profession. After
all, what else would he do? Clear tables at a buffet, maybe?
Work behind the counter at Mickey D's like some of the more
desperate retirees that he knew, reduced to cleaning up after
mewling infants and careless teenagers? No, that wasn't for the
Guesser. He had been following this path for the best part of
forty years, and the way he felt, he figured he was good for a
few more yet, assuming he was spared by the great dealer in
the sky. His mind was still sharp, and his eyes, behind the black-
framed lenses, were still capable of taking in all that he needed
to know about his marks in order to continue to make his
modest living. Some might term what he had a gift, but he did
not call it that. It was a skill, a craft, honed and developed year
upon year, a vestige of a sense that was strong in our ancestors but had now been dulled by the comforts of the modern
world. What he had was elemental, like the tides and currents
of the ocean.

Dave 'the Guesser' Glovsky had first arrived in Old Orchard
Beach in 1948, when he was thirty-seven years old, and since
then both his pitch and the tools of his trade had remained
largely unchanged. His little concession on the boardwalk was
dominated by an old wooden chair suspended by chains from
a set of R. H. Forschner scales. A yellow sign, hand-painted
roughly with a squiggly line drawing of Dave's face, advertised

his occupation and his location, just for those folks who maybe weren't entirely sure where they were or what they were seeing once they got there. The sign read: THE GUESSER, PALACE PLAYLAND, OLD ORCHARD BEACH, ME.

The Guesser was a fixture at Old Orchard. He was as much a part of the resort as the sand in the soda and the saltwater taffy that sucked the fillings from teeth. This was his place, and he knew it intimately. He had been coming here for so long, plying his trade, that he was acutely aware of seemingly inconsequential changes to his environment: a fresh coat of paint here, a mustache shaved there. Such things were important to him, for that was how he kept his mind keen, and that, in turn, was how he put food on the table. The Guesser noticed all that went on around him, filing the details away in his capacious memory, ready to extract that knowledge at the very moment when it would most profit him to do so. In a sense, his nickname was a misnomer. Dave Glovsky did not guess. Dave Glovsky noticed. He estimated. He gauged. Unfortunately, Dave 'the Noticer' Glovsky did not have quite the same ring about it. Neither did Dave 'the Estimator,' so Dave 'the Guesser' it was, and Dave 'the Guesser' it would stay.

The Guesser would guess your weight to within three pounds, or you won a prize. If that didn't salt your bacon – and there were folks who didn't particularly want their weight broadcast to a good-humored crowd on a bright summer's day, thank you for asking and be about your business, just as the Guesser wasn't overly anxious to test the strength of his scales by dangling three hundred pounds of all-American womanhood from them just to prove a point – then he was equally happy to take a swing at your age, your birth date, your occupation, your choice of car (foreign or domestic), even the brand of cigarettes that you favored. If the Guesser proved to be incorrect, then you went on your merry way clutching a plastic hair clip or a small bag of rubber bands, happy in the knowledge that you'd beaten the funny little man with his crooked, childlike signs – weren't you the smart one? – and it might take you a while to figure out that you'd just paid the man fifty cents for the pleasure of knowing something that you already knew before you arrived, with the added bonus of receiving ten rubber bands that cost about one cent wholesale. And it could be that maybe you looked back at the Guesser, wearing his white 'Dave the Guesser' T-shirt, the letters ironed on in black at the T-shirt concession farther along the boardwalk as a favor to Dave because everybody knew the Guesser, and you figured that maybe the Guesser was a very smart guy indeed.

Because the Guesser *was* smart, smart in the way that Sherlock Holmes was smart, or Dupin, or the little Belgian Poirot. He was an observer, a man who could ascertain the main circumstances of another's existence from his clothes, his shoes, the way he carried his cash, the state of his hands and his fingernails, the things that caught his interest and attention as he walked along the boardwalk, even the minute pauses and hesitations, the vocal inflections and unconscious gestures by which he revealed himself in a thousand different ways. He paid attention in a culture that no longer put any value upon such a simple act. People did not listen or see, but only *thought* that they listened and saw. They missed more than they perceived, their eyes and ears constantly adjusting to novelty, to the next new thing that might be thrown at them by TV, the radio, the movies, discarding the old before they had even begun to understand its meaning and its value. The Guesser was not like them. He belonged to a different order, to an older dispensation. He was attuned to sights and smells, to whispers that sounded loud in his ears, to tiny odors that tickled at the hairs in his nose and showed up as lights and colors in his mind. His sight was only one of the faculties that he used, and often it played a subsidiary role to the rest. Like early man, he did not rely on his eyes as his primary source of information. He trusted all of his senses, utilizing them to the fullest. His mind was like a radio, for ever tuned to even the faintest transmissions of others.

Some of it was easy, of course: age and weight were relatively simple for him. Cars were pretty much a done deal too, at least at the beginning when most of the people who came to Old Orchard for their vacations did so in American-made cars. It was only later that imports would become more prevalent, but even then, the odds were still about fifty-fifty in the Guesser's favor.

Occupations? Well, sometimes useful details might emerge in the course of the pitch, as the Guesser listened to their greetings, their answers, the way they responded to certain key words. Even while he was listening to what they were saying, Dave was examining their clothes and skin for telltale signs: a worn or stained shirt cuff on the right hand indicated someone who might have a desk job, and a lowly one if they had to wear their work shirt on vacation, while a closer examination of their hands might reveal the impression of a pen upon the thumb and index finger. Sometimes there was a slight flattening to the fingertips on one or both hands, the former perhaps suggesting that here was someone who was used to pounding an adding machine, the latter almost certainly the sign of a typist. Chefs always had little burns on their forearms, grill marks on their wrists, calluses upon the index fingers of their knife hands, healed and semihealed lines upon their flesh where the blades had nicked them, and the Guesser had yet to meet a mechanic who could scrub every trace of oil from the grooves of his skin. He could tell a cop simply by looking at him, and military types might just as well have arrived in full regalia.

But observation without memory was useless, and the Guesser was constantly taking in details from the crowds that thronged the seashore, from fragments of conversations to flashes of possessions. If you decided to light up, then Dave would remember that the pack was Marlboro and that you were wearing a green tie. If you parked your car within sight of his concession, then you were 'red suspenders Ford.' Everything was compartmentalized in case it might prove useful, for although the Guesser never really lost out on his bets, there was the small matter of professional pride and also the necessity of providing a good show for the watching folks. The Guesser hadn't survived at Old Orchard for decades just by guessing wrong, then fobbing off the tourists with rubber bands by way of apology.

He pocketed his earnings and took a last look around before he prepared to close up. He was tired, and his head hurt a little, but he would miss being here once the crowds were gone. The Guesser knew that there were those who bemoaned the state of Old Orchard, and felt that the beautiful beach had been ruined by a century of development, by the arrival of roller coasters and fun houses and merry-go-rounds, by the smell of cotton candy and hot dogs and suntan lotion. Maybe they were right, but there were plenty of other places for folks like that to go, while there weren't so many where people could come for a week with their kids and live relatively cheaply while enjoying the sea, the sand, and the pleasure of trying to beat men like the Guesser. True, Old Orchard wasn't like it once was. The kids were tougher, maybe even a little more dangerous. The town was looking more tawdry than before, and there was a sense of innocence lost rather than innocence recaptured. Ocean Park, the family-oriented religious resort that was part of Old Orchard, now looked increasingly like a throwback to another era, when education and self-improvement were as much a part of one's vacation time as amusement and relaxation. He wondered how many of those who came here to drink cheap beer and eat lobster from paper plates knew of the Methodists who had formed the Old Orchard Campground Association back in the 1870s, sometimes attracting crowds of ten thousand or more to hear speakers extol the benefits of a virtuous, sin-free life. Good luck trying to convince today's tourists to give up an afternoon of sunbathing to listen to stories from the Bible. You didn't have to be Dave the Guesser to figure out the odds on that one.

Nevertheless, the Guesser loved Old Orchard. Through his little concession, he had been privileged to meet men like Tommy Dorsey and Louis Armstrong, and he had the pictures on his wall to prove it. But while those encounters represented the great peaks of his career, his dealings with ordinary people had given him consistent pleasure and allowed him to stay young and sharp inside. Without people, Old Orchard would have meant far less to him, sea or no sea.

The Guesser was already putting away his signs and his scales when the man approached; or perhaps it would be truer to say that the Guesser became aware of his approach before he even saw the man, for his long-departed ancestors had not relied on their senses to play guessing games in flame-lit caves. No, they had required those senses to stay alive, to warn them of the coming of predators and enemies, and so their continued survival was dependent upon their engagement with the world around them.

Immediately, the Guesser turned casually and began taking in the stranger: late thirties, but looking older than his years; his blue jeans looser than was the current fashion; his T-shirt white but stained slightly at the belly; his boots heavy and suited to a motorcycle, not a car, yet without the wear on the soles that might have come from riding a hog; his hair dark and greased back in a D.A.; his features sharp and almost delicate; his chin small, his head compressed as if from long endurance of a great weight placed upon it, the bones in his face shaped like a kite beneath his skin. He had a scar below his hairline: three parallel lines, as though the tines of a fork had been inserted into his flesh and dragged down toward the bridge of his nose. His mouth was crooked, permanently downturned on one side and upturned slightly on the other, giving the impression that the symbolic masks of drama had been bisected and their disparate halves fused together over his skull. The lips were too big. They might almost have been called sensuous, but this was not a man whose demeanor spoke of such things. His eyes were brown, but flecked with tiny white flaws, like stars and planets suspended in their darkness. He smelled of eau de cologne and, lurking beneath, the rank stink of rendered animal fats, of blood and decay and waste voided in the final moment when living became dying.

Suddenly, Dave the Guesser wished that he had decided
to pack up fifteen minutes earlier, that his concession stand
were firmly locked and bolted, and that he had already put
as much distance between him and his beloved scales and
signs as it was possible for a man of his advancing years to
do. But even as he tried to break eye contact with the new
arrival, he still found himself analyzing him, drawing information from his movements, his clothing, his scent. The man
reached into one of the front pockets of his denims and drew
from it a steel comb, which he raked through his hair with
his right hand, his left following along behind to smooth down
any stray strands. He cocked his head slightly to the right as
he did so, as though sizing himself up in some mirror visible
only to him, and it took the Guesser a moment to realize that
he himself was that mirror. The stranger knew all about Dave
and his 'gift,' and even as he willed himself to stop, the Guesser
was separating the preening man into his constituent parts,
and the man was aware of what was being done and was
enjoying seeing himself refracted through the older man's
perceptions.

Clean, pressed denims, but with dirt on the knees. The stain
on the T-shirt like dried blood. The earth beneath the nails. The
smell. Sweet God, the smell . . .

And now the stranger was in front of him and the comb was
being eased back into the tight sheath of his pocket. The smile
widened, all false bonhomie, and the man spoke.

'You the guessin' man?' he asked. His accent had a hint of
the South to it, but there was Down East there as well. He was
trying to hide it, but Dave's ear was too acute.

The touch of Mainer to it wasn't native, though. No, this
was a man who could blend in when he chose, who picked up
the speech patterns and mannerisms of those around him,
camouflaging himself the way—

The way predators did.

'I'm all done for today,' the Guesser said. 'Tired out. I got
nothing left.'

'Ah, you got time for one more,' came the reply, and the Guesser knew that he was not being cajoled. He was being told.

He looked around, seeking a distraction, an excuse to depart, but now it seemed as if the stranger had created a space for himself, for there was no one else within earshot and the attention of those who passed was clearly directed elsewhere. They looked at the other concessions, at the sea, at the shifting sands. They looked at distant cars and the unfamiliar faces of those who passed them by. They looked at the boardwalk and at their feet and deep into the eyes of husbands and wives whom they had long since ceased to find interesting but who now held inside them some previously unsuspected, if fleeting, source of fascination. And had one suggested to them that they had somehow decided to turn their attention away from the little Guesser and the man who now stood before him, they would have dismissed the idea without appearing to give it a moment's serious thought. But to an observant person – to someone like Dave the Guesser – the fleeting expression of unease upon their faces as they spoke would have been enough to give the lie to their protestations. In that moment, they had become a little like the Guesser, some ancient, primal instinct woken from dormancy on a bright summer evening with the sun setting bloodily in the west. Maybe they truly didn't realize that they were doing it, or perhaps self-respect and self-preservation prevented them from acknowledging it, even to themselves, but they were giving space to the man with the slicked-back hair. He exuded menace and threat and harm, and just to acknowledge his existence was to risk drawing attention to oneself. Better, then, to look away. Better for another to suffer, for a stranger to incur his displeasure, than to have him take an interest in one's own affairs. Better to keep walking, to get into one's car, to drive away without a single backward glance for fear that one might find him staring into one's eyes, his lazy half smile slowly widening as he memorized faces, the numbers on a license plate, the color of the paintwork, the dark hair of a wife, the budding body of an adolescent daughter.

Better to pretend, then. Better not to notice. Better that than to wake up in the night to find such a man staring down at you, blood warm upon him and a telltale light coming from a nearby bedroom, something dripping softly upon the bare floorboards within, something that was once alive there now alive no longer . . .

Dave knew then that this man was not so different from himself. He was an observer, a cataloger of human characteristics, but in the stranger's case the observations were a prelude to harm. And now there were only the sounds of waves breaking, and voices fading, and the noises of the fairground rides dulling and muting as the stranger spoke, his tone insisting upon the attention of the listener to the exclusion of all else.

'I want you to guess somethin' about me,' he said.

'What do you want to know?' said the Guesser, and all pretence of goodwill departed from his own voice. It would serve no purpose here. They were equals, of a sort.

The man closed his right hand into a fist. Two quarters rose from between his white knuckles. He raised the hand toward Dave, and Dave removed the coins with fingers that barely trembled.

'Tell me what I do for a livin',' said the stranger. 'And I want you to make your best guess. Your very best guess.'

Dave heard the warning. He could have come up with something harmless, something innocent. You dig roads, maybe. You're a gardener. You—

You work in an abattoir.

No, too close. Mustn't say that.

You tear things apart. Living things. You hurt and you kill and you bury the evidence beneath the ground. And sometimes they fight back. I see the scars around your eyes, and in the soft flesh beneath your jaw. There's a cluster of rough strands just above your fore-head, and an inflamed patch of red at its base where the hair hasn't grown back properly. What happened? Did a hand get free? Did fingers grasp in desperation and tear a clump from your head? And even in your pain, was there not a part of you that relished the struggle, that enjoyed having to work for its prize? And what of those incisions below your hairline, what of them? You are a violent man, and violence has been visited upon you. You have been marked as a warning to others, so that even those who are foolish and distracted might know you when you come. Too late for the one who did it, perhaps, but a warning nonetheless.

A lie might be the death of him. Maybe not now, maybe not even a week from now, but the man would remember, and he would return. Some night, Dave the Guesser would go back to his room and the stranger would be sitting in an easy chair in the darkness opposite the window, taking long drags from a cigarette in his left hand, his right toying with a blade.

'Glad you could make it at last. I been waitin' for you. You remember me? I asked you to guess somethin' about me, but you guessed wrong. You gave me a child's toy as a prize, a prize for beating the Guesser, but that ain't prize enough for me, and you was wrong to think it. I figure I ought to correct your misapprehension. I figure you really ought to know what I do for a livin'. Here, let me show you . . .'

The stranger turned his hands slowly for Dave, displaying the palms, then the backs of the hands, and finally the almost delicate fingers, a thin sliver of dirt visible beneath the tip of each nail.

'So tell me,' he said. 'Tell me true.'

Dave looked him in the eye.

'You cause pain,' said Dave.

The stranger looked amused.

'Is that so?' he said.

'You hurt people.'

'Uh-huh?'

'You've killed,' and Dave both heard himself say the words and saw himself from without. He was floating apart from the scene unfolding before him, his soul already anticipating the separation from this life that was to come.

The stranger shook his head and looked at his own hands, as though quietly astonished at what they had revealed.

'Well,' he said at last, 'I reckon that's worth fifty cents of any man's money, and no mistake. That's quite the tale. Quite the tale.' He nodded to himself. 'Uh-huh,' he said softly. 'Uh-huh.'

'You want to claim a prize?' said Dave. 'You can have a prize if I guessed wrong.'

He gestured behind him at the rubber bands, the hair clips, the packs of balloons.

Take one. Please take one. Take 'em all, anything you want, just get away from me. Walk away and keep walking and never, ever come back here. And if it's any consolation, know that I'll never forget the smell of you or the sight of you. Not ever. I'll keep it with me, and I'll always be watching for you in case you come again.

'Nah,' said the stranger. 'You keep 'em. I was entertained. You entertained me.'

He backed away from Dave the Guesser, still nodding, still softly 'uh-huh'-ing.

Just as the Guesser felt certain he was about to be rid of him, the stranger stopped.

'Professional pride,' he said suddenly.

'Pardon me?' said the Guesser.

'I think that's what we got in common: we take pride in what we do. You could have lied to me, but you didn't. I could have lied to you and taken one of them shitty balloon packs, but I didn't do that either. You respected me, and I respected you in return. We're men, you and I.'

The Guesser didn't reply. There was nothing to say. He tasted something in his mouth. It was sour and unpleasant. He wanted to open his mouth and breathe in the salt sea air, but not yet, not while the stranger was nearby. He wanted to be rid of him first, for fear that some of his essence might enter him in that single breath, polluting his being.

'You can tell folks about me, if you like,' said the stranger. 'I don't much care either way. I'll be long gone before anybody takes it into his head to come looking for me, and even if they do find me, what are they gonna say? That some little sideshow huckster in a cheap T-shirt told them to look me up, that maybe I might have somethin' to hide or a story to tell?'

His hands busied themselves retrieving his pack of cigarettes from his jeans. The pack was battered, and slightly flattened. He shook a slim brass lighter from within, then followed it with a cigarette. He rolled the cigarette between his finger and thumb before lighting up, the lighter and the pack disappearing back into his pocket.

'Maybe I'll be through here again someday,' he said. 'I'll look you up.'

'I'll be here,' said the Guesser.

Come back if you like, then, you animal. Make no mistake, I'm scared of you, and I believe that I have good cause to be, but don't think I'm going to show it. You won't get that satisfaction, not from me.

'I hope so,' said the stranger. 'I surely do hope so.'

But the Guesser never saw him again, although he thought of him often, and once or twice in his remaining years, as he stood on the boardwalk and appraised the passing crowds, he was conscious of eyes upon him and he felt certain that, somewhere nearby, the stranger was watching him, perhaps in amusement or, as the Guesser often feared, perhaps with regret for ever allowing the truth about himself to be revealed in such a way, and with the desire to undo that mistake.

Dave 'the Guesser' Glovsky died in 1997, nearly fifty years after he had first arrived in Old Orchard Beach. He spoke of the stranger to those who would listen, of the stink of fats that arose from him and the dirt beneath his nails and the copper stains upon his shirt. Most of those who heard merely shook their heads at what they believed was just another attempt by the showman to add to his own legend; but some listened, and they remembered, and they passed on the tale so that others might be watchful for such a man in case he returned.

The Guesser, of course, had been right: the man did come back in the years that followed, sometimes for his own purposes and sometimes on the orders of others, and he both took and created life. But when he returned for the last time, he drew the clouds around him like a cloak, darkening the skies as he came, seeking death and the memory of a death in the faces of others. He was a broken man, and he would break others in his wrath.

He was Merrick, the revenger.

I

It was an overcast late November morning, the grass splintered by hoarfrost, and winter grinning through the gaps in the clouds like a bad clown peering between the curtains before the show begins. The city was slowing down. Soon the cold would hit hard, and like an animal, Portland had stored its fat for the long months ahead. There were tourist dollars in the bank; enough, it was hoped, to tide everyone over until Memorial Day. The streets were quieter than they once were. The locals, who coexisted sometimes uneasily with the leaf peepers and outlet shoppers, now had their home almost to themselves once more. They claimed their regular tables in diners and coffee shops, in restaurants and bars. There was time to pass idle conversation with waitresses and chefs, the professionals no longer run ragged by the demands of customers whose names they did not know. At this time of year, it was possible to feel the true rhythm of the small city, the slow beating of its heart untroubled by the false stimulus of those who came from away.

I was sitting at a corner table in the Porthole, eating bacon and fried potatoes and not watching Kathleen Kennedy and Stephen Frazier talking about the secretary of state's surprise visit to Iraq. There was no sound from the TV, which made ignoring it a whole lot easier. A stove fire burned next to the window overlooking the water, the masts of the fishing boats bobbed and swayed in the morning breeze, and a handful of people occupied the other tables, just enough to create the kind of welcoming ambience that a breakfast venue required, for such things rely on a subtle balance.

The Porthole still looked like it did when I was growing up, perhaps even as it had since it first opened in 1929. There were green-marbled linoleum tiles on the floor, cracked here and there but spotlessly clean. A long wooden counter topped with copper stretched almost the entire length of the room, its black-cushioned metal stools anchored to the floor, the counter dotted with glasses, condiments, and two glass plates of freshly baked muffins. The walls were painted light green, and if you stood up you could peer into the kitchen through the twin serving hatches divided by a painted *Scallops* sign. A chalkboard announced the day's specials, and there were five beer taps, serving Guinness, a few Allagash and Shipyard ales, and for those who didn't know any better, or who did and just didn't give a rat's ass, Coors Light. There were buoys hanging from the walls, which in any other dining establishment in the Old Port might have come across as kitsch but here were simply a reflection of the fact that this was a place frequented by locals who fished. One wall was almost entirely glass, so even on the dullest of mornings the Porthole appeared to be flooded with light.

In the Porthole you were always aware of the comforting buzz of conversation, but you could never quite hear all of what anyone nearby was saying, not clearly. This morning about twenty people were eating, drinking, and easing themselves into the day the way Mainers will do. Five workers from the Harbor Fish Market sat in a row at the bar, all dressed identically in blue jeans, hooded tops, and baseball caps, laughing and stretching in the warmth, their faces bitten red by the elements. Beside me, four businessmen had cell phones and notepads interspersed with their white coffee mugs, making out as if they were working but, from the occasional snatches that drifted over to me and could be understood, seemingly more interested in singing the praises of Pirates coach Kevin Dineen. Across from them, two women, a mother and daughter, were having one of those discussions that required a lot of hand gestures and shocked expressions. They looked as if they were having a ball.

I like the Porthole. The tourists don't come here a lot, certainly not in winter, and even in summer they hadn't tended to disturb the balance much until someone strung a banner over the wharf advertising the fact that there was more to this seemingly unpromising stretch of waterfront than met the eye: Boone's Seafood Restaurant, the Harbor Fish Market, the Comedy Connection, and the Porthole itself. Even that hadn't exactly led to an onslaught. Banner or no banner, the Porthole didn't scream its existence, and a battered soda sign and a fluttering flag were the only actual indication of its presence visible from the main drag of Commercial. In a sense, you kind of needed to know that it was there to see it in the first place, especially on dark winter mornings, and any lingering tourists walking along Commercial at the start of a bitter Maine winter's day needed to have a pretty good idea of where they were headed if they were going to make it to spring with their health intact. Faced with a bracing nor'easter, few had the time or the inclination to explore the hidden corners of the city.

Still, off-season travelers sometimes made their way past the fish market and the comedy club, their feet echoing solidly on the old wood of the boardwalk that bordered the wharf to the left, and found themselves at the Porthole's door, and it was a good bet that the next time they came to Portland they would head straight for the Porthole again; but maybe they wouldn't tell too many of their friends about it because it was the kind of place that you liked to keep to yourself. There was a deck outside overlooking the water, where people could sit and eat in summer, but in winter they removed the tables and left the deck empty. I think I liked it better in winter. I could take a cup of coffee in hand and head out, safe in the knowledge that most folks preferred to drink their coffee inside where it was warm and that I wasn't likely to be disturbed by anyone. I would smell the salt and feel the sea breeze on my skin, and if the wind and the weather were right the scent would remain with me for the rest of the morning. Mostly, I liked that scent. Sometimes, if I was feeling bad, I didn't care so much for it, because the taste of the salt on my lips reminded me of tears, as if I had recently tried to kiss away another's pain. When that happened, I thought of Rachel and of Sam, my daughter. Often, too, I thought of the wife and daughter who had gone before them.

Days like that were silent days.

But today I was inside, and I was wearing a jacket and tie. The tie was a deep red Hugo Boss, the jacket Armani, yet nobody in Maine ever paid much attention to labels. Everyone figured that if you were wearing it, then you'd bought it at a discount, and if you hadn't and had paid ticket instead, then you were an idiot.

I hadn't paid ticket.

The front door opened, and a woman entered. She was wearing a black pantsuit and a coat that had probably cost her a lot when she bought it but was now showing its age. Her hair was black, but colored with something that lent it a hint of red. She looked a little surprised by her surroundings, as though, having made her way down past the battered exteriors of the wharf buildings, she had expected to be mugged by pirates. Her eyes alighted on me and her head tilted quizzically. I raised a finger, and she made her way through the tables to where I sat. I rose to meet her, and we shook hands.

'Mr Parker?' she said.

'Ms. Clay.'

'I'm sorry I'm late. There was an accident on the bridge. The traffic was backed up a ways.'

Rebecca Clay had called me the day before, asking if I might be able to help her with a problem she was having. She was being stalked, and not surprisingly, she didn't much care for it. The cops had been able to do nothing. The man, she said, seemed almost to sense their coming, because he was always gone by the time they arrived, no matter how stealthily they approached the vicinity of her house when she reported his presence.

I had been doing as much general work as I could get, in

part to keep my mind off the absence of Rachel and Sam. We had been apart, on and off, for about nine months. I'm not even sure how things had deteriorated so badly, and so quickly. It seemed like one minute they were there, filling the house with their scents and their sounds, and the next they were leaving for Rachel's parents' house, but of course it wasn't like that at all. Looking back, I could see every turn in the road, every dip and curve, that had led us to where we now were. It was supposed to be a temporary thing, a chance for both of us to consider, to take a little time out from each other and try to recall what it was about the other person with whom we shared our life that was so important to us we could not live without it. But such arrangements are never temporary, not really. There is a sundering, a rift that occurs, and even if an accommodation is reached, and a decision made to try again, the fact that one person left the other is never really forgotten, or forgiven. That makes it sound like it was her fault, but it wasn't. I'm not sure that it was mine either, not entirely. She had to make a choice, and so did I, but her choice was dependent upon the one that I made. In the end, I let them both go, but in the hope that they would eventually return. We still talked, and I could see Sam whenever I wanted to, but the fact that they were over in Vermont made that a little difficult. Distances notwithstanding, I was careful about visiting, and not just because I didn't want to complicate an already difficult situation. I took care because I still believed that there were those who would hurt them to get at me. I think that was why I let them leave. It was so hard to remember. The last year had been . . . difficult. I missed them a great deal, but I did not know either how to bring them back into my life, or how to live with their absence. They had left a void in my existence, and others had tried to take their place, the ones who waited in the shadows.

The first wife, and the first daughter.

I ordered coffee for Rebecca Clay. A beam of morning sunlight shone mercilessly upon her, exposing the lines in her face, the gray seeping into her hair despite the color job, the dark patches beneath her eyes. Some of that was probably down to the man she claimed was bothering her, but it was clear that much of it had deeper origins. The troubles of her life had aged her prematurely. From the way her makeup had been applied, hurriedly and heavily, it was possible to guess that here was a woman who didn't like looking in the mirror for too long, and who didn't like what she saw staring back at her when she did.

'I don't think I've ever been here before,' she said. 'Portland has changed so much these last few years, it's a wonder that this place has survived.'

She was right, I supposed. The city was changing, but older, quirkier remnants of its past somehow contrived to remain: used bookstores, and barbershops, and bars where the menu never changed because the food had always been good, right from the start. That was why the Porthole had survived. Those who knew about it valued it, and made sure to pass a little business its way whenever they could.

Her coffee arrived. She added sugar, then stirred it for too long.

'What can I do for you, Ms. Clay?'

She stopped stirring, content to begin speaking now that the conversation had been started for her.

'It's like I told you on the phone. A man has been bothering me.'

'Bothering you how?'

'He hangs around outside my house. I live out by Willard Beach. I've seen him in Freeport too, or when I've been shopping at the mall.'

'Was he in a car, or on foot?'

'On foot.'

'Has he entered your property?'

'No.'

'Has he threatened you, or physically assaulted you in any way?'

'No.'

'How long has this been going on?'

'Just over a week.'

'Has he spoken to you?'

'Only once, two days ago.'

'What did he say?'

'He told me that he was looking for my father. My daughter and I live in my father's old house now. He said he had some business with him.'

'How did you respond to that?'

'I told him that I hadn't seen my father in years. I told him that as far as I was aware, my father was dead. In fact, since earlier this year he's been legally dead. I went through all of the paperwork. I didn't want to, but I suppose it was important to me, and to my daughter, that we finally achieved some kind of closure.'

'Tell me about your father.'

'He was a child psychiatrist, a good one. He worked with adults too, sometimes, but they had usually suffered some kind of trauma in childhood and felt that he could help them with it. Then things started to change for him. There was a difficult case: a man was accused of abuse by his son in the course of a custody dispute. My father felt that the allegations had substance, and his findings led to custody being granted to the mother, but the son subsequently retracted his accusations and said that his mother had convinced him to say those things. By then it was too late for the father. Word had leaked out about the allegations, probably from the mother. He lost his job, and got beaten up pretty badly by some men in a bar. He ended up shooting himself dead in his bedroom. My father took it badly, and there were complaints filed about his conduct of the original interviews with the boy. The Board of Licensure dismissed them, but after that my father wasn't asked to conduct any further evaluations in abuse cases. It shook his confidence, I think.'

'When was this?'

'About 1998, maybe a little before. It got worse after that.' She shook her head in apparent disbelief at the memory. 'Even talking about it, I realize how crazy it all sounds. It was just a mess.' She looked around to reassure herself that nobody was listening, then lowered her voice a little. 'It emerged that some of my father's patients were sexually abused by a group of men, and there were questions asked again about my father's methods and his reliability. My father blamed himself for what happened. Other people did too. The Board of Licensure summoned him to appear for an initial informal meeting to discuss what had happened, but he never made it. He drove out to the edge of the North Woods, abandoned his car, and that was the last anyone ever saw or heard of him. The police looked for him, but they never found any trace. That was in late September 1999.'

Clay. Rebecca Clay.

'You're Daniel Clay's daughter?'

She nodded. Something flashed across her face. It was an involuntary spasm, a kind of wince. I knew a little about Daniel Clay. Portland is a small place, a city in name only. Stories like Daniel Clay's tended to linger in the collective memory. I didn't know too many of the details, but like everyone else I'd heard the rumors. Rebecca Clay had summarized the circumstances of her father's disappearance in the most general terms, and I didn't blame her for leaving out the rest: the whispers that Dr Daniel Clay might have known about what was happening to some of the children with whom he was dealing, the possibility that he might have colluded in it, might even have engaged in abuse himself. There had been an investigation of sorts, but there were records missing from his office, and the confidential nature of his vocation made it difficult to follow up leads. There was also the absence of any solid evidence against him. But that didn't stop people from talking and drawing their own conclusions.

I looked closer at Rebecca Clay. Her father's identity made her appearance a little easier to understand. I imagined that she kept herself to herself. There would be friends, but not many. Daniel Clay had cast a shadow upon his daughter's life, and she had wilted under its influence.

'So you told this man, the one who's been stalking you, that you hadn't seen your father for a long time. How did he react?'

'He tapped the side of his nose and winked.' She replicated the gesture for me. 'Then he said, "Liar, liar, pants on fire." He told me that he'd give me some time to think about what I was saying. After that, he just walked away.'

'Why would he call you a liar? Did he give any indication that he might know something more about your father's disappearance?'

'No, nothing at all.'

'And the police haven't been able to trace him?'

'He melts away. I think they believe I'm making up stories to get attention, but I'm not. I wouldn't do that. I—'

I waited.

'You know about my father. There are those who believe that he did something wrong. I think the police are among them, and sometimes I wonder if they think I know more than I do about what happened, and that I've been protecting my father for all this time. When they came to the house, I knew what was on their minds: that I did know where he was, and somehow I've been in contact with him over the years.'

'And have you?'

She blinked hard, but she held my gaze.

'No.'

'But now it seems like the police aren't the only ones who doubt your story. What does this man look like?'

'He's in his sixties, I think. His hair is black. It looks dyed, and it's in kind of a quiff, the way those 'fifties rock stars used to wear their hair. He has brown eyes, and there's scarring here.' She pointed to her forehead, just below her hairline. 'There are three parallel marks, like someone dug a fork into his skin and dragged it down. He's short, maybe five-five or so, but stocky. His arms are real big, and there are folds of muscle at the back of his neck. He mostly wears the same clothes: blue jeans and a T-shirt, sometimes with a black suit jacket, other times with an old black leather jacket. He has a paunch, but he's not fat, not really. His nails are very short, and he keeps himself real clean, except—'

She stopped. I didn't disturb her as she tried to figure out the best way of formulating what she wanted to say.

'He wears some kind of cologne. It's wicked strong, but when he was speaking to me, it was like I caught a hint of whatever it was masking. It was a bad smell, a sort of animal stench. It made me want to run away from him.'

'Did he tell you his name?'

'No. He just said that he had business with my father. I kept telling him my father was dead, but he shook his head and smiled at me. He said he wouldn't believe any man was dead until he could smell the body.'

'Have you any idea why this man should have turned up now, so many years after your father's disappearance?'

'He didn't say. It could be that he heard news of the legal declaration of my father's death.'

For probate purposes, under Maine law, a person was presumed dead after a continuous absence of five years during which time he had not been heard from and his absence had not been satisfactorily explained. In some cases, the court could order a 'reasonably diligent' search, the notification of law enforcement and public welfare officials about the details of the case, and require that a request for information be posted in the newspapers. According to Rebecca Clay, she had complied with all of the conditions that the court had set, but no further information about her father had emerged as a result.

'There was also a piece about my father in an art magazine earlier this year, after I sold a couple of his paintings. I needed the money. My father was a pretty talented artist. He spent a lot of time in the woods, painting and sketching. His work doesn't go for much by modern standards – the most I ever got for one was a thousand dollars – but I've been able to sell some from time to time when money was scarce. My father didn't exhibit, and he only produced a relatively small body of work. He sold by word of mouth, and his paintings were always sought after by those collectors familiar with him. By the end of his life he was receiving offers to buy work that didn't even exist yet.'

'What kind of paintings are we talking about?'

'Landscapes, mostly. I can probably show you some photographs, if you're interested. I've sold them all now, apart from one.'

I knew some people in Portland's art scene. I thought I might ask them about Daniel Clay. In the meantime, there was the matter of the man who was bothering his daughter.

'I'm not just concerned for my own sake,' she said. 'My daughter, Jenna, she's just eleven. I'm afraid to let her out of the house alone now. I've tried to explain a little of what's been happening to her, but I don't want to frighten her too much either.'

'What do you want me to do about this man?' I said. It seemed like a strange question to ask, I knew, but it was necessary. Rebecca Clay had to understand what she was getting herself into.

'I want you to talk to him. I want you to make him go away.'

'That's two different things.'

'What?'

'Talking to him and making him go away.'

She looked puzzled. 'You'll have to excuse me,' she said. 'I'm not following you.'

'We need to be straight on some things before we begin. I can approach him on your behalf, and we can try to clear all of this up without trouble. It could be that he'll see reason and go about his business, but from what you've told me it sounds like he's got some notions fixed in his head, which means that he might not go without a fight. If that's the case, either we can try to get the cops to take him in, and look for a court order preventing him from approaching you, which can be hard to get and even harder to enforce, or we can find some other way to convince him that he should leave you alone.'

'You mean threaten him, or hurt him?'

She seemed to quite like the idea. I didn't blame her. I had met people who had endured years of harassment from individuals, and had seen them worn down by tension and distress. Some of them had resorted to violence in the end, but it usually just led to an escalation of the problem. One couple I knew had even ended up being sued by the wife's stalker after the husband threw a punch in frustration, further entangling their lives with his.

'They're options,' I said, 'but they leave us open to charges of assault, or threatening behavior. Worse, if the situation is not handled carefully, then this whole affair could just deteriorate. Right now, he hasn't done more than make you uneasy, which is bad enough. If we strike at him, he may decide to strike back. It could put you in real danger.'

She almost slumped with frustration.

'So what can I do?'

'Look,' I said, 'I'm not trying to make out that there's no hope of resolving this painlessly. I just want you to understand that if he decides to stick around, then there are no quick fixes.'

She perked up slightly. 'So you'll take the job?'

I told her my rates. I informed her that, as a one-man agency, I wouldn't take on other jobs that might conflict with my work on her behalf. If it became necessary to call on outside help, I would advise her of any additional costs that might arise. At any point, she could call a halt to our arrangement, and I would try to help her find some other way of handling her problem before I left the job. She seemed content with that. I took payment up front for the first week. I didn't exactly need the money for myself – my lifestyle was pretty simple – but I made a point of sending some money to Rachel every month, even though she said it wasn't necessary.

I agreed to start the following day. I would stay close to Rebecca Clay when she headed out to work in the mornings. She would inform me when she was leaving her office for lunch, for meetings, or to go home in the evening. Her house was fitted with an alarm, but I arranged to have someone check it out and to fit extra bolts and chains if necessary. I would be outside before she left in the morning, and I would remain within sight of the house until she went to bed. At any time she could contact me, and I would be with her within twenty minutes.

I asked her if, by any chance, she might have a photograph of her father that she could give me. She had anticipated the request, although she appeared slightly reluctant to hand it over after she had taken it from her bag. It showed a thin, gangly man wearing a green tweed suit. His hair was snow white, his eyebrows bushy. He wore a pair of steel-rimmed spectacles, and he had a stern, old-fashioned air of academia about him. He looked like a man who belonged amid clay pipes and leather-bound volumes.

'I'll have some copies made and get it back to you,' I said.

'I have others,' she replied. 'Hold on to it for as long as you need to.'

She asked me if I would keep an eye on her while she was in town that day. She worked in real estate and had some business to attend to for a couple of hours. She was worried that the man might approach her while she was in the city. She offered to pay me extra, but I declined. I had nothing better to do anyway.

So I followed her for the rest of the day. Nothing happened, and there was no sign of the man with the dated quiff and the scars upon his face. It was tedious and tiring, but at least it meant that I did not have to return to my house, my not-quite-empty house. I shadowed her so that my own ghosts could not shadow me.

2

The revenger walked along the boardwalk at Old Orchard, close to where the Guesser's concession had stood for summer upon summer. The old man was gone now, and the revenger supposed that he was probably dead; dead, or no longer capable of performing the feats that he once had, his eyes unable to see as clearly, his hearing muffled and decayed, his memory too fragmentary to record and order the information being fed to it. The revenger wondered if the showman had remembered him until the end. He thought that might have been the case, for was it not in the man's nature to forget little, to discard nothing that might prove useful?

He had been fascinated by the Guesser's talent, had watched him discreetly for an hour or more before he had eventually approached him for the first time on that cool evening close to summer's end. It was an extraordinary talent to find in such a small, strange-looking little man, surrounded by cheap trinkets in a simple booth: to be able to tell so much at a glance, to deconstruct an individual almost without thinking, forming a picture of his life in the time that it took most people to glance at a clock. From time to time he had come back to this place, and had hidden himself in the crowds, watching the Guesser from a distance. (And even then, had the little man not been aware of him? Had he not seen him scan the crowds uneasily, seeking the eyes that examined him too closely, his nostrils twitching like a rabbit sensing the approach of the fox?) Perhaps that was why he had come back here, as if by some faint chance the Guesser had chosen to remain in this place, seeing out the winter close by the water's edge instead of fleeing it for warmer climes.

If the revenger had found him here, what would he have said? *Teach me. Tell me how I may know the man whom I seek. I will be lied to. I want to learn how to recognize the lie when it comes.* Would he have explained why he had come back to this place, and would the little man have believed him? Of course he would, for a lie would not slip past him.

But the Guesser was long gone, and so the revenger was left only with the memory of their single meeting. There had been blood on his hands that day. It had been a comparatively simple task to accomplish: a vulnerable man laid to rest, a man who might have been tempted to barter what he knew for protection from those who sought him. From the moment that he had fled, his time left on this earth had been counted in seconds and minutes, hours and days, and no more than that. As five days became six, he had been found and he had been killed. There was fear at the end, but little pain. It was not for Merrick to torture or torment, though he did not doubt that, in those final moments, as the victim understood the implacable nature of the one who had come for him, there had been torment enough. He was a professional, not a sadist.

Merrick. That was his name then. It was the name on his record, the name that he had been given at birth, but it now meant nothing to him. Merrick was a killer, but he killed for others, not himself. It was an important distinction. A man who killed for his own purposes, his own ends, was a man at the mercy of emotions, and such men made mistakes. The old Merrick had been a professional. He was detached, disengaged, or so he told himself, although in the quiet after the kill, he sometimes allowed himself to acknowledge the pleasure that it gave him.

But the old Merrick, Merrick the killer, no longer existed. Another man had taken his place, dooming himself in the process, but what choice was there? Perhaps the old Merrick had been dying from the moment his child was born, his will weakened and ultimately broken by the knowledge that she was in the world. The revenger thought again of the Guesser, and of the moments they had passed together in this place.

If you looked at me now, old man, what would you see? You would see a man without a name, a father without a child, and you would see the fire of his rage consuming him from within.

The revenger turned his back on the sea, for there was work to be done.

The house was silent when I returned, a brief welcome back from Walter, my dog, apart, and I was grateful for that. Since Rachel and Sam had left, it seemed that those other presences, long denied, had found ways to colonize the spaces once occupied by the two who had taken their place. I had learned not to answer their call, to ignore the creaking of boards or the sound of footsteps upon the bedroom ceiling, as though presences paced the attic space, seeking what was once theirs among the boxes and cases that filled the room; to dismiss the gentle tapping upon the windows when darkness came, choosing instead to call it something other than what it was. It sounded like branches stirred by the wind, their very tips glancing against the glass, except that there were no trees near my windows, and no branch had ever tapped with such regularity or such insistence. Sometimes I would awaken in the darkness without quite knowing what had disturbed my rest, conscious only that there had been sound where no sound belonged, and perhaps faintly aware of whispered words trailing off as my conscious mind began reerecting the barriers that sleep had temporarily lowered.

The house was never truly empty. Something else had made its home there.

I should, I know, have spoken to Rachel about it long before she left. I should have been honest with her and told her that my dead wife and my lost daughter, or some phantasms that were not quite them, would not give me peace. Rachel was a psychologist. She would have understood. She loved me, and she would have tried to help me. It may be that she would have spoken of residual guilt, of the mind's delicate balance, of how some suffering is so great and so terrible that a full recovery is simply beyond the capacities of any human being. And I would have nodded and said, Yes, yes, it is so, knowing that there was some truth in what she said and yet that it was not enough to explain the nature of what had occurred in my life since my wife and child were taken from me. But I did not say those words, afraid that to speak them aloud would be to give what was occurring a reality I did not want to acknowledge. I denied their presence, and in doing so tightened their grip upon me.

Rachel was very beautiful. Her hair was red, her skin pale. There was much of her in Sam, our daughter, and just a little of me. When last we spoke, Rachel told me that Sam was sleeping better now. There were times, while we had lived together beneath this roof, when her sleep had been disturbed, when Rachel or I would wake to the sound of her laughter, and occasionally her tears. One or the other of us would check on her and watch as she reached out with her small hands, snatching at unseen things in the air before her, or as she turned her head to follow the progress of figures that only she could see, and I would notice that the room was cold, colder than it should have been.

And Rachel, I thought, although she said nothing, noticed it too.

Three months before, I had attended a talk at the Portland Public Library. Two people, a doctor and a psychic, had debated the existence of supernatural phenomena. Frankly, I was slightly embarrassed to be there. I seemed to be keeping company with some people who didn't wash often enough and who, judging by the questions that followed the session, were intent upon accepting as true every manner of mumbo jumbo, of which the spirit world appeared merely to be one small part, taking its place alongside angels who looked like fairies, UFOs, and alien lizards in human form.

The doctor spoke of auditory hallucinations that, he said,

were by far the most common experienced by those who spoke of ghosts. Older people, he continued, particularly those with Parkinson's, sometimes suffered from an ailment called Lewy body dementia, which caused them to see foreshortened bodies. That explained the prevalence of stories in which the spirits allegedly glimpsed appeared to be cut off at the knees. He spoke of other possible triggers, of diseases of the temporal lobe, of tumors and schizophrenia, and of depression. He described hypnagogic dreams, those vivid images that come to us in the spaces between sleeping and waking; and yet, he concluded, he still could not entirely explain away all reported supernatural experiences using science alone. There was too much that we did not know, he said, about the workings of the brain, about stress and depression, about mental illness and the nature of grief.

The psychic, by contrast, was an old fraud, full of the nonsense that seems to come with the worst of her kind. She spoke of beings with unfinished business, of seances and messages from the 'world beyond.' She had a cable TV show and a premium-rate telephone line, and she performed her routine for the poor and the gullible at community halls and Elk lodges across the Northeast.

She said that ghosts haunt places, not people. I think that is a lie. Someone once told me that we create our own ghosts, that, as in dreams, each one of them is a facet of ourselves: our guilt, our regrets, our grief. Perhaps that may be an answer, of sorts. Each of us has our ghosts. Not every one of them is of our own creation, and yet they find us all, in the end.

Rebecca Clay sat in her kitchen. There was a glass of red wine before her, although it remained untouched, and all of the lights were extinguished.

She should have asked the detective to stay with her. The man had never tried to enter her house, and she was confident in the security of its doors and windows and the efficiency of its alarms, particularly after they had been checked by a consultant recommended by the detective, but as the night had drawn in such precautions began to seem insufficient, and now she was aware of every noise in the old building, every settling of boards and rattling of cupboards as the wind played through the house like an errant child.

The window above the kitchen sink was very dark, quartered by the white frame with nothing visible beyond. She might have been floating through the blackness of space, with only the thinnest of barriers separating her from the vacuum outside, were it not for the gentle exclamation of unseen waves breaking upon the beach. For want of something better to do, she brought the glass to her lips and sipped carefully, noticing just too late the musty smell that arose from the wine. She grimaced, then spit it back into the glass and rose from the table. She walked to the sink and poured the liquid away before turning on the faucet and washing the red splashes from the metal. Leaning down, she sipped water straight from the flow, cleansing her mouth of the taste. It reminded her, uncomfortably, of the way her ex-husband had tasted, and the rankness of his kisses in the night as their marriage entered its final, terminal decline. She knew that he had detested her then just as much as she now hated him, and he had wanted to be rid of this burden that they shared. Rebecca had no longer wished to offer her body to him, and had felt not even the tiniest residue of the attraction she had once enjoyed, but he had found a way to separate love and need. She wondered, sometimes, of whom he fantasized as he moved upon her. Sometimes, his eyes grew vacant, and she knew that even as his body was bound to hers, his true self was far away. At other times, though, there was an intensity to his gaze, a kind of loathing as he stared down at her that made the sexual act feel like a violation. There was no love in it then, and as she looked back upon those years, she found it hard to remember if there had ever been love there.

She had tried to do the same, of course, to conjure up images of past or potential lovers to make the experience less unpleasant, but they were too few, and they brought with them their own troubles, and in the end she had simply given up. Her appetites had faded to such a degree that it was easier just to think of other things entirely, or to look forward to the time when this man would be gone from her life. She could not even recall why she had wanted to be with him to begin with, and he with her. She supposed that, with a young daughter and all that had happened with her father, she had just desired some stability for a time, but he had not been the man to give it to her. There had been a debased element to his attraction to her, as though he saw something within her that was corrupted and he had enjoyed touching it by entering her.

He had not even liked her daughter, the product of a relationship begun before she was fully ready to have one. (And who knows? Perhaps she was never meant to have a proper relationship, not really.) Jenna's father had drifted away. He had seen his child only a handful of times, and then only in the early years. He would not even recognize her now, Rebecca thought, then realized that she was thinking of him as if he were still alive. She tried to feel something for him, but she could not. His life had ended prematurely on a dark minor road far from home, his body dumped in a ditch, his hands tied roughly behind his back with fuse wire, blood soaking into the soft ground to feed the small scurrying things that burrowed up from below to scavenge upon him. He had not been good for her. He had probably not been good for very much at all, which was why he had ended up the way he did. He had never been one to keep his promises, to make good on his commitments. It was inevitable, she supposed, that one day he would encounter someone who would not forgive him his trespasses and would instead extract a final, grim payment from him.

For a time Jenna had asked a lot of questions about him, but in recent years they had become fewer and fewer until at last they were either forgotten, or she elected to keep them unspoken. She had not yet worked out how to inform Jenna that her father was dead. He had been killed earlier that year, and she had not found the right opportunity to talk with Jenna of his death. She was deliberately putting it off, she knew, yet still she waited. Now, in the darkness of her kitchen, she decided that when Jenna next raised the subject of her father she would tell her the truth about him.

She thought again about the private detective. In a sense, Jenna's father was the reason that she had approached him. Jenna's paternal grandfather had talked of Parker. He had wanted him to look for his son, but the detective had turned him down. She thought that the old man might have felt bitterness toward the detective, especially after the way things had worked out, but he had not. Perhaps he understood that his son was already a lost cause, even if he refused to surrender himself to the consequences of that understanding. If he had no faith in his son, then how could he expect another to believe in him instead? So he did not blame the detective for declining to help him, and Rebecca had remembered his name when the stranger came asking about her own father.

The faucet was still running, so she began to pour the rest of the bottle down the sink. The water circled around the drain, stained with red. Jenna was asleep upstairs. Rebecca was making plans to send her away if the detective could not quickly rid her of the stranger's attentions. So far, the man had not approached Jenna, but she was concerned that such a situation might not last, and he would use the daughter to get at the mother. She would tell Jenna's school that the child was sick, and she would deal with the repercussions when the time came. Then again, perhaps she might simply tell them the truth: that a man was bothering her, that Jenna might be at risk if she stayed in Portland. Surely they would understand.

Why now? she wondered. It was the same question the detective had asked her. Why, after so many years had gone by, would someone come asking about her father? What did he know about the circumstances of his disappearance? She had tried to ask him, but he had only tapped his forefinger against his nose in that knowing way of his before saying:

'It ain't his disappearance I'm interested in, missy. It's another's. He'll know, though. He'll know.'

The stranger had spoken of her father as though he were certain that he was still alive. More to the point, he seemed to think that she knew it too. He wanted answers she could not give him.

She lifted her head and saw herself reflected in the window. The sight gave her a sudden shock so that she jerked slightly, the face before her turning from a single image to a double through a flaw in the glass. But when she had regained her composure, the second image still remained. It was like her, yet not like her, as though she had somehow shed her skin as a snake might, and the discarded membrane had settled upon the features of another. Then the figure outside drew closer and the impression of a doppelgänger faded, leaving only the stranger in a leather jacket, his hair slick with grease. She heard his voice, distorted by the thickness of the glass, but she could not understand his words.

He pressed his hands against the glass, then slid the palms down until the tips of his fingers were resting against the window frame. He pushed, but the lock inside held. His face contorted in anger and he bared his teeth.

'You get away from me,' she said. 'You get away now, or so help me—'

His hands withdrew, and then Rebecca saw a fist punch its way through the glass, shaking the frame and showering the sink with fragments. She screamed, but the sound was caught up in the screeching of the alarm. Blood coursed down the shattered pane as the stranger pulled his hand back through the glass, not even attempting to avoid the jagged edges that ripped at his skin, tearing red channels across his palms and severing veins. He stared at the wounded fist, as if it were a thing beyond his control, surprising him with its actions. She heard the phone ring and knew that it was the monitoring company. If she didn't reply, the police would be called. Someone would eventually be sent to check on her.

'I shouldn't ought to have done that,' said the man. 'I apologize.' But she could barely hear him over the shrieking of the alarm. He tilted his head to her. It was a strangely respectful gesture, almost old-fashioned in its courtliness. She stifled the urge to giggle, fearful that if she started to laugh she would never stop, that she would descend into hysteria and never surface from it again.

The phone stopped, then began to ring again. She made no move toward it. Instead, she watched as the stranger retreated, leaving her sink covered with his blood. She smelled it as, slowly, it combined with the stink of the corked wine to create something terrible and new, lacking only a chalice from which it might be sipped.

3

I sat at Rebecca Clay's kitchen table, watching as she cleaned the broken glass from the sink with a brush and pan. There was still blood on the windowpane. She had notified the cops immediately after calling me, and a South Portland cruiser had arrived shortly before I did. I had identified myself to the patrolman and listened as Rebecca gave her statement, but otherwise I had not interfered in any way. Her daughter, Jenna, sat on a sofa in the living room, clutching a china doll that looked like it might once have belonged to her mother. The doll had red hair and wore a blue dress. It was obvious that it was an old and cherished possession. The mere fact that the girl was seeking comfort from it at this time attested to its value. She did not seem as shaken as her mother, appearing more puzzled than disturbed. She also struck me as both older and younger than her years – older in appearance yet younger in her demeanor – and I wondered if perhaps her mother sheltered and protected her a little too much.

There was another woman sitting with Jenna. Rebecca introduced her as April, a friend who lived nearby. She shook my hand and said that, since I was there and Jenna seemed okay, she'd go home so that she wouldn't be in the way. Rebecca kissed her on the cheek and they hugged, then April leaned back and held Rebecca at arm's length. A look passed between them, one that spoke of shared knowledge, of years of friendship and loyalty.

'You call me,' said April. 'Anytime.'

'I will. Thanks, hon.'

April kissed Jenna good-bye, then left.

I watched Jenna while Rebecca walked the cop around the outside of the house, pointing out the place where the stranger had stood. The child would grow up to be a very beautiful young woman. There was something of her mother in her, but it was rendered more striking by a slim, aquiline grace that came from elsewhere. I thought I saw a little of her grandfather in her as well.

'You doing okay?' I asked her.

She nodded.

'When something like this happens, it can be kind of scary,' I continued. 'It's happened to me, and I was scared.'

'I wasn't scared,' she said, and her tone was so matter-of-fact that I knew she wasn't lying.

'Why not?'

'The man didn't want to hurt us. He's just sad.'

'How do you know that?'

She just smiled and shook her head. 'It doesn't matter.'

'Have you spoken to him?'

'No.'

'Then how do you know that he doesn't mean you harm?'

She looked away, that almost beatific smile still on her face. The conversation was clearly over. Her mother came back inside with the cop, and Jenna told her that she was going back to bed. Rebecca hugged her and told her that she'd check on her later. She said good-bye to the cop and me, then went upstairs to her room.

Rebecca Clay lived in an area known as Willard. Her house, a compact but impressive nineteenth-century structure in which she had grown up, and to which she had returned after her father's disappearance, stood on Willard Haven Park, a dead end that ran perpendicular to Willard Beach, a few steps across Willard Haven Road. When the cop eventually left, promising that a detective would call either later that night or the next morning, I took a look around, walking in his footsteps, but it was clear that the man who had broken the glass was long gone. I followed a trail of blood to Deake Street, which ran parallel to Willard Haven Park on the right, then lost it where he had climbed into a car and driven away. I called Rebecca Clay from the sidewalk, and she gave me the names of some of the neighbors who lived within sight of where the car had been parked. Only one of them, a middle-aged woman named Lisa Hulmer, who sported the kind of look that suggested she might consider the description 'whorish' a compliment, had seen anything, and even that wasn't much help to me. She remembered a dark red car parked across the street, but she couldn't tell me the make or the tag number. She did invite me into her home, though, and suggested that I might like to join her for a drink. I had clearly disturbed her in the act of consuming a jug of something fruity and alcoholic. When she closed the front door behind me, it reminded me uncomfortably of a cell slamming shut on a condemned man.

'It's a little early for me,' I said.

'But it's after ten-thirty!'

'I'm a late sleeper.'

'Me too.' She grinned and arced an eyebrow in what would only have passed for a suggestive manner if you were especially susceptible to suggestion, like a dog or a small child. 'Once you get me into bed you just can't get me out of it.'

'That's . . . nice,' I said, for want of a better word.

'You're nice,' she said. She swayed a little and fiddled with a seashell chain that hung between her breasts, but by then I had opened the door and was backing out of the house before she shot me with a dart and chained me to a wall in her basement.

'Did you find out anything?' Rebecca Clay asked me when I got back to her house.

'Not much, apart from the fact that one of your neighbors is in heat.'

'Lisa?' She smiled for the first time since I'd arrived. 'She's *always* in heat. She even propositioned me once.'

'You're making me feel less special,' I said.

'I suppose I should have warned you about her but – ' She waved a hand at the broken window.

'Well, she was the only one who saw anything. She said there was a red car parked outside her house for a while, but the lighting isn't so good there. She could be mistaken.'

Rebecca threw the last of the glass in her trash can and put the brush and pan in a closet. She then called a glazier, who promised to be out to her first thing in the morning. I helped her to tape some plastic over the damaged pane, and when all of that was done, she made a pot of coffee and poured each of us a cup. We both stayed standing while we drank.

'I don't trust the police to do anything about this,' she said.

'Can I ask why?'

'They haven't been able to do anything about him so far. Why should this time be any different?'

'This time he busted through a window. That's criminal damage. It's escalating. There's blood, and the blood could be useful to the cops.'

'How? So they can use it to identify him if he kills me? By then it may be a little late for me. This man isn't scared of the police. I was thinking about what you told me when we first met, about how this man might have to be forced to leave me alone. I want you to do that. I don't care how much it costs. I have some money. I can afford to pay you to do it, and whomever else you want to hire to help you. Look at what he did here. He's not going to go away, not unless someone makes him. I'm afraid for myself, and I'm afraid for Jenna.'

'Jenna seems like a very self-possessed girl,' I said, hoping to distract her from the subject until she had calmed down.

'What do you mean?'

'I mean that she didn't seem particularly frightened or shaken by what happened.'

Rebecca frowned. 'I guess she's always been that way. I'll talk to her later, though. I don't want her bottling something up just because she doesn't want to upset me.'

'Can I ask where her father is?'

'Her father's dead.'

'I'm sorry to hear that.'

'It's okay. He never had much to do with her anyway, and we weren't married. But I meant what I said: I want this man stopped, whatever it takes.'

I didn't reply. She was angry and frightened. Her hands were still shaking from the shock of the incident. There would be time to talk in the morning. I told her that I'd stay if it made her feel better. She thanked me and made up the sofa bed in her living room.

'Do you carry a gun?' she asked as she prepared to head up the stairs to her bedroom.

'Yes.'

'Good. If he comes back, use it to kill him.'

'That'll cost extra.'

She looked at me and for a moment I could see that she was wondering if I was serious. Worryingly, I thought that she might even have been willing to pay.

The glazier arrived shortly after seven to replace the broken pane. He took a look at the sleeper couch, the busted window, and me, and clearly decided that he was entering the aftermath of a domestic dispute.

'It happens,' he whispered to me conspiratorially. 'They throw stuff, but they don't mean it to hit you, not really. Still, always pays to duck.'

I thanked him. It was probably good advice in any case. He nodded pleasantly to Rebecca and went about his work.

When he was done, I followed Rebecca's Hyundai as she drove Jenna to school, then kept behind her all the way to her office. She worked a stone's throw from where she lived, at Willard Square, just by the junction of Pillsbury and Preble. She had told me that she planned to be in the office until lunchtime, then had properties to visit in the afternoon. I watched her go inside. I had tried to keep a discreet distance from her while she drove. I hadn't yet seen any sign of the man who was following her, but I didn't want him to spot me with her, not yet. I wanted him to try to get close to her again, so that this time I could be waiting. If he was good, though, he'd pick me out easily, and I had already resigned myself to the fact that I would need to bring in more bodies if this thing was to be done right.

While Rebecca worked in her office, I drove back to Scarborough, walked and fed Walter, then showered and changed my clothes. I switched cars, substituting the Mustang for a green Saturn coupe, bought coffee and a Danish in Foley's Bakery on Route 1, and headed back to Willard. Willie Brew's auto shop in Queens had sourced the coupe for me and sold it on for what seemed like less than it must have cost to buy the tires. It was useful as a backup at times like this, but driving it made me feel like a rube.

'Somebody die in it?' I had asked Willie when he had first presented it to me as a possible second car.

Willie had made a show of sniffing the interior.

'I think it's damp,' he had answered. 'Probably. Maybe. Anyway, at what I'm asking for it, the corpse could be stuck to the seat and it would still be a bargain.'

He was right, but it remained kind of embarrassing to drive. Then again, it was hard to be inconspicuous in a 1969 Mustang Boss 302. Even the dumbest criminal is likely to look in his rearview at some point and think, I wonder, is that the same '69 Mustang with go-faster stripes that was behind me earlier? Hey, maybe I'm being followed!

I checked in with Rebecca by phone, then took a walk around Willard to clear my head a little more and to pass some time. Sleeping on a couch with a cold wind whistling through a broken window wasn't conducive to a good night's sleep. Even after my shower, I still felt out of sync.

People across the water in Portland tended to look down some on South Portland. It had been a city for only a hundred years or so, which made it a baby by Maine standards. The building of the Million Dollar Bridge, the construction of Interstate 295, and the opening of the Maine Mall had taken away some of its charm by forcing local businesses to close, but it still had a character all its own. The area in which Rebecca Clay lived used to be called Point Village, but that was way back in the 1800s, and by the time South Portland became a separate entity from Cape Elizabeth in 1895, it had become known simply as Willard. It was home to ships' captains and fishermen, descendants of whom still lived in the area to this day. During the last century, a man named Daniel Cobb used to own a lot of the land around here. He grew tobacco and apples and celery. It was also said that he was the first person to grow iceberg lettuce in the East.

I walked down Willard Street to the beach. The tide was out, and the sand changed color dramatically from white to dark brown where the sea's advance had halted. To the left, the beach stretched in a half-moon, ending at the Spring Point Ledge Light, which marked the dangerous ledge on the west side of the main shipping channel into Portland Harbor. Beyond lay Cushing Island and Peaks Island, and the rust-streaked façade of Fort Gorges. To the right, a set of concrete steps led up to a pathway along the promontory that ended in a small park.

A trolley line used to run down Willard Street to the beach in summer. Even after the trolley stopped running, an old refreshment stand remained near what used to be the end of the line. It dated back to the 1930s, and it was still selling food as late as the 1970s, when it was called the Dory and the Carmody family passed out hot dogs and fries through its window to the beachgoers. My grandfather sometimes brought me there as a child, and he told me that the stand had once been part of the empire of Sam Silverman, who was kind of a legend in his time. It was said that he kept a monkey and a bear in a cage in order to attract people to his businesses, including the Willard Beach Bath House and Sam's Lunch. The Carmodys' hot dogs had been pretty good, but they couldn't really match up to a bear in a cage. After we had spent a little time on the beach, my grandfather would always take me over to Mr and Mrs B's store, the Bathras Market, on Preble Street, where he would order some Italian sandwiches to bring home for supper and Mr B. would carefully record the sale on my grandfather's tab. The Bathras family had the most famous tab in South Portland, so that it seemed like every customer settled bills there on a weekly or biweekly basis, with cash rarely changing hands for small items.

I wondered if it was nostalgia that caused me to reflect warmly on something as simple as a grocery store or an old refreshment stand. That was part of it, I supposed. My grandfather had shared these places with me, but now both he and they were gone, and I would not have the opportunity to share them with another. Still, there were other places and other people. Jennifer, my first child, had never been given the chance to see them, not really. She was too young when she and her mother came up here with me, and before she was old enough to appreciate what she was encountering, she was dead. But there was still Sam. Her life was just beginning. If I could keep her safe from harm, then in time she might be able to join me on a stretch of sand, or on a quiet street along which trolleys used to rumble, or by a river or on a mountain path. I could pass on some of these secrets to her, and she could hold them to herself and know that the past and the present were speckled with brightness, and that there was light as well as shade in the honeycomb world.

I turned back toward Willard Haven Road, following the slatted path across the sand, then stopped. Halfway up Willard Street, a red car sat idling by the curb. The windshield was almost reflective, so that when I looked at it I saw only the sky. As I began to approach, the driver put it into reverse, backing slowly up Willard, keeping the distance between us constant, then found space to turn and headed for Preble. The car was a Ford Contour, probably a mid-nineties model. I didn't get the number of the plate. I couldn't even be sure that inside was the man who was stalking Rebecca Clay, but I had a feeling it was he. I guessed that it had been too much to hope that he might not have connected me to her yet, but it wasn't a disaster. My presence might be enough to rattle his cage. It wouldn't frighten him off, but it might make him try to frighten me off instead. I wanted to meet him face-to-face. I wanted to hear what he had to say. Until then, I couldn't begin to solve Rebecca Clay's problem.

I walked back up Willard Street to where my car was parked. If the guy had made me, then at least I wouldn't have to drive the Saturn any longer, so that was some cause for celebration. I called Rebecca and told her that I thought the man who was bothering her might be nearby. I gave her the color and the make of the car and told her not to leave the office, even for a short time. If her plans changed suddenly she was to call me, and I would come and get her. She informed me that she planned to eat lunch at her desk, and she had called Jenna's principal and asked that Jenna be allowed to wait with his secretary until she arrived to pick her up. The fact that Rebecca was staying at her office for a while gave me an hour or so to play around with. While she had told me a little about her father, I wanted to find out more, and I thought I knew someone who might be able to help.

I headed into Portland and parked across from the Public Market. I picked up two coffees and some scones from the Big Sky Bakery, on the grounds that it always paid to arrive somewhere with a bribe in hand, and headed over to the Maine College of Art on Congress. June Fitzpatrick owned a pair of galleries in Portland, and a black dog that took a dim view of anyone who wasn't June. I found June in her gallery space in the college, setting up an exhibition of new work against its pristine white walls. She was a small, enthusiastic woman with a voice that had lost only a little of its English accent during her years in Maine, and a good memory for faces and names in the art world. Her dog barked at me from a corner, then contented itself with keeping a close eye on me in case I decided to snatch a canvas.

'Daniel Clay,' she said, as she sipped her coffee. 'I remember him, although I've only ever seen a couple of examples of his work. He fell into the category of the gifted amateur. It was all very . . . *tortured* initially, I suppose you'd say: intermingled bodies, pale with eruptions of reds and blacks and blues, and all sorts of Catholic iconography going on in the background. Then he stopped doing those and moved on to landscapes. Misty trees, ruins in the foreground, that kind of thing.'

Rebecca had shown me some slides of her father's work earlier that day, along with the single canvas she had retained. It was a painting of Rebecca as a child, although it was a little dark for my liking, the child a pale blur amid gathering shadows. I confessed to June that I hadn't been very impressed with the rest of his work either.

'They're not to my taste, it must be said. I always thought his later work was one step above paintings of moose and yachts, but then it wasn't really an issue. He sold privately and didn't exhibit, so I never had to find a polite way of saying "No." There are one or two people in Portland who were quite serious collectors of his work, though, and I know he gave away a lot of his paintings to friends. His daughter occasionally sells some of those that are still in her possession, and a couple of potential buyers usually come out of the woodwork. I think most of those who collect him probably knew him personally, or are attracted by the mystery surrounding him, for want of a better term. I heard that he stopped painting entirely sometime before he went missing, so I suppose they have a certain rarity value.'

'You remember anything about his disappearance?'

'Oh, there were rumors. There wasn't much in the newspapers about the circumstances – the local press tends to be circumspect about such things at the best of times – but most of us knew that some of the children he'd been trying to help were subsequently abused again. There were people who wanted to blame him, I suppose, even among those who were prepared to believe that he wasn't directly involved.'

'You have an opinion on it?'

'There can be only two views: Either he was involved or he wasn't. If he was, then there's nothing more to say. If he wasn't, well, I'm no expert, but it can't have been easy getting some of those kids to talk about what happened to them to begin with. Perhaps the additional abuse just pushed them further and further into their shells. I really can't say.'

'Did you ever meet Clay?'

'Here and there. I tried to speak with him at a dinner we both attended, but he didn't say very much. He was quiet and distant, very soft-spoken. He appeared overburdened by life. That would have been very shortly before he vanished, so in this case appearances may not have been deceptive.'

She broke off to give instructions to a young woman who was hanging up a canvas by the window.

'No, no, that's upside down!'

I looked at the canvas, which appeared to be a painting of mud, and not pretty mud either. The young woman looked at the canvas. The young woman then looked at me.

'How can you tell?' I said, and heard my words echoed. The young woman and I had both spoken at precisely the same moment. She smiled at me, and I smiled back. I then did a rough calculation of the difference in our ages and decided that I should limit myself to smiling at people who were born before 1980.

'Philistines,' said June.

'What's it supposed to be?' I asked her.

'It's an untitled abstract.'

'Does that mean the artist doesn't know what it is either?'

'Possibly,' June conceded.

'Back to Daniel Clay. You said that the people who collected his work probably knew him. Any idea who some of those people might be?'

She walked over to the corner and absentmindedly scratched her dog behind the ear. The dog barked at me again, just to disabuse me of any notions I might have had about joining in.

'Joel Harmon is one.'

'The banker?'

'Yes. Do you know him?'

'I know of him,' I said.

Joel Harmon was the retired president of IBP, the Investment Bank of Portland. He was one of those credited with rejuvenating the Old Port during the eighties, and his picture still appeared in newspapers whenever the city threw a celebration of something or other, usually with his wife on one arm and a crowd of slavering admirers surrounding them, all aroused by the lingering smell of fresh dollar bills. His popularity could fairly be ascribed to his wealth, his power, and the attraction those two elements generally arouse in those with significantly less of either. It was whispered that he had an 'eye for the ladies,' even though his looks came pretty far down on the list of his attributes, probably somewhere between 'can carry a tune' and 'cooks spaghetti.' I'd seen him around, but we'd never been introduced.

'He and Daniel Clay were friends. I believe they might have met at college. I know that Joel bought a couple of Clay's paintings after he died, and was given others as gifts during his lifetime. I suppose he passed Clay's test of suitability. Clay was very particular about those to whom he sold or gave his work. I can't imagine why.'

'You really didn't like his paintings, did you?'

'Or him, I guess. He made me uneasy. There was something peculiarly joyless about him. Joel Harmon is having a dinner party in his house later this week, by the way. They're a pretty regular occurrence, and I have a standing invitation anytime I wish to attend. I've put some interesting artists his way. He's a good customer.'

'Are you asking me to be your date?'

'No, I'm offering to be yours.'

'I'm flattered.'

'You should be. Perhaps you'll get to see some of Clay's paintings. Just try not to offend Joel too grievously, there's a dear. I have bills to pay.'

I assured June that I would be on my best behavior. She didn't look impressed.

4

I drove back to Scarborough and dumped the Saturn, instantly feeling ten years younger in the Mustang, or at least ten years less mature, which wasn't the same thing at all. I called Rebecca to confirm that she was still planning to leave at the agreed time, then asked her to get someone to walk her to her car. She was due to look at a vacant storefront on Longfellow Square, so I waited for her in the parking lot behind Joe's Smoke Shop. There were fifteen or sixteen cars parked there, none of them occupied. I found a space that allowed me a view of Congress and the square, bought a grilled chicken sandwich with green peppers at Joe's sandwich counter, then ate in the car while I waited for Rebecca to arrive. A couple of homeless guys with shopping carts stood smoking in the alley beside the lot. Neither of them matched the description of the man who was following Rebecca.

She called me when she was passing the bus depot at St John, and I told her to park in front of the building she was visiting. The woman who was trying to rent the first-floor space was waiting outside for her when she arrived. The two of them entered together and the door closed safely behind them. The windows were large and clean and I could see both of them clearly from where I sat.

I didn't notice the squat man until he went through an odd routine while lighting a cigarette. He seemed to have appeared from out of nowhere to take up a spot on one of the metal crash barriers outside the lot. He was holding a cigarette vertically between the thumb and forefinger of his right hand and rotating it gently, probably to get a smoother draw, and his attention was entirely fixed on the women across the street. Still, there was something sensual about the motion of his fingers, a product, perhaps, of the way he was staring so intently at Rebecca Clay through the window of the store. After a time he slid the cigarette slowly into his mouth, wetting it against his lips for a moment before applying a match to the tip. Then, instead of simply throwing the match away, or blowing it out, he held it between the same thumb and forefinger as before and allowed the flame to burn down toward the tips of his fingers. I waited for him to discard it as the pain increased, but he did not. When the end of the match was no longer visible, he released his grip upon it and allowed it to fall into the palm of his hand, where it burned into blackness against his skin. He turned his hand, allowing the charred wood to fall upon the ground. I clicked off a picture of him on the little digital camera that I kept in the car. As I did so, he looked around, seemingly aware now that the attention of another was fixed upon him in turn. I slid down farther in my seat, but I had caught a glimpse of his face, and had seen the three parallel scars on his forehead of which Rebecca had spoken. When I looked back he appeared to be gone, but I sensed that he had merely retreated into the shade offered by Joe's building, for I saw a wisp of smoke carried out upon the street by a stray breeze.

Rebecca emerged from the store, carrying some papers. The other woman was beside her, talking and smiling. I called Rebecca on her cell and told her to keep smiling as she listened.

'Turn your back to Joe's Smoke Shop,' I said. I didn't want the watcher to see her reaction when I told her that I had spotted him. 'Your fan is over at Joe's. Don't look in that direction. I want you to cross the street and go into Cunningham Books. Just act casual, like you have some time to kill. Stay there until I come and get you, okay?'

'Okay,' she said. She sounded only a little frightened. To her credit, she did not pause or even betray any emotion by a change of expression. She shook hands with her client, glanced left, then right, and proceeded to cross casually to the bookstore.

She walked straight inside, as though that had been her intention all along. I got out of my car and headed quickly to the front of Joe's. There was nobody outside. Only the butt of a cigarette and the fragmented remains of a match indicated that the squat man had ever been there. The tip had been squeezed flat. Something told me that it might well have been glowing redly when the fingers were applied to it. I could almost smell the scorching of skin.

I looked around and saw him. He had crossed Congress and was walking toward the center of town. He turned right onto Park, and I lost sight of him. I figured that his car was probably there and he would wait for Rebecca to leave the bookstore before either following her or approaching her again.

I walked to the corner of Park and risked a glance down the street. The squat man was at the door of the red Ford, his head down. I stayed low and used the parked cars to approach him from the opposite side of the street. I had my .38 in a holster at my belt – it was a little more discreet than my big Smith 10 for work like this – but I was reluctant to show it. If I was forced to confront the watcher with a gun in my hand, then whatever chance I had of reasoning with him would evaporate and the situation would deteriorate before I had even begun to understand its nature. I had an image of this man burning himself, and the apparent ease with which he had done it. It suggested an individual who had a considerable tolerance for pain, and such tolerance was usually hard-earned. A face-to-face with him would have to be delicately handled.

A Grand Cherokee turned down Park, an archetypal soccer mom at the wheel, and as it passed I slipped behind it and approached the Ford from the driver's side. I could make out the outline of his quiff and the big folds of muscle at the back of his neck as he sat at the wheel, fumes already emerging from the exhaust. His hands rested on the steering wheel, the fingers of the left tapping a rhythm upon the plastic. The right hand was roughly bandaged. Bloodstains showed through the fabric. At last, I let him see me approach. I kept my arms out and my fingers splayed slightly, but I was ready to scuttle for cover if his hands left the wheel. The problem for me was that once I got close enough to talk to him, there would be nowhere for me to run. I was relying on the fact that there were people around, and the hope that he would see no percentage in reacting with hostility until he heard what I had to say.

'How you doing?' I said.

He peered lazily at me, as though it were all that he could do just to rouse himself enough to respond. He had another cigarette between his lips, and a blue pack of American Spirit rested on top of the dashboard in front of him.

'Fine,' he said. 'Just fine.'

He raised his right hand to his mouth, drawing on the cigarette so that the tip glowed brightly. He looked away from me and stared through the windshield.

'Thought someone was paying me mind,' he said. 'I see you got a gun.'

The bulge of the .38 was barely visible beneath my jacket, unless someone knew what he was looking for.

'Can't be too careful,' I said.

'You don't need to worry about me. I don't carry a gun. I got no call for one.'

'I guess you're just a gentle soul.'

'Nah, I can't claim that. The woman hire you?'

'She's concerned.'

'She has no cause to be. If she tells me what I want to know, I'll be on my way.'

'And if she doesn't, or if she can't?'

'Well, that's two different things, ain't it? One can't be helped, and one can.'

His fingers shifted from the wheel. Instantly, I was reaching for the gun at my waist.

'Whoa, whoa!' he said. He held his hands up in mock surrender. 'I done told you, I got no gun.'

I kept my hand close to the butt of the pistol. 'I'd still prefer it if your hands stayed where I can see them.'

He shrugged exaggeratedly, then allowed his palms to rest against the top of the wheel.

'Do you have a name?' I asked.

'I have lots of names.'

'That's very mysterious of you. Try one and see how it fits.'

He seemed to give the issue some thought.

'Merrick,' he said at last, and something in his face and his voice told me that this was as much as I was likely to get from him where names were concerned.

'Why are you bothering Rebecca Clay?'

'I ain't *bothering* her. I just want her to be straight with me.'

'About what?'

'About her father.'

'Her father's dead.'

'He ain't dead. She got him declared dead, but that don't mean nothing. You show me the worms crawling in the sockets of his eyes, then I'll believe he's dead.'

'Why are you so interested in him?'

'I got my reasons.'

'Try sharing them.'

His fingers tightened on the wheel. There was a small india ink tattoo on the knuckle of his left middle finger. It was a crude blue cross, a jailhouse mark.

'I don't think so. I don't like strangers questioning me about my business.'

'Well, then you'll know just how Ms. Clay feels.'

His teeth worried at the inside of his lower lip. He kept his gaze fixed straight ahead. I could feel the tension building up inside him. I had allowed my hand to drift to the butt of my gun, and my own forefinger was now extended above the trigger guard, ready to slip into place if necessary. Then the tightness released itself from Merrick's body. I heard him exhale, and he seemed to grow smaller and less threatening.

'You ask her about the Project,' he said softly. 'You see what she says.'

'What is the "Project"?'

He shook his head.

'Ask her, then come back to me. Maybe y'ought to talk to her ex-husband too, while you're about it.'

I didn't even know that Rebecca Clay had been married. I was only aware that she hadn't married the father of her child. Some investigator I was.

'Why would I do that?'

'A husband and wife, they share things. *Secret* things. You talk to him, and it could be you'll spare me the trouble of talking to him myself. I'll be around. You won't have to come looking for me, because I'll find you. You got two days to make her tell me what she knows, then I lose my patience with y'all.'

I gestured at his wounded hand.

'It seems to me like you lost your patience once already.'

He looked at the bandaged limb and stretched the fingers, as if testing the pain in the wounds.

'That was a mistake,' he said softly. 'I didn't mean to strike out like that. I'm being sorely tested by her, but I don't mean to do her harm.'

Maybe he believed that was true, but I didn't. There was a rage inside Merrick. It pulsed redly, animating his eyes and keeping every muscle and sinew in his body taut with barely suppressed emotion. Merrick might not mean to hurt a woman, might not set out to do it, but the blood on his hand said all that needed to be said about his capacity to control his impulses.

'I lost my temper, is all,' he continued. 'I need her to tell me what she knows. It's important to me.' He drew on his cigarette again. 'And since we're getting all friendly here, you didn't give me your name.'

'It's Parker.'

'What are you, a private cop?'

'You want to see my license?'

'No, a piece of a paper won't tell me nothing that I don't already know. I don't want trouble from you, sir. I've come here with business to conduct, business of a personal nature. Maybe you can make that little lady see reason so I can conclude it and be on my way. I hope so, I surely do, because if you can't, then you're no good to either of us. You'll just be in my path, and I might have to do something about that.'

He still had not looked at me again. His eyes were fixed on a small photograph that hung from the rearview mirror. It was a picture of a girl with dark hair, perhaps Jenna Clay's age or a little older, the image encased in plastic to protect it. A cheap crucifix dangled beside it.

'Who is she?' I asked.

'That doesn't concern you.'

'Nice-looking kid. How old is she?'

He didn't reply, but I had clearly struck a nerve. This time, though, there was no anger, just a kind of disengagement.

'If you told me something of why you're here, then maybe I could help you,' I persisted.

'Like I told you, sir, my business is personal.'

'Then I guess we've nothing left to discuss,' I said. 'But you need to stay away from my client.' The warning sounded hollow and unnecessary. Somehow, the balance had shifted.

'I won't trouble her no more, least of all, not until you talk to me again.' He reached down and turned the ignition key, no longer intimidated by the gun, if he had ever really been in the first place. 'But here's two warnings for you in return. The first is that when you start asking about the Project, you'd best keep a keen eye in your head because the others are going to hear about it and they won't like it that people are looking into it. They won't like it one little bit.'

'What others?'

The engine roared as he hit the gas.

'You'll find out soon enough,' he said.

'And the second warning?'

He raised his left hand and clenched it into a fist, so that the tattoo stood out starkly against the white of his knuckle.

'Don't interfere. You do, and I'll leave you for dead. Mark me now, *boy*.'

He pulled away from the curb, the exhaust pumping thick

blue smoke into the clear fall air. Before it was entirely engulfed by fumes, I caught a glimpse of his license plate.

Merrick. Now, I thought, we'll see what we can find out about *you* in the next two days.

I walked back to the bookstore. Rebecca Clay was seated in a corner, flicking through an old magazine.

'Did you find him?' she asked.

'Yes.'

She flinched. 'What happened?'

'We talked, and he went away. For now.'

'What does that mean, "for now"? I hired you to get rid of him, to make him leave me alone permanently.'

Her voice was steadily rising, but there was a tremor beneath it. I walked her from the store.

'Ms Clay,' I said, 'I told you that a warning might not be enough. This man has agreed to stay away from you until I make some inquiries. I don't know enough about him to trust him entirely, so I'd suggest that, for the moment, we continue to take every precaution. I have people whom I can call so there will always be someone watching over you while I try to find out more about him, if that will make you rest any easier.'

'Fine. I think I'll send Jenna away for a while, though, until this is all over.'

'That's a good idea. Does the name Merrick mean anything to you, Miss Clay?'

We had reached her car.

'No, I don't believe so,' she said.

'That's our friend's name, or that's what he told me. He had a photograph of a little girl in his car. It might have been his daughter. I was wondering if she was one of your father's patients, assuming she shared his surname.'

'My father didn't discuss his patients with me. I mean, not by name. If she was referred to him by the state, then there might be a record of her somewhere, I guess, but you'll have trouble getting anyone to confirm it. It would be breach of confidentiality.'

'What about your father's patient records?'

'My father's files were placed with the court after his disappearance. I remember that there was an attempt to get an order authorizing some of his colleagues to examine them, but it failed. Access can only be obtained through an in camera review, and they're rare. The judges have been reluctant to grant them in order to protect the privacy of the patients.'

It seemed time to broach the subject of her father and the accusations made against him.

'This is a difficult question for me to ask, Miss Clay,' I began.

She waited. She knew what was coming, but she wanted to hear me say it aloud.

'Do you believe that your father abused the children in his care?'

'No,' she said firmly. 'My father didn't abuse any of those children.'

'Do you think he enabled others to do so, perhaps by feeding them information about the identities and whereabouts of vulnerable patients?'

'My father was devoted to his work. When they stopped sending children to him for evaluation, it was because it was felt that he was no longer sufficiently objective. His inclination was to believe the children from the outset, and that was what got him into trouble. He knew what adults were capable of doing.'

'Did your father have many close friends?'

Her brow furrowed.

'A few. There were some professional colleagues too, although most didn't stay in touch after he disappeared. They wanted to put as much distance as possible between my father and themselves. I didn't blame them.'

'I'd like you to make a list: business associates; college buddies; people from the old neighborhood; anyone with whom he maintained regular contact.'

'I'll do it as soon as I get home.'

'By the way, you didn't tell me that you were once married.'

She looked surprised. 'How did you find out?'

'Merrick told me.'

'Jesus. It didn't seem important to tell you. It didn't last long. I don't see him anymore.'

'What's his name?'

'Jerry. Jerry Legere.'

'And he wasn't Jenna's father?'

'No.'

'Where would I find him?'

'He's an electrician. He works all over. Why do you want to talk to him?'

'I'm going to talk to a lot of people. That's how these things work.'

'But that's not going to make this man, this Merrick, go away.' Her voice was rising again. 'That's not why I hired you.'

'He's not going to go away, Miss Clay, not yet. He's angry, and that anger has something to do with your father. I need to find out the connection between your father and Merrick. To do that, I'm going to have to ask a lot of questions.'

She folded her arms on the roof of her car and laid her forehead against them.

'I don't want this to drag on,' she said, her voice slightly muffled by her posture. 'I want things to go back to the way they were. Do what you have to do, talk to whomever, but make it stop. Please. I don't even know where my ex-husband lives anymore, but he used to do some work for a company called A-Secure and he probably still does. They install security systems in businesses and homes. A friend of Jerry's, Raymon Lang, does a lot of the maintenance on the systems, and he used to put business Jerry's way. You'll probably find Jerry through A-Secure.'

'Merrick thinks that you and your ex-husband might have spoken about your father sometime in the past.'

'Well, of course we did, but Jerry doesn't know anything

about what happened to him. I can tell you that for sure. The only person Jerry Legere ever cared about was himself. I think he believed that my father would turn up dead somewhere and he could start spending the money that would come to me.'

'Was your father wealthy?'

'There's a good six-figure sum still tied up in probate, so, yes, I suppose you could say that he was comfortable. Then there's the house. Jerry wanted me to sell it, but obviously I couldn't because it wasn't mine to sell. In the end, Jerry just got tired of waiting, and of me. It was mutual, though. Jerry wasn't exactly a great catch.'

'One last thing,' I said. 'Did you ever hear your father mention something about a "project," or "*the* Project"?'

'No, never.'

'Have you any idea what that might mean?'

'None.'

She raised her head and got into her car. I stayed behind her all the way to her office, then remained there until it was time for her to collect Jenna. The principal escorted the girl to the door of the school, and Rebecca spent a little time talking to him, presumably to explain why Jenna would not be at school for a while, then I followed them both back to the house. Rebecca parked in the drive and kept the car doors locked while I checked every room. I went back to the front door and indicated that everything was okay. Once she was inside, I sat in the kitchen and watched while she put together a list of her father's friends and colleagues. It wasn't very long. Some, she said, were dead, and others she could not remember. I asked her to let me know if she thought of any additions and she assured me that she would. I told her that I would deal with the issue of extra protection that evening, and would call her with the details before she went to bed that night. With that, I left her. I heard her turning the key in the lock behind me, and a series of electronic beeps as she entered the alarm code to secure the house.

Already, the daylight had departed. The waves broke on the

shore as I walked to my car. Usually, I found it restful, but not now. There was an element missing, something out of kilter, and the late-afternoon air carried the scent of burning upon it. I turned to the water, for the smell was coming off the sea, as though a distant ship were aflame. I looked for its glow upon the horizon, but there was only the rhythmic pulse of the lighthouse, the movement of a ferry upon the bay, and the lit rooms in the houses on the islands beyond. Everything spoke of calm and routine, and yet I could not shake my sense of unease as I made my way home.

II

Shape without form, shade without colour
Paralysed force, gesture without motion;

Those who have crossed
With direct eyes, to death's other Kingdom
Remember us – if at all – not as lost
Violent souls, but only
As the hollow men . . .

T. S. Eliot, *The Hollow Men*

Merrick had promised us two days of peace, but I wasn't prepared to gamble the safety of Rebecca and her daughter on the word of a man like that. I had seen his kind before: Merrick was a simmerer, his temper always on the verge of boiling over. I recalled the way he had reacted to my comment about the girl in the picture, and the warnings about his 'personal' business. Despite his assurances, there was always the chance that he might go to a bar, down a couple of drinks, and decide now was the time to have another word with Daniel Clay's daughter. On the other hand, I couldn't spend all my time watching her. I needed to call in some help. I had few options. There was Jackie Garner, who was big and strong and well-meaning, but also had a couple of screws loose. In addition, where Jackie went two meat wagons on legs called the Fulci brothers usually followed, and the Fulcis were to subtlety what an egg beater was to an egg. I wasn't sure how Rebecca Clay would take it if she found them standing on her doorstep. In fact, I wasn't sure how the doorstep would take it either.

Louis and Angel would be preferable, but they were over on the West Coast for a couple of days, wine tasting in the Napa Valley. Clearly, I had sophisticated friends, but I couldn't afford to leave Rebecca unprotected until they returned. It seemed that I had no other choice.

Reluctantly, I called Jackie Garner.

I met him at Sangillo's Tavern, a little place on Hampshire that was always lit up like Christmas inside. He was drinking a Bud Light, but I tried not to hold that against him. I joined him at the bar and ordered a sugar-free Sprite. Nobody laughed, which was kind of them.

'You on a diet?' asked Jackie. He was wearing a long-sleeved T-shirt that bore the logo of a Portland bar that had closed down so long ago its patrons had probably paid for their drinks in wampum. His hair was shaved close to his skull and there was a faded bruise beside his left eye. His belly pressed tightly against the shirt so that a casual observer might have dismissed him as another fat guy at a bar, but Jackie Garner wasn't that at all. In all the time that I'd known him no one had ever knocked him down, and I didn't like to think about what had happened to whomever had left that bruise on Jackie's face.

'I'm not in the mood for beer,' I said.

He raised his bottle, squinted at me, and announced, in a deep baritone: 'This isn't beer. This is Bud.'

He looked pleased with himself.

'That's very catchy,' I said.

He smiled widely. 'I've been entering competitions. You know, the ones where you think up a slogan. Like, "This isn't beer. This is Bud".' He picked up my Sprite. 'Or, "This isn't soda. This is Sprite." "These aren't nuts. These are – " ' Well, these *are* nuts, but you get the point.'

'I see a pattern emerging.'

'I figure it's adaptable to any product.'

'Except nuts in bowls.'

'Pretty much.'

'Don't see how it can fail. You busy these days?'

Jackie shrugged. As far as I could tell, he was never busy. He lived with his mother, did a little bar work a couple of days a week, and spent the rest of the time manufacturing home-made munitions in a tumbledown shack in the woods behind his house. Occasionally, someone would report hearing an explosion to the local cops. Even less occasionally, the cops would send a car along in the faint hope that Jackie had blown himself up. So far, they had been sorely disappointed.

'You need something done?' he asked. His eyes gleamed with new light at the prospect of potential mayhem.

'Just for a couple of days. There's a woman who's being bothered by a guy.'

'You want us to hurt him?'

'Us? Who's us?'

'You know.' He gestured with his thumb at some indefinable place beyond the confines of the bar. Despite the cold, I felt a prickle of sweat on my forehead and aged about one year in an instant.

'They're here? What are you, joined at the hip?'

'I told them to wait outside. I know they make you nervous.'

'They don't make me nervous. They scare the hell out of me.'

'Well, they're not allowed in here no more anyway. They're not allowed anywhere, I guess, not since the, uh, the *thing*.'

There was a 'thing.' Where the Fulcis were concerned, there was always a 'thing'.

'What thing?'

'The thing over at the B-Line.'

The B-Line was just about the roughest joint in the city, a dive bar that offered a free drink to anyone who could produce a one-month AA badge. Getting banned from the B-Line for causing trouble was like getting thrown out of the Eagle Scouts for being too good with knots.

'What happened?'

'They hit a guy with a door.'

By comparison with some of the stories I had heard about the Fulcis, and the B-Line, that seemed comparatively minor.

'You know, that doesn't sound so bad. For them.'

'Well, it was really a couple of guys. And two doors. And they took the doors off their hinges so they could hit the guys with them. Now they can't go out so much no more. They were kind of sore about it. Still are. But they don't mind sitting in the lot here. They think the lights are pretty, and I bought them a couple of family-style takeouts from Norm's.'

I took a deep, calming breath.

'I don't want anybody hurt, which means, I'm not sure that I want the Fulcis near this.'

Jackie scowled. 'They'll be disappointed. I told them I was meeting you and they asked to come along. They like you.'

'How can you tell? Because they haven't hit me with a door yet?'

'They don't mean no harm. It's just that the doctors keep changing their medication and sometimes it don't take like it should.'

Jackie spun his bottle sorrowfully. He didn't have a lot of friends, and it was clear that he felt society had misjudged the Fulcis on a great many levels. Society, by contrast, was certain that it had the Fulcis down pat, and had taken all appropriate steps to ensure that contact with them was kept to a minimum.

I patted Jackie on the arm.

'We'll find something for them to do, okay?'

He brightened. 'They're good guys to have around when things get messy,' he said, conveniently ignoring the fact that things tended to get messy precisely because they were around.

'Look, Jackie, this guy's name is Merrick, and he's been following my client for a week now. He's been asking about her father, but her father has been missing for a long time, so long that he's been declared legally dead. I cornered Merrick yesterday and he said that he'd ease off for a couple of days, but I'm not inclined to trust him. He's got a temper.'

'Was he carrying?'

'I didn't see one, but that doesn't mean anything.'

Jackie sipped his beer.

'How come he's only showing up now?' he asked.

'What?'

'If this guy's been missing so long, how come this other guy is only asking about him now?'

I looked at Jackie. That was the thing about him. Something definitely rattled in his head when he walked, but he wasn't dumb. I'd considered the question of why Merrick was asking about Daniel Clay now, but not what might have prevented

him from doing so before. I thought of the tattoo on his
knuckle. Could Merrick have been doing time since Clay
disappeared?

'Maybe I can find that out while you're watching the woman.
Her name is Rebecca Clay. I'll introduce you to her tonight.
And look: keep the Fulcis away from face-to-faces with her,
but if you want to have them close by, then that's okay with
me. In fact, it might not be a bad idea to let them be seen
keeping an eye on the house.'

Even a man like Merrick was likely to be discouraged from
approaching Rebecca by the sight of three big men, two of
whom made the third look undernourished.

I gave Jackie a description of Merrick and his car, including
the tag number.

'Don't bank on the car, though. He may ditch it now that
it's been connected with him.'

'Century and a half a day,' said Jackie. 'I'll look after Tony
and Paulie out of it.' He finished his beer. 'Now, you gotta come
out and say hello. They'll be offended if you don't.'

'And we wouldn't want that,' I said, and I meant it, too.

'Damn straight.'

Tony and Paulie hadn't arrived in their monster truck, which
was why I hadn't spotted them when I'd parked. Instead they
were sitting in the front of a dirty white van that Jackie sometimes used for what he euphemistically termed his 'business.'
As I approached, the Fulcis opened the van doors and climbed
out. I wasn't even sure how Jackie had managed to get them
in there to begin with. It looked like the van had been assembled around them. The Fulcis weren't tall, but they were wide,
even double-wide. The kind of places in which they shopped
for clothes opted for practical over fashionable, so they were
twin visions in polyester and cheap leather. Tony clasped my
hand in one of his paws, smearing it with barbecue sauce, and
I felt something pop. Paulie patted me softly on the back and
I almost coughed up a lung.

'We're back in business, fellas,' announced Jackie proudly.

And for a brief moment, before common sense prevailed, I felt strangely happy.

I drove with Jackie over to Rebecca Clay's house. She looked relieved to see me again. I made the introductions and told Rebecca that Jackie would be looking after her for the next few days, but that I'd also be around if anything came up. I think Jackie looked more like her idea of a bodyguard than I did, so she didn't object. In the interests of almost full disclosure, I also told her that there would be two other men nearby in case of trouble, and gave her a rough description of the Fulcis that erred on the side of flattery without resorting to outright lies.

'Are three men really necessary?' she asked.

'No, but they come as a package. They'll cost one-fifty a day, which is cheap, but if you're worried about the cost we can work something out.'

'It's okay. I think I can afford it for a while.'

'Good. I'm going to try to find out more about Merrick while we have breathing space, and I'm going to talk to some of the people on your list. If we're no closer to figuring out Merrick at the end of this two-day grace period, and he still won't accept that you can't help him, we'll go to the cops again and try to have him picked up before running the whole thing by a judge. Right now, I know you'd prefer a more physical approach, but we need to exhaust the other possibilities first.'

'I understand.'

I asked after her daughter, and she told me that she'd arranged for Jenna to go to D.C. with her grandparents for a week. Her absence had been cleared with the school, and Jenna would leave first thing in the morning.

She walked me to the door, and touched my arm.

'Do you know why I hired you?' she asked. 'I used to date a guy called Neil Chambers. He was Jenna's father.'

Neil Chambers. His father, Ellis, had approached me earlier in the year, seeking help for his son. Neil owed money to some men in Kansas City, and there was no way that he could pay the debt. Ellis wanted me to act as an intermediary, to find some way to solve the problem. I couldn't help him, not then. I had suggested some people I thought might be able to work something out, but it was too late for Neil. His body was dumped in a ditch as a warning to others shortly after Ellis and I had spoken.

'I'm sorry,' I said.

'Don't be. Neil didn't see Jenna much, hadn't seen her in years, to tell the truth, but I'm still close to Ellis. He and his wife, Sara, are the ones who are looking after Jenna this week, and he was the one who told me about you.'

'I turned him down. I couldn't give him help when he asked for it.'

'He understood. He didn't blame you. He still doesn't. Neil was lost to him. Ellis knew that, but he loved him nevertheless. When I told Ellis about Merrick, he said that I should talk to you. He's not the kind of man to bear a grudge.'

She released her hold on my arm. 'Do you think they'll ever get the men who killed Neil?' she asked.

'*Man*,' I said. 'It was one man who was responsible. His name was Donnie P.'

'Will anything ever be done about it?'

'Something was done,' I said.

She stared at me silently for a time.

'Does Ellis know?' she asked.

'Would it help him if he did?'

'No, I don't think so. Like I told you, he's not that kind of man.'

Her eyes shone, and something uncurled itself deep inside her, stretching sinuously, its mouth soft and red.

'But you are,' she said, 'aren't you?'

We found the girl in a glorified kennel in Independence, east of Kansas City and within sight and sound of a small airport. Our information had been good. The girl didn't open the door when I knocked. Angel, small and apparently unthreatening, was beside me and Louis, tall, dark, and very, very threatening, was at the back of the house in case she tried to run. We could hear someone moving inside. I knocked again.

'Who's there?' *The voice sounded cracked and strained.*

'Mia?' *I said.*

'There's nobody called Mia here.'

'We want to help you.'

'I told you: there's no Mia here. You have the wrong address.'

'He's coming for you, Mia. You can't keep one step ahead of him forever.'

'I don't know what you're talking about.'

'Donnie, Mia. He's closing in, and you know it.'

'Who are you? Cops?'

'You ever hear of a guy named Neil Chambers?'

'No. Why would I have?'

'Donnie killed him over a bad debt.'

'So?'

'He left him in a ditch. He tortured him, then he shot him. He'll do the same to you, except in your case nobody is going to come knocking on doors to try to even things out later. Not that it will matter to you. You'll be dead. If we can find you, then he can find you too. You don't have much time left.'

There was no reply for so long that I thought she might have slipped away from the door. Then there was the sound of a security chain being removed, and the door was unlocked. We stepped into semidarkness. All the drapes were closed, and no lights burned in the room. The door slammed shut behind us and the girl named Mia retreated into the shadows so that we couldn't see her face, the face that Donnie P. had beaten on for some offense that she had given him, real or imagined.

'Can we sit down?' *I asked.*

'You can sit, if you like,' *she said.* 'I'll stay here.'

'Does it hurt?'

'Not so much, but I look bad.' *Her voice cracked further.* 'Who told you I was here?'

'It doesn't matter.'

'It does to me.'

'Someone who's concerned for you. That's all you need to know.'

'What do you want?'

'We want you to tell us why Donnie did this to you. We want you to share what you know about him.'

'What makes you think I know something?'

'Because you're hiding from him, and because the word is he wants to find you before you talk.'

My eyes were growing accustomed to the gloom. I could make out some of her features now. They looked distorted, her nose misshapen and her cheeks swollen. A shard of light from beneath the door caught the edge of her bare feet and the hem of a long red dressing gown. The varnish on her toenails was red too. It looked freshly applied. She removed a pack of cigarettes from a pocket of her gown, tapped one out, and lit it with a cigarette lighter. She kept her head down, her hair hanging over her face, but I still caught a glimpse of the scars that ran across her chin and her left cheek.

'I should have kept my mouth shut,' she said softly.

'Why?'

'He came around and threw two grand in my face. After all that he'd done to me, a lousy two grand. I was angry. I told one of the other girls that I had a way of getting even with him. I told her that I'd seen something I shouldn't have. Next I hear, she's sharing Donnie's bed. Donnie was right. I am just a dumb whore.'

'Why didn't you go to the cops with what you know?'

She drew on the cigarette. Her head was no longer lowered. Absorbed by the details of her story, she had briefly forgotten to hide her face from us. Beside me, I heard Angel hiss in sympathy as he caught sight of her ruined features.

'Because they wouldn't have done anything about it.'

'You don't know that.'

'Oh, but I do,' she said.

She took another drag on the cigarette and toyed with her hair. Nobody said anything. Eventually, Mia broke the silence.

'So now you say you're going to help me.'

'That's right.'

'How?'

'Look outside. Back window.'

She put her hand to her face and stared at me for a moment, then walked to the kitchen. I heard a soft swishing sound as she parted the curtains. When she returned, her demeanor had changed. Louis had that effect on people, especially if it seemed like he might be on their side.

'Who is he?'

'A friend.'

'He looks . . .' She tried to find the right word. '. . . intimidating,' she said at last.

'He is *intimidating*.'

She tapped her foot on the floor.

'Is he going to kill Donnie?'

'We were hoping to find another way of dealing with him. We thought that you might be able to assist us.'

We waited for her to make her decision. There was a TV on in another room, probably her bedroom. It struck me that she might not be alone, and that we should have checked the house first, but it was too late now. Finally, she reached into the pocket of her gown and withdrew her cell phone. She tossed it across the room to me. I caught it.

'Open the picture file,' she said. 'The ones you want are five or six photos in.'

I flicked through images of young women smiling together at a dinner table, of a black dog in a yard, and a baby in a high chair, until I came to the pictures of Donnie. The first showed him standing in a car park with another man, taller than he was and wearing a gray suit. The second and third pictures were different shots of the same scene, but this time the faces of the two men were a little clearer. The photos must have been taken from inside a car because the frame of a door and a side mirror were visible in two of them.

'Who is the second man?' I asked.

'I don't know,' she said. 'I followed Donnie because I thought he was cheating on me. Hell, I *knew* he was cheating on me. He's a dog. I just wanted to find out who he was cheating with.'

She smiled. The effort seemed to cause her pain.

'*You see, I thought I loved him. How stupid is that?*'

She shook her head. I could tell that she was crying.

'*And this is what you have on him? This is why he wants to find you: because you have pictures of him on your phone with a man whose name you don't know?*'

'*I don't know his name, but I know where he works. When Donnie left him, the guy was joined by two other people, a woman and a man. They're in the next picture.*'

I flicked on, and saw the trio. They were all dressed for business.

'*I thought they looked like cops,*' *said Mia.* '*They got in the car and drove away. I stayed with them.*'

'*Where did they go?*'

'*To Thirteen Hundred Summit.*'

And then I knew why Donnie wanted Mia found, and why she couldn't go to the cops with what she had – Thirteen Hundred Summit was the FBI's Kansas City field office.

Donnie P. was an informer.

In a field off a deserted road in Clay County, where cars rarely traveled and only birds kept vigil, Donnie P., the man who killed Neil Chambers over a meat-and-potatoes debt, now lay buried in a shallow grave. It had taken one phone call to his bosses, one phone call and a handful of blurred photographs sent from an untraceable e-mail account.

It was revenge, revenge for a boy I barely knew. His father wasn't aware of what had happened, and I would not tell him, which raised the question of why I had done it. It didn't matter to Neil Chambers, and it wouldn't bring him back to his father. I guess I did it because I needed to strike out at something, at someone. I chose Donnie P., and he died for it.

As Rebecca Clay said, I was that kind of man.

That night, I sat on my porch with Walter asleep at my feet. I wore a sweater under my jacket, and drank coffee from a Mustang travel cup that Angel had given me as a birthday present. The plumes of my breath mingled with the steam that rose from the coffee with each sip. The sky was dark, and there was no moon to guide the way through the marshes, no light to turn its channels to silver. The air was still, but there was no peace to the stillness, and once again I was aware of a faint smell of burning in the distance.

And then everything changed. I couldn't say how, or why, but I sensed the sleeping life around me wake for an instant, the natural world troubled by a new presence yet afraid to move for fear of attracting attention to itself. Birds beat their wings in a flurry of concern, and rodents froze in the shadows cast by tree trunks. Walter's eyes opened, and his muzzle twitched warily. His tail beat nervously upon the boards, then abruptly ceased, for even that slight disturbance in the night seemed too much.

I stood, and Walter whined. I walked to the porch rail and felt a breeze arise from the east, blowing in across the marshes, troubling the trees and causing the grass to flatten slightly as it passed over the blades. It should have brought with it the smell of sea, but it did not. Instead, there was only the scent of burning, stronger now, and then that faded, to be replaced by a dry stench, as of a hole in the ground that had recently been opened to reveal a hunched, wretched thing lying dead in the earth. I thought of dreams that I had had, dreams of a great mass of souls following the shining pathways of the marshes to lose themselves at last in the sea, like the molecules of river water drawn inexorably to the place where all things were born.

But now something had emerged, traveling from, not to, moving away from that world and into this one. The wind appeared to separate, as though it had encountered some obstacle and been forced to seek alternative paths around it, but it did not come together again. Its constituent parts flowed away in different directions, then, as suddenly as it had arisen, it was gone, and there was only that lingering odor to indicate that it had ever existed. Just for a moment, I thought I caught sight of a presence among the trees to the east, the figure of a man in an old tan coat, the details of his features lost in the gloom, his eyes and mouth dark patches against the pallor of his skin. Then just as quickly he was gone, and I wondered if I had truly seen anything at all.

Walter rose to his feet and walked to the porch door, using his paw to ease it open before disappearing into the safety of the house. I stayed, waiting for the night creatures to settle once more. I sipped at my coffee, but now it tasted bitter. I walked onto the lawn and emptied my cup on the grass. Above me, the attic window at the top of the house moved slightly in its frame, the rattle that it made causing me to turn around. It could have been the house settling, adjusting itself after the sudden breeze, but as I looked up at the window, the clouds briefly parted and moonlight at last shone upon the glass, creating the impression of movement in the room beyond. Then the clouds came together again, and the movement ceased a fraction after.

Just a fraction.

I went back inside and took the flashlight from the kitchen. I checked the batteries, then climbed the stairs to the top of the house. Using a hook on the end of a pole, I pulled down the steps leading to the attic. The light from the hallway penetrated reluctantly into the space, revealing the edges of forgotten things. I climbed up.

This attic was used for storage, nothing more. There were still some of Rachel's things here, packed away into a pair of old suitcases. I kept meaning to send them on to her, or to take them with me when next I visited her and Sam, but to do so would be to admit, finally, that she was not coming back. I had left Sam's cot as it was in her room for the same reason, another link to them that I did not wish to see disappear.

But there were other items here too, belonging to those who preceded Rachel and Sam: clothes and toys, photographs and drawings, cheap plastic jewelry, even gold and diamonds. I had not kept much, but what I did keep was here.

I could almost hear the word spoken, as though a child's voice had whispered softly in my ear, fearful of being heard yet anxious to communicate. Something small scuttled through the darkness, disturbed by the coming of the light.

They were not real. That was what I told myself again. A fragment of my sanity was jarred loose on the night that I found them, the night that they were taken from me. My mind was shaken up and was never the same again. They were not real. I created them. I conjured them up out of grief and loss.

They were not real.

But I could not convince myself, for I did not believe that it was true. I knew that this was their place, the refuge of the lost wife and the lost daughter. Whatever traces of them remained in this world clung tenaciously to the possessions stored amid the dirt and cobwebs, the fragments and relics of lives now almost gone from this world.

The flashlight chased shadows across the wall and floor. A thin layer of dust lay over everything: on boxes and cases, on old crates and old books. My nose and throat itched, and my eyes began to water.

afraid

That patina of dust lay also on the glass of the window, but it was not undisturbed. The flashlight picked out lines upon it as I approached, a pattern that formed itself into a message, carefully written in what might have been a child's hand.

make them go away

My fingers touched the glass, tracing the curves and the uprights, following the shapes of the letters. There were tears in my eyes, but I could not tell if it was the dust that brought them or the possibility that here, in this room filled with regret and loss, I had found some trace of a child long gone, that her finger had made these letters and that, by touching them, I might in turn touch something of her.

please, daddy

I stood back. The flashlight's beam showed me the dirt upon my fingers, and all of my doubts returned. Were the letters really there before I came, written by another who lived in this dark place, or had I given deeper meaning to random scratches upon the dirt perhaps left by Rachel or me, and in moving my finger upon them somehow found a way to communicate something of which I was afraid, to give form and identity to a previously nameless fear? The rational side of me reasserted itself, providing explanations, however unsatisfactory, for all that had occurred: for smells on the breeze, for a pale figure at the edge of the forest, for movement in the attic and words scratched in the dust.

Now the flashlight shone on the message, and I saw my face reflected in the glass, hovering in the night as though I were the unreal element, the lost being, so that the words were written across my features.

so afraid

They read:

HOLLOW MEN

6

I slept badly that night, my dreams punctuated by recurrent images of eyeless men who yet could somehow see, and a faceless child curled up in a ball in a darkened attic, whispering only the single word 'afraid' to herself, over and over again. I checked in with Jackie Garner first thing. It had been a quiet night in Willard, and for that much I was grateful. Jenna had departed for D.C. with her grandparents shortly after seven, and Jackie had stayed with their car as far as Portsmouth, while the Fulcis remained with Rebecca. There was no sign of Merrick, or of anyone else showing an unhealthy interest in the Clay family.

I went for a run to Prouts Neck, Walter racing ahead of me in the still morning air. This part of Scarborough was still relatively rural, the presence of the yacht club and the country club ensuring that the area retained a certain exclusivity, but elsewhere the town was changing rapidly. It had begun as far back as 1992, when Wal-Mart arrived near the Maine Mall, bringing with it minor irritations like the RV owners who were allowed to park overnight on the store's lot. Soon, other big-box retailers followed Wal-Mart's lead, and Scarborough started to become like many other satellite towns on the edge of larger cities. Now residents at Eight Corners were selling out to allow Wal-Mart to expand further, and despite a cap on residential building permits, more and more families were moving into the area to take advantage of its schools and the town's recreational pursuits, pushing property prices up and causing increases in taxes to pay for the infrastructure needed to support the new arrivals, who were taking root at four times the county average. In my darker moments, I sometimes saw what was once a fifty-four-square-mile town encompassing six distinct villages, each with its own local identity, and the largest salt marsh in the state, becoming a single homogenous sprawl populated almost entirely by those with no concept of its history and no respect for its past.

There was one message on my answering machine when I returned, and the result of my InforMe search on Merrick's vehicle plate was in my computer mailbox. According to him, Merrick's car was a company vehicle recently registered to a law office down in Lynn, Massachusetts. I didn't recognize the name of the firm, Eldritch and Associates. I scribbled the details on a notepad. Merrick could have stolen a lawyer's car – and a call to the firm would quickly confirm whether or not a theft had occurred – or he might have been employed by the attorney or attorneys, which didn't seem very likely. There was a third option: that the firm had provided Merrick with a car, either out of choice or at the instigation of a client, thereby offering at least some degree of protection if someone came around asking questions about what Merrick was doing, as the firm could offer client confidentiality as a defence. Unfortunately, if that was the case, the individual involved had underestimated Merrick's capacity for causing trouble, or just didn't care.

I thought again about Merrick's sudden appearance so many years after Daniel Clay had vanished. Either some evidence had been revealed to convince Merrick that Clay was still alive, or Merrick had been out of the loop for a long time and had just emerged to rattle a few cages. Increasingly, I was drawn to the view that Merrick might have been in jail, but I didn't have his first name, assuming Merrick even was his real name. If I had it, I could run searches in corrections.com and bop.gov in the hope of turning up a release date. Still, I could make some calls and see if the name rang any bells, and there was always Eldritch and Associates, although, in my experience, lawyers tended to be unhelpful at best in these situations. I wasn't even sure that

Merrick's pursuit of Rebecca Clay and the broken pane of glass would be enough to force some information out of them.

The second message was from June Fitzpatrick, confirming our dinner at Joel Harmon's house the following night. I had almost forgotten about Harmon. It might be a wasted evening. Then again, I still knew next to nothing about Daniel Clay, apart from what his daughter had told me and the little extra that I had found out from June. I would drive down to the Commonwealth early the next morning, see what I could wring out of Eldritch and Associates, and try to fit in a conversation with Rebecca Clay's ex-husband before Harmon's dinner. I remained aware that a clock was ticking, slowly counting down the minutes to Merrick's promised return and what was certain to be an escalation of his campaign of intimidation against Daniel Clay's daughter.

Rebecca Clay sat in her employer's washroom and wiped away her tears. She had just spoken to her daughter on the phone. Jenna had told her that she missed her already. Rebecca had told her that she missed her too, but she knew that sending her away was the right thing to do.

The night before, she had walked into Jenna's bedroom to make sure that she had packed everything that she needed for her trip. Jenna was downstairs reading. From her daughter's bedroom window, Rebecca could see the man named Jackie sitting in his car, probably listening to the radio, judging by the slight glow that came from the dashboard, illuminating his features. His presence made her feel a little better. She had also briefly met the other two men, the massive brothers who gazed adoringly at Jackie, hanging on his every word. Although big, they did not fill her with the same sense of assurance as Jackie did. They were intimidating, though, she had to give them that. One of her neighbors had been so disturbed by their presence that she had called the police. The cop who drove by in response had taken one look at the pair, recognized them for who they were, and immediately driven away without exchanging a single word with either of them. Nobody had seen a cop in the vicinity since.

All in Jenna's room was neat and in its place, because that was the kind of girl her daughter was. Rebecca looked down at the little desk that Jenna used for homework, and for her painting and drawing. She had clearly been working on something quite recently, a sketch of some kind, for a pack of colored pencils lay open beside a couple of sheets of paper. Rebecca picked up one of the sheets. It was a drawing of their house, and two figures stood beside it. They were dressed in long tan coats, and their faces were pale, so pale that her daughter had used a white wax crayon to accentuate it, as though the paper itself was not sufficient to convey the depth of their pallor. Their eyes and mouths were black circles, draining light and air from the world. The same figures appeared in each of the drawings. They looked like shadows given form, and the fact that her daughter was imagining such beings had made Rebecca shudder. Perhaps Jenna had been more disturbed by the actions of the man named Merrick than she had pretended to be, and this was some manifestation of that fear.

Rebecca had gone downstairs to Jenna and shown her the drawings.

'Who are they supposed to be, honey?' she said, but Jenna had merely shrugged.

'I dunno.'

'I mean, are they supposed to be ghosts? They look like ghosts.'

Jemma had shaken her head. 'No, I saw them.'

'You saw them? How? How could you have seen something like this?'

She had knelt beside her daughter, genuinely troubled by what she was hearing.

'Because they're real,' Jenna had replied. She had looked puzzled for a moment, then had corrected herself. 'No, I *think* they're real. It's hard to explain. You know, it's like when there's a little fog, and it makes everything fuzzy, but you can't see what's making it fuzzy. Then I took a nap this evening after packing, and it was almost like I dreamed them, but I was awake because I was drawing them at the same time that I saw them. It was like I woke up with them still in my mind, and I had to put their images down on paper, and when I looked out the window they were there, except – ' She had paused.

'Except what? Tell me, Jenna.'

The girl had looked uncomfortable. 'Except I could only see them if I didn't look directly at them. I know it makes no sense, Mom, but they were there and also not there.' She took the drawing from her mother. 'I think they're kind of cool.'

'They were *here*, Jenna?'

Jenna had nodded. 'They were outside. What did you think I meant?'

Rebecca's hand went to her mouth. She felt ill. Jenna rose and hugged her and kissed her on the cheek.

'Don't worry, Mom. It was probably just some weird mind thing. If it helps, I didn't feel scared or anything. They don't mean us any harm.'

'How do you know?'

'I just do. I kind of heard them, in my head, while I was sleeping or waking or whatever it was I was doing. They weren't interested in us.'

Then, for the first time, Jenna had looked thoughtful, as though she had only just begun to understand how truly odd her words sounded.

Rebecca tried to stop her voice from trembling when she spoke. 'Honey, who are they?'

The question distracted Jenna. She giggled. 'That's the weirdest part of all. I woke knowing who they were, like sometimes I'll have a painting and a title in my head, both at the same time, and I won't know where they came from. I made this first drawing, and I knew who those figures were almost before the pencil touched the paper.'

She held the drawing up before her, both admiring it and yet slightly concerned at what she had created.

'They're the Hollow Men.'

7

I had strawberries and coffee for breakfast. There was a Delgados CD, *Universal Audio*, in the stereo, and I let it play while I ate. Walter fooled around in the garden, relieved himself in the bushes, then came back inside and fell asleep in his basket.

When I was done eating, I spread the list of Daniel Clay's former associates on the kitchen table, and added 'Eldritch' to the bottom. Then I worked out a rough order in which to approach them all, starting with those who were local yet farthest from town. I began to make calls to arrange appointments, but the first three were washouts. The people in question had moved, or were dead, or in the case of a third man, a former professor of Clay's who had retired to Bar Harbor, was suffering from such severe Alzheimer's that, according to his daughter-in-law, he no longer even recognized his own children.

I had better luck, of a sort, with the fourth name, an accountant named Edward Haver. He had died a decade earlier, but his wife, Celine, said that she wouldn't mind talking about Clay, even over the phone, particularly when I explained that I had been hired by Clay's daughter. She told me that she had always liked Dan, and had never found him to be anything other than good company. She and her husband had attended his wife's funeral, back when Rebecca was only four or five. His wife had died of cancer. Then, twenty years later, her own husband had succumbed to a form of the same illness, and Daniel Clay had attended that funeral. For a time, she admitted, she thought that there might have been a chance that they would get together, for they had similar tastes and she liked

Rebecca, but it seemed that Clay had become used to living without a partner.

'And then he vanished,' she concluded.

I was about to press her about the circumstances of his disappearance, but in the end I didn't have to.

'I know what people said about him, but that wasn't Dan, not the Dan that I knew,' she said. 'He cared about the children he counseled, maybe too much. You could see it in his face when he spoke about them.'

'He talked about his cases with you?'

'He never mentioned names, but sometimes he'd tell me about what a child had been through: beatings, neglect, and, well, you know, other things too. It was clear that it troubled him. He couldn't bear to see a child hurt. I think that brought him into conflict with people sometimes.'

'What kind of people?'

'Other professionals, doctors who didn't always see things the way that he did. There was one man named – oh, what was it again? I've seen his name somewhere recently – Christian! That's it: Dr Robert Christian, over at the Midlake Center. He and Dan were always disagreeing about things in papers that they wrote, or at conferences. I guess it was a small field that they worked in, so they were forever encountering each other and arguing over how best to deal with the children who came to them.'

'You seem to have a good memory for events that were sometime in the past, Mrs Haver.' I tried not to make it sound like I was doubting her, or that I was suspicious in any way, although I felt a little of both.

'I liked Dan a lot, and we shared parts of our life over the years.' I could almost see her smiling sadly. 'He rarely got angry, but I can still remember the look that used to come over his face when the subject of Robert Christian was raised. They were competing, in a way. Dan and Dr Christian were both involved in evaluating allegations of child abuse, but each had a very different approach. I think Dan was a little less cautious than Dr Christian, that's all. He was inclined to believe the child from the start, on the grounds that his priority was the protection of children from harm. I admired that about him. He had a crusading impulse, and you don't see that kind of devotion much anymore. Dr Christian didn't see his calling in the same way. Dan said Robert Christian was too skeptical, that he confused objectivity with distrust. Then there was some trouble. Dan gave an evaluation that turned out to be wrong, and a man died, but I guess you probably know about all that already. Afterward, I think, Dan was offered fewer evaluations, or maybe they stopped altogether.'

'Do you remember the name of the man who died?'

'I think it was a German name. Muller, perhaps? Yes, I'm almost sure that was the name. I would imagine that the boy involved must be in his late teens by now. I can't imagine what his life has been like, knowing that his allegations led to his father's death.'

I wrote down the name Muller and drew a line connecting it to Dr Robert Christian.

'Then, of course, the rumors started,' she said.

'The rumors of abuse?'

'That's right.'

'Did he discuss them with you?'

'No, we weren't really seeing much of each other by that time. After the death of Mr Muller, Daniel became less sociable. Don't get me wrong: he was never what you might call a party animal, but he would attend dinners, and sometimes he would come over here for a coffee or a glass of wine. That all stopped after the Muller incident. It did something to his confidence, and I can only imagine that the allegations of abuse shattered it entirely.'

'You didn't believe them?'

'I saw how committed he was to his work. I could never believe the things some people said about Dan. It sounds like a cliché, but his problem was that he cared too much. He wanted to protect them all, but he couldn't, in the end.'

I thanked her, and she told me to call her anytime. Before she hung up, she gave me some names of people to whom I might talk, but they were all on Rebecca's list. Still, she was helpful, which was more than could be said for the next two people I called. One was a lawyer named Elwin Stark, who had acted for Clay as well as being his friend. I knew Stark to see around town. He was tall and unctuous, and favored the kind of dark striped suits beloved of old-style mobsters and upmarket antiques dealers. It was true to say that he wasn't the pro bono kind when it came to legal matters, and he seemed to apply the same principle to telephone conversations for which he wasn't being paid. It was Stark who had dealt with the paper-work surrounding the declaration of Clay's death.

'He's gone,' Stark told me, after his secretary had left me hanging in the ether for a good fifteen minutes, then advised me that Stark wouldn't have time to see me in person but might, just might, have two minutes free during which he could squeeze in a brief word on the phone. 'There's nothing more to be said about it.'

'His daughter is having trouble with someone who disagrees. He doesn't seem willing to accept that Clay is dead.'

'Well, his daughter has a piece of paper that says otherwise. What do you want me to tell you? I knew Daniel. I went fishing with him a couple of times a year. He was a good guy. A bit intense, maybe, but that came with the territory.'

'Did he ever speak about his work with you?'

'Nope. I'm a business lawyer. That kid shit depresses me.'

'Do you still act for Rebecca Clay?'

'I did that one thing as a favor for her. I didn't expect to be chased up by a PI for doing it, so you can safely say that I won't be doing her any more favors. Look, I know all about you, Parker. Even talking to you makes me uneasy. No good can come from a lengthy conversation with you, so I'm ending this one now.'

And he did.

The next conversation, with an M.D. named Philip Caussure,

was even shorter. Caussure was Clay's former physician. It seemed like Clay had a lot of relationships that blended the personal with the professional.

'I have nothing to say,' said Caussure. 'Please don't bother me again.'

Then he hung up too. It seemed like a sign. I made one more call, but this time it was to secure an appointment with Dr Robert Christian.

The Midlake Center was a short drive from where I used to live, just off the Gorham Road. It stood in a tree-shrouded lot, and looked like any other anonymous office building. It could have housed a lawyer's office or a realtor's. Instead, it was a place for children who had suffered abuse or neglect, or who had made such allegations, or who were having those claims made on their behalf by others. Inside the main door was a waiting area painted in bright yellow and orange, with books for children of various ages lying on tables, and a play area in one corner, trucks and dolls and packets of Crayolas lying on its foam matting. There was also a rack of information leaflets on the wall, slightly higher than a small child could reach, containing contact details for the local Sexual Assault Response Team and assorted social services.

The secretary behind the desk took my name and made a call. A minute or two later, a small, spry man with white hair and a neatly trimmed beard appeared at the door connecting the reception area to the clinic. He was probably in his early fifties, and dressed in chinos and an open-collared shirt. His handshake was firm, but he seemed a little cautious. He led me to his office, which was furnished in yellow pine and dominated by shelves of books and reports. I thanked him for seeing me at such short notice, and he shrugged.

'Curiosity,' he said. 'It's a long time since anyone has mentioned Daniel Clay to me, at least outside this branch of the medical community.' He leaned forward in his chair. 'Just so we're clear, I'll be straight with you if you're straight with me. Clay and I disagreed on certain matters. I don't think he cared much for me. I didn't care much for him. Professionally, most people believed that his heart was in the right place, for what it's worth, at least until the rumors began circulating, but that element needed to be balanced by objectivity, which I don't think Daniel Clay had in sufficient quantities for his opinions to be taken seriously.'

'I heard that you'd clashed,' I said. 'That's why I'm here. His daughter hired me. Someone has been asking about her father. She's worried.'

'So now you're going back over the trail, trying to find out why someone should be concerned about him so many years after his disappearance?'

'Something like that.'

'Am I under suspicion?' He smiled.

'Should you be?'

'There were certainly times when I would cheerfully have strangled him. He had a way of getting under my skin, both personally and professionally.'

'Would you care to explain?'

'Well, I guess to understand him, and what happened prior to his disappearance, you need to know something about what we do here. We perform medical examinations and psychological evaluations in cases where there are allegations of abuse of children, whether that abuse is physical or sexual, emotional or the result of neglect. A call comes through to Central Intake in Augusta. It's referred to a supervisor, screened, then a decision is made on whether or not to send out a social worker. Sometimes that call may have originated with local law enforcement, or Child Protection Services. It may have come from a school, a parent, a neighbor, even from the child in question. The child is then referred to us for evaluation. We're the main provider for this service in the state. When Daniel Clay first started performing evaluations, we were still finding our feet a little. Hell, everyone was. Now, things are a little better organized. We can do everything in this one building: examination, evaluation, initial counseling, interviewing of the child and the alleged perpetrator. It can all be handled here.'

'And before the center opened?'

'The child might have been examined by a doctor, then sent elsewhere for an interview and evaluation.'

'Which is where Clay came in.'

'Yes, but, again, I don't think Daniel Clay was careful enough. It's a delicate business, what we do, and there are no easy answers. Everyone wants a definite yes or no – the prosecutors, the judges, obviously the people directly involved, like the parents or guardians – and they're disappointed when we can't always give it.'

'I'm not sure that I understand,' I said. 'Isn't that why you're here?'

Christian sat forward in his chair and opened his hands. They were very clean, the nails cut so short that I could see the soft, pale flesh at the fingertips.

'Look, we deal with eight to nine hundred children every year. In terms of sexual abuse, maybe five percent of those children will have positive physical findings – say, small tears in the hymen or rectum. Many of those kids will be teenagers, and even if there are indications of sexual activity, it can be hard to tell if it was consensual or not. A lot of adolescent females can even be penetrated and still have a normal exam that reveals an unbroken hymen. If we do establish nonconsensual sex, then we often can't tell who did it, or when. All we can say is that sexual contact did occur. Even in a very young child, there may be little or no evidence, especially taking into account the normal anatomical variations that may occur in children's bodies. Physical findings that used to be considered abnormal have now come to be regarded as nonspecific. The only sure-fire way to establish sexual abuse is to test for STDs, but that assumes that the perpetrator was infected. If the test is positive, then abuse is a done deal, but even then you're no closer to establishing who did it, not unless you have DNA marking. If the perpetrator wasn't infected with an STD, then you have nothing.'

'But what about the child's behavior. Wouldn't that change after abuse?'

'The effects vary, and there are no specific behavioral indicators to suggest abuse. We may see anxiety, difficulty sleeping, sometimes night terrors, where the child wakes up screaming, inconsolable, yet will have no memory of the event in the morning. There may be nail biting, the pulling out of hair, refusal to go to school, an insistence on sleeping with a trusted parent. Boys will tend to act out, becoming more aggressive, while girls will tend to act in, becoming withdrawn and depressed. But those types of behavior may also occur if, say, the parents are going through a divorce and the child is stressed. By themselves, they don't offer proof one way or the other of abuse. At least a third of abused children will have no symptoms whatsoever.'

I took off my jacket, then continued making notes. Christian smiled. 'More complicated than you thought, isn't it?

'A little.'

'That's why the evaluation process and the interview techniques employed for it are so important. The professional can't lead the child, which is what I believe Clay did in a number of cases.'

'Like the Muller case?'

Christian nodded. 'The Muller case should be offered as a textbook example of all the things that can go wrong during the investigation of alleged child abuse: a child being manipulated by a parent, a professional who sets aside his objectivity as part of some misguided crusading impulse, a judge who prefers black-and-white to shades of gray. There are those who believe that the vast majority of sexual abuse allegations that arise during custody disputes in divorce cases are fabricated. There's even a term for the child's behavior in such disputes: Parental Alienation Syndrome, where a child identifies with one parent and in so doing alienates the other. The negative behavior toward the alienated parent is a reflection of the alienating parent's own feelings and perceptions, not the child's. It's a theory, and not everyone accepts it, but looking back at the Muller case, it should have been clear to Clay that the mother was hostile, and had he asked more questions about her own medical background, he would have discovered that there were indications of personality disorder. Instead, he sided with her and appeared to accept the child's version of events unquestioningly. The whole affair was a disaster for everyone concerned, and damaged the standing of those who work in the field. Worst of all, though, a man lost not only his family, but his life.'

Christian realized how tense he had become. He stretched and said: 'Sorry, I got us kind of sidetracked there.'

'Not at all,' I said. 'I asked you about the Mullers. You were talking about interview techniques.'

'Well, it's pretty simple, in one way. You can't ask questions like "Has something bad happened to you?" or "Did X touch you somewhere special or somewhere private?" That's particularly the case when you're dealing with very young children. They may try to please the evaluator with the right answer just so they can leave. We also have instances of what's called "source misattribution," where a kid may have heard something and applied it to himself, perhaps as a way of seeking attention. Sometimes, you may get a good disclosure from a younger child initially but find that the child then recants under pressure from, say, family members. It happens also with teenagers, where Mom has a new boyfriend who starts abusing the daughter but Mom doesn't want to believe it because she doesn't want to lose the guy who's supporting her and would rather blame the child for telling lies. Teenagers in general bring with them their own challenges. They may lie about abuse for gain, but generally they're pretty resistant to suggestion. The problem with them is that, if they have been abused, it can take a couple of sessions just to get the details from them. They won't want to talk about it, maybe out of guilt or shame, and the *very* last thing they'll want to discuss with a stranger is oral or anal abuse.

'So the evaluation has to be conducted with all of these

elements borne in mind. My position is that I don't believe
anybody: I only believe the data. That's what I present to the
police, to the prosecutors, and to the judges if the case gets to
court. And you know what? They get frustrated with me. Like
I said, they want definite answers, but a lot of the time we can't
give them those answers.

'That's where Daniel Clay and I differed. There are some
evaluators out there who have almost a political position on
abuse. They believe that it's rampant, and they interview children with the presumption that abuse has occurred. It colors
everything that follows. Clay became the go-to guy to confirm
abuse allegations, whether in the first instance or where a lawyer
decided to seek a second opinion on abuse. That was what got
him into trouble.'

'Okay, can we go back to the Muller case for a moment?'

'Sure. Erik Muller. It's a matter of record. The papers reported
a lot of the details at the time. It was a nasty divorce case, and
the wife wanted custody. It seems like she may have pressured
her son, who was then twelve, into making allegations against his
father. The father denied the allegations, but Clay offered a pretty
damning evaluation. There still wasn't enough evidence for the
D.A. to indict, so it went to Family Court, where the burden of
proof is lower than at criminal level. The father lost custody and
killed himself a month later. Then the child recanted to a priest,
and it all came out. Clay went before the Board of Licensure. It
took no action against him, but the whole thing looked bad, and
he ceased to do case evaluations shortly afterward.'

'Was that his decision, or was it forced upon him?'

'Both. He decided not to conduct evaluations again, but he
would not have been offered them even had he decided to
continue. By that time, we had been up and running for some
time, so the burden of evaluation in most cases fell on us. Well,
I say "burden," but it was one that we were willing to accept.
We're as committed to child welfare as Daniel Clay ever was,
but we never lose sight of our responsibilities to all of those
involved and, most of all, to the truth.'

'Do you know where the Muller boy is now?'

'Dead.'

'How?'

'He became an addict and died of a heroin overdose. That was, um, about four years ago, up in Fort Kent. I don't know what happened to the mother. Last I heard, she was living somewhere in Oregon. She married again, and I think she has another child now. I hope she does better with this one than the last.'

It sounded like the Muller angle wasn't going to lead anywhere. I moved on to the subject of the abuse of some of Clay's patients. Christian seemed to have the details at his fingertips. Maybe he had gone over them before I arrived, or it could simply have been one of those cases that nobody was very likely to forget.

'Two cases of alleged abuse were referred to us in the space of three months,' said Christian, 'each with similar elements: alleged stranger abuse, or abuse by someone apparently unknown to the child, and the use of masks.'

'Masks?'

'Bird masks. The abusers – three in one case, four in the other – disguised their faces with bird masks. The kids – the first a twelve-year-old girl, the second a fourteen-year-old boy – were abducted, one on the way home from school, the other while drinking beer by a disused railroad track, taken to an unknown location, systematically abused over a period of hours, then dumped close to where they'd been abducted. The alleged abuse had occurred some years back, one in the mid eighties and another at the start of the nineties. The first case emerged after a suicide attempt by the girl shortly before she was due to be married at the tender age of eighteen. The second came about when the boy went before the courts on a whole range of misdemeanor offenses and the lawyer decided to use the alleged abuse as mitigation. The judge wasn't inclined to believe him, but when the two cases came to us the similarities were impossible to ignore. These kids didn't know each other and came from towns fifty miles apart. Yet the details of their stories matched perfectly, even down to details of the masks used.

'You know what else they had in common? Both children had been treated by Daniel Clay in the past. The girl had made allegations of abuse against a teacher that turned out to be untrue, motivated by a belief that the teacher was secretly attracted to one of her friends. It was one of the rare instances where Clay's evaluation did not find reason to support the allegations. The boy was sent to Clay after he'd engaged in inappropriate sexual contact with a ten-year-old girl in his class. Clay's evaluation suggested possible indicators of abuse in the boy's past, but went no further. Since then, we've uncovered six more cases with the bird element to them: three of those involved were former patients of Daniel Clay, but none of the cases took place after his disappearance. In other words, there have been no new reports of similar incidents since late 1999. That doesn't mean that they haven't occurred, but we haven't heard about them. Most of the children involved were also, um, slightly troublesome in certain ways, which is why the allegations took so long to emerge.'

'Troublesome?'

'Their behavior was antisocial. Some had made allegations of abuse before, which may or may not have been true. Others had engaged in criminal activity, or had simply been allowed to run wild by parents or foster parents. Taken together, it might have made authority figures less willing to believe them, even if they had made an effort to talk about what had taken place, and police, especially male cops, tend to be reluctant to believe allegations of abuse from teenage girls in particular anyway. It also made the children in question vulnerable since nobody was inclined to look out for them.'

'Then before anyone could ask Clay about all of this in detail, he disappeared?'

'Well, most of the cases emerged subsequent to his disappearance, but that's about right,' said Christian. 'The problem for us is that we've had to wait for indications of similar abuse to come to us instead of being able to seek out the children for ourselves. There are issues of patient confidentiality, sealed records, even the natural dispersal of families and children that occurs over time. Any child who had undergone abuse similar to that I've outlined to you would be in his or her late teens or early twenties at least by now, given that the victims of whom we're aware were aged between nine and fifteen at the time when the abuse is alleged to have occurred. To put it simply, we can't really place an advertisement in the newspapers asking people who may have been abused by men in bird masks to come forward. It just doesn't work that way.'

'Any suggestion that Clay could have been one of the abusers?'

Christian let out a long breath. 'That's the big question, isn't it? There were certainly rumors, but did you ever meet Daniel Clay?'

'No.'

'He was a tall man, very tall, six-six at least. Very thin. All in all, he was quite distinctive-looking. When we went back over those cases, none of the children involved described any of their alleged abusers in terms that could be applied to Daniel Clay.'

'So it could be a coincidence that some of these kids were his patients?'

'It's certainly possible. He was well known for dealing with children who claimed to have been abused. If someone was sufficiently committed, then it's possible that children could have been targeted because they were his patients. Perhaps someone among the various professions involved with the children along the way might also have leaked details, whether deliberately or accidentally, although our own inquiries have proved negative on that front. It's all supposition, though.'

'Do you have any idea where these children are now?'

'Some of them. I can't give you any details. I'm sorry. I could, perhaps, show you some reports of their allegations with the identities removed, but it won't tell you much more than you already know.'

'I'd appreciate it if you would.'

He led me back to the reception area, then returned to his office. Twenty minutes later he returned with a handful of printed pages.

'This is all that I can give you, I'm afraid.'

I thanked him for the papers, and for his time. He told me to contact him if I needed anything more, and gave me his home number.

'Do you think Daniel Clay is dead, Dr Christian?' I asked.

'If he was involved – and I'm not saying that he was – then he would not have wanted to face ruin, disgrace, and imprisonment. We may have disagreed on most things, but he was a proud, cultured man. Under the circumstances, he might have taken his own life. If he wasn't involved in some way, well, why did he run? Perhaps the two events, the revelations of possible abuse and Clay's disappearance, were entirely unconnected, and we are besmirching an innocent man's reputation. I simply don't know. It is strange, though, that no trace of Daniel Clay has ever been found. I work with the available data, and nothing more, but from the data I have before me, I'd have to say that Clay is dead. The question then is, did he take his own life, or did someone deprive him of it?'

I left the Midlake Center and drove home. At my kitchen table, I read the sections of the case reports that Christian had given to me. As he had promised, they added little to what he had told me, except to make me despair, if I ever needed reminding, at what adults were capable of doing to children. The details of the abusers' bodies were vague, especially given that, in a number of cases, the children had been blindfolded throughout the abuse, or had been so traumatized by it that they were unable to recall anything about the men themselves, but Christian was right: none of the available descriptions matched the physical appearance of Daniel Clay.

When I was done, I took Walter for a walk. He had matured a lot in the last year, even for a young dog. He was quieter and

less skittish, although he was still but a shadow of his ancestors, the big hunting dogs owned by the original planters and
settlers of Scarborough. My grandfather once told me of a traveling showman who stopped for a night at the house of the
local ferryman. The showman was carrying a lion east, and a
hunter proposed, after some liquor was taken, to match one of
his dogs against the lion for a wager of a barrel of rum. The
showman agreed, and in front of a gathering of townsmen,
the dog was put in the lion's cage. The dog took one look at
the lion, sprang for its throat, then forced it onto its back and
set about killing it. The showman intervened and paid the hunter
the barrel of rum and $50 to be allowed to shoot the dog in
the cage before it tore the lion apart. Walter wasn't the lion-
killing kind, but he was my dog, and I loved him nonetheless.
My neighbors, Bob and Shirley Johnson, looked after him for
me if I had to go away for a few days. Walter didn't mind
staying with them. He was still free to roam his territory, and
they spoiled him. They were retired and didn't have a dog of
their own, so Bob was always happy to take Walter for a stroll.
It worked out well for everybody.

By now, we had reached Ferry Beach. It was late, but I
needed the air. I watched Walter tentatively dip a paw into the
water, then withdraw it rapidly. He barked once in reproof then
looked at me as if there was something that I could do to raise
the temperature of the sea so he could splash away. He wagged
his tail, then all of the hairs on his back seemed to rise at once.
He grew very still and stared past me. His lips parted, exposing
his sharp white teeth. He growled low in his throat.

I turned. A man appeared to be standing among the trees.
If I looked directly at him I could see only branches and spots
of moonlight where I thought he was standing, but he seemed
to appear more clearly when I found him with my peripheral
vision, or if I tried not to focus on him at all. He was there,
though. Walter's reaction was evidence of that, and I still recalled
the events of the night before: the glimpse I had caught of
something at the edge of the forest before it faded away; a

child's voice whispering from the shadows; words scrawled on a dusty windowpane.

Hollow Men.

I didn't have my gun. I had left the .38 in the car while I was talking to Dr Christian and had not retrieved it before taking Walter out, while the Smith 10 was in my bedroom. I now wished I had either one of them with me, or maybe both.

'How you doing?' I called. I raised my hand in greeting. The man didn't move. His coat was a dirty tan in color, so that it blended with the shadows and the sandy earth. Only a little of his face was visible: a hint of pale cheek, of white forehead and chin. His mouth and eyes were black pools, fine wrinkles visible where the lips might have been and at the edges of the dark sockets, as though the skin in those places had become shrunken and dried. I walked closer, Walter advancing beside me, hoping to see him more clearly, and he began to retreat into the trees, the darkness embracing him.

And then he was gone. Walter's growls ceased. Warily, he approached the spot where the figure had been standing and sniffed at the ground. Clearly he didn't like what he smelled there because his muzzle wrinkled, and he ran his tongue over his teeth as though trying to rid it of a bad taste. I walked on through the trees until I came to the boundary of the beach area, but there was no sign of anyone. I didn't hear a car start. All seemed quiet and still.

We left the beach and walked home, but Walter stayed close to me all the way, only pausing at times to stare into the trees to our left, his teeth slightly bared as though waiting for the approach of some threat as yet unknown.

8

I drove down to Lynn the next morning. The sky was clear and blue, the color of summer, but the deciduous trees were bare, and the workers employed on the never-ending turnpike extension were wrapped in hooded sweaters and wore thick gloves to ward off the cold. I drank coffee on the ride and listened to an album of North African protest music. It drew disapproving looks when I stopped for gas in New Hampshire, where the sound of Clash songs being bellowed in Arabic was clearly regarded as evidence of unpatriotic leanings. The songs kept my mind off the figure glimpsed in the trees at Ferry Beach the night before. The memory of it evoked a curious response, as though I had witnessed something that I was not really meant to see, or had broken some taboo. The strangest part of it was that the figure had seemed almost familiar to me, as if I had at last encountered a distant relative about whom I had heard a great deal but whom I had never before met.

I left the interstate for Route 1, as ugly a stretch of uncontrolled commercial development as could be found anywhere in the Northeast, and then took 107 North, which wasn't much better, heading through Revere and Saugus toward Lynn. I passed the huge Wheelabrator waste management plant on the right, then GE-Aviation, the big employer in the area. Used car lots and vacant sites dotted the landscape as I entered Lynn, its streetlights adorned with Stars and Stripes banners welcoming all comers, each sponsored by a local business. Eldritch and Associates wasn't among them, and when I came to their offices it wasn't hard to see why. It didn't look like a particularly prosperous operation, occupying the top two floors

of an ugly gray building that squatted defiantly on the block
like a mongrel dog. Its windows were filthy and nobody had
refreshed the gold lettering upon them announcing the presence of a lawyer within in a long, long time. The premises were
sandwiched between Tulley's bar on the right, itself a pretty
austere place that appeared to have been built to repel a siege,
and some gray-green condos with businesses on the lower level:
a nail salon, a store called Angkor Multi Services with signs in
Cambodian, and a Mexican restaurant advertising pupusas,
tortas, and tacos. At the end of the block was another bar that
made Tulley's look like it had been designed by Gaudi. It was
little more than a doorway and a pair of windows, with the
name above the entrance painted in jagged white letters by
someone who might have been suffering from serious delirium
tremens at the time, and who had offered to do the job in return
for a hand-steadying drink. It was called Eddys, without the
apostrophe. Maybe if they'd called it Steady Eddys they might
have gotten away with the sign on ironic grounds.

I wasn't optimistic about Eldritch and Associates as I parked
in Tulley's lot. In my experience, lawyers didn't tend to open up
much for private investigators, and the previous day's conversation with Stark hadn't done much to change my opinion. In fact,
now that I thought about it, my encounters with lawyers had
been almost uniformly negative. Maybe I wasn't meeting enough
of them. Then again, maybe I was just meeting too many.

The street-level door of Eldritch's building was unlocked,
and a narrow flight of battered steps led to the upper floors.
The yellow wall to the right of the stairs had an extended greasy
smear at the level of my upper arm where countless coat sleeves
had brushed against it over the years. There was a musty smell
that grew stronger the farther up I went. It was the odor of old
paper slowly decaying, of dust piled upon dust, of rotting carpet
and law cases that had dragged on for decades. It was the stuff
of Dickens. Had the problems of Jarndyce and Jarndyce found
their way across the Atlantic, they would have enjoyed familiar
surroundings in the company of Eldritch and Associates.

I reached a door marked *Bathroom* on the first landing. Ahead of me, on the second floor, was a frosted-glass door with the firm's name etched upon it. I climbed on, careful not to place too much faith in the carpet beneath my feet, which was fatally undermined by an absence of enough tacks to hold it in position. To my right, a further flight of steps led up into the dimness of the top floor. The carpet there was less worn, but it wasn't much of a claim.

Out of politeness, I knocked on the glass door before entering. It seemed like the Olde Worlde thing to do. Nobody answered, so I opened the door and went in. There was a low wooden counter to my left. Behind it was a large desk, and behind the large desk was a large woman with a pile of big black hair balanced precariously on her head like dirty ice cream on a cone. She was wearing a bright green blouse with frills at the neck, and a necklace of yellowing imitation pearls. Like everything else there, she looked old, but age had not dimmed her affection for cosmetics or hair dye, even if it had deprived her of some of the skills required to apply both without making the final effect look less like an act of vanity than an act of vandalism. She was smoking a cigarette. Given the amount of paper surrounding her it seemed an almost suicidal act of bravado, as well as indicating an admirable disregard for the law, even for someone who worked for a lawyer.

'Help you?' she said. She had a voice like puppies being strangled, high and gasping.

'I'd like to see Mr Eldritch,' I said.

'Senior or Junior?'

'Either.'

'Senior's dead.'

'Junior it is, then.'

'He's busy. He's not taking on any new clients. We're run off our feet already.'

I tried to imagine her even getting to her feet, let alone being run off them, and couldn't. There was a picture on the wall behind her, but the sunlight had faded it so much that only a hint of a tree was visible in one corner. The walls were yellow, just like those on the stairway, but decades of nicotine accumulation had given them a disturbing brown tint. The ceiling might once have been white, but only a fool would have placed a bet on it. And everywhere there was paper: on the carpet, on the woman's desk, on a second, unoccupied desk nearby, on the counter, on a pair of old straight-backed chairs that might once have been offered to clients but was now assigned to more pressing storage duties, and on the full-length shelves that stood against the walls. Hell, if they could have found a way to store paper on the ceiling, they probably would have covered that as well. None of the documents looked like they'd been moved much since quills went out of fashion.

'It's about someone who may be a current client,' I replied. 'His name is Merrick.'

She squinted at me through a plume of cigarette smoke.

'Merrick? Doesn't ring a bell.'

'He's driving a car registered to this firm.'

'How'd you know it's one of ours?'

'Well, it was hard to tell at first because it wasn't filled with paper, but it checked out in the end.'

Her squint grew narrower. I gave her the tag number.

'Merrick,' I said again. I pointed at her phone. 'You may want to call someone who isn't dead.'

'Take a seat,' she said.

I looked around.

'There isn't one.'

She almost smiled, then thought better about cracking the makeup on her face.

'Guess you'll have to stand, then.'

I sighed. Here was more proof, if proof were needed, that not all fat people were jolly. Santa Claus had a lot to answer for.

She lifted the receiver and pressed some buttons on her beige phone.

'Name?'

'Parker. Charlie Parker.'

'Like the singer?'

'Saxophonist.'

'Whatever. You got some ID?'

I showed her my license. She looked at it distastefully, like I'd just taken my weenie out and made it do tricks.

'Picture's old,' she said.

'Lot of stuff's old,' I replied. 'Can't stay young and beautiful forever.'

She tapped her fingers upon her desk while she waited for an answer at the other end of the line. Her nails were painted pink. The color made my teeth hurt. 'You sure he didn't sing?'

'Pretty sure.'

'Huh. So who was the one who sang? He fell out of a window.'

'Chet Baker.'

'Huh.'

She continued drumming her nails.

'You like Chet Baker?' I asked. We were forming a relationship.

'No.'

Or maybe not. Mercifully, somewhere above us a phone was answered.

'Mr Eldritch, there's a' – she paused dramatically – '*gentleman* here to see you. He's asking about a Mr Merrick.'

She listened to the answer, nodding. When she hung up she looked even unhappier than before. I think she had been hoping for an order to release the hounds on me.

'You can go up. Second door at the top of the stairs.'

'It's been a blast,' I said.

'Yeah,' she said. 'You hurry back now.'

I left her, like an overweight Joan of Arc waiting for the pyre to ignite, and went up to the top floor. The second door was already open and a small old man, seventy or more, stood waiting for me. He still had most of his hair, or most of someone's hair. He wore gray pinstripe trousers and a black jacket over a white shirt and a gray pin-stripe vest. His tie was black silk. He looked vaguely unhappy, like an undertaker who had just mislaid a corpse. A faint patina of dust seemed to have settled upon him, a combination of dandruff and paper fragments, paper mostly. Wrinkled and faded as he was, he might almost have been made of paper himself, slowly crumbling away along with the accumulated detritus of a lifetime in the service of the law.

He stretched out a hand in greeting, and conjured up a smile. Compared to his secretary, it was like being greeted with the keys of the city.

'I'm Thomas Eldritch,' he said. 'Please come in.'

His office was tiny. There was paper here too, but less of it. Some of it even looked like it had been moved recently, and box files were stored alphabetically on the shelves, each carefully marked with a set of dates. They went back a very long time. He closed the door behind me and waited for me to sit before he took his own seat at his desk.

'Now,' he said, steepling his hands before him. 'What's this about Mr Merrick?'

'You know him?'

'I am aware of him. We provided him with a car at the request of one of our clients.'

'Can I ask the name of the client?'

'I'm afraid I can't tell you that. Is Mr Merrick in some kind of trouble?'

'He's getting there. I've been employed by a woman who seems to have attracted Merrick's attentions. He's stalking her. He broke a window in her house.'

Eldritch tut-tutted. 'Has she informed the police?'

'She has.'

'We've heard nothing from them. Surely a complaint of this kind would have made its way back to us by now?'

'The police didn't get to talk to him. I did. I took the tag number from his car and traced it back to your firm.'

'Very enterprising of you. And now, instead of informing the police, you are here. May I ask why?'

'The lady in question is not convinced that the police can help her.'

'And you can.'

It sounded like a statement, not a question, and I had an uneasy sensation that Eldritch already knew who I was before I arrived. I treated it as a question anyway.

'I'm trying. We may have to involve the police if this situation persists, which I imagine might be embarrassing, or worse, for you *and* your client.'

'Neither we nor our client are responsible for Mr Merrick's behavior, even if what you say is true.'

'The police may not take that view if you're acting as his personal car rental service.'

'And they'll get the same reply that I have just given you. We simply provided a car for him at a client's request, and nothing more.'

'And you can't tell me anything at all about Merrick?'

'No. I know very little about him, as I've said.'

'Do you even know his first name?'

Eldritch considered. His eyes were cunning and bright. It struck me that he was enjoying this.

'I believe it's Frank.'

'Do you think that "Frank" might have served some time?'

'I couldn't possibly say.'

'There doesn't seem to be very much that you can say.'

'I am a lawyer, and therefore a certain degree of discretion is to be expected by my clients. Otherwise, I would not have remained in this profession for as long as I have. If what you say is true, then Mr Merrick's actions are to be regretted. Perhaps if your own client were to sit down with him and discuss the matter, then the situation could be resolved to everyone's satisfaction, as I can only assume that Mr Merrick believes she may be of some assistance to him.'

'In other words, if she tells him what he wants to know, then he'll go away.'

'It would be logical to assume so. And does she know something?'

I let the question dangle. He was baiting me, and wherever

you found bait, you could be pretty certain that there was a
hook hidden somewhere within it.

'He seems to think so.'

'Then it would appear to be the natural solution. I'm sure
that Mr Merrick is a reasonable man.'

Eldritch had remained impossibly still throughout our discussions. Only his mouth moved. Even his eyes appeared reluctant
to blink. But when he said the word 'reasonable' he smiled slightly,
imbuing the word with an import that was entirely the opposite
of its apparent meaning.

'Have you met Merrick, Mr Eldritch?'

'I have had that pleasure, yes.'

'He seems to have a lot of anger in him.'

'It may be that he has just cause.'

'I notice that you haven't asked me the name of the woman
who is employing me, which suggests to me that you already
know it. In turn, that would seem to indicate that Merrick has
been in touch with you.'

'I have spoken to Mr Merrick, yes.'

'Is he also a client of yours?'

'He was, in a sense. We acted on his behalf in a certain
matter. He is a client no longer.'

'And now you're helping him because one of your other
clients has asked you to.'

'That is so.'

'Why is your client interested in Daniel Clay, Mr Eldritch?'

'My client has no interest in a Daniel Clay.'

'I don't believe you.'

'I will not lie to you, Mr Parker. If I cannot answer a question, for whatever reason, then I will tell you so, but I will not
lie. I will repeat myself: to my knowledge, my client has no
interest in any Daniel Clay. Mr Merrick's line of inquiry is
entirely his own.'

'What about his daughter? Is your client interested in her?'

Eldritch seemed to consider confirming it, then decided
against it, but his silence was enough. 'I could not possibly

say. That is something you would have to discuss with Mr Merrick.'

My nostrils itched. I could feel the molecules of paper and dust settling in them, as though Eldritch's office were slowly making me part of itself, so that in years to come a stranger might enter and find us here, Eldritch and me, still batting questions and answers back and forth to no end, a thin layer of white matter covering us as we ourselves dwindled into dust.

'Do you want to know what I think, Mr Eldritch?'

'What would that be, Mr Parker?'

'I think Merrick is a dangerous man, and I think somebody has set him on my client. You know who that person is, so maybe you'll pass on a message for me. You tell him, or her, that I'm very good at what I do, and if anything happens to the woman I've been hired to protect, then I'm going to come back here and someone will answer for what has taken place. Am I making myself clear?'

Eldritch's expression did not alter. He was still smiling benignly like a little wrinkled Buddha.

'Perfectly, Mr Parker,' he said. 'This is purely an observation and nothing more, but it appears to me that you have adopted an adversarial position with regard to Mr Merrick. Perhaps, if you were to be less confrontational, you might find that you have more in common with him than you think. It may be that you and he share certain common goals.'

'I don't have a goal, beyond ensuring that no harm comes to the woman in my care.'

'Oh, I don't think that's true, Mr Parker. You are thinking in the specific, not the general. Mr Merrick, like you, may be interested in a form of justice.'

'For himself, or for someone else?'

'Have you tried asking him?'

'It didn't work out so well.'

'Perhaps if you tried without a gun on your belt?'

So Merrick had spoken to him recently. Otherwise, how

could Eldritch have known of my confrontation with him, and the gun?

'You know,' I said, 'I don't think I want to meet Merrick unless I have a gun close at hand.'

'That is, of course, your decision. Now, if there's nothing else . . .'

He stood, walked to the door, and opened it. Clearly, our meeting was at an end. Once more, he extended his hand for me to shake.

'It's been a pleasure,' he said gravely. In an odd way, he seemed to mean it. 'I'm delighted that we've had a chance to meet at last. I've heard so much about you.'

'Would that be from your client as well?' I asked, and for an instant the smile almost slipped, fragile as a crystal glass teetering on the edge of a table. He rescued it, but it was enough. He seemed about to reply, but I answered for him.

'Let me guess,' I said. 'You couldn't possibly say.'

'Precisely,' he replied. 'But if it's any consolation, I expect that you'll meet him again, in time.'

'Again?'

But the door had already closed, sealing me off from Thomas Eldritch and his knowledge just as surely as if a tomb door had closed upon him, leaving him with only his paper and his dust and his secrets for company.

9

My visit to Thomas Eldritch hadn't contributed significantly to my sense of inner well-being, although it had at least given me Merrick's first name. Eldritch had also carefully avoided any denial that Merrick might have done time, which meant that somewhere in the system there was probably a closetful of bones just waiting to be rattled. But Eldritch's hint that I knew his client made me uneasy. I had enough ghosts in my past to know that I didn't relish the prospect of any of them being raised.

I stopped for coffee and a sandwich at the Bel Aire Diner on Route 1. (I gave Route 1 this much: at least it had no shortage of spots where a man could eat.) The Bel Aire had survived in its current spot for over half a century, a big old 'Diner' sign outside advertising its presence from the top of a forty-foot pole, the name written beneath in the original fifties cursive. The last I heard, a guy called Harry Kallas was running the Bel Aire, and Harry had taken over the place from his father. Inside it was burgundy red vinyl booths and matching stools at the counter, and a gray-and-white tiled floor that boasted the kind of wear and tear associated with generations of customers. There were rumors that it was due to close for redecoration, which I supposed was necessary if kind of sad. A TV was built into the wall at one end, but nobody was watching it. The kitchen was noisy, the waitresses were noisy, and the construction workers and locals ordering blue plate specials were noisy too.

I was finishing my second cup of coffee when the call came through. It was Merrick. I recognized his voice the moment I heard it, but no number was displayed on my cell phone.

'You're a smart sonofabitch,' he said.

'Is that meant to be a compliment? If it is, you need to work on your technique. All that time in the can must have made you rusty.'

'You're fishing. The lawyer didn't give you shit.'

I wasn't surprised that Eldritch had made some calls. I just wondered who had touched base with Merrick: the lawyer, or his client?

'Are you telling me that if I go searching for you in the system, I won't find a record?'

'Search away. I ain't gonna make it easy for you, though.'

I waited a heartbeat before asking my next question. It was a hunch, and nothing more.

'What's the name of the girl in the picture, Frank?'

There was no reply.

'She's the reason why you're here, isn't she? Was she one of the children seen by Daniel Clay? Is she your daughter? Tell me her name, Frank. Tell me her name, and maybe I can help you.'

When Merrick spoke again, his voice had changed. It was filled with quiet yet lethal menace, and I knew with certainty that this was a man who not only was capable of killing, but who had killed already, and that a line had been crossed at the mention of the girl.

'Listen to me,' he said. 'I told you once before: my business is my own. I gave you time to convince that little missy to come clean, not to go nosing around in matters that don't concern you. You'd better get back up to where you came from and talk her around.'

'Or what? I'll bet that whoever called you about my visit to Eldritch told you to take it down a couple of notches. You keep harassing Rebecca Clay, and your friends are going to cut you loose. You'll end up back in the can, Frank, and what good will you be to anyone then?'

'You're wasting time,' he said. 'You seem to think I was funnin' with you about that deadline.'

'I'm getting close,' I lied. 'I'll have something for you by tomorrow.'

'Twenty-four hours,' he said. 'That's all the time you have left, and I'm being generous with you. Let me tell you something else: you and missy better start worrying if'n I am cut loose. Right now, that's the only thing holding me in check, apart from my general good nature.'

He hung up. I paid the check and left my coffee to grow cold. Suddenly, it didn't seem like I had the time to linger over it after all.

My next visit was to Jerry Legere, Rebecca Clay's ex-husband. I contacted A-Secure and was told that Legere was out on a job in Westbrook with Raymon Lang, and after only a little cajoling the receptionist let me know the location.

I found the company van parked in an industrial wasteland of mud and seemingly deserted premises, with a rutted track leading between them. It wasn't clear if the site was half finished or in terminal decline. Building work had ceased some time before on a couple of incomplete structures, leaving sections of the steel supports jutting from the concrete like bones from the stumps of severed limbs. Puddles of filthy water stank of gas and waste, and a small yellow cement mixer was lying on its side in a patch of weeds, slowly decaying into rust.

Only one warehouse was open, and inside I found two men on the first floor of the empty two-story interior, a blueprint spread out on the ground in front of them as they knelt over it. This building, at least, had been finished, and there was fresh wire screening to protect its windows from any stones that might be thrown. I knocked on the steel door, and the men both looked up.

'Help you?' said one. He was about five years older than I was, big and strong-looking, but balding badly on top, although he kept his hair cut short enough to disguise the worst of it. It was petty and childish, I knew, but I always felt a brief surge of warmth inside when I met someone close to my own age who had less hair than I did. You could be king of the world and own a dozen companies, but every morning when you stared in the mirror your first thought would be, Damn, I wish I still had my hair.

'I'm looking for Jerry Legere,' I said.

It was the other man who answered. He was silver-haired and ruddy-cheeked. Rebecca was six or seven years younger than I was, I guessed, and this man had a good ten or fifteen years on me. He was carrying some weight, and his jowls were sagging. He had a big, square head that looked a little too heavy for his body and the kind of mouth that was always poised to find something to scowl about: women, kids, modern music, the weather. He was wearing a checkered lumberjack shirt tucked into old blue jeans and muddy work boots with mismatched laces. Rebecca was an attractive woman. True, we couldn't always choose those with whom we fell in love, and I knew looks weren't everything, but the union, however temporary, of the houses of Clay and Legere suggested that sometimes looks might actually be a real disadvantage.

'My name's Charlie Parker,' I said. 'I'm a private investigator. I'd like to talk to you, if you can spare a few minutes.'

'Did she hire you?'

From the tone of his voice, 'she' didn't sound like anyone for whom he retained a high degree of affection.

'I'm working for your ex-wife, if that's what you mean,' I replied.

His face cleared, but only slightly. At least it took a little weight off his scowl. It looked like Legere was having troubles with someone other than Rebecca. The effect didn't last long, though. If there was one thing that could be said for Jerry Legere, it was that he wasn't a man capable of keeping his thoughts hidden behind a poker face. He went from concern to relief, then descended into worry that bordered on a kind of panic. Each transition was clearly readable in his features. He was like a cartoon character, his face engaged in a constant game of catch-up with his emotions.

'What does my ex-wife need with a detective?' he asked.

'That's why I'd like to talk to you. Maybe we could step outside.'

Legere glanced at the younger man, who nodded and returned to checking the blueprint. The sky was clear blue, and the sun shone down upon us, giving light but no warmth.

'So?' he said.

'Your wife hired me because a man has been bothering her.'

I waited for Legere's face to conjure up a surprised expression, but I was disappointed. Instead, he settled for a leer that could have come straight from a villain in a Victorian melodrama.

'One of her boyfriends?' he asked.

'Does she have boyfriends?'

Legere shrugged.

'She's a slut. I don't know what sluts call them: fucks, maybe.'

'Why would you call her a slut?'

'Because that's what she is. She cheated on me when we were married, then lied about it. She lies about everything. This guy you're talking about, he's probably some jerk who was promised a good time, then got upset when it didn't arrive. I was a fool to marry a woman who was soiled goods, but I took pity on her. I won't make that mistake again. Now I'll screw 'em, but I won't marry 'em.'

He leered once more. I waited for him to nudge me in the ribs, or give me an 'Aren't we men of the world?' wink, like in that Monty Python sketch. Your wife, eh? She's a liar and a slut, right? They all are. Put like that, it wasn't quite so funny. I recalled Legere's earlier question – *Did she hire you?* – and the relief on his face when I told him that I was working for his wife. What did you do, Jerry? Who else did you annoy so much that she might require the services of a private detective?

'I don't think this man is a rejected suitor,' I said.

Legere appeared to be about to ask what a suitor was, but then took the trouble to work it out for himself.

'He's been asking about Rebecca's father,' I continued. 'He's under the impression that Daniel Clay might still be alive.'

Something flickered in Legere's eyes. It was like watching a djinn momentarily try to break free from the bottle, only to have the cork forcefully rammed home upon it.

'That's bullshit,' said Legere. 'Her father's dead. Everyone knows that.'

'Everyone?'

Legere looked away. 'You know what I mean.'

'He's missing, not dead.'

'She had him declared. Too late for me, though. There's money in the bank, but I won't see any of it. I could have done with some of it right about now.'

'Times hard?'

'Times are always hard for the working man.'

'You ought to put that to music.'

'I reckon it's been done before. It's old news.'

He turned on his heel and looked back at the warehouse, clearly anxious to be done with me and return to work. I couldn't blame him.

'So what makes you so sure that Daniel Clay is dead?' I asked.

'I don't think I like your tone,' he replied. His fists clenched involuntarily. He became conscious of the reflex and allowed them to relax, then wiped the palms dry on the seams of his jeans.

'There's nothing in it. I just meant that you seem pretty certain that he's not coming back.'

'Well, he's been gone a long time, right? Nobody has seen him in years, and from what I hear, he left with the clothes on his back and nothing else. Didn't even pack an overnight bag.'

'Did your ex-wife tell you that?'

'If she didn't, I read it in the newspapers. It's no secret.'

'Were you seeing her when her father went missing?'

'No, we hooked up later, but it didn't last more than six months. I found out she was seeing other men behind my back, and I let the bitch go.'

He didn't seem embarrassed to be telling me this. Usually

when men discussed the infidelities of their wives or girlfriends, it came with a greater degree of shame than Legere was showing, the memories of the relationship underscored by an abiding sense of betrayal. They were also careful to whom they told their secrets, because what they feared most of all was that they would somehow be held accountable, that it would be adjudged that their failings had forced their women to seek their pleasures elsewhere, that they had been lacking in the ability to satisfy them. Men tended to see these matters distorted through the prism of sex. I'd known women to wander out of desire, but I'd known more who had cheated because with it came the affection and attention that they weren't getting at home. Men, by and large, sought sex. Women traded it.

'I guess I wasn't no innocent either,' he said, 'but that's the way of men. She had everything she needed. She had no call to do what she did. She threw me out of the house when I objected to how she was behaving. I told you: she's a whore. They hit a certain age, and that's it. They become sluts. But instead of admitting it, she turned it on me. She said I was the one who done wrong, not her. Bitch.'

I wasn't sure that this was any of my business, but Rebecca Clay's version of her marital difficulties was very different from her ex-husband's. Now Legere was claiming that he was the injured party, and while Rebecca's story had more of the ring of truth about it, perhaps that was simply because Jerry Legere made my skin crawl. But I could see no reason for him to lie. The story didn't reflect well on him, and there was no mistaking his bitterness. There was a little truth somewhere in his story, however distorted it might have become in the telling.

'Have you ever heard of a man named Frank Merrick, Mr Legere?' I asked.

'No, I can't say that I have,' he replied. 'Merrick? No, it doesn't ring a bell. Is he the guy who's been bothering her?'

'That's right.'

Legere looked away again. I couldn't see his face, but his

posture had changed, as though he had just tensed to avoid a blow. 'No,' he repeated. 'I don't know who you're talking about.'

'Strange,' I said.

'What is?'

'He seems to know you.'

I had his full attention now. He didn't even bother to hide his alarm.

'What do you mean?'

'He was the one who told me to talk to you. He said you might know why he was looking for Daniel Clay.'

'That's not true. I told you, Clay's dead. Men like him don't just drop off the face of the earth only to pop up again later someplace else under a different name. He's dead. Even if he wasn't, there's no way he'd be in contact with me. I never even met the guy.'

'This man, Merrick, was of the opinion that your wife might have told you things that she kept from the authorities.'

'He's mistaken,' he said quickly. 'She didn't tell me nothing. She didn't even speak about him much.'

'Did you think that was odd?'

'No. What was she gonna say? She just wanted to forget him. Nothing good would come from talking about him.'

'Could she have been in contact with him without you knowing, assuming that he was still alive?'

'You know,' said Legere, 'I don't think she's that smart. You see this man again, you tell him all that.'

'The way he was talking about you, it sounded like you might get the chance to tell him yourself.'

The prospect didn't appear to give him much pleasure. He spit on the ground, then rubbed the spittle into the dust with his shoe just to give himself something to do.

'One more thing, Mr Legere: what was the Project?'

If it was possible to freeze a man with a word, then Jerry Legere froze.

'Where did you hear that?'

The words were spoken almost before he realized it, and I

could see instantly that he wished he could retract them. There was no anger left now. It had disappeared entirely, overwhelmed by what might almost have been wonder. He was shaking his head, as if in disbelief.

'It doesn't matter where. I'd just like to know what it is, or was.'

'You got it from that guy, right? Merrick.' Some of his belligerence was already returning. 'You come here, making accusations, talking about men I've never met, listening to lies from strangers, from that bitch I married. You got some nerve.'

His right hand shoved me hard in the chest. I took a step back and he started to advance. I could see him preparing to land another blow, this one harder and higher than the first. I raised my hands in a placatory gesture, and positioned my feet, my right foot slightly forward of the left.

'I'll teach you some—'

I came off my left foot and hit him in the stomach with a doorbreaker kick, following through with the full weight of my body. The force of the impact drove the air from him and sent him sprawling backward in the dirt. He lay there gasping, clutching his hands to his belly. His face was contorted in pain.

'You bastard,' he said. 'I'll kill you for that.'

I stood over him.

'The Project, Mr Legere. What was it?'

'Fuck you. I got no idea what you're talking about.'

He forced the words out through gritted teeth. I took one of my cards from my wallet and dropped it on him. The other man appeared at the entrance to the warehouse. He had a crowbar in his hand. I raised a finger of warning to him, and he paused.

'We'll talk again. You might want to think some on Merrick and what he said. You're going to end up discussing this again with one of us, whether you like it or not.'

I started to walk back to my car. I heard him get to his feet. He called after me. I turned around. Lang was standing at the entrance to the warehouse, asking Legere if he was okay, but Legere ignored him. The expression on his face had changed again. It was still red, and he was having trouble breathing, but a look of low cunning had taken shape upon it.

'You think you're clever?' he said. 'You think you're hard? Maybe you ought to make some inquiries, see what happened to the last guy who started asking about Daniel Clay. He was a private *dick* too, just like you.'

He put a lot of emphasis on the word 'dick.'

'And you know where he is?' Legere continued. 'He's in the same fucking place as Daniel Clay, is where he is. Somewhere, there's a hole in the fucking ground with Daniel Clay in it, and right next to it is another hole with a fucking snoop rotting to hell inside. So you go right ahead, you keep asking questions about Daniel Clay and "projects." There's always room for one more. It don't take much effort to dig a hole, and it takes less to fill it up again once there's a body in it.'

I walked toward him. I was pleased to see him take a step back.

'There you go again,' I said. 'You do seem certain that Daniel Clay is dead.'

'I got nothing more to say to you.'

'Who was the detective?' I asked. 'Who hired him?'

'Fuck. You,' he said, but then he reconsidered. A broad, bitter grin creased his face. 'You want to know who hired him? That bitch hired him, just like she hired you. She was fucking him too. I could tell. I could smell him on her. I bet that's how she pays you too, but don't think you're the first.

'And he asked *all* the same questions that you did, about Clay and "projects" and what she said or didn't say to me, and you're gonna go the way he did. Because that's what happens to people who go asking after Daniel Clay.'

He snapped his fingers.

'They disappear.' He wiped the dirt from his jeans. Some of his false courage began to dissipate as his adrenaline failed him, and for a moment he looked like a man who had glimpsed his own future, and what he saw frightened him. 'They disappear . . .'

10

I touched base with Jackie Garner when I got home. He told me that all was quiet. He sounded vaguely disappointed. Rebecca Clay said the same when I called her. There had been no sign of Merrick. He seemed to be keeping his word, and his distance, the phone call to me apart.

Rebecca was working in her office, so I drove over to speak to her, acknowledging Jackie's presence outside with a small wave when I arrived. We ordered coffee at the little market beside the realtor's, and sat at the single table outside to drink it. Passing motorists looked at us curiously. It was too cold to be dining al fresco, but I wanted to talk to her while my conversation with her ex-husband was still fresh in my mind. It was time to clear the air.

'He said all that?' Rebecca Clay looked genuinely shocked when I told her of what had passed between Jerry and me. 'But they're all lies! I was never unfaithful to him, never. That wasn't why we broke up.'

'I'm not saying he was telling the truth, but there was real bitterness behind his words.'

'He wanted money. He didn't get it.'

'Is that why you think he married you? For money?'

'Well, it wasn't for love.'

'And what about you? What was your reason?'

She shifted in her seat, her discomfort at discussing the subject manifesting itself physically. She looked even more tired and drawn than when I had first met her. I didn't think she would be able to take the strain of what was happening for much longer without breaking in some way.

'I told you part of it,' she said. 'After my father disappeared, I just felt completely alone. I was like a pariah because of the rumors about him. I met Jerry through Raymon, who installed the alarm system in my father's house. They come back once a year to check that everything is working okay, and Jerry was the one who arrived to do the maintenance a few months after my father went away. I guess I was lonely, and one thing led to another. He was okay, at the start. I mean, he was never exactly a charmer, but he was good with Jenna, and he wasn't a deadbeat. He was surprising too, in some ways. He read a lot, and knew about music and old movies. He taught me stuff.' She laughed humorlessly. 'Looking back, I guess I replaced one father figure with another.'

'And then?'

'We got married kind of fast, and he moved into my father's house with me. Things were fine for a couple of months. Jerry was hung up on money, though. It was always a big thing with him. He felt that he'd never been given an even break. He had all kinds of big plans, and no way to make them happen until he met me. He smelled cash, but there was none, or none that he could get his hands on. He started to harp on it a lot, and that caused arguments.

'Then I came home one night and he was bathing Jenna. She was six or seven at the time. He'd never done that before. It's not like I had made it clear to him that he shouldn't, or anything, but I just kind of assumed that he wouldn't. She was naked in the bath and he was kneeling beside her, outside the tub. His feet were bare. That was what freaked me out: his bare feet. Makes no sense, huh? Anyway, I screamed at him, and Jenna started crying, and Jerry stormed out and didn't come back until late. I tried talking to him about what had happened, but he'd run up a head of steam by that point, fueled by a lot of booze, and he slapped me. It wasn't hard or painful, but I wasn't going to take a slap from any man. I told him to get out, and he did. He came back a day or two later, and he apologized and I guess we made up. He was real careful around me and Jenna after that, but I couldn't shake off that image of him with my daughter naked beside him. He had a computer that he used for work sometimes, and I knew his password. I'd seen him enter it once when he was showing Jenna something on the Internet. I went into his files and, well, there was a lot of pornography. I know men look at that kind of stuff. I suppose some women do too, but there was so much of it on Jerry's computer, just so much.'

'Adults or children?' I asked.

'Adults,' she replied. 'All adults. I tried to stay quiet about it, but I couldn't. I told him what I'd done and what I'd seen. I asked him if he had a problem. At first he was ashamed, then he got real angry, real, real angry. He screamed and shouted. He threw stuff. He started calling me all these names, like the ones he used when he was talking to you. He told me I was "soiled," that I was lucky anyone would want to touch me. He said other things too, things about Jenna. He said that she'd end up like me, that the apple never fell far from the tree. That was it, as far as I was concerned. He left that night, and things came to an end. He had a lawyer for a time, and he was trying to get an order made against my assets, but I didn't really have any assets. After a while, it all dried up, and I didn't hear from him or the lawyer again. He didn't contest the divorce. He just seemed happy to be rid of me.'

I finished my coffee. A wind blew, sending dead leaves scurrying like children fleeing the approach of rain. I knew she hadn't told me everything, that aspects of what had occurred would remain private, but some of what she had said explained Jerry Legere's animosity toward his ex-wife, especially if he felt that he was not entirely to blame for what had occurred. There were truth and lies bound up together in what each of them was saying, though, and Rebecca Clay had not been entirely honest with me from the start. I pressed on.

'I mentioned the Project that Merrick had spoken about to your ex-husband,' I said. 'It looked like he had heard it referred to before.'

'It could have been something private that my father was engaged in – he was always doing research and reading journals, trying to keep up with changes in his profession – but it wouldn't make sense for Jerry to have information about it. I mean, they didn't know each other, and I don't even remember Jerry coming to check out the security system before my father died. They never met.'

But mention of the Project led me to the final question, and the one that was troubling me the most.

'Jerry told me something else,' I said. 'He claimed that you hired a private investigator once before, to look into your father's disappearance. Jerry said that the man you hired disappeared in turn. Is that true?'

Rebecca Clay bit some dry skin from her bottom lip.

'You think I lied to you, don't you?'

'By omission. I'm not blaming you, but I'd like to know why.'

'Elwin Stark suggested that I hire someone. It was about eighteen months after my father had vanished, and the police seemed to have decided that there wasn't anything more that they could do. I spoke to Elwin because I was worried about Jerry's lawyer, and I didn't know what could be done to protect my father's estate. There was no will, so it was going to be messy anyway, but Elwin said that a first step, if my father didn't reappear, would be to have him declared legally dead after five years. Elwin's view was that it would be helpful to hire someone to make further inquiries, as a judge might take that into account when it came to making the declaration. I didn't have a whole lot of money, though. I was just starting out as a junior realtor. I guess that determined the kind of person I could afford to hire.'

'Who was he?' I asked.

'His name was Jim Poole. He was just starting out too. He had done some work for someone I knew – it was my friend April: you met her at the house – who suspected that her husband was cheating on her. It turned out that he wasn't. He was gambling instead, although I don't know if that was better or worse for her, but she seemed happy with Jim's work. So I hired him and asked him to look into things, even see if he could discover anything new. He spoke to some of the same people that you did, but he didn't find out anything more than we already knew. Jim might have mentioned something about a project at one point, but I probably didn't pay a whole lot of attention. My father really did always seem to have some kind of article or essay on the back burner. He was never short of ideas for things to write about and research.

'Then, after a couple of weeks, Jim called me to tell me that he was heading out of town for a few days and that he might have some news for me when he got back. Well, I waited for Jim to call again, and he never did. About a week later, the police came to see me. Jim's girlfriend had reported him missing, and they were talking to his friends and his clients, although he didn't have very many of either. They found my name among the files in his apartment, but I couldn't help them. Jim hadn't told me where he was going. They weren't happy about that, but what more could I do? Jim's car was found down in Boston shortly after, parked in one of the long-term lots near Logan. They found some drugs in the car – a bag of coke, I think – enough to suggest that he might have been dealing on the side. I think they figured that he'd gotten into some kind of trouble over the drugs, maybe with a supplier, and that he'd either fled because of it or been killed. His girlfriend told the police that he wasn't that kind of guy, and he would have found a way to get in touch with her, even if he was running from something, but he never did.'

'And what do you think?'

She shook her head. 'I stopped looking for my father after that,' was all she said. 'Is that enough of an answer for you?'

'And you didn't tell me about Poole because you thought it might dissuade me from helping you?'

'Yes.'

'Was your relationship with Jim Poole purely professional?'

She stood up quickly, almost knocking over her cup. It splashed coffee between us that dripped through the holes in the table and stained the ground below.

'What kind of question is that? I bet that came from Jerry too, right?'

'It did, but now isn't the time to get self-righteous.'

'I liked Jim,' she said, as if that answered the question. 'He was having problems with his girlfriend. We talked, had a drink together once or twice. Jerry saw us in a bar – he used to call me sometimes when he'd been drinking, asking for another chance – and decided that Jim was getting in the way, but Jim was younger and stronger than him. There was some shouting, and a bottle was broken, but nobody got hurt. I guess Jerry's still sore about it, even after all this time.'

She straightened the skirt of her business suit. 'Look, I'm grateful for what you've done, but I can't let this go on for much longer.' She gestured toward Jackie, as if he symbolized all that was wrong in her life. 'I want my daughter home, and I want Merrick off my back. Now that you know about Jim Poole, I'm not sure that I want you to keep asking questions about my father either. I don't need to feel guilty about any more people, and every day seems to cost me, like, at least a day's pay. I'd appreciate it if we could get this whole thing wrapped up as soon as possible, even if it means going to a judge.'

I told her that I understood, and I'd talk to some people about her options and call her to go through them with her as soon as I could. She headed back to her office to collect her things. I chatted with Jackie Garner and told him about the call from Merrick.

'What happens when our time runs out?' asked Jackie. 'We just gonna wait for him to make a move?'

I told him it wouldn't come to that. I also told him that I didn't think Rebecca Clay would keep paying us for much longer and that I was going to bring in some extra help.

'The kind of help that comes from New York?' asked Jackie.

'Maybe,' I said.

'If the woman don't want to pay you, then how come you want to keep working?'

'Because Merrick isn't going away, whether he gets what he wants from Rebecca or not. Plus I'm going to shake his tree a whole lot over the next day or two, and he's not going to like it.'

Jackie looked amused. 'Well, you need a hand, you let me know. It's the boring stuff you have to pay me for. The interesting stuff I do for free.'

Walter was still wet with salt water from his walk with Bob Johnson when I got home, and seemed content to sleep in his basket away from the cold. I had a couple of hours to kill before I was to meet June Fitzpatrick for dinner so I went on to the *Press-Herald*'s web site and browsed its archive for anything I could find on Daniel Clay's disappearance. According to the reports, allegations of abuse had been received from a number of children who had been patients of Dr Clay. At no point was there any implication that he was involved, but questions were clearly being asked about how he could have failed to notice that children whom he was assisting, each of whom had been abused before, were being abused again. Clay had declined to comment, other than to say that he was 'very distressed' by the allegations, that he would make a full statement in due course, and that his main priority was assisting the police and social services with their own investigations with a view to finding the culprits. A couple of experts had come, somewhat reluctantly, to Clay's defence, pointing out that sometimes it could take months or years to get an abuse victim to reveal the depth of what he or she had endured. Even the police were careful not to apportion blame on Clay, but reading between the lines of the story it seemed clear that Clay was taking some of that blame on himself anyway. There was such a scandal brewing that it was hard to see how Clay could have continued to practice, no matter what the outcome of any investigation. One piece described him variously as 'ashen-faced,' 'hollow-eyed,' 'gaunt,' and 'close to tears.' There was a picture of Clay beside the piece, taken outside his house. He looked thin and stooped, like a wounded stork.

The detective quoted in one of the newspaper articles was Bobby O'Rourke. He was still a detective with the Portland P.D., although he worked out of Internal Affairs. I got him at his desk just before he left for the day, and he agreed to meet me for a beer over in Gritty's within the hour. I parked on Commercial and found him seated in a corner, flipping through some photocopies and eating a hamburger. We had met a couple of times in the past, and I'd helped him to fill in the blanks in a case involving a Portland P.D. cop named Barron who had died under what could euphemistically be termed 'mysterious circumstances' a few years before. I didn't envy O'Rourke his job. The fact that he was with IA meant that he was good at his work. Unfortunately, it was work at which some of his fellow cops didn't want him to be good.

He wiped his hands on a napkin and we shook.

'You eating?' he asked.

'Nope. Going to dinner in an hour or two.'

'Anyplace flash?'

'Joel Harmon's house.'

'I'm impressed. We're going to be reading about you in the society columns.'

We spoke a little about the annual IA report that was about to be published. It was the usual stuff, mainly use-of-force allegations and complaints about the operation of police vehicles. The patterns remained pretty consistent. The complainants were typically young males, and the use-of-force incidents mostly related to breaking up fights. The cops had used only their hands to subdue the combatants, and the guys involved were mostly white and under thirty, so it wasn't like senior citizens or the Harlem Globetrotters were being rousted. Nobody had been suspended for longer than two days as a result of complaints. All told, it wasn't a bad year for IA. Meanwhile, the Portland P.D. had a new chief. The old chief had stepped down earlier in the year, and the city council had been considering two candidates, one who was white and local, and one who was black and from the South. Had the council gone for the black candidate it would have increased by 100 percent the number of black cops in Portland, but instead it had opted for local experience, and some minority leaders were still sore. The old chief, meanwhile, was rumored to be considering a run for governor.

O'Rourke finished his burger and took a sip of his IPA. He was a slim, fit guy who didn't look like burgers and beer usually accounted for too many of his calories.

'So, Daniel Clay,' he said.

'You remember him?'

'I remember the case, and what I didn't recall I checked before I came over here. I only met Clay twice before he went missing, so there's a limit to what I can tell you.'

'What did you think of him?'

'He seemed genuinely upset by what had happened. He looked to be in shock. He kept referring to them as his "kids." We started investigating, along with the state police, the sheriffs, the local cops, social services. The rest you probably know already: some points of correspondence came up in other cases over a period of time, and a number of those cases could be traced back to Clay.'

'You think it was a coincidence that Clay had worked with the kids?'

'There's nothing to indicate that it wasn't. Some of the children were particularly vulnerable. They'd been abused before, and most of them were in the very early stages of therapy and intervention. They hadn't even got around to talking about the first series of abuses before the next began to happen.'

'Ever come close to an arrest?'

'No. A girl, thirteen years old, was found wandering in fields outside of Skowhegan at three in the morning. Barefoot, clothes torn, bleeding, no underwear. She was hysterical, babbling about men and birds. She was disoriented and didn't seem to know where she'd been held or what direction she'd walked from, but she was clear on the details: three men, all masked, taking turns with her in what seemed to be an unfurnished room in a house. We got some DNA samples from her, but most of them were pretty messed up. Only a couple were clean, and they didn't match anything on the databases. About a year ago we tried again as part of a cold case review, but still zip. It's bad. We should have done better on it, but I don't see how.'

'What about the kids?'

'I haven't kept track of all of them. Some have come back on the radar. They were screwed-up kids, and they became screwed-up adults. I always felt sorry for them when I saw their names appear. What the hell kind of chance did they have after what was done to them?'

'And Clay?'

'He literally vanished. His daughter called us, said she was worried about him, that he hadn't been home in two days. They found his car outside Jackman, up by the Canadian border. We thought he might have fled the jurisdiction, but there was no reason for him to do that, apart from shame, maybe. He's never been seen again.'

I leaned back in my chair. I wasn't much wiser than before I'd sat down. O'Rourke recognized my dissatisfaction.

'Sorry,' he said. 'Bet you were hoping for a revelation.'

'Yeah, a blinding flash of light.'

'So how did this come up?'

'Clay's daughter hired me. Someone has been asking questions about her father. It has her rattled. You ever hear of a man named Frank Merrick?'

Bingo. O'Rourke's face lit up like the Fourth of July.

'Frank Merrick,' he said. 'Oh yeah. I know all about Frank. Fatal Frank, they used to call him. He's the guy, the one who's shaking up Clay's daughter?'

I nodded.

'Makes sense, in a way,' said O'Rourke.

I asked him why.

'Because Merrick's daughter was also a patient of Daniel Clay's, except she went the same way he did. Lucy Merrick, that was her name, although he never married the mother.'

'The daughter disappeared?'

'Reported missing two days after Clay, but it looks like she was gone for longer than that. Her foster parents were animals. Told the social workers she was always running away, and they'd just gotten tired of chasing her ass down. From what they could recall, they'd last seen her four or five days earlier. She was fourteen. I don't doubt she was a handful, but you know, she was still a kid. There was talk of pressing charges against the foster parents, but nothing ever happened.'

'And where was Merrick when all this was going on?'

'In jail. Let me tell you: Frank Merrick is an interesting guy.' He loosened his tie. 'Order me another beer,' he said. 'Better get something for yourself too. It's that kind of story.'

Frank Merrick was a killer.

That word had become so devalued through overuse that every mean little kid with a knife who overstepped the line and gutted a drinking buddy in a bar fight over some girl in a too-tight dress, every jobless no-hoper who ever held up a liquor store, then shot the guy earning seven bucks an hour behind the counter, whether through panic or boredom or just because he had a gun in his hand and it seemed a shame not to see what it could do, every one of them received the title of 'killer'. It was used in the newspapers to drive up sales, in the court-rooms to drive up sentences, on cell blocks to make reputations and buy some breathing space from assaults and challenges. But it didn't mean anything, not really. Killing someone didn't make you a killer, not in the world through which Frank Merrick walked. It wasn't something you did once, either by accident or design. It wasn't even a lifestyle choice, like vegetarianism or nihilism. It was something that lay in your cells, waiting for a moment of awakening, of revelation. In that way, it was possible to be a killer even before you took your first life. It was part of your nature, and it would show itself in time. All that it took was a catalyst.

Frank Merrick had lived what seemed to be a regular guy's life for the first twenty-five years or so. He'd grown up in a rough part of Charlotte, North Carolina, and he'd run with a tough crowd as a kid, but he straightened himself out. He trained as a mechanic, and no clouds followed him through life and no shadows trailed in his wake, although it was said that he stayed in touch with elements from his past and that he was a man who could be relied upon to supply or dispose of a car at short notice. It was only later, when his true self, his secret self, began to emerge, that people remembered men who had crossed Frank Merrick and fallen between the cracks in the sidewalk, never to be seen or heard from again. There were stories of calls made, of trips to Florida and Atlanta and New Orleans, of guns used once, then disassembled and thrown into canals and levees.

But they were just stories, and people will talk . . .

He married an ordinary girl, and he might have stayed married to her had it not been for the accident that changed Frank Merrick beyond all recognition, or perhaps it merely allowed him to shed the veneer of a quiet, introverted man who was good with his hands and knew his way around a car and to become something altogether odder and more frightening.

Frank Merrick was struck by a motorcycle one night as he crossed a street in the suburb of Charlotte where he lived. He was carrying a carton of ice cream that he had bought for his wife. He should have waited for the signal but he was worried that the ice cream would melt before he could get it home. The motorcyclist, who was not wearing a helmet, had been drinking, but he was not drunk. He had also been smoking a little dope, but he was not high. Peter Cash had told himself both of those things before he climbed on his bike after leaving his buddies watching porn on the Betamax.

To Cash, it seemed as if Frank Merrick had materialized out of thin air, suddenly assuming form on the empty street, assembling himself out of atoms of night. The bike hit Merrick full on, breaking bones and rending flesh, the impact catapulting the motorcyclist on to the hood of a parked car. Cash was lucky to escape with a busted pelvis, and had he hit the windshield of the car with his unprotected head instead of his ass he would, most assuredly, have died there and then. Instead, he remained conscious for long enough to see Merrick's mangled body jerking like a stranded fish on the road.

Merrick was released from hospital after two months, when his broken bones had healed sufficiently and his internal organs were no longer deemed to be in imminent danger of failure or collapse. He scarcely spoke to his wife and spoke even less to his friends until those friends finally ceased to trouble him with their presence. He slept little, and rarely ventured into the marital bed, but when he did he fell upon his wife with such ferocity that she grew to fear his advances and the pain that came with them. Eventually, she fled the house and, after a year or two, filed for divorce. Merrick signed everything without comment or complaint, seemingly content to discard every aspect of his old life, something within him cocooning itself while it transformed. His wife later changed her name and remarried in California, and never told her new husband the truth about the man who had once shared her life.

And Merrick? Well, it was believed that Cash was the first victim of the transformed man, although no evidence was ever produced linking him to the crime. Cash was stabbed to death in his bed, but Merrick had an alibi, supplied by four men out of Philly who, it was said, obtained some services from Merrick in return. In the years that followed he picked up a little work with various crews, mainly on the East Coast, and gradually became the go-to guy when someone needed to be taught a last, fateful lesson, and when the necessity of deniability meant that the job had to be farmed out. The tally of bodies that had fallen at his hands began to mount. He had embraced at last his natural aptitude for killing, and it served him well.

In the meantime, he had other appetites. He liked women,

and one of them, a waitress in Pittsfield, Maine, found herself pregnant after a night in his company. She was in her late thirties, and had despaired of ever finding a man, or of having a child of her own. She never even considered an abortion, but had no way of contacting the man who had impregnated her, and eventually she gave birth to a seemingly ordinary child. When Frank Merrick returned to Maine and looked the waitress up, she feared how he might respond to the news that he was a father, but he had held the child in his arms and asked her name ('Lucy, after my mom,' he was told), and he had smiled and told her that Lucy was a fine name, and he had left money in the child's cradle. Thereafter, on a regular basis, cash would arrive, sometimes delivered in person by Merrick, at other times arriving in the form of a money order. The child's mother recognized that there was something dangerous about this man, something that should remain unexplored, and it always surprised her to see the devotion he showed toward the little girl, although he never stayed long with her. His daughter grew into a child who sometimes had bad dreams, but nothing worse than that. Then the little girl's dreams began to filter into her waking life. She became difficult, even disturbed. She hurt herself and she tried to hurt others. When her mother died – a massive pulmonary embolism took her as she swam in the sea, so that her body was taken out by the tide and found days later on a beach, bloated and half eaten by scavengers – Lucy Merrick was put into care. In time, the child was sent to Daniel Clay in an effort to curb her aggression and tendency toward self-harm, and he seemed to be making some progress with her, until both he and the girl disappeared.

By then, her father had been in jail for four years. His luck ran out when he picked up five years for reckless conduct with a dangerous weapon, five years for criminal threatening with the use of a dangerous weapon, and ten years for aggravated assault, all to be served concurrently, after one of his prospective victims managed to shoot his way out of his home as Merrick was closing in on him with a knife, only for the vic to be hit by a patrol car as he was fleeing. Merrick only avoided a further forty-to-life after the state failed to prove premeditation in fact, and because he had no previous convictions for crimes using deadly force against the person. It was during this period that his daughter disappeared. The sentence wasn't all served in the general population, either. A chunk of it, according to O'Rourke, was spent in Supermax, and that was real hard time right there.

After his release, he was sent for trial in Virginia for the killing of an accountant named Barton Riddick, who was shot once in the head with a .44 in 1993. Merrick was charged on the basis of bullet lead analysis by the FBI of rounds found in his car following his arrest in Maine. There was nothing to indicate that he had been at the scene of the killing in Virginia, or to link him physically to Riddick in any other way, but the chemical composition of the bullet that had passed through the victim, taking a chunk of skull and brain with it as it exited, matched bullets from the box of ammunition discovered in Merrick's trunk. Merrick was facing the possibility of spending the rest of his life in prison, maybe even a death sentence, but his case was one of a number taken up by some law firms that believed the Bureau's examiners had overstated the bullet lead analysis test results in a number of instances. The case against Merrick had been further weakened when the gun used in the killing was subsequently used in the murder of a lawyer in Baton Rouge. Reluctantly, the prosecutor in Virginia decided not to follow through on the charges against Merrick, and the FBI had since announced that it was abandoning bullet lead analysis. He had been released in October and was now, to all intents and purposes, a free man, as he had served his sentence in full in the state of Maine, and no conditions had been applied to his release on the assumption that the Riddick charges would ensure he would never taste the air as a free man again.

'And now he's back here,' concluded O'Rourke.

'Asking after the doctor who was treating his daughter,' I said.

'Sounds like a man with a grudge. What are you going to do?'

I took out my wallet and laid some bills on the table to cover our tab. 'I'm going to have him picked up.'

'Will the Clay woman press charges?'

'I'll talk to her about it. Even if she doesn't, the threat of imprisonment might be enough to keep Merrick off her back. He won't want to go back to jail. Who knows, the cops may even turn up something in his car.'

'Has he threatened her at all?'

'Only verbally, and just in the vaguest of ways. He broke her window, though, so he's capable of more.'

'Any sign of a weapon?'

'None.'

'Frank's the kind of guy who might feel a little naked without a gun.'

'When I met him he told me he wasn't armed.'

'You believed him?'

'I think he's too smart to carry a gun with him. As a convicted felon, he can't be found in possession, and he's already attracting a lot of attention to himself. He can't find out what happened to his daughter if he's locked up again.'

'Well, it sounds plausible, but I wouldn't want to bet my life on it. The Clay woman still live in the city?'

'South Portland.'

'I can make some calls if you want me to.'

'Every little helps. It would be good if we could have a temporary order in place by the time Merrick is picked up.'

O'Rourke said that he didn't think it would be a problem. I had almost forgotten about Jim Poole. I asked O'Rourke about him.

'I remember something about it. He was an amateur, a correspondence-college private eye. Liked using a little weed, I think. Cops down in Boston figured there might have been a drug connection to his death, and I guess people up here were happy enough to go along with that.'

'He was working for Rebecca Clay when he disappeared,' I said.

'I didn't know that. It wasn't my case. Sounds like she might be unlucky to be around. She vanishes more people than the Magic Circle.'

'I don't imagine lucky people attract the interest of men like Frank Merrick.'

'If they do, they don't stay lucky for long. I'd like to be there when they bring him in. I've heard a lot about him, but I've never met him face-to-face.'

His beer glass had left a circle of moisture on the table. He traced patterns in it with his index finger.

'What are you thinking?' I asked.

'I'm thinking it's a shame you have a client who believes she's at risk.'

'Why?'

'I don't like clusters. Some of Clay's patients were being abused. Merrick's daughter was one of his patients.'

'Hence Merrick's daughter was being abused? It's possible, but it doesn't necessarily follow.'

'Then Clay disappears and so does she.'

'And the abusers are never found.'

He shrugged. 'I'm just saying: having a man like Merrick asking questions about old crimes might make some people worried.'

'Like the people who committed those old crimes.'

'Exactly. Could be useful. You never know who might decide to take offense and make themselves known along the way.'

'The problem is that Merrick isn't like a dog on a leash. He can't be controlled. I've got three men looking out for my client as things stand. My priority is to keep her safe.'

O'Rourke stood. 'Well, talk to her. Explain what you intend to do. Then let's get him picked up and see what happens.'

We shook hands again, and I thanked him for his help.

'Don't get carried away,' he said. 'I'm in this because of the kids. And hey, forgive me for being blunt, but if this thing goes up in smoke, and I find you lit the fuse, I'll arrest you myself.'

*　*　*

It was time for me to drive out to Joel Harmon's house. Along the way, I called Rebecca and shared with her most of what O'Rourke had told me of Merrick and what I was hoping to do the next day. She seemed to have calmed down a little since we last talked, although she was still intent on wrapping up our business with each other as soon as possible.

'We'll arrange a meeting, then have him picked up by the cops,' I said. 'The state's protection-from-harassment law says that if you've been intimidated or confronted three or more times by the same person, then the cops have to act. I figure that incident with the window may also fall under terrorizing, and I spotted him watching you that day at Longfellow Square, so we have him for stalking as well. Either one of those would be enough to bring us under the cover of the law.'

'Does that mean I'll have to go to court?' she asked.

'Make the harassment report first thing tomorrow. The report has to be made before a court complaint can be filed anyway. Then we can go to the District Court and get it to issue a temporary order for emergency protection after you've filed the complaint. I've already talked to someone about this, and everything should be in place for you by tomorrow evening.' I gave her O'Rourke's name and number. 'A date and time will be set for a hearing, and the summons and complaint will have to be served on Merrick. I can do that, or if you prefer, we can get the sheriff's department to do it instead. If he approaches you again once the order has been served, then that's a Class D crime with a penalty of up to one year in jail and a maximum fine of a thousand dollars. Three convictions and he's looking at five years.'

'It still doesn't sound like enough,' she said. 'Can't they just put him away immediately?'

'It's a delicate balance,' I said. 'He's overstepped the line, but not enough to justify serving time. The thing is, I believe that doing more time is the last thing he wants to risk. He's a dangerous man, but he's also had years to think about his daughter. He failed her, but he wants someone else to blame. I think he's decided to start with your father, because he heard the rumors about him and wonders if something similar might have happened to his own child while she was in his care.'

'And because my father's not around, he's moved on to me.' She sighed. 'Okay. Will I have to be there when they arrest him?'

'No. The police may want to talk to you later, though. Jackie will stay close to you, just in case.'

'Just in case it doesn't go the way you've planned?'

'Just in case,' I repeated, not committing to anything. I felt that I'd let her down, but I couldn't see what more I could have done. True, I could have banded together with Jackie Garner and the Fulcis to beat Merrick to a pulp, but that would have been to descend to his level. And now, after my conversation with O'Rourke, there was one more thing stopping me from using force against Frank Merrick.

In a strange way, I felt sorry for him.

11

There were calls made that night. Perhaps that was what
Merrick wanted all along. That was why he had made his
presence at Rebecca Clay's house so obvious, that was why
he had left his blood on her window, and that was why he
had set me on Jerry Legere. There were other incidents, too,
that I did not yet know about. Four dead crows had been
strung together and hung outside the offices occupied by
Rebecca's former lawyer, Elwin Stark, the previous night.
Sometime that same night, the Midlake Center had been
burglarized. Nothing was taken, but someone must have spent
hours going through whatever files were at hand, and it would
be a long time before it became clear what, if anything, had
been removed. Clay's former physician, Dr Caussure, had been
approached on his way to a bridge tournament by a man
fitting Merrick's description. The man had boxed in Caussure's
car, then had rolled down the window of his red Ford and
asked Caussure if he liked birds and if he was aware that his
late patient and friend Dr Daniel Clay had consorted with
pedophiles and deviants.

It didn't matter to Merrick if these individuals were involved
or not. He wanted to create a climate of fear and doubt. He
wanted to slip in and out of lives, sowing rumors and half-
truths, knowing that, in a small city like Portland, word would
spread, and the men he was hunting would soon be buzzing
like bees in the presence of an imminent threat to the hive.
Merrick thought that he had everything under control, or that
he could deal with whatever arose, but he was wrong. He was

being manipulated, just as I was, and nobody was really in control, not even Eldritch's mysterious client.

Soon, people would start to die.

Joel Harmon lived in a big house off Bayshore Drive in Falmouth, with its own private jetty and a white yacht berthed close by. Portland used to be called Falmouth, back from the late seventeenth century when the Basque, St Castin, led the natives in a series of attacks against the English settlements that resulted eventually in the burning of the town, until the end of the eighteenth century, when the city came into its own. Now the area that bore the old name was one of Portland's most affluent suburbs, and the center of its boating activity. The Portland Yacht Club, one of the oldest in the country, was located on Falmouth Foreside, sheltered by the long, narrow Clapboard Island, which was itself home to two private estates, throwbacks to the late nineteenth century when the railroad magnate Henry Houston built a ten-thousand-square-foot summer cottage on the island, his own small contribution to rendering the word 'cottage' meaningless in this part of the world.

Harmon's house stood on a raised promontory from which a green lawn sloped down to the water's edge. There were walls on either side for privacy, and a lot of rosebushes in carefully regimented and sheltered beds. June had told me that Harmon was a fanatical rose grower, fascinated by hybridization, and that the soil in his garden was constantly monitored and adjusted to facilitate his obsession. There were said to be roses in his beds that simply did not exist elsewhere, and unlike his peers, Harmon saw no reason to share his discoveries with others. The roses were for his pleasure, and his alone.

It was an unusually mild night, a trick of the season to lull the unwary into a false sense of security, and as June and I stood in his garden with the other guests, sipping pre-dinner drinks, I took in Harmon's house, his yacht, his roses, and his wife, who had greeted us as we arrived, her husband being occupied elsewhere in the party. She was in her early sixties, which made her about the same age as her husband, her gray hair interwoven with carefully dyed blond strands. Up close, her skin looked like molded plastic. She seemed to have trouble stretching it into any semblance of an expression, although her surgeon had clearly anticipated this problem and had carved her mouth into a permanent half smile, so that someone could have been telling her about the systematic drowning of puppies and kittens and she would merely have looked slightly amused at the whole affair. There was a relic of the beauty that she might once have had still visible in her face, but it had been debased by her grim determination to hold on to it. Her eyes were dull and glassy, and her conversational skills would have made a passing child seem like Oscar Wilde.

Her husband, by contrast, was the model of a perfect host, dressed casually but expensively in a blue wool blazer and gray trousers, with a red cravat to add a touch of carefully cultivated eccentricity to the whole look. He was shadowed, as he shook hands and exchanged gossip, by a beautiful Asian-American girl, young and slim with the kind of figure that caused male jaws spontaneously to unhinge. According to June, she was Harmon's latest squeeze, although officially she was his personal assistant. He had a habit of picking up young women, dazzling them with his wealth, then dropping them as soon as a new prospect appeared on the horizon.

'Doesn't look like his wife objects to her presence too much,' I said. 'Then again, it doesn't look like she's aware of anything beyond the promise of her next fix of prescription medication.'

Mrs Harmon's empty gaze swept across the guests at regular intervals, never resting on any of them but merely bathing them in the dull light of her regard, like the beam of a lighthouse picking out the ships in its ambit. Even when she had greeted us at the door, her hand like the cold, desiccated remains of a long-dead bird in my palm, she had barely made eye contact.

'I feel sorry for her,' said June. 'Lawrie was always the kind of woman who was destined to marry a powerful man and provide him with children, but she had no inner life, or none that anyone could detect. Now her children are all grown-up, and she fills her days as best she can. She was beautiful once, but beauty was all she had. She just sits motionless on the boards of various charities and spends her husband's money, and he doesn't object as long as she doesn't interfere with the way he lives his life.'

I felt that I had Harmon down to a T: a self-indulgent man, with money enough to enable him to pursue his appetites and to sate them, even as his needs grew greater with each bite that he took. He came from a politically well-connected family, and his father had been an adviser to the Democrats, although the failure of a number of his businesses had left enough of a whiff of scandal on him that he never managed to get close enough to the bowl to feed with the big dogs. Harmon himself had been very politically active once, working on Ed Muskie's campaign as a young man in '71, even traveling with him on his visit to Moscow thanks to his father's efforts, until it became clear that not only was Muskie not going to win the nomination but it was probably a good thing that McGovern was going to clean his clock in the primaries. Muskie couldn't keep his temper. He railed at journalists and staffers, and he did it in public. Had he won the nomination, it wouldn't have been long before that side of him was revealed to the voters. So Joel Harmon and his family had quickly and quietly ditched Muskie, and any political idealism that he might have had was left by the wayside as he moved on to the pressing business of accumulating wealth and making up for his father's business failings.

But according to June, Harmon was much more complex than he appeared: he gave generously to charity, not only publicly but privately. His views on welfare and social security made him almost a socialist by most American standards, and he remained a powerful, if discreet, voice in that regard, enjoying the ear of successive governors and state representatives. He was passionate about the city and state in which he lived, and it was said that his children were mildly disturbed by the ease with which he was dissipating what they considered to be their inheritance, their social conscience being considerably less well developed than their father's.

I wanted to keep my head clear, so I sipped orange juice while the other guests drank champagne. I recognized one or two of those whom Harmon had invited. There was a writer named Jon Lee Jacobs, who penned novels and poems about lobstermen and the call of the sea. He had a big red beard and dressed like the men in his books, except he came originally from a family of accountants in Massachusetts, and was rumored to get seasick when he stepped in a puddle. The other familiar face was Dr Byron Russell, a young shrink who made occasional appearances on Maine Public Radio and on local TV channels whenever a serious talking head was needed on matters relating to mental health. To Russell's credit, he tended to be the voice of reason whenever he participated, often at the expense of some treacle-voiced woman with a bum degree in psychology from a college that operated out of a trailer, and who believed in the kind of touchy-feely platitudes that made depression and suicide seem like attractive alternatives to actually listening to her. Also present, interestingly, was Elwin Stark, the lawyer who had been so reluctant to speak to me earlier that week. I felt like telling him about Eldritch, who had talked to me for a lot longer, albeit without actually telling me a great deal more than I'd learned from a fraction of the time spent speaking with Stark, but initially Stark didn't seem any happier to meet me in person than he had been to talk with me on the phone. Nevertheless, he eventually managed to be civil for a couple of minutes. He even apologized, in a way, for his earlier brusqueness. I could smell whiskey on his breath, even though he had champagne in his glass. Clearly, he had started earlier than the rest of the guests.

'I was having a hell of a day when you called,' he said. 'The timing wasn't great.'

'My timing is often bad,' I said. 'And timing is everything.'

'You got it. You still nosing around in the Clay business?'

I told him that I was. He made a face, as though someone

had just offered him a piece of bad fish. It was then that he told me about the dead crows.

'Freaked my secretary the hell out,' he said. 'She thought it was the work of Satanists.'

'And what about you?'

'Well, it was different, I'll give it that. Worst that ever happened to me before was a golf club being put through the windshield of my Lexus.'

'Any idea who was responsible?'

'I can guess who *you* think was responsible: the same guy who's been giving Rebecca Clay a hard time. I knew you were bad luck the minute I heard your voice.' He tried to laugh it off, but it was clear that he meant it.

'Why would he target you?'

'Because he's desperate, and my name was all over the documentation relating to her father. I passed on dealing with the probate, though. Enough was enough.'

'Are you concerned?'

'No, I'm not. I've done my share of swimming with sharks, and I've lived. I've got people I can call on if I have to. Rebecca, on the other hand, only has people for as long as she can afford to pay them. You ought to let the whole business go, Parker. You're just making things worse by stirring up the dirt at the bottom of the pond.'

'You're not interested in the truth?'

'I'm a lawyer,' he replied. 'What has the truth got to do with anything? My concern is the protection of my clients' interests. Sometimes, the truth just gets in the way.'

'That's a very, um, pragmatic approach.'

'I'm a realist. I don't do criminal work, but if I had to defend you on a charge of murder, and you decided to plead not guilty, what would you expect me to do? Tell the judge that, all things considered, I thought you'd done it, because that was the truth? Be serious. The law doesn't require truth, only the appearance of it. Most cases simply rest on a version of it that's acceptable to both sides. You want to know what the only truth is?

Everybody lies. That's it. *That's* truth. You can take that to the preacher and get it baptized.'

'So do you have a client whose interests you're protecting in the matter of Daniel Clay?'

He wagged his finger at me. I didn't like the gesture, just like I didn't care much for him calling me by my last name.

'You're a piece of work,' he said. 'Daniel was my client. So too, briefly, was his daughter. Now Daniel is dead. It's done and dusted. Let him rest, wherever he is.'

He left us to go over and speak with the writer Jacobs. June imitated Stark's finger wag.

'He is right,' she said. 'You really are a piece of work. Do you have any conversations that end happily?'

'Only with you,' I replied.

'That's because I don't listen to you.'

'There is that,' I conceded, as a waiter rang a bell, summoning us to dinner.

It seemed like there were to be twelve of us, all told, including Harmon and his wife, the additional numbers being made up by a female collage artist of whom even June had never heard, and three banker friends of Harmon's from way back. Harmon spoke to us properly for the first time as we were walking to the dining room, apologizing for taking so long to get to us.

'Well, June,' he said, 'I had despaired of ever seeing you again at one of my little evenings. I was worried that I might have offended you somehow.'

June waved him away with a smile. 'I know you far too well ever to be offended by anything but your occasional lapses in taste,' she said.

She stepped aside so that Harmon and I could shake hands. He had it down to a fine art. He could have given lessons in the proper duration, the force of the grip, the width of the smile that accompanied it.

'Mr Parker, I've heard a great deal about you. You lead an interesting life.'

'It's not as productive as yours. You have a beautiful house, and a fascinating collection.'

The walls were decorated with an incredible variety of art, the positioning of each clearly the subject of considerable thought, so that paintings and drawings appeared both to complement and echo one another, even occasionally clashing where their juxtaposition would have a particular impact on the beholder. On the wall to the right of where we stood, a beautiful, if slightly sinister, nude of a young woman on a bed hung across from a much older painting of an aged man on the point of expiring on a very similar bed, his final moments witnessed by a physician and a gathering of relatives and friends, some bereft, some pitying, and some merely avaricious. Among them was a young woman whose face startlingly resembled the features of the nude opposite. Similar beds, similar women, seemingly separated by centuries but now part of the same narrative due to the proximity of the two images.

Harmon beamed appreciatively. 'If you would enjoy it, I'll happily show you around after dinner. One of the benefits of having somewhat eclectic taste, whatever June's opinion of the direction it may sometimes take, is that there is usually something to satisfy everyone within its limits. I should be most interested to see what catches your eye, Mr Parker, most interested indeed. Now come, dinner is about to be served.'

We took our seats at the dinner table. I was between Harmon's girlfriend, whose name was Nyoko, and the collage artist. The artist had green streaks through her blond hair, and was attractive in a willowy, vaguely disturbing way. She looked like the kind of girl who had wrist-slashing potential, and not just her own wrists either. She told me her name was Summer.

'Summer,' I said. 'Really?'

She scowled. I had barely sat down, and already someone was unhappy.

'It's my true name,' she said. 'My given name was an imposition. Discarding it in favor of my real identity freed me to pursue my art.'

'Uh-huh,' I said. Flake.

Nyoko was a little more in touch with objective reality. She was an art history graduate, and had only recently returned to Maine after two years spent working in Australia. When I asked her how long she had known Harmon, she had the self-awareness to blush slightly.

'We met at a gallery opening a few months back. And I know what you're thinking.'

'Do you?'

'Well, I know what I'd be thinking if our positions were reversed.'

'You mean if I was seeing Joel Harmon? He's not really my type.'

She giggled.

'You know what I mean. He's older than I am. He's married, sort of. He's wealthy and I drive a car that probably cost less than the brandy Joel will have decanted after dinner. But I like him: he's funny, he's got good taste, and he's lived a little. I let people think what they want.'

'Even his wife?'

'You're pretty blunt, aren't you?'

'Well, I'm sitting beside you. If his wife starts throwing knives around after her second glass of wine, I'd like to be sure that they're aimed at you, not me.'

'She doesn't care what Joel does. I'm not even sure that she notices.'

As if on cue, Lawrie Harmon glanced in our direction and managed to eke an extra quarter of an inch out of her smile. Her husband, who was sitting at the head of the table, patted her left hand reflexively, the way he might have petted a dog. But for a moment, I thought some of the dullness disappeared from her eyes, and something lanced through the fog, like a camera lens fixing on the perfect moment of clarity before an exposure. For the first time that night, her gaze lingered, but only on Nyoko. Then the smile leveled out slightly, and her attention moved on. Nyoko hadn't noticed, distracted as she was by something Summer had said to her, although I wondered if she would even have registered the change, had she been watching.

Harmon nodded to one of the waiters who stood like white compass points in a circle around us, and dishes began to appear before us with quiet efficiency. There were still two empty chairs at the end of the table.

'Are we missing someone, Joel?' asked Jacobs. He had a repu-tation as someone who, given half a chance, would declaim endlessly about his own status as a visionary, someone who was in touch with nature and the grandeur of the ordinary man. Clearly, he'd sized up the rest of us and figured that we were going to be no competition, but he didn't want some unknown quantity arriving and upstaging him. His beard twitched, as though something living within it had briefly shifted position, and then he was distracted by the arrival of his duck terrine and commenced eating instead of wondering.

Harmon looked at the chairs, as if noticing them for the first time.

'Our children,' he said. 'We had hoped that they might join us, but you know how kids are. There's a party down at the yacht club. No offense meant to anyone here, but I think they decided that it provided more opportunities for mischief than a dinner with the folks and their guests. Now, please eat.'

It came a little late for Jacobs, who was already halfway through. To his credit, he paused awkwardly, then did a little shrug and continued working on the terrine. The food was good, although terrine of anything tended to leave me un-impressed. The main course of venison was fine, though, served as a *navarin* with juniper berries. There was a mousse of choc-olate and lime for dessert, and coffee with petits fours to finish. The wine was a Duhart-Milon '98, which Harmon described as *costaud,* or powerfully built, from one of the lesser Lafitte properties. Jacobs nodded sagely as if he understood what Harmon was talking about. I sipped at my glass to be polite. It tasted a little rich for my blood, in every sense.

The conversation moved from local politics to art and,

inevitably, to literature, the latter largely a result of Jacobs's intervention, at which point he began to preen as he waited for someone to inquire about his latest magnum opus. Nobody seemed very keen to open the floodgates, but in the end Harmon asked, apparently more out of a sense of duty than any real interest. Judging from the summary that followed, Jacobs had not yet bored of mythologizing the common man, even if he had yet to get around to either understanding him or liking him.

'That man,' June whispered, as the plates were cleared and the guests began to move through a pair of double doors into a room furnished with comfortable chairs and couches, 'is the most insufferable bore.'

'Someone gave me one of his books once,' I replied.

'Did you read it?'

'Started it, then figured I'd want the time back on my deathbed and I wouldn't get it. I managed to lose the book instead. I think I dropped it in the sea.'

'A wise decision.'

Harmon appeared at my elbow.

'How about that tour, Mr Parker? June, will you accompany us?'

June demurred. 'We'll only start fighting, Joel. I'll let your new guest enjoy your collection without being bothered by my prejudices.'

He bowed to her, then turned back to me. 'Can I offer you another drink, Mr Parker?'

I lifted my half-finished wine. 'I'm good, thank you.'

'Well, let's proceed, then.'

We moved from room to room, Harmon pointing out pieces of which he was particularly proud. I didn't recognize many of the names, but that was probably due more to my ignorance than anything else. I couldn't say that much of Harmon's collection was to my taste, though, and I could almost hear June's expressions of dismay at some of the more outlandish works.

'I hear you have a number of pieces by Daniel Clay,' I said, as we gazed at something that might have been a sunset or a suture.

Harmon grinned.

'June told me that you might ask after them,' he said. 'I have two in a back office. Some of the others are in storage. I have a revolving collection, you might say. Too many pieces and too little space, even in a house this size.'

'Did you know him well?'

'We were at college together, and we kept in touch after graduation. He was a guest here on many occasions. I liked him a lot. He was a sensitive man. What happened was just terrible, both for him and for the children involved.'

He led me to a room at the back of the house, with high, recessed windows looking out over the sea. It was a combination of office and small library, with floor-to-ceiling oak shelves and an enormous matching desk. Harmon told me that Nyoko used it on the days when she was working in the house. There were only two paintings on the walls, one perhaps two feet by five feet, the other much smaller. The latter depicted a church steeple set against a backdrop of receding pines. It was hazy, the edges dulled, as though the whole scene was being filtered through a Vaseline-smeared lens. The larger painting showed the bodies of men and women writhing together, so that the canvas was a mass of twisting, shadowy flesh. It was startlingly unpleasant, more so because of the degree of artistry that had gone into its creation.

'I think I prefer the landscape,' I said.

'Most people do. The landscape is a later work, created perhaps two decades after the other. Both are untitled, but the larger canvas is typical of Daniel's earlier work.'

I turned my attention back to the landscape. There was something almost familiar about the shape of the steeple.

'Is this a real place?' I asked.

'It's Gilead,' said Harmon.

'As in the "children of Gilead"?'

Harmon nodded. 'Another of the dark spots on our state's

history. That's why I keep it back here. I suppose I hold on to it more out of tribute to Daniel's memory and the fact that he gave it to me than anything else, but it's not something I'd want displayed in the more public areas of the house.'

The community of Gilead, named after one of the biblical cities of refuge, had been founded in the fifties by a minor timber baron named Bennett Lumley. Lumley was a God-fearing man, and he worried about the spiritual well-being of the men who worked in the forests below the Canadian border. He thought that if he could establish a town in which they and their families could live, a town without the distraction of booze and whores, then he could keep them on the straight and narrow. He instituted a building program, the most conspicuous element of which was a massive stone church designed to act as the centerpiece of the settlement, a symbol of its citizens' devotion to the Lord. Gradually, the houses Lumley had built began to fill with timber workers and their families, some of whom were probably genuinely committed to a community based on Christian principles.

Unfortunately, not all of them felt the same way. Rumors began to emerge about Gilead, and about some of the things that went on there in the dark of night, but those were different times and there was little that the police could do, especially as Lumley hampered any investigations, anxious to preserve the façade of his ideal community.

Then, in 1959, a hunter tracking deer through the woods near Gilead came across a shallow grave that had been partially disturbed by animals. The corpse of a newborn child was revealed: a boy, barely a day old when he died. He had been stabbed repeatedly with, it was later surmised, a knitting needle. Two other similar graves were later found nearby, each holding a small corpse, one male and one female. This time, the police arrived in force. Questions were asked; gentle and not-so-gentle interrogations took place, but a number of the adults who had been living at the settlement had already fled by that stage. Three girls, one aged fourteen and two aged fifteen, were examined by doctors and found to have given birth to children in the previous twelve months. Lumley was forced to act. Meetings were convened, and influential men spoke to one another in the corners of clubs. Quietly, and without fuss, Gilead was abandoned and the buildings were either destroyed or began to fall into decay, all but the great, unfinished church, which was gradually colonized by the forest, its steeple turning to a pillar of green beneath layers of twisting ivy. Only one person was jailed in connection with what had occurred: a man named Mason Dubus, who was regarded as the senior figure in the community. He served time for child abduction and sex with a minor, after one of the girls who had given birth told police she had been a virtual prisoner of Dubus and his wife for seven years, having been taken from near her family home in West Virginia while out picking berries. Dubus's wife escaped jail by claiming that she had been coerced by her husband into all that had occurred, and it was her evidence that helped to secure his conviction. She declined, or was unable, to tell the police anything more of what had taken place at Gilead, but it was clear from the testimony of some of the children, both male and female, that they had been subjected to continuous and sustained abuse both before and during the establishment of the Gilead settlement. It was, as Harmon had said, a dark chapter in the state's history.

'Did Clay create many paintings like this one?' I asked.

'Clay didn't create many paintings, period,' replied Harmon, 'but of those that I've seen, a number certainly contain images of Gilead.'

Gilead had been situated just outside Jackman, and Jackman was where Clay's car had been found abandoned. I reminded Harmon of that fact.

'I think Gilead was certainly an interest of Daniel's,' he said cautiously.

'An interest, or more than that?'

'Do you mean was Daniel obsessed by Gilead? I don't think so, but given the nature of his own work it's hardly surprising that he was curious about its history. He interviewed Dubus, you know. He told me about it. Daniel had an idea for a project concerning Gilead, I think.'

'A project?'

'Yes, a book about Gilead.'

'Was that the term he used? "Project"?'

Harmon thought for a moment. 'I couldn't say for sure, but it might have been.' He finished the last of his brandy and set the glass down on his desk. 'I'm afraid I'm neglecting my other guests. We should return to the fray.'

He opened the door, allowed me to pass, then closed and locked it behind us.

'What do you think happened to Daniel Clay?' I asked him, the buzz of conversation from the other guests growing louder as we drew nearer to the room in which they were gathered.

Harmon stopped at the door.

'I don't know,' he said. 'I can tell you only this: Daniel wasn't the kind of man to commit suicide. He might have blamed himself for what happened to those children, but he wouldn't have killed himself over it. Yet if he was still alive, I believe he would have made contact with someone in the years since his disappearance, either with me or his daughter, or one of his colleagues. He hasn't, though, not once.'

'Then you think he's dead?'

'I believe he was killed,' Harmon corrected me. 'I just have no idea why.'

12

The party, if that was the right word for it, broke up shortly after ten. I spent most of the time in the company of June, Summer, and Nyoko, trying to sound like I knew a little about art, and failing, and considerably less time with Jacobs and two of the bankers, trying to sound like I knew a little about finance, and failing there too. Jacobs, the people's writer, was very knowledgeable about high-risk bonds and currency speculation for someone who claimed to have the common touch. His hypocrisy was so blatant as to be almost admirable.

Slowly, the guests began to drift toward their cars. Harmon stood on his porch, despite the fact that it had grown suddenly colder, and thanked each of us for coming. His wife had disappeared after wishing us a polite good night. Nyoko was excluded from the farewells, and once again I was aware that, despite appearances, Lawrie Harmon was not quite as disengaged from the real world as the young Asian-American believed.

When it came to my turn to leave, Harmon placed his left hand upon my upper arm as his right hand gripped mine.

'You tell Rebecca that if there's anything I can do for her, she just has to let me know,' he said. 'There are a lot of people who would like to find out what happened to Daniel.' His face darkened, and his voice dropped in volume. 'And not just his friends,' he added.

I waited for him to continue. He had a taste for the enigmatic.

'At the end, before he disappeared, Daniel changed,' Harmon went on. 'It wasn't just his troubles: the Muller case, the revelations of abuse. There was something else. He was certainly preoccupied the last time I saw him. Perhaps it was research, but what sort of research could have left him shaken in that way?'

'When did you last see him?'

'A week or so before he went missing.'

'And he gave you no indication of what was bothering him, his known difficulties apart?'

'None. It was just an impression that I got.'

'Why didn't you mention this back in your office?'

Harmon shot me a look that told me he wasn't used to his decisions being questioned.

'I'm a careful man, Mr Parker. I play chess, and I'm pretty good at it. It's probably why I was a good businessman too. I've learned that it pays to take a little time to think before making a move. Back in the office, part of me wanted nothing more to do with Daniel Clay. He was my friend, but after what happened, after the rumors and the whispered allegations, I felt that it was best to distance myself from him.'

'But now you've changed your mind.'

'No, I haven't. I still believe that no good can come of your nosing around in this, but if it uncovers the truth about Daniel and lays the suspicions to rest, and gives his daughter some peace of mind along the way, then it could be that you'll prove me wrong.'

He released his grip upon my hand and my arm. It seemed that we were done. Harmon was watching the writer's car pull out of its parking slot on the driveway. It was an old Dodge truck – it was said that he drove a Mercedes back in Massachusetts, where he kept an apartment near Harvard – and Jacobs maneuvered it like it was a Panzer tank. Harmon shook his head in baffled amusement.

'You mentioned some others who might be interested in what happened to Clay, people apart from his friends or acquaintances.'

Harmon didn't look at me.

'Yes. It's not hard to figure out. There are people who believe that Daniel colluded in the abuse of children. I have two children. I know what I would do to anyone who harmed them, or anyone who allowed others to do so.'

'And what would that be, Mr Harmon?'

He tore himself away from Jacobs's increasingly frantic attempts to make a turn unaided by power steering.

'I'd kill him,' he said, and there was something in the way he said it, something so matter-of-fact, that I didn't doubt him, not for one moment. I knew then that for all of his bonhomie, all of his fine wines and his pretty pictures, Joel Harmon was a man who would not hesitate to crush those who crossed him. And I wondered, for a moment, if Daniel Clay might not have been such a person, and if Joel Harmon's interest in him was not entirely benign. Before I had a chance to follow that train of thought any further, Nyoko came over and whispered something in Harmon's ear.

'Are you sure?' Harmon said.

She nodded.

Harmon immediately called to those who had reached their cars to stop. Russell, the shrink, patted the hood of Jacobs's truck, indicating that he should cut the engine. Jacobs looked almost relieved to do so.

'It seems that there is an intruder in the grounds,' said Harmon. 'It might be best if you all stepped into the house for a moment, just to be safe.'

Everyone did as Harmon asked, albeit with some grumbling from Jacobs, who clearly felt a poem coming on and was anxious to commit it to paper before it was lost to posterity; that, or he was trying to hide his embarrassment at screwing up a simple turn. We all shuffled back into the library. Jacobs and Summer went to one of the windows and looked out on the expanse of neatly mown lawn at the back of the house.

'I can't see anyone,' said Jacobs.

'Maybe we should stay away from the windows,' said Summer.

'He's an intruder, not a sniper,' said Russell.

Summer didn't seem convinced. Jacobs placed a reassuring

arm around her shoulders and let it linger there. She didn't object. What was it with poets? I wondered. It seemed that there was a certain type of woman who just buckled at the suggestion of an internal rhyme.

Harmon's driver, housekeeper, and maid all lived in quarters adjoining the main house. The waiters, who were huddled together like startled doves, had been hired for the evening, and the cook lived in Portland and commuted to the house each day. The driver, whose name was Todd, joined us in the hallway. He was dressed casually in jeans and a shirt. He wore a leather jacket over the shirt and was carrying a gun. It was a Smith & Wesson nine-millimeter in a glitzy finish, but he held it in a way that suggested he knew how to use it.

'Mind if I tag along?' I asked Harmon.

'I don't mind at all,' he said. 'It's probably nothing, but best to be sure.'

We walked through to the kitchen, where the cook and the maid were standing by a sink, staring out at the grounds through the little window above it.

'What is all this about?' asked Harmon.

'Maria saw someone,' said the cook. She was an attractive older woman, her dark hair tied back and covered with a white cap, her body lean and athletic. The maid was Mexican, and also slim and good-looking. Joel Harmon clearly allowed aesthetics to influence his hiring procedures.

Maria pointed. 'Over by the trees, at the east wall,' she said. 'A man, I think.'

She looked even more frightened than Summer. Her hands were shaking.

'Did you see anyone?' Harmon asked the cook.

'No, I was working. Maria called me over to the window. He could have taken off before I got there.'

'If there was someone out there, then he'd have set off the motion sensors,' Harmon said. He turned back to Maria. 'Did the lights come on?'

She shook her head.

'Lot of shadow back there,' said Todd. 'You sure you weren't mistaken?'

'No mistake,' she said. 'I see him.'

Todd gave Harmon a look that was more resigned than concerned.

'We're not going to find out anything in here,' I said.

'Bring up all of the lights,' Harmon told Todd. Todd went to a box of switches on the kitchen wall and flicked a line of them. Instantly the grounds were illuminated. Todd led the way out. I followed, picking up a flashlight from a rack on the wall along the way. Harmon hung back. After all, he didn't have a gun. Regrettably, I didn't have a gun either. It seemed rude to bring one to a stranger's dinner party.

The lights took out most of the shadows in the garden, but there were still patches of dark under the trees by the walls. I used the flashlight to probe them, but there was nothing there. The ground was soft, but there was no sign of footprints. The surrounding wall was eight or nine feet high, and covered in ivy. Anyone climbing the wall would have damaged the ivy, but it appeared to be intact. We made a cursory search of the rest of the grounds, but it was obvious that Todd believed Maria had been mistaken.

'She's kinda jittery at the best of times,' he said, as we walked back to where Harmon waited for us. 'Everything is "*Jesus*" and "*Madre de Dios*". She's a looker, though, I'll give her that, but you got a better chance of getting laid by a busload of nuns.'

Harmon raised his hands in a 'What's happening?' gesture.

'Nada,' said Todd. 'Not a sign.'

'A lot of fuss over nothing,' said Harmon. He headed back into the kitchen, shot Maria a disapproving glance, then went to release his guests. Todd followed. I stayed behind. Maria was putting plates into a big dishwasher. Her chin was trembling slightly.

'Can you tell me what you saw?' I said.

She shrugged.

'Maybe Mr Harmon is right. Maybe I no see,' she said, although I could tell from the expression on her face that she didn't believe her own words.

'Try me,' I said.

She stopped what she was doing. A tear caught in her eyelash, and she brushed it away.

'It was a man. He dress in clothes. Brown, I think. *Muy sucio.* His face? White. *Pálido, sí?*'

'Pale?'

'*Sí*, pale. Also—'

Now she looked frightened again. She touched her hands to her face and mouth.

'Here and here, *nada*. Empty. *Hueco*.'

'*Hueco?* I don't understand.'

Maria glanced over my shoulder. I turned to find the cook watching us.

'Della,' said Maria, '*ayudame explicarle lo que quiere decir "hueco".*'

'You speak Spanish?' I asked her.

'Some,' she said.

'So, any idea what *hueco* might mean?'

'Uh, I'm not sure. I can try to find out.'

Della exchanged some words with Maria, who made gestures and signs to help her along. Eventually, she picked up a decorated ostrich egg that was used to hold pens and tapped her fingers lightly on the shell.

'*Hueco*,' said Maria, and the cook's face briefly brightened before she too looked troubled, as though she had somehow misunderstood what was being said.

'*Hueco* means "hollow,"' she said. 'Maria says he was a hollow man.'

Back in the hallway, June was waiting for me. Harmon hovered nearby, seemingly anxious to be rid of us all. Todd was on the phone. I heard him thank someone before he hung up. He clearly wanted to tell Harmon something, but wasn't sure if he should wait until we were gone. I decided to nudge him.

'Anything wrong?'

He glanced at Harmon for permission to speak in the company of others.

'Well?' said his boss. 'What did they say?'

'I called the Falmouth P.D.,' said Todd, directing the explanation to me as well as his employer. 'Just seemed like it was worth checking to see if they'd spotted anything out of the ordinary. They usually keep a close eye on the houses along here.' By that, I presumed that he meant they kept a close on Joel Harmon's house. He could have bought and sold most of his neighbors ten times over. 'Someone reported a car cruising the area, maybe even parked for a while over by the eastern wall of the property, and got suspicious. By the time the cops came, the car was gone, but could be that it was connected to what Maria saw.'

'They get a make, a number?' I asked him.

Todd shook his head. 'Just a medium-sized red car,' he said.

Harmon must have seen something in my face.

'Does that ring a bell with you?' he asked.

'Maybe,' I said. 'Frank Merrick, the man who was bothering Rebecca Clay, drives a red car. If I found the connection between you and Clay, then so could he.'

'Friendship,' Harmon corrected me, 'not connection. Daniel Clay was my friend. And if this man Merrick wants to talk to me about him, then I'll tell him just what I told you.'

I walked to the door and looked out at the pebbled driveway, illuminated by the lights of the house and the lamps that stood along the verge. It was Merrick, it had to be. But Merrick's description did not match that given by Maria of the man whom she had glimpsed in the garden. Merrick had come here, but he had not been alone.

Hollow.

'I'd be careful for the next few days, Mr Harmon,' I said. 'If you go out, keep Todd with you. I'd have your security system checked too.'

'All because of this one man?' asked Harmon. He sounded slightly incredulous.

'He's dangerous, and he may not be just one man. As you said yourself, better to be safe.'

With that, June and I departed. I drove, the electronic gates opening silently before us as we left the Harmon house behind.

'My,' said June, 'you do lead an interesting life.'

I looked at her. 'You think that was my doing?'

'You told Joel that the man in the car might have made the same connection that you did – or, rather, that *I* made for you – but there is another possibility.'

There was only the slightest hint of a rebuke in her voice. I didn't need her to tell me why. I had figured it out for myself, even though I was reluctant to say it aloud in front of Harmon and had instead forced it back like bile in my throat. Just as I had tracked Merrick, so, too, perhaps Merrick was now tracking me, and I had led him straight to Joel Harmon.

But I was also troubled by the appearance of the man in Harmon's garden. It appeared that Merrick's inquiries about Daniel Clay had drawn something else, a man – no, *men*, I corrected myself, remembering a feeling like foul breezes separating before me, and letters scrawled in dust by a child-like hand – shadowing his movements. Was he aware of them, or was their presence something to do with Eldritch's client? Yet it was hard to see half-glimpsed men climbing the rickety stairs to an ancient lawyer's office, or dealing with the harridan who guarded the gateway to the upper levels of Eldritch's business. What had seemed at first like a simple case of stalking had become infinitely stranger and more complex, and I was glad that Angel and Louis would soon be with me. Merrick's deadline was about to expire, and while I had set in motion a plan for dealing with him, I was aware that he was, in a sense, the least of my worries. Merrick I could deal with. He was dangerous, but he was a known quantity. The Hollow Men were not.

13

Early the next morning, I was standing by the Portland Public Market's parking lot. The temperature had plummeted overnight, and the weathermen were saying that it was likely to stay that way for the foreseeable future, which, in Maine terms, meant that it might begin to improve sometime around April. It was a damp cold, the kind that left clothing moist to the touch, and the windows of coffeeshops, diners, even passing cars were steamed up as the heat caused the moisture to evaporate, lending an uncomfortably claustrophobic atmosphere to anywhere but the least crowded of places.

While most people had the option of seeking shelter indoors, there were some who were not so fortunate. Already a queue had formed outside the Preble Street Resource Center, where the city's poorest gathered each day to be served breakfast by volunteers. Some would be hoping to take a shower or do their laundry while they were there, or to pick up some fresh clothing and use a telephone. The working poor who couldn't make it back for midday would be served a bag lunch so they wouldn't go hungry later. In this way the center and its partners, the Wayside and Saint Luke's soup kitchens, served over three hundred thousand meals every year to those who might otherwise have starved or have been forced to redirect money from rent or essential medicines just to keep body and soul together.

I watched them from where I stood, the line made up mostly of men, a few of them obviously veterans of the street, their layers of clothing filthy, their hair unkempt, while others were still a couple of steps away from homelessness. Some of the women scattered among them were hard-faced and large, their features distorted by alcohol and difficult lives, their bodies swollen by cheap, fatty foods and cheaper booze. It was possible too to pick out the new arrivals, the ones who had yet to grow accustomed to supporting themselves and their families with handouts. They did not talk or mix with the rest, and kept their heads down or faced the wall, fearful of making eye contact with those around them, like new prisoners on a cell block. Perhaps, too, they were afraid to look up and lock eyes with a friend or neighbor, maybe even an employer who might decide that it wasn't good for business to give work to someone who had to beg for breakfast. Nearly all of those in the line were in their thirties or older. It gave a false impression of the nature of the poor in a city where one in five of those under the age of eighteen lived below the poverty line.

Nearby were the Salvation Army's Adult Rehabilitation Center, the Midtown Community Policing Center, and the city's department of probation and parole. This area was a narrow channel through which most of those with a history of legal problems inevitably flowed. So I stood drinking a coffee from the market to keep me warm and waited to see if a familiar face might appear. Nobody paid me much attention. After all, it was too cold to worry about anyone but oneself.

After twenty minutes, I saw the man I was looking for. His name was Abraham Shockley, but on the street he was known only as 'Mr In-Between,' or 'Tween' for short. He was, by any definition, a career criminal. The fact that he wasn't very good at his chosen career hardly mattered to the courts. He had been charged in his time with possession of Class A drugs with intent to supply, theft by deception, larceny, operating under the influence, and night hunting, among other offenses. Tween had been fortunate that violence had never played a part in his crimes, so that he had, on more than one occasion, benefited from the fact that the offense in question fell into the category of 'wobblers,' or crimes that were not statutorily defined as either felonies or misdemeanors, so that some offenses prosecuted as felonies were later reduced to misdemeanors by the trial court. The local cops had also put in a good word for Tween, when required, because Tween was everybody's friend. He knew people. He listened. He remembered. Tween wasn't a snitch. He had his own standards of behavior, his own principles, and he adhered to them as best he could. Tween wouldn't rat anyone out, but he was the man to ask if you wanted a message passed on to someone who was keeping a low profile, or if you wanted to find an individual of ill repute for purposes other than putting him behind bars. In his turn, Tween acted as a go-between for those who were in trouble and wanted to cut a deal with a cop or a parole officer. He was a small but useful cog in the machinery of the unofficial justice system, the shadow courts in which deals were struck and blind eyes turned so that valuable time could be spent on more pressing matters.

He saw me as he took his place in the queue. I nodded to him, then walked slowly down Portland Street. After a few minutes, I heard footsteps approaching from behind, and Tween fell into step beside me. He was in his late forties and dressed cleanly, if shabbily, in yellow sneakers, jeans, two sweaters, and an overcoat with a vent that had split neatly halfway up his back. His reddish brown hair was unevenly cut; people in Tween's position didn't waste their money on barbers. He lived rent-free in a one-room basement off Forest Avenue thanks to an absentee landlord who relied on Tween to keep an eye on his more unruly tenants, and to feed the building's resident cat.

'Breakfast?' I said.

'Only if it's Bintliff's,' he replied. 'I hear they do a wicked good lobster eggs Benedict.'

'You do have a taste for the finer things in life,' I said.

'I was born with a silver spoon in my mouth.'

'Yeah, but you stole it from the kid in the next cradle.'

To their credit, nobody in Bintliff's gave us a second glance. We were seated in a booth upstairs, and Tween ordered enough food to fill him up for a day at least: fruit and OJ to begin, followed by toast, the lobster eggs Benedict of which he'd heard so much, extra home fries, then some muffins to finish, three of which were squirreled away in the pockets of his overcoat 'for my buddies,' as he explained. While we ate, we spoke about books and local news and just about anything else that came to mind, except the reason why I had brought Tween here. It was the gentlemanly way to conduct business and Tween was always a gentleman, even when he was trying to steal the sole from somebody's shoe.

'So,' he said, as he finished a fifth coffee, 'you just bring me here to enjoy the pleasure of my company?' The coffee didn't appear to have made him jittery, or at least no more jittery than he had been to begin with. If you handed Tween a bowl of cream to hold, it would turn to butter in the time it took to wind your wristwatch. He had so much nervous energy that it was tiring to be in his immediate vicinity for too long.

'Not just that,' I replied. 'I'd like you to ask around, see if you can find anyone who might have known a guy called Frank Merrick, either in Thomaston or in Supermax. He did ten years, the final two or three in the Max, then got released and sent for trial in Virginia.'

'He anything special?'

'He's not the kind of guy you're going to forget easily. He had a reputation as a button man.'

'Rumor or solid?'

'I'm inclined to believe what I've heard.'

'Where is he now?'

'He's here.'

'Renewing old acquaintances?'

'Could be. If he is, I'd like to know the names.'

'I'll ask around. Shouldn't take me too long. You got some quarters so I can call you?'

I gave him my business card, the change from my pocket, and fifty dollars in tens, fives, and ones so he could buy beer and sandwiches to oil the wheels. I knew how Tween worked. He'd helped me in the past. When he found someone who could cast some light on Merrick, as I was sure he would, he would hand me back my change and a handful of receipts, and only then would he look for payment. That was the way Tween worked in his 'official' capacity, operating by one simple rule: you didn't rip off anyone who looked like they might be on your side.

Merrick called me at midday. I'd been checking for signs of him all morning, but I didn't see him or his red car. If he was smart, he'd have changed the car, but that assumed that Eldritch and his client were still prepared to bankroll him. I'd taken all of the precautions I could in case Merrick, or someone else, was keeping an eye on my movements. I was satisfied that no one was, not that day. In addition, Jackie Garner confirmed that all was still quiet where Rebecca Clay was concerned. Now Merrick was on the phone, threatening to shatter that silence.

'Time's up,' he said.

'You ever consider that you might get further with honey than vinegar?'

'Feed a man honey, and you get his love. Feed him vinegar, and you get his attention. Helps if you grab him by the balls too, and squeeze him some.'

'That's very profound. You learn that in jail?'

'Hope you didn't waste all that time finding out about me, else we're going to have us a problem.'

'I didn't come up with much, not on you and not on Daniel Clay either. His daughter doesn't know any more than you do, but then she told you that already. You just didn't want to listen.'

Merrick forced air through his nose in an imitation of amusement.

'Well, that's unfortunate. You tell missy I'm disappointed in her. Better yet, I'll tell her myself.'

'Wait. I didn't say that I'd found nothing.' I needed leverage, something to draw him in. 'I have a copy of the police file on Daniel Clay,' I lied.

'So?'

'It mentions your daughter.'

Now Merrick was silent.

'There's some material in it that I don't understand. I don't think the cops did either.'

'What is it?' His voice sounded husky, as though something had suddenly caught in his throat.

I should have felt bad about lying. I was playing on Merrick's feelings for his missing child. There would be consequences when he found out the truth.

'Uh-uh,' I said. 'Not over the phone.'

'So what do you suggest?' he asked.

'We meet. I give you a look at the file. I'll tell you what I've learned. Then you go and do what you have to do, as long as it doesn't involve Rebecca Clay.'

'I don't trust you. I seen those cavemen you got guarding the woman. What's to stop you from trying to turn them loose on me? I got no problem killing them if it comes down to it, but it would kind of hinder my investigations, you might say.'

'I don't want their blood on my hands either. We meet in a public place, you read the file, and we go our separate ways. I'm warning you, though: I'm giving you a break because of your daughter. You show up again around Rebecca Clay and this is all going to step up a notch. I guarantee that you won't like what happens then.'

Merrick gave a theatrical sigh. 'Now that you got the pissing competition out of the way, maybe you'd like to name a place.'

I told him to meet me at the Big 20 Bowling Center on Route 1. I even gave him directions. Then I started making my calls.

Tween got back to me at three o'clock that afternoon.

'I've found someone for you. He comes at a price.'

'Which is?'

'A ticket to tonight's hockey game, and fifty bucks. He'll meet you there.'

'Done.'

'Just leave his ticket for collection with my name on the envelope. I'll take care of the rest.'

'How much do I owe you?'

'Hundred dollars sound fair?'

'It sounds fine.'

'I got some change for you too. I'll give it to you when you pay me.'

'Has he got a name, this guy?'

'He has, but you can call him Bill.'

'Is he the nervous type?'

'He wasn't until I mentioned Frank Merrick. I'll see you around.'

Candlepin bowling is a New England tradition. The balls are smaller and lighter than in tenpin, and the pins are thinner: three inches in the middle and one and a half at the top and bottom. Getting a strike is more a matter of luck than skill, and it's said that nobody has ever bowled a perfect ten-strike candlepin game. The best score recorded in Maine is 231 out of a possible 300. I'd never bowled over 100.

The Big 20 in Scarborough had been in existence since 1950, when Mike Anton, an Albanian by birth, founded it as Maine's largest and most modern bowling house, and it didn't seem to have changed much since then. I sat on a pink plastic chair, sipped a soda, and waited. It was four-thirty on a Friday afternoon and every lane was already in use, the players ranging from teenagers to seniors. There was laughter and the smell of beer and fried food and the distinctive sound of the balls rolling along the wooden alleys. I watched two old guys who barely spoke ten words to each other close in on 200 each, and when they failed to break the double century one of them expressed his disappointment in a single 'Ayuh.' I sat in silence, the only lone male among groups of men and women, knowing that I was about to cross a line with Merrick.

My cell phone rang shortly before five, and a voice said, 'We got him.'

Outside there were two Scarborough police cruisers and a trio of unmarked cars, one each from the Portland P.D., the South

Portland P.D., and the Scarborough cops. A handful of people had gathered to watch the show. Merrick was facedown in the parking lot, his hands cuffed behind his back. He looked up at me as I approached. He didn't appear angry. He just seemed disappointed. I saw O'Rourke nearby, leaning against a car. I nodded to him and made a call. Rebecca Clay answered. She was at the courthouse, and the judge was about to issue the temporary protection order against Merrick. I told her that we had him and that I'd be at Scarborough P.D. headquarters if she needed to contact me when she was done.

'Any problems?' I asked O'Rourke.

He shook his head.

'He walked right into it. Didn't even open his mouth to ask what was going on.'

As we watched, Merrick was hauled to his feet and put in the back of one of the unmarked cars. He stared straight ahead as it pulled out.

'He looks old,' said O'Rourke. 'He's got something, though. I wouldn't like to cross him. And I hate to tell you this, but I think you just have.'

'It didn't seem like I had a whole lot of choice.'

'Well, at least we can hold him for a while and see what we get out of him.'

The length of time for which Merrick could be held would depend on the charges brought against him, if any. Stalking, defined as engaging in conduct that would cause a person to suffer intimidation, annoyance, or alarm, or to fear bodily injury, either to that person or a member of that person's immediate family, was defined as a Class D crime. Similarly, terrorizing was a Class D, and harassment was a Class E. There was always the possibility of adding trespassing and criminal damage to the list, but taken altogether it meant that Merrick could be held only until the following Tuesday evening, assuming he didn't get lawyered up, since D and E offenses allowed a suspect to be held only for forty-eight hours without charge, excluding weekends and holidays.

'You think your client will want to take this all the way?' asked O'Rourke.

'Do you want her to?'

'He's a dangerous man. Seems kind of rude to lock him up for just sixty days, which is what he'll get if the judge buys all the arguments in favor of putting him away. Might even be counterproductive, although if anyone asks, I didn't say that.'

'You never struck me as the gambling type, you know that?'

'It's not a gamble. It's a calculated risk.'

'Based on what?'

'Based on Frank's reluctance to be jailed and your ability to protect your client.'

'So what's the compromise?'

'We warn him off, make sure the order is ready to be served, and set him free. It's a small city. He's not going to disappear. We'll arrange for someone to stick close to him for a while, and see what happens.'

It didn't sound like the perfect plan. Nevertheless, it looked like I had just been given an extra ninety-six hours at most without Merrick to worry about. It was better than nothing.

'Let's hear what he's got to say for himself first,' I said. 'You cleared it for me to watch?'

'Didn't take much doing. Seems like you still have friends in Scarborough. You spot anything in what he says, then you let me know. You think he'll call a lawyer?'

I thought about it. If he did decide to lawyer himself up, it would have to be through Eldritch, assuming the old man was licensed to practice in Maine, or had someone in the state who was prepared to do a little quid pro quo work when necessary. But I had a feeling that Eldritch's support for Merrick had always been conditional, and Merrick's recent actions might have forced the lawyer to reconsider his position.

'I don't think he's going to talk much anyway.'

O'Rourke shrugged. 'We could hit him with a telephone book.'

'You could, but I'd have to report you to IA.'

'Yeah, there's that. I'd have to lose the paperwork on myself. Still, it's Scarborough's turf, and South Portland's problem. We can stand back and see how they handle it.'

He got in his car. The Scarborough cruisers were pulling away, the Portland cops close behind.

'You coming?' he asked.

'I'll follow.'

He left, the crowd dispersed, and suddenly I was the only person in the parking lot. The cars rolled by on Route 1, and the neon Big 20 sign illuminated the lot, but behind me was the darkness of the marshes. I turned, gazing into it, and I couldn't shake the feeling that, from its deepest reaches, something stared back at me. I walked to my car, started the engine, and tried to leave that sensation behind.

Merrick was seated in a small square room furnished with a white table bolted to the floor. There were three blue chairs around it, and Merrick sat in the one facing the door, the two empty chairs across from him. A wipe-clean board was attached to one wall, its surface covered with children's doodles. There was a phone beside the door and, high in one corner, a video camera. The room was also wired for sound recording.

One of Merrick's hands had been cuffed, and the cuff had been chained through a D-ring on the table. He had been given a soda to drink from the machine beside the evidence technician's office, but he hadn't touched it. While the room didn't have a two-way mirror, we were able to watch him on the computer monitor in a partitioned office close by the interview room. We weren't alone. Although the alcove was big enough for four people at best, almost three times that number were crowded around the screen, trying to catch a glimpse of their new guest.

Detective Sergeant Wallace MacArthur was one of them. I knew him from way back. Through Rachel, I'd introduced him to his wife, Mary. In a way, I had nearly been responsible for her death too, but Wallace had never held that against me, which was pretty Christian of him, all things considered.

'Not often we get a living legend in here,' he said. 'Even the Feds have joined us.'

He jerked a thumb in the direction of the door, where Pender, the new SAC of the small Portland field office, was talking with a man whom I didn't recognize but whom I took to be another agent. I had been introduced to Pender once at some policeman's benefit in Portland. As far as the Feds went, he seemed okay. Pender nodded to me. I nodded back. At least he hadn't tried to have me thrown out, which was reason to be thankful.

MacArthur shook his head in something like admiration. 'Merrick's old-school,' he said. 'They don't make 'em like him anymore.'

O'Rourke grinned emptily. 'Yeah, what have we come to when we can look at someone like him and think, Hell, he's not so bad? He just popped them, neatly and cleanly. No torture. No sadism. No kids. Just men that somebody figured had it coming.'

Merrick kept his head down. He did not look up at the camera, even though he must have known that we were watching him.

Two Scarborough detectives entered the room, a beefy guy named Conlough and a woman named Frederickson, who had made the formal arrest at the Big 20. As soon as they began to question him, Merrick, contrary to expectations, looked up and answered them in soft, civil tones. It was almost as though he felt the need to justify and defend himself. Perhaps he was correct. He had lost his daughter. He had the right to ask where she might be.

CONLOUGH: *What's your interest in Rebecca Clay?*

MERRICK: *None, beyond who her daddy is.*

C: *What's her father to you?*

M: *He treated my little girl. Now she's gone. I want to find out where she is.*

C: *You think you can do that by threatening a woman? Real big guy, huh, stalking a defenseless woman?*

M: *I didn't threaten anyone. I didn't stalk anyone. I just wanted to ask her some questions.*

C: *So you do that by trying to bust into her house, breaking her window?*

M: *I didn't try to bust into her house, and the window was an accident. I'll pay for the damage.*

C: *Who put you up to this?*

M: *Nobody. I don't need no one to tell me that what happened ain't right.*

C: *What's not right?*

M: *That my daughter could disappear and nobody give a rat's ass about finding her.*

FREDERICKSON: *Maybe your daughter ran away. From what we hear, she was having problems.*

M: *I told her I'd look out for her. She had no cause to run away.*

C: *You were in jail. How were you going to look out for her from a cell?*

M (silent)

F: *Who gave you the car?*

M: *A lawyer.*

F: *Which lawyer?*

M: *The lawyer Eldritch, down in Massachusetts.*

F: *Why?*

M: *He's a good man. He thinks I got the right to ask questions. He got me out of trouble in Virginia, then helped me when I came back up here.*

C: *So he gives you a car out of the goodness of his heart. What is he, St Vincent de Paul's lawyer?*

M: *Maybe you should ask him.*

C: *Don't worry, we will.*

'We'll talk to the lawyer,' said O'Rourke.

'You won't get much from him,' I said.

'You've met him?'

'Oh yeah. He's old-school too.'

'How old?'

'So old they built the school out of wattle and daub.'

'What did he tell you?'

'Pretty much what Merrick just said.'

'You believe him?'

'That he's a good guy who gives away cars to deserving causes? No. Still, he said that Merrick had been one of his clients, and there's no law against loaning a car to your client.'

I didn't tell O'Rourke that Eldritch had another client, one who seemed to be covering Merrick's tab. I figured he could find that out for himself.

A call came through from the evidence technician. Merrick's car was clean. There were no weapons, no incriminating papers, nothing. Frederickson emerged from the interview room to consult with O'Rourke and the FBI man, Pender. The man who had been talking with Pender listened in, but said nothing. His eyes flicked to me, regarded me for a moment, then returned to Frederickson. I didn't like what passed between us with that look. O'Rourke asked me if there was anything that I thought we should put to Merrick. I suggested asking him if he was working alone, or if he had brought other men with him. O'Rourke seemed puzzled, but agreed to suggest the question to Frederickson.

F: *Ms. Clay has taken out a court order against you. Do you understand what that means?*

M: *I understand. It means I can't go near her no more, else you put my ass back in jail.*

F: *That's right. You going to abide by that order? You don't plan to, and you can save us all some time right now.*

M: *I'll abide by it.*

C: *Maybe you'll think about leaving the state too. We'd like you to do that.*

M: *I can't promise nothing on that front. I'm a free man. I done my time. Got a right to go where I choose.*

C: *That include hanging around houses up in Falmouth?*

M: *I ain't never been to Falmouth. Hear it's real nice, though. I like being by the water.*

C: *Car like yours was seen around there last night.*

M: *Lots of cars like mine. Red is a real popular color.*

C: *Nobody said it was a red car.*

M: (silent)

C: *You hear me? How come you knew it was a red car?*

M: *Car like mine, what else would it be? If'n it was a blue car, or a green car, then it wouldn't be like mine. Have to be a red car to be like mine, just the way you said it.*

F: *You loan your car out to other people, Mr Merrick?*

M: *No, I don't.*

F: *So if we find out that it was your car – and we can do that, you know; we can take casts, canvass witnesses – then it would have to be you behind the wheel, right?*

M: *I guess so, but since I wasn't there, it's moot.*

F: *Moot?*

M: *Yeah, you know what 'moot' means, officer. Don't need me to explain it to you.*

F: *Who are the other men with you?*

M: (confused) *Other men? The hell you talking about?*

F: *We know you're not here alone. Who did you bring with you? Who's helping you? You're not doing all this without others.*

M: *I always work alone.*

C: *And what kind of work would that be?*

M: (smiling) *Problem solving. I'm a lateral thinker.*

C *You know, I don't think you're being as cooperative as you should be.*

M: *I'm answering your questions, ain't I?*

F: *Maybe you'll answer them better after a couple of nights in jail.*

M: *You can't do that.*

C: *Are you telling us what we can and can't do? Listen, you may have been a big shot once upon a time, but that doesn't count for anything up here.*

M: *You got no more cause to hold me. I told you I'd abide by that order.*

F: *We think you need some time to reflect on what you've been doing, to, uh, meditate on your sins.*

M: *I'm done talking to you. I want to call me a lawyer.*

That was it. The interrogation was over. Merrick was given access to a phone. He called Eldritch, who, it emerged, had taken the Maine bar exam, along with its equivalents in New Hampshire and Vermont. He told Merrick not to answer any more questions, and arrangements were made to transfer Merrick to the Cumberland County Jail, since Scarborough no longer had holding cells of its own.

'The lawyer won't be able to get him out until Monday morning at the earliest,' said O'Rourke. 'The judges do like to keep their weekends clear.'

Even if Merrick was charged, it was likely that Eldritch would arrange bail for him if it was still in the interests of Eldritch's other client that Merrick should be free, just as it seemed to be in O'Rourke's interests. The only person whose interests might not be well served by Merrick's freedom was Rebecca Clay.

'I have some people keeping watch over Ms. Clay,' I told O'Rourke. 'She wants to cut them loose, but I think she may need to reconsider, just until we get a sense of how Merrick reacts to all this.'

'Who are you using?'

I shifted awkwardly in my seat.

'The Fulcis, and Jackie Garner.'

O'Rourke laughed, attracting surprised glances from the men around him.

'No way! That's like using a pair of undercover elephants *and* their ringmaster.'

'Well, I kind of wanted him to see them. The object of the exercise was to keep him away.'

'Hell, they'd keep me away. Probably kept the birds away too. You really do pick entertaining friends.'

Yeah, I thought, but he didn't know the half of it. The really entertaining ones had just arrived.

14

The streets were thick with buses by the time I made it back
from Scarborough to the Cumberland County Civic Center:
yellow school buses, Peter Pan Trailways, in fact just about
anything that had wheels and could accommodate more than
six people. The Pirates were on a roll. Under coach Kevin
Dineen they were at the top of the Atlantic Division of the
AHL's Eastern Conference. Earlier in the week they had beaten
their nearest rivals, the Hartford Wolf Pack, 7–4. Now it was
the turn of the Springfield Falcons and it looked like about
five thousand fans had made their way to the Civic Center
for the game.

Inside the arena, Crackers the Parrot was entertaining the crowd.
To be more accurate, he was entertaining most of the crowd.
There were some people just didn't want to be entertained.

'This has got to be the dumbest game ever,' said Louis. He
was dressed in a gray cashmere coat over a black jacket and
trousers, his hands thrust deep into the pockets of the coat, his
chin buried in the folds of his red scarf. He acted like he'd just
been forced out of a train somewhere in the middle of Siberia.
His mildly Satanic beard had been dispensed with, and his hair
was even more ruthlessly cut back than usual, its gray touches
now barely visible. He and Angel had arrived earlier that day.
I had bought a couple of extra tickets in case they wanted to
come along to the game, but Angel had somehow managed to
pick up a cold in Napa and was back at my place feeling sorry
for himself. That left Louis as my reluctant escort for the
evening.

Things between us had changed over the last year. In a way,

I had always been closer to Angel. I knew more about his past,
and when I was, however briefly, a cop, I had done what I
could to help and protect him. I had seen something in him –
even now I found it hard to explain precisely what it was, but
perhaps it was a kind of decency, an empathy with those who
had suffered, albeit one filtered murkily through his criminality
– and had responded to it. I had seen something in his partner
too, but it was very different. Long before I had fired a gun in
anger, Louis had killed. At first, he had done so out of a rage
of his own, but he had quickly discovered he had a talent for
it, and there were those who had been willing to pay him to
utilize that ability on their behalf. He was once, I thought, not
so different from Frank Merrick, although his moral compass
had become surer than Merrick's had ever been.

Yet Louis was also, I knew, not so different from me. He
represented a side of me that I had long been reluctant to
acknowledge – the urge to strike out, the impulse toward violence
– and his presence in my life had forced me to come to terms
with it, and, through that accommodation, to control it. In turn,
I thought that I had given him an outlet for his own anger, a
way of engaging with and altering the world that was worthy
of him as a man. We had seen things in this last year that had
changed both of us, confirming suspicions that we had both
held about the nature of the honeycomb world, but had rarely
shared. We had found a common ground, however hollow it
might have sounded beneath our feet.

'You know why you don't see no black men playing this
game?' he continued. '*(A)* Because it's slow. *(B)* Because it's
dumb. And *(C)* Because it's cold. I mean, look at these guys.'
He flicked through the pages of the official program. 'Most of
them ain't even American. They're Canadian. Like you don't
have enough slow-ass white men of your own, you got to import
them from Canada.'

'We like giving jobs to Canadians,' I said. 'It gives them the
chance to earn some real dollars.'

'Yeah, I bet they send it back to their families, like in the

Third World.' He watched with obvious disdain as the mascots frolicked on the ice. 'Parrot is more of an athlete than they are.'

We were seated in Block E, right in the center overlooking the circle. There was no sign of Bill, the man Tween was putting our way, although it was clear from what Tween had said that he was likely to be the cautious type where Merrick was concerned. If he was smart, he would be watching us even now. He would be reassured to learn that Merrick was behind bars for a few days. It had bought us all a little more time, for which I was grateful, at least until I was forced to explain the subtle nuances of hockey to a man who thought sport started and finished on a basketball court or an athletics track.

'Come on,' I said. 'That's not fair. Wait until they get on the ice. Some of these guys are pretty fast.'

'Get the fuck out of here,' said Louis. 'Carl Lewis was fast. Jesse Owens was fast. Even Ben Johnson was fast on his chemical ass. The Popsicles, on the other hand, are not fast. They like snowmen on flat tin cans.'

An announcement was made advising spectators that 'obscene or abusive language' would not be tolerated.

'You can't swear?' said Louis incredulously. 'The fuck kind of sport is this?'

'It's just for appearances,' I said, as a man with kids on either side of him glanced up at Louis disapprovingly from below, considered saying something, then thought better of it and contented himself with pulling his kids' hats down over their ears.

Queen's 'We Will Rock You' was played, followed by Republica's 'Ready to Go.'

'Why is so much sports music shit?' asked Louis.

'This is white people's music,' I explained. 'It's supposed to suck. That way, black people can't show them up by dancing to it.'

The teams hit the ice. There was more music. As usual, prizes were given out all through the first period: free burgers and mall discounts, the occasional T-shirt or cap.

'Give me a break,' said Louis. 'They got to give shit away just to keep folks in their seats.'

By the end of the first period, the Pirates were 2-0 up from Zenon Konopka and Geoff Peters. There was still no sign of Tween's guy.

'Maybe he's asleep somewhere,' suggested Louis. 'Like here.'

Just as the teams emerged for the second period, a small, hard-looking man in an ancient Pirates jacket moved into the row from the right. He had a goatee and wore silver-rimmed glasses. His head was covered by a black Pirates hat and his hands were hidden in the pockets of his jacket. He looked like any one of hundreds of other people in the crowd.

'Parker, right?' he said.

'That's right. You're Bill?'

He nodded but didn't take his hands out of his pockets.

'How long have you been watching us?' I asked.

'Since before the first period,' he replied.

'You're being pretty careful.'

'I figure it doesn't hurt.'

'Frank Merrick's in custody,' I said.

'Yeah, well I didn't know that, did I? What did they get him for?'

'Stalking.'

'They're going to charge Frank Merrick with *stalking*?' He snorted in disbelief. 'Give me a break. Why don't they add jaywalking, or not having a license for his dog?'

'We wanted him held for a while,' I said. 'The "why" didn't matter.'

Bill looked past me to where Louis was sitting. 'No offense meant, but a black guy kind of stands out at a hockey game.'

'This is Maine. A black guy stands out just about anywhere.'

'I suppose, but you could have made him blend in some.'

'Does he look like the kind of guy who's gonna wear a pirate's hat and wave a plastic cutlass?'

Bill looked away from Louis.

'I guess not. A real cutlass, maybe.'

He sat back and didn't say anything more for a time. With 3:18 to go in the second period, Shane Hynes hit a rocket from the right point. A minute and a half later, Jordan Smith made it 4-0. It was all over.

Bill stood.

'Let's go get a beer,' he said. 'That's four consecutive wins, nine wins in ten games. Best start since the ninety-four-to-ninety-five inaugural, and I had to watch that in jail.'

'That count as cruel and unusual punishment?' asked Louis.

Bill gave him the eye.

'He's not a fan,' I said.

'No shit.'

We walked outside and picked up three microbrews in plastic glasses. There was a steady stream of people already leaving the arena now that it looked like the Pirates had sewn everything up.

'I appreciated the ticket, by the way,' he said. 'I don't always have the funds to come here no more.'

'No problem,' I said.

He waited expectantly, his eyes fixed on the bulge in my jacket where my wallet was visible. I took it out and paid him the fifty. He folded the bills carefully and placed them in a pocket of his jeans. I was about to ask him about Merrick when, from inside the arena, came the unmistakable response to a Falcons' goal.

'Goddammit!' said Bill. 'We jinxed 'em by leaving.'

So it was back to our seats to wait for the start of the third period, but at least Bill was content to talk for a while about his time in Supermax while we did so. The Supermax system was designed to take out of the general population prisoners who were deemed to be especially violent, or escape risks, or a threat to others. Often, it was used as a form of punishment for those who broke the rules, or who were found with contraband. The Maine Supermax was opened in 1992 in Warren. It had a hundred maximum-security, solitary-confinement cells. With the closure of the old Thomaston State Prison at the start of the century, the new eleven-hundred-inmate prison was eventually built around the Supermax, like fortress walls around a citadel.

'We were both in the Max at the same time, Merrick and me,' he said. 'I was doing twenty for burglary. Well, *burglaries*. You believe that? Twenty years. Goddamn killers get out in less. Anyway, the cops busted me for possession of a screwdriver and some wire. I only had the stuff to repair my goddamn radio. Told me I was an escape risk and sent me to the Max. After that, things got crazy. I hit a cop. I was pissed at him. I paid for it, though. I stayed in the Max for the duration. Fuckin' cops. I hate them.'

Inmates routinely referred to the prison guards as 'cops.' After all, they were part of the same law enforcement edifice as the police, the prosecutors, and the judges.

'Bet you've never seen the inside of the SMU,' said Bill.

'Nope,' I said. The Supermax was off-limits to just about everyone who wasn't a prisoner or a guard, but I'd heard enough about it to know that it wasn't a place I ever wanted to be.

'It's bad,' said Bill, and from the way he said it I knew that I wasn't going to hear some exaggerated, hard-luck ex-con's story. He wasn't trying to sell me anything. He just wanted someone to listen.

'It stinks: shit, blood, puke. Stuff is on the floor, on the walls. Snow comes under the doors in winter. The vents make this noise all the time, and there's something about it. You can't block it out. I used to stuff toilet paper in my ears to try to stop myself from hearing it. I thought it was going to drive me nuts. It's twenty-three-hour lockdown with one hour a day, five days a week, in the kennel. That's what we call the exercise yard: thing is six feet wide, thirty feet long. I should know: I measured it myself for five years. Lights are on twenty-four/seven. There's no TV, no radio, just noise and white light. They don't even allow a man a toothbrush. They give you this useless fucking piece of plastic for your finger, but it's not worth a damn.'

Bill opened his mouth and pointed with his finger at the gaps in his yellow teeth.

'I lost five teeth in there,' he said. 'They just fell out. When you get down to it, the Max is a form of psychological torture. You know why you're in there, but not what you can do to get out again. And that's not the worst of it. You fuck up badly enough and they send you to the chair.'

That I knew about. The 'chair' was a restraining device used on those who managed to push the guards too far. Four or five guards wearing full body armor and carrying shields and Mace would storm a prisoner's cell to perform the 'extraction.' He would be Maced, pushed to the floor or onto his bed, then handcuffed. The cuffs would be connected to leg irons and his clothes cut from his body, and then the prisoner would be carried, naked and screaming, to an observation room, and there bound to a chair with straps, where he would be left for hours in the cold. Incredibly, the prison authorities argued that the chair wasn't used for punishment but only as a means of controlling inmates who were a threat to themselves or others. The *Portland Phoenix* had obtained a tape of an extraction, as all such operations were recorded by the prison, ostensibly to prove that the prisoners were not being mistreated. According to those who had seen it, it was hard to imagine how extractions and the chair qualified as anything other than state-sanctioned violence bordering on torture.

'They did it to me once,' said Bill, 'after I cold-cocked the cop. Never again. I kept my head down after that. That was no way to treat a man. They did it to Merrick too, more than once, but they couldn't break Frank. It was always the same reason, though. It never varied.'

'What do you mean?'

'Merrick was always being punished for the same thing. There was a kid in there, name of Kellog, Andy Kellog. He was crazy, but it wasn't his fault. Everybody knew it. He'd been fucked with as a child and he never recovered. Spoke about birds all the time. Men like birds.'

I interrupted Bill.

'Wait a minute, this kid Kellog had been abused?'

'That's right.'

'Sexually abused?'

'Uh-huh. I guess the men who did it wore masks or something. I recalled Kellog from his time in Thomaston. Some of the others in the Max did too, but nobody ever seemed to know for sure what had happened to him. All we knew was that he'd been taken by the "men like birds," and not once either. A couple of times, and that was after others had been at him already. What was left when they were done with him wasn't worth a nickel curse. Kid was medicated to hell and back. Only man who seemed to get through to him was Merrick, and I got to tell you, that was a surprise to me. Merrick wasn't no social worker. He was hard. But this kid, man, Merrick tried to look out for him. It wasn't no faggot thing either. First man who said that to Merrick was also the last. Merrick near took his head off, tried to force it through the bars of his cell. Nearly succeeded, too, until the cops came and broke it up. Then Kellog got transferred to the Max for throwing shit at guards, and Merrick, he found a way to go there too.'

'Merrick deliberately got himself transferred to the Supermax?'

'Yep, that's what they say. Until Kellog went, Merrick had minded his own business, kept his head down, apart from those occasions when someone stepped out of line and threatened the kid or, if he was really dumb, tried to move up the order by knocking heads with Merrick. But after Kellog was transferred, Merrick did everything he could to rile the cops until they had no choice but to send him to Warren. Wasn't much that he could do for the kid there, but he didn't give up. He talked to the cops, tried to get them to send a mental health worker to check up on Kellog, even managed to talk the kid down once or twice when it seemed like he was going to get himself sent to the chair again. Guards took him out of his cell on occasion just so he could reason with the kid, but it didn't always work. I tell you, Kellog lived in that chair. Maybe he still does, for all I know.'

'Kellog is still in there?'

'I don't think he's ever gonna get out, not alive. I think the kid wants to die. It's a miracle he isn't dead already.'

'What about Merrick? Did you talk to him? Did he tell you anything about himself?'

'Nah, he was a loner. Only man he had time for was Kellog. I got to talk to him some, when our paths crossed on the way to the infirmary or to and from the kennel, but over the years we talked about as much as you and I have done tonight. I knew about his daughter, though. I think that was why he was looking out for Kellog.'

The final period started. I could see Bill's attention immediately transfer itself to the ice.

'I don't understand,' I said. 'What did Merrick's daughter have to do with Kellog?'

Reluctantly, Bill turned away from the action for the last time.

'Well, his daughter had gone missing,' he said. 'He didn't have much to remember her by. A couple of photographs, a drawing or two that the girl sent to him in jail before she disappeared. It was the drawings that attracted him to Kellog because Kellog and Merrick's daughter, they'd drawn the same thing. They'd both drawn men with the heads of birds.'

III

I myself am Hell,
nobody's here—

Robert Lowell, *Skunk Hour*

15

It didn't take long to find out the name of the lawyer who had represented Andy Kellog during his most recent brushes with the law. Her name was Aimee Price, and she had an office in South Freeport, about three miles away from the tourist-trap bustle of Freeport itself. The contrast between the towns of Freeport and South Freeport was striking. While Freeport had largely given up the ghost to the joys of outlet shopping, its side streets now converted to extended parking lots, South Freeport, which extended from Porter Landing to Winslow Park, had preserved most of its old, nineteenth-century homes, built when the shipyards on the Harraseeket were booming. Price worked out of a small complex that had been created from a pair of carefully restored ship captains' houses on Park Street, part of an area two blocks square that constituted the town center, situated just above the Freeport Town Landing. She shared the space with an accountant, a debt restructuring service, and an acupuncturist.

Although it was Saturday, Price had told me that she would be working on case files until about one. I picked up some fresh muffins at the Carharts' Village Store and strolled over to her office shortly before noon. I entered the reception area, and the young woman behind the desk pointed me in the direction of a hallway to my left, after calling ahead to inform Price's secretary that I had arrived. Her secretary was male, and in his early twenties. He wore suspenders and a red bow tie. In someone else his age, it might have come across as an imitation of eccentricity, but there was something about the crumpled cotton of his shirt and the ink stains on his tan pants that suggested his eccentricity was pretty genuine.

Price herself was in her forties, with red curly hair cut short in a style that might have suited a woman twenty years older. She wore a navy suit, the jacket of which was slung across her chair, and had the tired look of someone who was fighting too many losing battles with the system. Her office was decorated with pictures of horses, and while there were various files on the floor, the windowsill, and on her desk, it was still a lot more welcoming than the offices of Eldritch and Associates, mainly because the people here seemed to have figured out how to use computers and dispose of some of their old paper.

Instead of sitting at her desk, Price cleared some space on a couch and invited me to sit there, while she took an upright chair alongside it. There was a small table between us, and the secretary, whose name was Ernest, set down some cups and a coffeepot, and took one of the muffins for his trouble. The seating arrangement left me sitting slightly lower, and slightly less comfortably, than Price. It was, I knew, quite deliberate. It seemed like Aimee Price had learned the hard way always to assume the worst, and to take every advantage available in anticipation of the battles to come. She wore a large diamond engagement ring. It sparkled in the winter sunlight as if there were bright living things moving within the stones.

'Nice rock,' I said.

She smiled. 'Are you an appraiser as well as a detective?'

'I'm multitalented. In case the whole detecting thing doesn't work out, I'll have something to fall back on.'

'You seem to be doing okay at it,' she said. 'You make the papers a lot.' She reconsidered what she had just said. 'No, I guess that's not true. It's just that when you do make the papers, it kind of stands out. I bet you have all your press framed too.'

'I've built a shrine to myself.'

'Well, good luck attracting fellow worshipers. You wanted to talk to me about Andy Kellog?'

It was straight down to business.

'I'd like to see him,' I said.

'He's in the Max. It's off-limits to everyone.'

'Except you.'

'I'm his lawyer and even I have to jump through hoops to get near him in there. What's your interest in Andy?'

'Daniel Clay.'

Price's face grew stony. 'What about him?'

'His daughter hired me. She's been having some trouble with an individual who's anxious to trace her father. It seems this individual was an acquaintance of Andy Kellog's in jail.'

'Merrick,' said Price. 'It's Frank Merrick, isn't it?'

'You know about him?'

'I couldn't help but be aware of him. He and Andy were close.'

I waited. Price leaned back in her chair.

'Where to begin?' she said. 'I took on Andy Kellog pro bono. I don't know how much of his circumstances you're familiar with, but I'll give you a short summary. Abandoned as a baby, taken in by his mother's sister, brutalized by her and her husband, then passed around to some of the husband's buddies for the purposes of sexual abuse. He started running away at the age of eight, and was practically wild by twelve. Medicated from the age of nine; severe learning difficulties; never made it past third grade. Eventually, he ended up in a halfway house for severely disturbed children, run on a wing and a prayer with minimal state funding, and that's when he was referred to Daniel Clay. It was part of a pilot program. Dr Clay specialized in traumatized children, particularly those who had been victims of physical or sexual abuse. A number of children were selected for the program, and Andy was one of them.'

'Who decided which kids were admitted?'

'A panel of mental health workers, social workers, and Clay himself. Apparently, there was some improvement in Andy's condition right from the start. The sessions with Dr Clay seemed to be working for him. He grew more communicative, less aggressive. It was decided that he might benefit from inter-action with a family outside of the environment of the state home, so he began to spend a couple of days each week with a family in Bingham. They ran a lodge for outdoor pursuits: you know, hunting, hiking, rafting, that kind of thing. Eventually, Andy was allowed to live with them, with the mental health workers and child protection people keeping in regular touch with him. Well, that was the idea, but they were always over-stretched, so as long as he wasn't getting into any trouble, they left well enough alone and moved on to other cases. He was allowed a certain degree of freedom, but mostly he preferred to stay close to the family and the lodge. This was during the summer season. Then things got busier, there wasn't always time to watch Andy twenty-four/seven, and—'

She stopped.

'Do you have children, Mr Parker?'

'Yes.'

'I don't. I thought I might have wanted them once, but I don't think it's going to happen now. Maybe it's for the best, when you see the things that people are capable of doing to them.' She wet her lips, as though her system was trying to silence her by drying out her mouth. 'Andy was abducted from near the lodge. He went missing for a couple of hours one afternoon, and when he returned he was very quiet. Nobody paid too much heed. You know, Andy still wasn't like the other kids. He had his moods, and the folks who were looking after him had learned to let them blow over. They figured that it didn't hurt to allow him to explore the woods by himself. They were good people. I think they just let their guard down where Andy was concerned.

'Anyhow, it wasn't until the third or fourth time it happened that notice was taken. Someone, I think it was the mother, went to see how Andy was, and he just attacked her. He went wild, clawing at her hair, her face. Eventually, they had to sit on him and pin him down until the police came. He wouldn't go back to Clay, and the child-care workers could only get him to talk about fragments of what had occurred. He was returned to the institution, and he stayed there until he was seventeen. After that, he hit the streets and was lost. He couldn't afford the medication that he needed so he fell into dealing, robbery, violence. He's doing fifteen years, but he doesn't belong in the Max. I've been trying to get him admitted to Riverview Psychiatric. That's where he should really be. I've had no luck so far. The state has decided that he's a criminal, and the state is never wrong.'

'Why didn't he tell anyone about the abuse?'

Price nibbled at her muffin. I noticed that her hands moved when she was thinking, her fingers always beating out some pattern on the edge of her chair, testing her fingernails or, as in this case, pulling apart the muffin before her. It seemed to be an element of her thought processes.

'It's complicated,' she said. 'In part, it was probably a product of the earlier abuse, where the adults responsible for him were not only aware of what was happening but actively colluded in it. Andy had little or no trust in authority figures, and the foster couple in Bingham had only just begun to break down his barriers when the new abuse occurred. But from what he told me later, the men who abused him threatened to hurt the couple's eight-year-old daughter if he said anything about what was happening to him. Her name was Michelle, and Andy had grown very fond of her. He was protective of her, in his way. That was why he went back.'

'Went back?'

'The men told Andy where he should wait for them each Tuesday. Sometimes they came, sometimes they didn't, but Andy was always there in case they did. He didn't want anything to happen to Michelle. There was a clearing about half a mile from the house with a creek nearby, and a trail led down to it from the road, wide enough to take a single vehicle. Andy would sit there, and one of them would come for him. He was told always to sit facing the creek, and never to turn around when he heard someone arriving. He would be blindfolded, walked to the car, and driven away.'

I felt something in my throat, and my eyes stung. I looked away from Price. I had an image in my head of a boy sitting on a log, the sound of water rushing nearby, sunlight spearing through the trees and birds singing, then footsteps approaching, and darkness.

'I hear he's been taken to the chair a couple of times.'

She glanced at me, perhaps surprised at how much I knew.

'More than a couple. It's a vicious circle. Andy's medicated, but the medication needs to be monitored and the dosages adjusted. It isn't monitored, though, so the meds stop working as well as they should, Andy gets distressed, he lashes out, the guards punish him, he ends up more disturbed, and the meds have even less effect on him than before. It's not Andy's fault, but try explaining that to a prison guard who's just had Andy's urine thrown all over him. And Andy's not untypical: there's an escalating cycle occurring at the Supermax. Everyone can see it, but nobody knows what to do about it, or nobody even wants to do something about it, depending upon how depressed I'm feeling. You take a mentally unstable prisoner who commits some infraction of the rules while part of the general population. You confine him in a brightly lit cell without distractions, surrounded by other prisoners who may be even more disturbed than he is. Under the strain, he violates more rules. He's punished by being placed in the chair, which makes him even wilder than before. He commits more serious breaches of the rules, or assaults a guard, and his sentence is increased. The end result, in the case of someone like Andy, is that he's driven insane, even suicidal. And what does a threat of suicide get you? More time in the chair.

'Winston Churchill once said that you can judge a society by the way it treats its prisoners. You know, there was all of this stuff about Abu Ghraib and what we we're doing to Muslims in Iraq and in Guantánamo and in Afghanistan and wherever else we've decided to lock up those whom we perceive to be a threat. People seemed surprised by it, but all they had to do was look around them. We do it to our own people. We try children as adults. We lock up, even execute, the mentally ill. And we tie people naked to chairs in ice-cold rooms because their medication isn't working. If we can do that here, then how the hell can anybody be surprised when we don't treat our enemies any better?'

Her voice had grown louder as she became more angry. Ernest knocked on the door and poked his head in.

'Everything okay, Aimee?' he asked, looking at me as if I was to blame for the disturbance which I suppose, in a way, I was.

'It's fine, Ernest.'

'You want more coffee?'

She shook her head. 'I'm wired as it is. Mr Parker?'

'No, I'm good.'

She waited until the door had closed before continuing.

'Sorry about that,' said Aimee.

'For what?'

'For giving you the rant. I guess you probably don't agree with me.'

'Why would you say that?'

'Because of what I've read about you. You've killed people. You seem like a harsh judge.'

I wasn't sure how to respond. Part of me was surprised by her words, maybe even annoyed by them, but there was no edge to them. She was simply calling it as she saw it.

'I didn't think that I had a choice,' I replied. 'Not then. Maybe now, knowing what I know, I might have acted differently in some cases, but not all.'

'You did what you thought was right.'

'I've started to believe that most people do what they think is right. The problems arise when what they do is right for themselves, but not for others.'

'Selfishness?'

'Perhaps. Self-interest. Self-preservation. A whole lot of concepts with "self" in them.'

'Did you make mistakes when you did what you did?'

I realized that I was being tested in some way, that Price's questions were a way of gauging whether or not I should be allowed to see Andy Kellog. I tried to answer them as honestly as I could.

'No, not at the end.'

'So you don't make mistakes?'

'Not like that.'

'You never shot anyone who didn't have a gun in his hand, is that what you're saying?'

'No, because that's not true either.'

There was a silence then, until Aimee Price put her hands to her forehead and gave a growl of frustration.

'Some of that is none of my business,' she said. 'I'm sorry. Again.'

'I'm asking you questions. I don't see why you can't ask some back. You frowned when I mentioned Daniel Clay's name, though. Why?'

'Because I know what people say about him. I've heard the stories.'

'And you believe them?'

'Somebody betrayed Andy Kellog to those men. It wasn't a coincidence.'

'Merrick doesn't think so either.'

'Frank Merrick is obsessed. Something inside him broke when his daughter disappeared. I don't know if it makes him more dangerous or less dangerous than he was.'

'What can you tell me about him?'

'Not much. You probably know all that you need to about his conviction, and the stuff in Virginia: the killing of Barton Riddick, and the bullet match that linked Merrick to the shooting. It doesn't interest me a great deal, to be honest. My main concern was, and remains, Andy Kellog. When Merrick first began forming some kind of bond with Andy, I thought what most people would: you know, a vulnerable younger man, an older, harder prisoner, but it wasn't like that. Merrick really seemed to be looking out for Andy as best he could.'

She had begun to doodle on the legal pad on her lap as she spoke. I don't think she was even fully aware of what she was doing. She didn't look down at the pad as the pencil moved across it, and she didn't look at me, preferring instead to gaze out at the cold winter light beyond her window.

She was drawing the heads of birds.

'I heard that Merrick got transferred to the Supermax just so he could stay close to Kellog,' I said.

'I'm curious to know the source of your information, but it's certainly right on the money. Merrick got transferred, and made it clear that anyone who messed with Andy would answer to him. Even in a place like the Max, there are ways and means. Except the only person from whom Merrick couldn't protect Andy was Andy himself.

'In the meantime, the AG's office in Virginia began setting in motion Merrick's indictment on the Riddick killing. It rattled on and on, and as the date of Merrick's release from the Max approached, the papers were served and he was notified of his extradition. Then something peculiar happened: another lawyer intervened on Merrick's behalf.'

'Eldritch,' I said.

'That's right. The intervention was troublesome in a number of ways. It didn't seem like Eldritch had ever had any previous contact with Merrick, and Andy told me that the lawyer had initiated the contact. This old man just turned up and offered to take on Merrick's case, but from what I found out later, Eldritch didn't seem to specialize in any kind of criminal work. He did corporate stuff, real estate, all strictly white collar, so he was an unusual candidate for a crusading attorney. Nevertheless, he tied Merrick's case in with a challenge to bullet matching being assembled by a group of liberal lawyers, and turned up evidence of a shooting involving the same weapon used to kill Riddick, but committed while Merrick was behind bars. The Feds began to backtrack on bullet matching, and Virginia came to the realization there wasn't enough evidence to get a conviction on the Riddick shooting, and if there's one thing a prosecutor hates to do, it's to pursue a case that looks like it's doomed from the start. Merrick spent a few months in a cell in Virginia, then was released. He'd served his full sentence in Maine, so he was free and clear.'

'Do you think he regretted leaving Andy Kellog in the Max?'

'Sure, but by then he seemed to have decided that there were things he needed to do outside.'

'Like find out what had happened to his daughter?'

'Yes.'

I closed my notebook. There would be other questions, but for now I was done.

'I'd still like to talk to Andy,' I said.

'I'll make some inquiries.'

I thanked her and gave her my card.

'About Frank Merrick,' she said, as I was about to leave. 'I think he did kill Riddick, and a whole lot of others too.'

'I know his reputation,' I said. 'Do you believe Eldritch was wrong to intervene?'

'I don't know why Eldritch intervened, but it wasn't out of a concern for justice. He did some good, though, even inadvertently. Bullet matching was flawed. The case against Merrick was equally flawed. If you let even one of those slip by, then the whole system falls apart, or crumbles a little more than it's crumbling already. If Eldritch hadn't taken the case, maybe I would have sought a pro hac vice order and taken it myself.' She smiled. 'I stress "maybe."'

'You wouldn't want Frank Merrick as a client.'

'Even hearing that he's back in Maine makes me nervous.'

'He hasn't tried to contact you about Andy?'

'No. You have any idea where he's staying while he's up here?'

It was a good question, and it set off a train of thought. If Eldritch had provided Merrick with a car, and perhaps funds too, he might also have supplied a place for him to stay. If that was the case, there might be a way to find it, and perhaps discover more about both Merrick and Eldritch's client.

I stood to leave. At the door of her office, Aimee Price said: 'So Daniel Clay's daughter is paying you to do all this?'

'No, not this,' I said. 'She's paying me to keep her safe from Merrick.'

'So why are you here?'

'For the same reason that you might have taken on Merrick's case. There's something wrong here. It bothers me. I'd like to find out what it is.'

She nodded. 'I'll be in touch about Andy,' she said.

Rebecca Clay called me, and I updated her on the situation with Merrick. Eldritch had informed his client that he would be unable to do anything for him until Monday, when he would petition a judge if Merrick continued to remain in custody without charge. O'Rourke wasn't confident that any judge would allow the Scarborough cops to continue to hold him if he had already spent forty-eight hours behind bars, even allowing for the fact that the letter of the law entitled them to keep him for a further forty-eight.

'What then?' asked Rebecca.

'I'm pretty certain that he's not going to bother you again. I saw what happened when they told him he was going to be locked up for the weekend. He's not afraid of jail, but he is afraid of losing his freedom to search for his daughter. That freedom is now tied up with your continued well-being. I'll serve him with the court order upon his release, but if you're agreeable, we'll keep an eye on you for a day or two after he's released, just in case.'

'I want to bring Jenna home,' she said.

'I wouldn't advise that just yet.'

'I'm worried about her. This whole business, I think it's affecting her.'

'Why?'

'I found pictures in her room. Drawings.'

'Drawings of what?'

'Of men, men with pale faces and no eyes. She said that she'd seen them or dreamed them, or something. I want her close to me.'

I didn't tell Rebecca that others had seen those men too, myself included. It seemed better to let her believe for now that they were a product of her daughter's troubled imagination, and nothing more.

'Soon,' I said. 'Just give me a few more days.'

Reluctantly, she agreed.

That evening, Angel, Louis, and I had dinner at Fore Street. Louis had gone to the bar to examine the vodka options, leaving Angel and me to talk.

'You've lost weight,' said Angel, sniffing and snowing fragments of tissue on the table. I had no idea what he had been doing in Napa to contract a cold, but I was pretty certain that I didn't want him to tell me. 'You look good. Even your clothes look good.'

'It's the new me. I eat well, still go to the gym, walk the dog.'

'Uh-huh. Nice clothes, eating well, going to the gym, owning a dog.' He thought for a moment. 'You sure you're not gay?'

'I can't be gay,' I said. 'I'm very busy as it is.'

'Maybe that's why I like you,' he said. 'You're a gay nongay.'

Angel had arrived wearing one of my cast-off brown leather bomber jackets, the material so worn in places that it had faded entirely to white. His aged Wranglers had an embroidered wave pattern on the back pockets, and he was wearing a Hall and Oates T-shirt, which meant that the time in Angel Land was approximately a quarter after 1981.

'Can you be a gay homophobe?' I asked.

'Sure. It's like being a self-hating Jew, except the food is better.'

Louis returned.

'I've been telling him how gay he is,' said Angel, as he buttered a piece of bread. A fragment of butter fell on his T-shirt. He carefully used a finger to remove it and licked the digit clean. Louis's face remained impassive, only the slightest narrowing of his eyes indicating the depth of the emotions he was feeling.

'Uh-huh,' he said. 'I don't think you're the right guy to front the recruitment drive.'

While we ate, we talked about Merrick, and what I had

learned from Aimee Price. Earlier that day, I had put in a call to Matt Mayberry, a realtor I knew down in Massachusetts whose company did business all over New England, asking him if there was a way he could find out about any properties in the greater Portland area with which Eldritch and Associates had been involved in recent years. It was a long shot. I had spent most of the afternoon making calls to hotels and motels, but I had drawn a blank every time I asked for Frank Merrick's room. Still, it would be useful to know where Merrick was likely to bolt once he was released.

'You seen Rachel lately?' asked Angel.

'A few weeks back.'

'How are things between you?'

'Not so good.'

'That's a shame.'

'Yeah.'

'You got to keep trying, you know that?'

'Thanks for the advice.'

'Maybe you should go see her, while Merrick is safe behind bars.'

I thought about it as the check arrived. I knew then that I wanted to see them both. I wanted to hold Sam, and talk to Rachel. I was tired of hearing about men who tormented children and the troubled lives they had left in their wake.

Louis began counting out bills.

'Maybe I will go to see them,' I said.

'We'll walk your dog,' said Angel. 'If he's secretly gay like you, he won't object.'

16

It was a long ride to the property Rachel and Sam now shared with Rachel's parents in Vermont, and I spent most of it driving in silence, going over all that I had learned about Daniel Clay and Frank Merrick, and trying to figure out where Eldritch's client fitted into the whole affair. Eldritch had told me that his client had no interest in Daniel Clay, yet they were both facilitating Merrick, who was obsessed with Clay. And then there were the Hollow Men, whatever they were. I had seen them, or perhaps it would be more true to say that they had entered my zone of perception. The maid at Joel Harmon's house had seen them too, and as I had learned from the brief conversation with Rebecca Clay the night before, her daughter Jenna had drawn pictures of them before she left the city. The connection appeared to be Merrick, but when he was asked during his interrogation if he was working alone, or if he had brought others with him, he had seemed genuinely surprised and had responded in the negative. The questions remained: who were they, and what was their purpose?

Rachel's parents had gone away for the weekend and weren't due back until Monday, so Rachel's sister had come to stay in order to help with Sam. Sam had grown so much, even in the few weeks since I had last seen her, or perhaps that was just the view of a father conscious of the fact that he was separated from his daughter and that the stages of her development would from now on be revealed to him in leaps rather than steps.

Was I simply being pessimistic? I didn't know. Rachel and I still spoke regularly on the phone. I missed her, and I thought that she missed me, but on the recent occasions when we had met, her parents were present, or Sam was acting up, or there was something else that seemed to get in the way of talking about ourselves and how things had become so bad between us. I couldn't figure out if we were allowing these intrusions to become obstacles in order to avoid some kind of final confrontation, or if they truly were what they seemed to be. A period apart to allow us both to figure out how we wanted to live this life had become something longer and more complicated and, it appeared, more final. Rachel and Sam had moved back to Scarborough for a time in May, but Rachel and I had fought, and there was a distance between us that had not existed before. She had been uncomfortable in the house that we had once shared more easily, and Sam had trouble sleeping in her room. Had we simply grown used to being without each other, even though I knew that I still craved her, and she me? We existed in a kind of strained limbo, where things were left unsaid for fear that to speak them aloud would cause the whole fragile edifice to collapse around us.

Rachel's parents had converted some old stables on their property into a large guest house, and that was where Rachel lived with Sam. She was working again, employed on a contract basis with the Psychology Department of the University of Vermont in Burlington, taking tutorials and lecturing on criminal psychology. She told me a little about it as I sat at her kitchen table, but in the casual, passing way that one might describe one's pursuits to a stranger at dinner. In the past, I would have been privy to every little detail, but not anymore.

Sam was squatting on the floor between us, playing with big plastic farm animals. She gripped two sheep in her chubby hands and pounded their heads together, then looked up and offered one to each of us. They were slick with baby drool.

'You think it's a metaphor for us?' I asked Rachel. She looked tired, but still beautiful. She caught me staring and brushed a strand of hair back over her ear, blushing slightly.

'I'm not sure that knocking our heads together would solve

anything,' she said. 'Although admittedly I'd get a sense of satisfaction from knocking your head against something.'

'Nice.'

She reached out and touched the back of my hand with her finger.

'I didn't mean it to sound quite as harsh as it did.'

'It's okay. If it's any consolation, I often feel like beating my head against a wall too.'

'What about beating mine?'

'You're too good-looking. And I'd be afraid of ruining your hair.'

I turned my hand palm up and held her finger.

'Let's go for a walk,' she said. 'My sister will look after Sam.'

We rose, and she called her sister's name. Pam entered the kitchen before I had a chance to release Rachel's finger, and she gave us both a knowing look. It wasn't disapproving, though, which was something. Had Rachel's father seen us like this, he might well have reached for his rifle. I didn't get on with him, and I knew that he hoped the relationship between his daughter and me was over for good.

'Why don't I take Sam for a ride?' said Pam. 'I have to go to the store anyway, and you know how she likes people-watching.' She knelt in front of Sam. 'You wanna go for a ride with Aunt Pammie, huh? I'll take you to the health section and show you all the stuff you're gonna need when you're a teenager and boys come calling. Maybe we can go look at guns too, huh?'

Sam let her aunt pick her up without complaint. Rachel followed them and helped her sister to get Sam ready, and to fit her into the child seat. Sam cried a little when the door closed and she realized that her mom wasn't joining them, but we knew that it wouldn't last long. She was fascinated by the car, and seemed to spend most of her time in it either watching the sky go by or just sleeping, lulled by the movement of the vehicle. We watched them drive off, then I followed Rachel across the garden and into the fields that bordered her parents' house. She kept her arms folded across her chest, as though uneasy about the fact that she had held my hand earlier.

'How have you been?' she asked.

'Busy.'

'Anything interesting?'

I told her about Rebecca Clay and her father, and the arrival of Frank Merrick.

'What kind of man is he?' asked Rachel.

It was a strange question. 'A dangerous one, and hard to read,' I replied. 'He thinks Clay is still alive, and that he knows what happened to his daughter. Nobody else seems to be able to say different, but the general wisdom is that Clay is dead; that, or his daughter is the best actress I've ever met. Merrick tends toward the latter view. He used to be a freelance button man, a hired killer. He's been in jail for a long time, but he doesn't strike me as being rehabilitated. There's more to him than that, though. He looked out for one of Clay's patients while he was in the can, even getting himself sent to the Max so he could be close to him. I thought at first that it might be a jail thing – older guy–younger guy – but it doesn't look like it was that way. Merrick's own daughter was one of Clay's patients at the time that she disappeared. That may be why there was a bond between him and this kid, Kellog.'

'Maybe Merrick also hoped to learn something from Kellog that might lead him to his daughter,' said Rachel.

'Probably, but he shadowed this kid for years, and he protected him. It wouldn't have taken him long to find out what Kellog knew, but he didn't cut him loose. He stood by him. He took care of him, as best he could.'

'He couldn't protect his own daughter, so he protected Kellog instead?'

'He's a complex man.'

'You sound almost as though you respect him.'

I shook my head. 'I pity him. I think I even understand him some. But I don't respect him, not in the way that you mean.'

'There's another way?'

I didn't want to utter it. After all, it would lead us back to one of the reasons why Rachel and I had parted.

'Well?' she pressed, and I knew that she had already guessed what I was going to say. She wanted to hear it spoken, as though to confirm something sad but necessary.

'He has a lot of blood on his hands,' I said. 'He doesn't forgive.'

I could have been talking about myself, and once again I was aware of how much like Merrick I once was, and might still be. It was as though I had been given an opportunity to witness a version of myself decades down the line, older and more solitary, trying to right a wrong through force and the infliction of harm upon others.

'And now you've crossed him. You brought in the police. You got in the way of his efforts to find out the truth about his daughter's disappearance. You respect him the way you'd respect an animal, because to do otherwise would be to under-estimate him. You think you're going to have to face him again, don't you?'

'Yes.'

Her brow wrinkled, and there was pain in her eyes. 'It never changes, does it?'

I didn't reply. What could I say?

Rachel didn't pursue an answer. Instead, she said: 'Is Kellog still in jail?'

'Yes.'

'Are you going to talk to him?'

'I'm going to try. I've spoken to his lawyer. From what I hear, he's not doing so good. Then again, he was never doing good, but if he stays in the Supermax for much longer he's going to be beyond rescuing. He was troubled before he got there. It sounds like he's bordering on insane now.'

'Is it true what they say about that place?'

'Yes, it's true.'

She didn't speak again for a time. We walked through dead leaves. Sometimes, they made a sound like a parent hushing a child, soothing it, consoling it. At other times, the noise was empty and dry, crackling with the promise of the passing of all things.

'What about the psychiatrist, Clay? You say there were suspicions that he might have been providing information on the children to the abusers. Was there anything to implicate him directly in the abuse itself?'

'Nothing, or nothing that I've been able to find. His daughter's view is that he couldn't live with the guilt of failing to prevent it. He believed that he should have spotted what was happening. The kids were damaged before he even began treating them, just like Kellog. He was having trouble getting through to them, but his daughter remembers that he was making progress, or thought he was. Kellog's lawyer confirmed as much about him. Whatever Clay did, it was working. I spoke to one of his peers too, a doctor named Christian who runs a clinic for abused children. His main criticism of Clay seems to have been that he was too anxious to spot abuse. He had an agenda, and he got into some trouble over it that prevented him from making any further evaluations on cases for the state.'

Rachel stopped and knelt down. She picked a piece of rabbit-foot clover, still with one of its fuzzy, grayish pink flowers in place.

'This is supposed to stop blooming in September or October,' she said. 'Yet here it is, still in flower. The world is changing.' She handed it to me. 'For luck,' she said.

I held it in my palm, then carefully slipped it into the plastic pocket of my wallet.

'The question still remains: if the same people were involved in the abuse of different children, then how did they target them?' she asked. 'From what you've told me, they picked the most vulnerable. How did they know?'

'Somebody told them,' I said. 'Somebody fed children to them.'

'If not Clay, then who was it?'

'There was a committee formed to select the children who

would be sent to Clay. It had health workers on it, and social workers. If I had to pick, I'd say it was one of them. But I'm sure the cops looked at that angle. They must have. Christian's people did too. They came up with nothing.'

'But Clay disappeared. Why? Because of what happened to the children, or because he was involved? Because he felt responsible, or because he *was* responsible?

'That's a big leap.'

'It just feels wrong, Clay disappearing like that. There are always exceptions, but I can't think of a doctor in that situation who would respond in a similar way. He's a psychiatrist, a specialist, not some ordinary Joe. He's not going to buckle, not in the space of a few days.'

'So either he ran away to avoid being implicated—'

'Which doesn't sound right either. If he was involved, he would have been smart enough to cover his tracks.'

'—or someone "disappeared" him, maybe one or more of those involved in the abuse.'

'Covering *their* tracks.'

'But why would he do it?'

'Blackmail. Or he may have had those tendencies himself.'

'You still think he might have been a participant in the abuse? It would be risky.'

'Too risky,' she agreed. 'It doesn't rule him out as a pedophile, though. Neither does it rule out blackmail.'

'We're still assuming he's guilty.'

'We're speculating, that's all.'

It was interesting, but it still didn't fit right. I just couldn't figure out what was wrong with the picture. We headed back toward the house, the moon already rising above us in the late-afternoon sky. I was facing the long ride home, and suddenly I felt unbearably lonely. I didn't want to drive away from this woman and the child we had made together. I didn't want to leave things this way. I couldn't.

'Rach,' I said. I stopped walking.

She paused and looked back to where I stood.

'What happened to us?'

'We've talked about this before.'

'Have we?'

'You know we have,' she said. 'I thought I could handle you, and what you did, but perhaps I was wrong. Something in me responded to it, the part of me that was angry and hurt, but in you it's so great that it frightens me. And—'

I waited.

'When I returned to the house, that time in May when we – I don't want to say "when we got back together," because it didn't last long enough for that, but when we lived together again – I realized how much I hated being there. I didn't notice it until I went away and came back, but there's something wrong with that place. I find it hard to explain. I don't think I've ever tried, not aloud, but I know there are things that you haven't told me. I've heard you sometimes, crying out names in your dreams. I've seen you walking through the house half asleep, carrying on conversations with people that I can't see, but I know who they are. I've watched you, when you think you're alone, responding to something in the shadows.' She laughed mirthlessly. 'Hell, I even saw the dog do it. You have him freaked out too. I don't believe in ghosts. Maybe that's why I don't see them. I think they come from within, not beyond. People create them. All that stuff about spirits with unfinished business, individuals taken before their time haunting places, I don't believe any of it. It's the living who have unfinished business, who can't let the past go. Your house – and it is *your* house – is haunted. Its ghosts are your ghosts. You brought them into being, and you can get rid of them too. Until you do, nobody else can be part of your life, because the demons in your head and the spirits in your heart will force them away. Do you understand? I *know* what you've been going through all of these years. I waited for you to tell me, but you couldn't. Sometimes, I think it's because you were afraid that by telling me you'd have to let them go, and you don't want to let them go. They fuel that rage within you.

That's why you look at this man Merrick and feel pity for him, and more than that: you feel empathy.'

Her face changed, the tone of her voice transforming with it, and her cheeks flushed red with anger.

'Well, be sure that you look closely at him, because that's what you'll become if all of this doesn't stop: an empty vessel motivated by hatred and revenge and frustrated love. In the end, we're not apart just because I'm afraid for Sam and myself, or scared for you and for what might happen to all of us as a consequence of your work. I'm frightened *of* you, of the fact that part of you is drawn to evil and pain and wretchedness, that the anger and hurt that you feel will always need to be fed. It will never end. You talk of Merrick as a man unable to forgive. Well, you can't forgive either. You can't forgive yourself for not being there to protect your wife and child, and you can't forgive them for dying on you. And maybe I thought that that might change, that having us in your life would enable you to heal a little, to find some peace with us, but there will be no peace. You want it, but you can't bring yourself to embrace it. You just—'

She was starting to cry now. I moved to her but she stepped away.

'No,' she said softly. 'Please don't.'

She walked away, and I let her go.

17

Eldritch arrived in Maine early on Monday morning, accompanied by a younger man who had the distracted yet slightly desperate air of an alcoholic who has forgotten where the bottle is hidden. Eldritch allowed his colleague to make all of the running in petitioning the judge, only contributing a few words on behalf of his client at the end of the submission, his soft, reasonable tones conveying the impression that Merrick was a peace-loving man whose actions, born out of a concern for the well-being of his lost child, had been cruelly misinterpreted by an uncaring world. Nevertheless, he gave a promise, on Merrick's behalf, for Merrick did not speak during the hearing, to adhere to any and all conditions of the court order about to be served, and requested, with all due deference, that his client be released forthwith.

The judge, whose name was Nola Hight, was no fool. In her fifteen years at the bench she had heard just about every excuse known to man, and she wasn't about to take Eldritch or Merrick at face value.

'Your client spent ten years in jail for attempted murder, Mr Eldritch,' she said.

'Aggravated assault, Your Honor,' Eldritch's young assistant corrected. Judge Hight glared at him so hard his hair started to singe.

'With respect, Your Honor, I'm not sure that is relevant to the matter before the court,' said Eldritch, attempting to smooth the judge's ruffled feathers through tone alone. 'My client served his time for that offense. He is a changed man, chastened by his experiences.'

Judge Hight gave Eldritch a look that would have reduced a lesser man to charred flesh. Eldritch merely wavered where he stood, as though his brittle form had been briefly buffeted by a gentle breeze.

'He will be chastened for the maximum term allowable under law if he comes before this court again in connection with the matter in hand,' she said. 'Am I making myself clear, counsel?'

'Indisputably,' said Eldritch. 'Your Honor is as reasonable as she is wise.'

Judge Hight debated finding him in contempt of court for sarcasm, then gave up.

'Get the hell out of my courtroom,' she said.

It was still early, barely after ten. Merrick was due for release at eleven once his paperwork had been processed. When they let him out of the Cumberland County lockup, I was waiting, and I served him with the court order forbidding further contact with Rebecca Clay on pain of imprisonment and/or a fine. He took it, read it carefully, then slipped it into the pocket of his jacket. He looked crumpled and tired, the way most people did after a couple of nights in a cell.

'That was low, what you did,' he said.

'You mean setting the cops on you? You were terrorizing a young woman. That also seems kind of low. You need to reconsider your standards. They're all screwed up.'

He might have heard me, but he wasn't really listening. He wasn't even looking at me. He was staring at a spot somewhere over my right shoulder, letting me know that I wasn't even worthy of eye contact.

'Men ought to deal with each other like men,' he continued, red rising into his face as though he were being boiled from below. 'You set the hounds on me when all I wanted to do was talk. You and missy both, you got no honor.'

'Let me buy you breakfast,' I said. 'Maybe we can work something out.'

Merrick waved a hand in dismissal.

'Keep your breakfast and your talk. The time for talking with you is over.'

'You may not believe this, but I have some sympathy for you,' I said. 'You want to find out what happened to your daughter. I know what that feels like. If I can help you, then I will, but scaring Rebecca Clay isn't the way to go about it. If you approach her again you'll be picked up and put back behind bars: the Cumberland County lockup if you're lucky, but Warren if you're not. That could be another year out of your life, another year spent not getting any closer to finding out the truth about your daughter's disappearance.'

Merrick looked at me for the first time since we'd begun talking.

'I'm done with the Clay woman,' he said. 'But I ain't done with you. I'll give you some advice, though, in return for what you just gave me. Stay out of this, and maybe I'll be merciful the next time our paths cross.'

With that he pushed past me and began walking toward the bus station. He looked smaller than before, his shoulders slightly hunched, his jeans stained from his time behind bars. Once again, I felt pity for him. Despite all that I knew about him, and all that he was suspected of doing, he was still a father seeking his lost child. Perhaps it was all he had left, but I knew the damage that could be caused by that kind of single-minded intensity. I knew because I had once wrought it myself. Rebecca Clay might be safe from him, at least for the present, but Merrick was not going to stop. He would keep looking until he found out the truth, or until someone forced him to desist. Either way, it could only end with a death.

I called Rebecca and told her that I didn't believe Merrick would trouble her for the time being, but there were no guarantees.

'I understand,' she said. 'I don't want men outside my house any longer, though. I can't live that way. Will you thank them for me, and bill me?'

'One last thing, Miss Clay,' I said. 'If the choice was given to you, would you want your father found?'

She thought about the question.

'Wherever he is, he made the choice that brought him there,' she said softly. 'I told you before: I think sometimes about Jim Poole. He went away, and he never came back. I like to pretend that I don't know if it was because of me, if he vanished because I asked him to look for my father, or if something else happened to him, something equally bad. But when I can't sleep, when I'm lying alone in my room in the darkness, I know it was my fault. In the daylight, I can convince myself that it wasn't, but I know the truth. I don't know you, Mr Parker. I asked you to help me, and you did, and I'll pay you for your time and your efforts, but we don't know each other. If something were to happen to you because you asked questions about my father, then we'd be bound by it, and I don't want to be bound to you, not like that. Do you understand? I'm trying to let it go. I want you to do the same.'

She hung up. Maybe she was right. Maybe Daniel Clay should be left wherever he was, either above or below ground. But it wasn't up to her, or me, not any longer. Merrick was out there, and so was the person who had instructed Eldritch to bankroll him. Rebecca Clay's part in this might have been over, but mine wasn't.

When the Maine State Prison was based in Thomaston it was hard to miss. It stood slap bang on the main road into town, a massive edifice on Route 1 that had survived two fires and, even after being rebuilt, renovated, extended, and occasionally updated, still resembled the early-nineteenth-century penitentiary that it had once been. It felt like the town itself had developed around the prison, although in truth there had been a trading post at Thomaston since the seventeenth century. Nevertheless, the prison dominated the landscape of the community, both physically and, perhaps, psychologically. If one mentioned Thomaston to anyone in Maine, the first thing that came to mind was the penitentiary. I wondered sometimes what it was like to live in a place whose principal claim to fame was the incarceration of human beings. It might have been that, after a while, you just forgot about it, or failed to notice the effect it had on the people and the town. Perhaps it was only those who visited Thomaston who immediately felt that an oppressive miasma hung over the place, as though the misery of those locked behind the prison's walls had seeped into the atmosphere, coloring it with gray, weighing it down like particles of lead in the air. Then again, it certainly kept the crime rate low. Thomaston was the kind of place where there was a violent crime once every two or three years, and its crime index was about one-third of the national average. It might have been that the presence of a huge prison on the doorstep made those tempted by a life of crime reconsider their career options.

Warren was different, though. The town was a little larger than Thomaston, and its identity was not so bound up with the penitentiary. The new state prison had grown gradually, beginning with the opening of the Supermax, then the Mental Health Stabilization Unit, and finally the transfer of the general population from Thomaston to the new facility. Compared to the old prison, it was a little harder to find, squirreled away on Route 97, or at least as squirreled away as a place with a thousand prisoners and four hundred employees can be. I drove along Cushing Road, past the Bolduc Correctional Facility on the left, until I came to the brick and stone sign to the right of the road announcing the Maine State Prison, with the years 1824 and 2001 beneath, the first commemorating the founding of the original prison, and the second the opening of the new facility.

Warren looked more like a modern industrial plant than a prison, an impression reinforced by the big maintenance area to the right that appeared to house the prison's power plant. Bird feeders made from buoys hung on the lawn outside the main entrance, and everything looked new and freshly painted.

It was the silence that gave away the true nature of the place, though; that, and the name, white on green above the door, and the razor wire on top of the double fencing, and the presence of the blue uniformed guards with their striped trousers, and the beaten-down look of those waiting in the lobby to visit their loved ones. All told, you didn't have to look too hard to figure out that, whatever cosmetic adjustments had been made to the façade, this was still as much a prison as Thomaston ever was.

Aimee Price had clearly pulled some strings to get me access to Andy Kellog. Visitor clearances could sometimes take up to six weeks. Then again, Price was entitled to see her client whenever she chose, and I wasn't exactly unknown to the prison authorities. I had visited the preacher Faulkner when he was incarcerated at Thomaston, an encounter that had been memorable for all the wrong reasons, but this was my first time at the new facility.

It wasn't a complete surprise, therefore, to see a familiar figure standing beside Price when I eventually cleared security and entered the body of the prison: Joe Long, the colonel of the guards. He hadn't changed much since last we'd met. He was still big, still taciturn, and still radiated the kind of authority that kept a thousand criminals on the right side of respectful. His uniform was starched and pressed, and everything that was supposed to gleam did so spectacularly. There was a little more gray in his mustache than before, but I decided not to point that out. Beneath his gruff exterior, I sensed there was a sensitive child just waiting to be hugged. I didn't want to hurt his feeling, singular.

'Back again,' he said, in a tone that suggested I was forever bothering him by knocking on the door at all hours of the day and night, demanding that I be let in to play with the other kids.

'Can't stay away from men in jails,' I said.

'Yeah, we get a lot of that here,' he replied.

That Joe Long. What a kidder. If he was any drier, he'd have been Arizona.

'I like the new place,' I said. 'It's institutional, but homey. I can see your hand at work in the decor: the institutional grays, the stone, the wire. It all just screams you.'

He allowed his gaze to linger on me for just a moment or two longer than was strictly necessary, then turned smartly on his heel and told us to follow him. Aimee Price fell into step beside me, and a second guard, named Woodbury, brought up the rear.

'You just have friends everywhere, don't you?' she said.

'If I ever end up in here as a guest, I'm hoping he'll look out for me.'

'Yeah, good luck with that. You ever find yourself in that much trouble, make a shank.'

Our footsteps echoed along the corridor. Now there was noise: unseen men talking and shouting, steel doors opening and closing, the distant sound of radios and TVs. That was the thing about prisons: inside, they were never quiet, not even at night. It was never possible to be anything but acutely aware of the men incarcerated around you. It was worse in the dark, after lights out, when the nature of the sound changed. It was then that the loneliness and desperation of their situation would hit prisoners, and the snores and wheezes would be interspersed with the cries of men enduring nightmares and the weeping of those who had not yet learned to accommodate themselves to the prospect of years in such a place, or who would never reach that accommodation. Tween had once told me that during his longest stretch inside – two years of a three-year B&E sentence – he did not get a single undisturbed night's sleep. It was that, he said, that wore him down. The irony was that when he was released, he was unable to sleep either, unaccustomed as he was to the comparative silence of the city.

'They're transferring Andy from the Supermax to a noncontact room for our meeting,' said Aimee. 'It's not ideal, and you won't get any sense of the Max for yourself, but it's the best that I could do. Andy is still considered a risk to himself and others.'

Price excused herself to use the bathroom before we sat down with Kellog. That left just me and Joe Long. Woodbury kept his distance, content to stare at the floor and the walls.

'Been a while since we've seen you,' said Long. 'What is it, three, four years?'

'You sound almost regretful.'

'Yeah, almost.' Long straightened his tie, carefully brushing away some flecks of lint that had had the temerity to affix themselves to him. 'You ever hear tell what happened to that preacher Faulkner?' he asked. 'They say he just plain disappeared.'

'That's the rumor.'

Long, finished with his tie, examined me from behind his glasses, and stroked his mustache thoughtfully.

'Strange that he never showed up again,' he continued. 'Hard for a man like that just to vanish, what with so many people looking for him. Kind of makes you wonder if they're looking in the wrong direction. Up, so to speak, instead of down. Above ground instead of below.'

'I guess we'll never know,' I said.

'Guess not. Probably for the best. The preacher would be no loss, but the law's the law. Man could find himself behind bars for something like that, and that wouldn't be a good place for him to be.'

If Long was expecting me to break down and confess something, he was disappointed.

'Yeah, I hear it hasn't been good for Andy Kellog,' I said. 'He seems to be having problems adjusting.'

'Andy Kellog has a lot of problems. Some of them he makes for himself.'

'Can't help Macing him in the middle of the night and tying him naked to a chair. I think someone in this place missed his vocation. There we are, spending taxpayers' money flying bad guys to Egypt and Saudi Arabia to be softened up, when we could just put them on a Trailways bus and send them here.'

For the first time, there was a flicker of emotion on Long's face.

'It's used for restraint,' he said, 'not torture.'

He said it very softly, almost as if he didn't believe what he was saying enough to enunciate it loudly.

'It's torture if it drives a man crazy,' I replied.

Long opened his mouth to say something else, but before he could speak Aimee Price reappeared.

'Okay,' she said. 'Let's see him.'

The door across from us was opened by Woodbury, and we entered a room divided in two by a thick pane of Plexiglas. A series of booths, each with its own speaker system, allowed a degree of privacy to those visiting, although it wasn't required that morning. Only one prisoner stood on the opposite side of the glass, two guards hovering stony-faced behind him. He wore an orange jumpsuit and a collar-and-tie arrangement of chains that kept his hands cuffed and his legs manacled. He was shorter than I was, and unlike a lot of men in prison he didn't seem to have put on any excess weight because of the diet and the lack of exercise. Instead, the jumpsuit seemed too big for him, the sleeves hanging down almost to the second line of knuckles on each hand. He had pale skin and fine black hair, cut unevenly so that the fringe sloped downward from left to right across his forehead. His eyes were set deep in his skull, overshadowed by a narrow but swollen brow. His nose had been broken more than once and had set crookedly. His mouth was small, the lips very thin. His lower jaw trembled constantly, as though he were on the verge of tears. When he saw Aimee he smiled widely. One of his front teeth was missing. The others were gray with plaque.

He sat when we sat and leaned into the speaker before him. 'How you doing, Miss Price?' he said.

'Good, Andy. And you?'

He nodded repeatedly but said nothing, as though she were still speaking and he were still listening. Up close, I could see bruising beneath his left eye and over his left cheekbone. His right ear was scarred, and dried blood was mixed with wax in the entrance to the canal.

'I'm doing okay,' he replied, eventually.

'You been in any trouble?'

'Uh-uh. I been taking my meds, like you asked me to, and I tell the guards if I'm not feeling good.'

'Do they listen?'

He swallowed and seemed about to look over his shoulder at the men behind him. Aimee caught the movement and addressed the two guards.

'Could you give us some space, please?' she asked.

They looked to Long for confirmation that it was permissible. He assented, and they retreated out of our line of sight.

'Some of 'em, the good ones,' continued Kellog. He pointed respectfully at Long. 'Colonel Sir, he listens, when I get to see him. Others, though, they got it in for me. I try to keep out of their way, but sometimes they just rile me, you know? They make me angry, then I have problems.'

He glanced at me. It was the third or fourth time that he'd done so, never staring long enough to catch my eye, but nodding to me each time in acknowledgment of my presence. The niceties over with, Aimee introduced me.

'Andy, this is Mr Parker. He's a private detective. He'd like to talk to you about some things, if you don't mind.'

'I don't mind at all,' said Kellog. 'Nice to meet you, sir.'

Now that the introductions had been made he was happy to look me in the eye. There was something childlike about him. I didn't doubt that he could be difficult, even dangerous under the wrong circumstances, but it was hard to understand how anyone could have met Andy Kellog, could have read his history and examined the reports of experts, and not have concluded that here was a young man with severe problems that were not of his own making, an individual who would never truly belong anywhere but still did not deserve to end up in a cell or, worse, tied naked to a chair in an ice-cold room because nobody had bothered to check that his meds were in order.

I leaned closer to the glass. I wanted to ask Kellog about

Daniel Clay, and about what had happened to him in the woods near Bingham, but I knew it would be difficult for him, and there was always the possibility that he might clam up entirely or lose his temper, in which case I wouldn't get the chance to ask him anything else. I decided to start with Merrick instead and work my way back to the abuse.

'I met someone who knows you,' I said. 'His name is Frank Merrick. You remember him?'

Kellog nodded eagerly. He smiled, exposing his gray teeth again. He wouldn't have them for much longer. His gums were purple and infected.

'I liked Frank. He looked out for me. Will he come visit me?'

'I don't know, Andy. I'm not sure he'll want to come back here, you understand?'

Kellog's face fell. 'I guess you're right. When I get out of here, I ain't never coming back here neither, not ever.'

He picked at his hands, opening a sore that immediately began to bleed.

'How did Frank look out for you, Andy?'

'He was scary. I wasn't afraid of him – well, maybe I was at first, not later – but the others were. They used to pick on me, but then Frank came along and they stopped. He knew how to get at them, even in the Max.' He smiled widely once more. 'He hurt some of them *real* bad.'

'Did he ever tell you why he looked out for you?'

Kellog looked confused. 'Why? Because he was my friend, that's why. He liked me. He didn't want anything bad to happen to me.' Then, as I watched, the blood began to pump into his face, and I was reminded uncomfortably of Merrick, as though something of him had transferred itself into the younger man while they were imprisoned together. I saw his hands form fists. A peculiar clicking sound came from his mouth, and I realized he was sucking at one of his loose teeth, the socket filling with spittle then emptying again, creating a rhythmic ticking like a time bomb waiting to go off.

'He weren't queer,' said Kellog, his voice rising slightly. 'If that's what you're saying, I'm telling you now that it's not true. He weren't a fag. Me neither. 'Cause if that's what you're trying to say—'

From the corner of my eye, I saw Long make a gesture with his right hand, and the guards quickly swam into view behind Kellog.

'It's all right, Andy,' said Aimee. 'Nobody's suggesting anything of the kind.'

Kellog was shaking slightly as he tried to keep his anger in check. 'Well, he weren't, that's all. He never touched me. He was my friend.'

'I understand, Andy,' I said. 'I'm sorry. I didn't mean to suggest anything different. What I meant to ask you was if he ever gave you any sign that you might have something in common. Did he ever mention his daughter to you?'

Kellog began to calm down, but there was now a gleam of hostility and suspicion in his eyes. I knew it would take a lot to make it go away.

'Yeah, some.'

'This was after he began to look out for you, right?'

'That's right.'

'She was a patient of Dr Clay's, wasn't she, just like you were?'

'Yeah. She disappeared while Frank was in jail.'

'Did Frank ever tell you what he thought might have happened to her?'

Kellog shook his head. 'He didn't like talking about her. It made him sad.'

'Did he ask about what happened to you up north?'

Kellog swallowed hard and looked away. The clicking noise came again, but this time there was no anger with it.

'Yes,' he said softly. Not 'yeah,' but 'yes.' It made him sound younger, as though by raising the subject of the abuse I was propelling him physically back into his childhood. His face grew slack and his pupils shrank. He seemed to grow even smaller, his shoulders hunching, his hands opening out in an unconscious gesture of supplication. The tormented adult faded away, leaving behind the ghost of a child. I didn't need to ask what had been done to him. It played out on his features in a series of trembles and winces and flinches, a dumb play of remembered pain and humiliation.

'He wanted to know what I saw, what I remembered,' he said. It was almost a whisper.

'And what did you tell him?'

'I told him what they done to me,' he said simply. 'He asked me if I'd seen their faces or heard a name spoke, but they wore masks and they never spoke no names.' He looked straight at me. 'They looked like birds,' he said. 'All different. There was an eagle, and a crow. A pigeon. A rooster.' He shivered. 'All different,' he repeated. 'They always wore them, and they never took them off.'

'Did you remember anything about where it happened?'

'It was dark. They used to put me in the trunk of a car, tie my arms and my legs, put a sack over my head. They'd drive for a time, then carry me out. When the bag came off I'd be in a room. There were windows, but they were all covered up. There was a propane heater, and storm lamps. I'd try to keep my eyes closed. I knew what was going to happen. I knew, 'cause it had happened before. It was like it was always going to happen to me, and it wasn't never going to stop.'

He blinked a couple of times, then closed his eyes as he relived it over again.

'Andy,' I whispered.

He kept his eyes closed, but he nodded to let me know that he'd heard.

'How many times did this happen?'

'I stopped counting after three.'

'Why didn't you tell anyone about it?'

'They said they'd kill me, and then they'd take Michelle and do it to her instead. One of them said they didn't care if they did it to a boy or a girl. He said it was just different for each, that was all. I liked Michelle. I didn't want nothing bad to happen to her. It had been done to me before, so I knew what to expect. I learned to block some of it out. I'd think of other things while it was happening. I'd imagine that I was somewhere else, that I wasn't in me. Sometimes, I'd be flying over the forest and I'd look down and see all of the people, and I'd find Michelle and I'd go to her and we'd play by the river together. I could do that, but Michelle, she wouldn't have been able to do that. She'd have been there with them, all the time.'

I leaned back. He had sacrificed himself for another child. Aimee had told me as much, but to hear it from Kellog himself was another matter. There was no boastfulness about his tale of self-sacrifice. He had done it out of love for a younger child, and it had come naturally to him. Once again, I was aware that here was a boy trapped in a man's body, a child whose development had ceased almost entirely, arrested by what had been done to him. Beside me, Aimee was silent, her lips clamped so tightly shut that the blood had drained from them. She must have heard this before, I thought, but it would never get any easier to listen to.

'But they found out, in the end,' I said. 'People discovered what was happening to you.'

'I got angry. I couldn't help it. They brought me to the doctor. He examined me. I tried to stop him. I didn't want them to come for Michelle. Then the doctor asked me questions. I tried to lie, for Michelle, but he kept tripping me up. I couldn't keep all the answers straight in my head. They brought me back to Dr Clay, but I didn't want to talk to him no more. I didn't want to talk to anyone, so I kept quiet. They put me away again, but then I got too old and they had to let me go. I fell in with some people, did some bad things, and they put me in the Castle.'

The Castle was the name given to the old Maine Youth Center in South Portland, a correctional facility for troubled youths built in the middle of the nineteenth century. It had since closed, but it was no great loss. Before the building of the new youth facilities in South Portland and Charleston, the recidivism rate for young inmates had been 50 percent. It was now down to 10 or 15 percent, largely because the institutions now focused less on incarceration and punishment than helping the kids, some as young as eleven or twelve, to overcome their problems. The changes had come too late for Andy Kellog, though. He was a walking, talking testament to everything that could go wrong in the state's dealings with a troubled child.

Now Aimee spoke. 'Can I show Mr Parker your pictures, Andy?'

He opened his eyes. There were no tears. I don't think he had any left to shed.

'Sure.'

Aimee opened her document case and removed a card-board wallet. She handed it to me. Inside were eight or nine pictures, most done in crayon, a couple in watercolor paint. The first four or five were very dark, painted in shades of gray and black and red, and populated by crude naked figures with the heads of birds. These were the pictures that Bill had told me about.

The rest of the artwork depicted variations on the same land-scape: trees, barren ground, decaying buildings. They were crude, with no great talent behind them, yet at the same time a huge amount of care had been lavished on some of them, while others were angry smears of black and green, still recog-nizably a version of the same locale, but created in a burst of anger and grief. Each picture was dominated by the shape of a great stone steeple. I knew the place, because I had seen it depicted before. It was Gilead.

'Why did you draw this place, Andy?' I asked.

'That's where it happened,' said Kellog. 'That's where they took me.'

'How do you know?'

'The second time, the bag slipped while they were carrying me in. I was kicking at them, and it nearly came off my head. That's what I saw before they pulled it back down again. I saw the church. I painted it so I could show it to Frank. Then they moved me to the Max and they wouldn't let me paint no more.

I couldn't even take them with me. I asked Miss Price to take care of them for me.'

'So Frank saw these pictures?'

'Uh-huh.'

'And you could remember nothing of the men who took you there?'

'Not their faces. I told you: they wore masks.'

'What about other marks? Tattoos maybe, or scars?'

'No.' He frowned. 'Wait. One of them had a bird, here.' He pointed to his left forearm. 'It was a white eagle's head, with a yellow beak. I think that was why he wore the eagle mask. He was the one who told the others what to do.'

'Did you tell the police this?'

'Yeah. I never heard nothing more, though. I guess it didn't help.'

'And Frank? Did you tell him about the tattoo?'

He screwed up his face. 'I think so. I don't remember.' His face relaxed.

'Can I ask a question?' he said.

Aimee looked surprised. 'Sure you can, Andy.'

He turned to me. 'You going to try to find these men, sir?' he asked. There was something in his voice that I didn't like. The boy was gone now, and what had taken its place was neither child nor adult but some perverse imp straddling both. His tone was almost mocking.

'Yes,' I said.

'You'd best hurry then,' he said.

'Why is that?'

Now the smile was back, but so was that hostile light.

'Because Frank promised to kill them. He promised to kill every one of them once he got out.'

And then Andy Kellog stood and threw himself face-first at the Plexiglas barrier. His nose broke immediately, leaving a smear of blood on the surface. He rammed it again, opening a wound on his forehead just below his scalp. And then he was shouting and screaming as the guards descended on him, and Aimee

Price was calling his name and begging them not to hurt him as an alarm sounded and more men appeared and Andy was submerged beneath a mass of bodies, still kicking and shouting, inviting new pain to drown the memory of the old.

18

The colonel of the guard was fuming quietly as we walked back to the reception lobby. There he left us for a time. Aimee took a seat and we waited in silence for Long to come back to us with news of Andy Kellog's condition. There were too many people around to enable us to talk about what had occurred. I looked at them, all caught up in their own pain and the misery of those whom they were visiting. Few spoke. There were older men who might have been fathers, brothers, friends. Some women had brought children along for the visit, but even the kids were quiet and subdued. They knew what this place was, and it frightened them. If they ran around, even if they spoke too loudly, they might end up in here like their daddies. They wouldn't be allowed to go home, and a man would take them and lock them up in the dark, because that was what happened to bad children. They got locked up, and their teeth rotted, and they beat their faces against Plexiglas screens to numb themselves into unconsciousness.

Long appeared at the lobby desk and gestured for us to join him. He told us that Andy's nose was badly broken, he had lost another tooth, and he had sustained some bruising during the attempt to subdue him, but otherwise he was as well as could be expected. The injury to his forehead had required five stitches, and he was now in the infirmary. They hadn't even Maced him, perhaps because his lawyer was present on the other side of the glass. There were no signs of concussion, but he would be kept under observation overnight, just in case. He had been restrained, though, to ensure that he didn't injure himself again, or try to hurt anyone else. Aimee retreated to use her cell phone in private, leaving me alone with Long, who was still angry at himself and the men under his command for what had happened to Andy Kellog.

'He's done that kind of thing before,' he said. 'I told them to keep a close eye on him.' He risked a glance at Aimee, an indication that he blamed her in part for making his men keep their distance.

'He doesn't belong in here,' I replied.

'Judge made that decision, not me.'

'Well, it was the wrong one. I know you heard what was said in there. I don't think he had much hope from the start, but what those men did to him took away what little there was. The Max is just making him crazier and crazier, and the judge didn't sentence him to gradual insanity. You can't keep a man locked up in a place like that with no possibility of release and expect him to stay balanced, and Andy Kellog was barely holding on to start with.'

Long had the decency to look embarrassed. 'We do what we can for him.'

'It's not enough.' I was railing at him, but I knew that it wasn't his fault. Kellog had been sentenced and imprisoned, and it wasn't Long's duty to question that decision.

'Maybe you think he was better off with his pal Merrick close by,' said Long.

'At least he kept the wolves at bay.'

'He wasn't much better than an animal himself.'

'You don't really believe that.'

He raised an eyebrow at me.

'You developing a soft spot for Frank Merrick? You better be careful or you're likely to find a knife in it.'

Long was both right and wrong about Merrick. I didn't doubt that he would hurt or kill without compunction, but there was an intelligence at work there. The problem was that Merrick was also a weapon to be wielded, and someone had found a way of using him to that end. But Long's words had struck home, just as Rachel's had. I did feel some sympathy for Merrick.

How could I not? I was a father too. I had lost a child, and I had stopped at nothing to hunt down the man responsible for her death. I knew too that I would do anything to protect Sam and her mother. How then could I judge Merrick for wanting to find out the truth behind his daughter's disappearance?

Still, such doubts aside, I now knew more than I had an hour before. Unfortunately, Merrick shared some of the same knowledge. I wondered if he had already begun scouting around Jackman and the ruins of Gilead for traces of the men who he believed were responsible for his daughter's disappearance, or if he had a lead on the man with the eagle tattoo. I would have to go to Gilead eventually. Each step that I took seemed to take me closer to it.

Aimee returned.

'I've made some calls,' she said. 'I think we can find a sympathetic judge who'll order a transfer to Riverview.' She turned her attention to Long. 'I'll be getting an independent psychiatric evaluation done on Andy Kellog over the next few days. I'd appreciate it if you could make the whole business as easy as possible.'

'It's got to go through the usual channels, but once I get the okay from the governor I'll hold the shrink's coat for him if it helps.'

Aimee seemed reasonably satisfied, and indicated that we should leave. As I moved to follow her, Long gently took my arm.

'Two things,' he said. 'First of all, I meant what I said about Frank Merrick. I saw what he was capable of doing. He near killed a guy who tried to take Andy Kellog's dessert once, left him in a coma over a plastic bowl of cheap ice cream. You're right: I heard what Andy Kellog had to say in there. Hell, I've heard it before. It's not news to me. You want to know what I think? I think Frank Merrick used Kellog. He stayed close to him so he could find out what he knew. He was always pumping him for information, trying to get him to remember all that he could about what those men did to him. In a way, he was responsible for winding Kellog up. He got him all upset, all riled up, and we had to deal with the consequences.'

That wasn't what I had been told at the hockey game, but I knew there was a tendency among ex-cons to sentimentalize some of those they had met. Also, in a place where kindnesses were at a premium, even small acts of human decency assumed monumental proportions. The truth, as in all things, probably lay in the gray area between what Bill and Long had said. I had seen how Andy Kellog had reacted to questioning about his abuse. Perhaps Merrick had managed to talk him down sometimes, but I didn't doubt that there were other occasions on which he had failed to do so, and Andy had suffered as a result.

'Second, about that tattoo your boy mentioned. You might be looking for a military man. That sounds like someone who could have been in the service once.'

'Any idea where I might start?'

'I'm not the detective,' said Long. 'But if I was, I might be looking south. Fort Campbell, maybe. Airborne.'

Then he left us, his bulk receding into the body of the prison.

'What was that about?' asked Aimee, but I didn't answer.

Fort Campbell, situated right on the border of Kentucky and Tennessee, home of the 101st Airborne Division.

The Screaming Eagles.

We separated in the parking lot. I thanked Aimee for her help, and asked her to let me know if there was anything I could do for Andy Kellog.

'You know the answer to that,' she said. 'You find those men, and you let me know when you do. I'll recommend the worst lawyer I can.'

I tried to smile. It died somewhere between my mouth and my eyes. Aimee knew what I was thinking.

'Frank Merrick,' she said.

'Yeah, Merrick.'

'I think you'd better find them before he does.'

'I could just leave them to him.'

'You could, except it's not just about him, or even Andy. In this case, justice has to be seen to be done. Someone has to answer publicly. Other children will have been involved. We need to find a way to help them too, or to help the adults they've become. We can't do that if these men are hunted down and killed by Frank Merrick. You still have my card?'

I checked my wallet. It was there. She tapped it with her finger.

'You get in trouble and you call me.'

'What makes you think I'm going to get in trouble?'

'You're a repeat offender, Mr Parker,' she said, as she climbed into her car. 'Trouble is your thing.'

19

Dr Robert Christian looked distracted and ill at ease when I called unexpectedly at his office on my way back from Warren, but he still agreed to give me a few minutes of his time. There was a patrol car parked outside when I arrived, a man seated in the back, his head resting against the screen dividing the interior of the car, the position of his hands indicating that he had been restrained. A policeman was talking to a woman in her thirties whose head kept moving from one point of a triangle to the next: from the cop, to two children seated in a big Nissan 4X4 to her right, then on to the man in the back of the patrol car. Cop, kids, man. Cop, kids, man. She had clearly been crying. Her kids still were.

'It's been a long day,' Christian said, as he closed the door of his office and collapsed into the chair behind his desk, 'and I haven't even eaten lunch yet.'

'The guy outside?'

'I can't really comment,' said Christian, only to relent a little. 'There is no easy aspect to what we do, but among the hardest, and the one that needs some of the most delicate handling, involves the moment when someone is forced to confront the accusations made against him. There was a police interview a couple of days back, and today the mother and children arrived here for a session with us only to find the father waiting for them outside. People react in different ways to allegations of abuse: disbelief, denial, rage. We don't often have to call the police, though. That was . . . a par-ticularly difficult moment for all involved.'

He began collecting papers from his desk, assembling them

into piles and inserting them into folders. 'So, Mr Parker, what can I do for you? I don't have much time, I'm afraid. I have a meeting up in Augusta in two hours with Senator Harkness to discuss the mandatory-sentencing issue, and I haven't prepared for it as well as I might have wished.'

State Senator James Harkness was a right-wing hawk with a sledgehammer attitude to just about every issue that came his way. Recently, he had been among those whose voices were raised loudest in favor of mandatory twenty-year sentences for those found guilty of gross sexual assault of a minor, even for those who copped a plea.

'Are you for, or against?'

'In common with most prosecutors, I'm against it, but to gentlemen like the good senator, that's a little like arguing against Christmas.'

'Can I ask why?'

'It's pretty simple: it's a sop to voters that will do more harm than good. Look, of every hundred allegations that get reported, about half will end up with law enforcement. Of that fifty, forty will get charged. Of that forty, thirty-five will plea-bargain, five will go to trial; and from that five, there will be two convictions and three acquittals. So, out of that initial hundred we have maybe thirty to forty sex offenders that we can register and of whom we can keep track.

'In the case of mandatory sentencing, there will be no incentive for alleged offenders to cop a plea. They might as well take their chances in court, and in general, prosecutors prefer not to go to trial on abuse allegations unless they have a solid case. The problem for us, as I told you when we last met, is that it can be very difficult to provide the kind of evidence necessary to secure a conviction in criminal court. So, if you introduce mandatory sentencing, there's a strong possibility that more offenders will slip through the net. We don't get them on the register, and they go back to doing whatever it was they were doing until someone catches them at it again. Mandatory sentencing allows politicians to appear tough on crime, but it's essentially counterproductive. Frankly, though, I'd have a better chance of making a chimp understand that than I will of convincing Harkness.'

'Chimps aren't concerned with reelection,' I said.

'I'd vote for a chimp over Harkness anyday. At least the chimp might evolve further at some stage. So, Mr Parker, have you made any progress?'

'A little. What do you know about Gilead?'

'I assume you're not testing my knowledge of biblical trivia,' he replied, 'so I take it you're referring to the Gilead community, and the "children of Gilead."'

He gave me a potted history, similar to what I already knew, although he believed that the scale of the abuse was greater than had previously been suspected. 'I've met some of the victims, so I know what I'm talking about. I think most of the people in Gilead knew what was happening to those children, and more of the men participated than was acknowledged at first.

'Then the families scattered after the bodies were found, and some of them were never heard from again. Others, though, cropped up in relation to other cases. One of the victims, the girl whose evidence led to the conviction of Mason Dubus, the man believed to be the ringleader of the abusers, did her best to keep track of them. A couple are in jail in other states, and the rest are dead. Dubus is the only one left alive, or the only one that we know of; even if others of whom we're not aware have survived, they're old, old men and women by now.'

'What happened to the children?'

'Some were taken away by their parents or guardians when the community disintegrated. We don't know where they went. The ones that were rescued were put in foster homes. A couple were taken in by Good Will Hinckley.'

Good Will Hinckley was an institution close to I-95 that provided a home and school environment for kids aged twelve to twenty-one who had suffered molestation, were homeless, or had been affected by substance or alcohol abuse, whether directly or as the result of the addictions of a family member. It had been in existence since the late nineteenth century, and graduated nine or ten seniors every year who might otherwise have found themselves in jail, or in the ground. It was not surprising that some of the children of Gilead had ended up there. It was probably the best thing that could have occurred, under the circumstances.

'How could it have happened?' I asked. 'I mean, the scale of it seems, well, almost incredible.'

'It was an isolated, secretive community in a state filled with isolated, secretive communities,' said Christian. 'From what we now know, it also seems to have been the case that the principal families involved had been aware of each other prior to their arrival at Gilead, and had worked together or maintained contact for a period of some years. In other words, there was already a structure in place that would have facilitated the kind of abuse that went on there. There was certainly a clear division between the four or five core families and those who arrived later: the women didn't mix with one another, the children didn't play with one another, and the men kept their distance as much as possible, apart from those occasions when work forced them together. The abusers knew exactly what they were doing, and were possibly even attuned to those who might share their tastes, so there was always new prey for them. It was a nightmare situation, but there was something about Gilead – bad luck, bad timing, bad location, or, well, let's call it a touch of evil and have done with it – that exacerbated it. You also have to take into account the fact that people weren't as aware of child abuse issues then as we are now. It wasn't until 1961 that a doctor named Henry Kempe wrote a paper called "The Battered Child Syndrome" and started a revolution on child abuse, but that paper concentrated principally on physical abuse, and even in the early seventies, when I started my training, sexual abuse was hardly mentioned. Then came feminism, and people began talking to women and children about abuse. In 1977, Kempe published "Sexual Abuse: Another Hidden

Pediatric Problem," and the realization that there was a real issue to be confronted probably stems from about then.

'Unfortunately, it could be said that the pendulum swung too far the other way. It created a climate of constant suspicion, because science hadn't caught up with the desire to deal with the problem. There was enthusiasm, but not enough skepticism. It led to a backlash, and decreased reporting in the nineties, but now we seem to be approaching some kind of equilibrium, even if we still sometimes concentrate on sexual abuse at the expense of other kinds of abuse. It's reckoned that twenty percent of children have been sexually abused by the time they reach adulthood, but the consequences of long-term neglect and physical abuse are actually much more severe. For example, a child who has been physically abused and neglected is much more likely to grow up to engage in criminal behavior than a child who has been sexually abused. Meanwhile, from data we know that sexual abusers of children are more likely to have been abused themselves, but most pedophiles have not been sexually abused. There,' he concluded. 'You got the lecture. Now, why the curiosity about Gilead?'

'Daniel Clay was interested in Gilead too. He created paintings of it. Someone told me that he even interviewed Mason Dubus, and he may have intended to write a book about what happened there. Then there's the fact that his car was found abandoned in Jackman, and Gilead isn't far from Jackman. It also appears that one of Clay's former patients was abused at or near Gilead by men wearing bird masks. All of that strikes me as more than a series of coincidences.'

'Well, it's probably not surprising that Clay was curious about Gilead,' said Christian. 'Most people in our field who work in Maine have at some point examined the available material, and a number of them would have interviewed Dubus, myself included.' He thought for a moment. 'I don't recall any descriptions of Gilead in the case reports relating to Clay, although there were mentions of rural settings. Some of the children caught sight of trees, grass, dirt. There were similarities too in their descriptions of the place in which they were abused – bare walls, a mattress on the floor, that sort of thing – although most of the victims were blindfolded for much of the abuse, so we're talking about snatched glimpses and nothing more.'

'Could these men have been drawn to Gilead because of what happened there in the past?' I asked.

'It's possible,' said Christian. 'I have a friend who works in the area of suicide prevention. He talks of "clusters of location," places that become sites of choice for suicide, largely because others have successfully committed suicide in those locations. One suicide facilitates another, or provides a stimulus for it. Equally, it might be that a place synonymous with the abuse of children could prove attractive to other abusers, but it would be quite a risk to take.'

'Could the risk have been part of the attraction?'

'Perhaps. I've been thinking a lot about this since you came to me. It's an unusual case. It sounds like stranger abuse on a significant scale, which is itself out of the ordinary. Children, unlike adults, are rarely victimized by strangers. Intrafamilial abuse accounts for fifty percent of the acts perpetrated against girls, and ten to twenty percent of those against boys. Generally, too, nonincestuous abusers fall into one of six categories based on their degree of fixation, from those who have frequent nonsexual contact with children to sadistic offenders who rarely have nonsexual contact with them. They're the kind who will typically view children unknown to them as victims, but the degree of violence inflicted on the children who mentioned the bird masks was minimal. In fact, only one child recalled being seriously physically injured, and she said the man who did it – he began choking her, to the point where she almost blacked out – was instantly rebuked by one of the others. That indicates a significant degree of control. These men weren't ordinary abusers, not by any means. There was planning, cooperation, and for want of a better word, restraint. Those elements make what happened particularly disturbing.'

'Are you sure that there have been no similar reports since Clay disappeared?'

'You mean reports of abuse that tally with those descriptions? Well, I'm as certain as I can be, given the information to hand. It was one of the reasons why suspicion fell on Clay, I suppose.'

'Could these men just have stopped abusing?'

'I don't think so. It's possible that some of them were jailed for other offenses, which would explain the cessation, but otherwise, no, I don't believe that they have stopped abusing. These men are predatory pedophiles. Their pattern of abuse might have altered, but their urges will not have gone away.'

'Why would they have altered their pattern?'

'Something could have happened, something that frightened them or caused them to realize that they risked drawing more attention to themselves if they continued to abuse in this way.'

'The daughter of a man named Frank Merrick drew pictures of men with the heads of birds,' I said.

'And Merrick's daughter is still missing,' said Christian, finishing my thought for me. 'I'm aware of the case.'

'The date of Clay's disappearance coincided roughly with the period when Lucy Merrick was last seen,' I said. 'And you've just told me that there were no more reports of children being abused by men in bird masks after that time.'

'None that I know of,' said Christian. 'I told you before, though: there's no easy way to track down those who might have been victims. It could be that such abuse did continue, but we didn't hear about it.'

But the more I considered it, the more it made sense. There was a connection between Clay's disappearance and that of Lucy Merrick, and perhaps a connection in turn between her disappearance and the fact that no other children had reported abuse by men masked as birds after that time.

'The death of a child: would that have been enough to frighten them, enough to make them stop what they were doing?' I asked.

'If it was accidental, then yes, possibly,' said Christian.

'And if it wasn't?'

'Then we would be looking at something else: not child abusers, but child killers.'

We were both silent then. Christian made some notes on a pad. I watched the day begin to fade, the angle of the light through the blinds on the window changing as the sun set. The shadows looked like prison bars, and I was reminded again of Andy Kellog.

'Does Dubus still live in the state?' I asked.

'He has a place near Caratunk. It's isolated. He's virtually a prisoner in his own home: he wears a satellite tracking device on his ankle, is medicated in an effort to subdue his sex drive, and is denied access to the Internet and cable television. Even his mail is monitored, and his telephone records are subject to examination as one of the conditions of his probation. Even though he's old, he's still a potential risk to children. You probably know that he served time for what happened at Gilead. He was subsequently incarcerated on three separate occasions for, off the top of my head, two counts of sexual assault, three counts of risk of injury to a minor, possession of child pornography, and a string of other offenses that all amounted to the same thing. He got twenty years the last time, suspended after ten with probation for life to ensure that he would be strictly monitored to the grave. Occasionally, graduate students or medical professionals will interview him. He makes a useful subject. He's intelligent, and clearheaded for a man in his eighties, and he doesn't mind talking. He doesn't have a whole lot of other ways to pass the time, I suppose.'

'Interesting that he should have stayed so close to Gilead.' Caratunk was only about thirty miles south of Gilead.

'I don't think he ever left the state again once he got here,' said Christian. 'When I interviewed him, he described Gilead as a kind of Eden. He had all the usual arguments at his fingertips: that children had a greater sexual awareness than we gave them credit for; that other societies and cultures looked more favorably on the union of children and adults; that the relationships at Gilead were loving, reciprocal ones. I hear variations on those themes all the time. With Dubus, though, I got the sense that he knew they were all a smoke screen. He understands what he is, and he enjoys it. There was never any hope that he might be rehabilitated. Now we just try to keep him under control, and use him to discover more about the nature of men like him. In that sense, he's been useful to us.'

'And the dead babies?'

'He blamed the women for that, although he wouldn't name any names.'

'Did you believe him?'

'Not for a moment. He was the dominant male figure in the community. If he didn't himself wield the weapon that killed those children, then he gave the order for their killing. But as I've said, those were different times, and you don't have to go very far back to find similar tales of the children of adulterous or incestuous relationships who conveniently die.

'Nevertheless, Dubus was still lucky to escape with his life when the people over in Jackman discovered what had been going on there. They might have had their suspicions, but when the bodies of the children were found, well, that changed everything. A lot of the buildings in the settlement were put to ruin. Only a couple were left standing, along with the shell of a half-completed church. Even those might be gone by now. I couldn't say. I haven't been up there in a long time, not since I was a student.'

There was a knock on his office door. The receptionist entered with a sheaf of messages and a cup of coffee for Christian.

'How would I get to talk to Mason Dubus?' I asked.

Christian took a huge draft of his coffee as he stood, his mind already moving on to other, more pressing matters, like bullish senators who valued votes over results.

'I can make a call to his probation officer,' he said, as he showed me out. 'There shouldn't be any problem with arranging a visit.'

When I got outside, the police car was gone. So too was the Nissan, but I saw it minutes later as I drove back to Scarborough. It was parked outside a doughnut shop, and through the window I thought I could see the children eating pink-and-yellow pastries from a box. The woman's back was to me. Her shoulders were hunched, and I thought she might have been crying.

I had one more house call to make that day. I had been thinking about the tattoo that Andy Kellog had mentioned, and of Joe Long's view that it might indicate someone who had served in the military, perhaps in an airborne division. I knew from experience that it was hard to track down that kind of information. The bulk of files pertaining to service records were kept at the National Personnel Records Center in St Louis, Missouri, but even if I did have a way to gain access to its database, which would be difficult to begin with, the access would be useless without some clue as to the possible identity of the man in question. If I had some suspicions, then it was possible that I could find someone to pull the 201 file, but it would mean calling in favors from outside, and I wasn't ready to do that yet. The Veterans Administration was also tight with information, and there weren't many people willing to risk a federal job with a pension by slipping files under the table to an investigator.

Ronald Straydeer was a Penobscot Indian from Oldtown who had served with the K-9 Corps during the Vietnam War. He lived out by Scarborough Downs, beside a bullet-shaped trailer that had once been home to a man named Billy Purdue but now served as a halfway house for the assorted drifters, ne'er-do-wells, and former comrades in arms who found their way to Ronald's door. He had been invalided out of the service, injured in the chest and left arm by an exploding tire on the day he left Nam. I was never sure what had hurt him more: the injuries he received, or the fact that he had been forced to

leave his German shepherd, Elsa, behind as 'surplus equipment.' He was convinced that the Vietnamese had eaten Elsa.
I think he hated that about them more than the fact that they
kept shooting at him when he was in uniform.

I knew that Ronald had a contact, a National Service officer
named Tom Hyland who worked with the Disabled American
Veterans, and who had helped Ronald to file his claim for benefits through the Veterans Administration. Hyland had handled
power of attorney for Ronald when he was trying to maneuver
his way through the system, and Ronald always spoke highly
of him. I had met him once, when he and Ronald were catching
up over chowder at the Lobster Shack by Two Lights State
Park. Ronald had introduced him to me as an 'honorable man,'
the highest praise that I had ever heard him accord to another
human being.

In his capacity as NSO, Hyland would have access to the
records of any veteran who had ever filed for benefits through
the VA, including those who might have served with an airborne
unit and who had enlisted from an address in the state of Maine,
or who were claiming benefits here. In turn, the DAV worked
with other service groups like the Vietnam Veterans of America,
the American Legion, and the Veterans of Foreign Wars. If I
could convince Ronald to tap Hyland, and Hyland in turn was
willing to do me a good turn, then I might be able to come up
with a potential shortlist.

It was almost dark when I got to Ronald's place, and the
front door was open. Ronald was sitting in his living room in
front of the TV, surrounded by cans of beer, some full but most
empty. There was a DVD of Hendrix in concert playing on the
TV, the sound turned down very low. On the couch across from
him sat a man who looked younger than Ronald, but infinitely
more worn. For his age, Ronald Straydeer was in good condition, with only a hint of gray to his short dark hair, and a frame
that had held off the onset of late-middle-age spread through
hard physical labor. He was a big man, but his friend was bigger
still, his hair hanging down in curls of yellow and brown, his

face grizzled with a three-day growth. He was also fried to the gills, and the smell of pot in the air made my head swim. Ronald seemed to be a little more together, but it was only a matter of time before he succumbed to the fumes.

'Man,' said his buddy, 'lucky you weren't the cops.'

'Helps if you lock the door,' I said, 'or even just close it. Makes it harder for them to enter.'

Ronald's friend nodded sagely. 'That is so right,' he said. '*Soooo* right.'

'This is my friend Stewart,' said Ronald. 'I served with his father. Stewart here fought in the Gulf first time around. We were talking about old times.'

'Fuckin' A,' said Stewart. He raised his beer. 'Here's to old times.'

Ronald offered me a beer, but I declined. He popped the tab on another Silver Bullet and almost drained it before letting it part from his lips.

'What can I do for you?' he asked.

'I'm looking for someone,' I said. 'He might have been in the service. He's got a tattoo of an eagle on his right arm, and a taste for children. I thought that if it didn't ring any bells for you, you might be able to ask around, or put in a word with your NSO friend, Hyland. This guy is bad news, Ronald. I wouldn't be asking otherwise.'

Ronald considered the question. Stewart's eyes narrowed as he tried to concentrate on what was being said.

'A man who likes children wouldn't go around advertising it,' said Ronald. 'I don't recall hearing about anyone who might have those tendencies. The eagle tattoo could narrow it down some. How do you know about it?'

'One of the children saw it on his arm. The man was masked. It's the only clue I have to his identity.'

'Did the kid get a look at the years?'

'Years?'

'Years of service. If he served, even if he just cleaned out latrines, he'd have added his years.'

I didn't recall Andy Kellog mentioning any numbers tattooed beneath the eagle. I made a note to ask Aimee Price to check it with him.

'And if there are no years?'

'Then he probably didn't serve,' said Ronald simply. 'The tattoo's just for show.'

'Will you ask around anyway?'

'I'll do that. Tom might know something. He's pretty straight but, you know, if there are kids involved . . .'

By now, Stewart had stood and was browsing Ronald's shelves, bopping gently to the barely heard sound of Hendrix, a fresh joint clasped between his lips. He found a photograph: a picture of Ronald in uniform squatting beside Elsa.

'Hey, Ron, man, was this your dog?' asked Stewart.

Ronald didn't even have to turn around to know what Stewart had found.

'Yes,' he said. 'That's Elsa.'

'Nice dog. It's a damn shame what happened to her.' He waved the photograph at me. 'You know, they ate his dog, man. They *ate* his *dog*.'

'I heard,' I said.

'I mean,' he continued, 'what kind of fucking people eat a man's dog?' A tear appeared in his eye and rolled down his cheek. 'It's all just one big damned shame.'

And it was.

20

Merrick had told the police that he was mostly sleeping in his car, but they didn't believe him, and I didn't either. That was why Angel had been detailed to follow him when he was released from jail. According to Angel, Merrick had picked up a cab at the rank beside the bus station, then had checked into a motel out by the Maine Mall before closing his drapes and, apparently, going to sleep. There was no sign of his red car at the motel, though, and when, after six hours, Merrick had still not made an appearance, Angel had taken it upon himself to find out what was going on. He had bought a takeout pizza, carried it into the motel, and knocked on the door of Merrick's room. When there was no reply, he broke into the room, only to find Merrick gone. There was a police cruiser at the motel too, probably dispatched for the same reason Angel had been, but the cop had enjoyed no more luck than Angel.

'He knew that someone might put a tail on him,' Angel said, as he and Louis sat in my kitchen, Walter, now returned once more from the care of the Johnsons, sniffing at Angel's feet and chewing on the ends of his laces. 'There must have been three or four different ways out of the place. That was probably why he chose it.'

I wasn't too surprised. Wherever Merrick had been holed up prior to his arrest, it wasn't at a shoppers' motel. I called Matt Mayberry to see if he had turned up anything useful.

'I've been kind of busy, otherwise I'd have called you myself,' Matt said when I eventually got through to him. He told me that he had concentrated his initial search on tax assessors' offices in the city of Portland and its immediate vicinity, before expanding it to a sixty-mile radius. 'I've found two so far. One is in Saco, but it's still tied up in litigation after nearly four years. Apparently, the city published a pending sale notice for its tax liens on some middle-aged man's property while he was receiving treatment for cancer, then without notice allegedly prematurely conducted a sealed-bid sale. Get this, though: when he refused to leave the property upon his release from the hospital they sent in a SWAT team to remove him forcibly. The man didn't even have hair! The hell is up with you people in Maine? The whole business is making its way through Superior Court at the moment, but it's moving at the pace of an arthritic tortoise. I've got copies of pretrial memoranda if you want to see them but they won't tell you much.'

'How is Eldritch involved in it?'

'He's the owner of record, as trustee. I ran a couple of additional searches on him, though, and I've found his name attached to various property sales as far west as California, but they're all old references and when I followed them up title had passed on again. The Maine sales are the most recent by a long shot, and, well, they don't follow the pattern of the others.'

'In what way?'

'Well, I couldn't swear to this, but it looks like at least part of Eldritch's business lies, or lay, in sourcing properties for individuals or companies who didn't want their names attached as owners. But, like I told you, most of the references I can find are prehistoric, which leads me to guess that Eldritch has since moved on to other things, or he's just not doing it as much, or he's simply learned to hide his tracks better. Some of these properties have a paper trail after them like you wouldn't believe, which could be a way of disguising the fact that, despite a blizzard of additional sales and transfers, de facto ownership of the premises in question remained the same. That's just a suspicion, though, and it would take a whole team of experts with a lot of time on their hands to prove it.

'The Saco sale looks like an error of judgment. Maybe Eldritch was instructed to find a property for a client, this one looked like a steal, then it all went to hell in a handcart because the city mishandled the whole business. It was probably just crossed wires, but the result was that Eldritch got caught up in the kind of legal quagmire that he seems to have spent so much time and effort trying to avoid.

'Which brings us to the second property, purchased within weeks of black flags rising over the Saco sale. It's near some place called Welchville. You ever hear of it?'

'Vaguely. I think it's somewhere between Mechanic Falls and Oxford.'

'Whatever. I couldn't even find it on a regular map.'

'It's not the kind of place that people put on regular maps. There's not a whole lot there. Hell, there's not a whole lot in Mechanic Falls, and Welchville makes it look like a metropolis.'

'Well, remind me to search someplace else for my retirement home. Anyhow, I found it eventually. The property is on Sevenoaks Road, close by Willow Brook. Doesn't look like there's much else nearby, which fits with what you just told me, so it shouldn't be hard to find. Number eleven-eighty. Don't know what happened to numbers one to eleven-seventy nine, but I guess they're out there somewhere. Those two properties are it for Maine so far. If you want me to widen the search it's going to take more time than I have, so I'll have to pass it on to someone else and he may not work for free like I do.'

I told Matt I'd let him know, but the Welchville property sounded like a good place to start. Welchville was close enough to Portland to make the city and its surrounds easily accessible, and far enough away to offer privacy, even a bolt-hole if necessary. People in places like Welchville and Mechanic Falls didn't go sticking their noses into other folk's business, not unless someone gave them a reason to do it.

The daylight was gone, but that suited us. It seemed wiser to approach the Welchville house under cover of night. If Merrick was there, then there was some chance that he might not see us coming. But I was also interested in the timing of Eldritch's purchase of the house. Merrick had been in jail when the house was bought, and was a long way from his eventual release, which meant either that Eldritch was planning very far ahead or the house was purchased for another purpose entirely. According to Matt, Eldritch was still the owner of record, but I couldn't see him spending much time in Welchville, which posed the question: who had been using the house for the last four years?

We took the Mustang, heading away from the coast, skirting Auburn and Lewiston until we left the bigger towns behind and entered rural Maine, even though it was within close reach of the state's largest city. Portland might have begun to sprawl, swallowing up smaller communities and threatening the identity of others, but out here the city could have been hundreds of miles away. It was another world of narrow roads and scattered houses, of small towns with empty streets, the quiet disturbed only by the rumble of passing trucks and the occasional car, and even they grew less and less frequent as we traveled farther west. Occasionally, a line of streetlights would appear, illuminating a stretch of road that was seemingly identical to all the rest yet, somehow, merited an individual touch courtesy of the county.

'Why?' asked Angel.

'Why what?' I said.

'Why would anyone live out here?'

We had barely left 495, and already he was feeling anxious for city lights. He was sitting in the backseat, his arms folded like a sulky child.

'Not everyone wants to live in a city.'

'I do.'

'Equally, not everyone wants to live close to people like you.'

Route 121 wound its lazy way through Minot and Hackett Mills, then Mechanic Falls itself, before intersecting with 26. There was less than a mile to go. Beside me, Louis removed a Glock from the folds of his coat. From behind, I heard the telltale sound of a round being chambered. If there was someone living on Sevenoaks Road, whether Merrick or an unknown other, we didn't expect him to be pleased to see us.

The house lay some way back from the road so that it remained invisible until we had almost passed it. I caught sight of it in the rearview: a simple, single-story dwelling, with a central door and two windows at either side of it. It was neither excessively run-down nor unusually well kept. It was simply . . . *there.*

We drove on for a time, following the upward slope of the road until I was certain that the sound of the engine would have faded from the hearing of anyone in the house. We stopped and waited. No other cars passed us on the road. Finally, I made a U-turn and allowed the car to coast back down the hill, then braked while the house was still out of sight. I pulled in to the side of the road, and we covered the rest of the distance on foot.

There were no lights burning in the house. While Louis and I waited, Angel scouted the perimeter to look for night-lights that might be activated by movement. He found none. He circled the house before signaling Louis and me to join him, using his Maglite, his fist wrapped tightly around it so that it was visible only to us.

'There's no alarm,' he said, 'not that I could see.'

It made sense. Whoever was using this place, whether it was Merrick or the person who was funding him, wouldn't want to give the cops an excuse to drop by while the place was unoccupied. Anyway, you could probably have counted the number of burglaries around here on the thumbs of one hand.

We drew closer to the house. I could see that slates on the roof had been repaired at some point over the last year or two, but the exterior paintwork was cracked and damaged in places. Weeds had colonized most of the yard, but the driveway had been sown with fresh gravel, and there was a weed-free space for one or two cars. The garage to one side of the house had a new lock on its door. The building itself had not been repainted, but neither did it seem in urgent need of any repair. In other words, all that was necessary to keep the property ready for use had been done, but no more. There was nothing to draw attention to it, nothing to attract a second glance. It was non-descript in the way that only the most purposeful self-effacement could be.

We checked the house one more time, avoiding the gravel and sticking to the grass in order to muffle our footsteps, but there was no sign of anyone inside. It took Angel a few minutes' work with a rake and a pick to open the back door, allowing us to enter a small kitchen with bare shelves and closets and a refrigerator that appeared to serve no purpose other than to add a comforting hum to the otherwise silent house. A trash can revealed the carcass of a roasted chicken and an empty plastic water bottle. The smell suggested that the chicken had been there for some time. There was also a crumpled pack of American Spirit cigarettes, Merrick's brand of choice.

We moved into the main hallway. Before us was the front door. To the left was a small bedroom furnished only with a worn sofa bed and a small table. The edge of an off-white sheet protruded from the innards of the sofa, the only splash of brightness visible in the gloom. Next to the bedroom was the main living area, but it had no furniture at all. Sets of fitted bookshelves occupied the alcoves at either side of the cold fireplace, but the only book that troubled them was a battered leather-bound Bible. I picked it up and leafed through it, but there were no markings or notes that I could see, and no name on the frontispiece to indicate the identity of its owner.

Angel and Louis had moved on to the rooms to the right: a bathroom, what might once have been a second bedroom, now also empty apart from the husks of insects trapped in the remains of last summer's webs like Christmas tree decorations left up past their time, and a dining room that bore traces of its past in the form of the marks of a table and chairs in the dust, as though the furniture had been spirited away without the intervention of any human agency, vanishing into the air like smoke.

'Here,' said Angel. He was in the hallway, pointing his Mag at a square door in the floor close by the side wall of the house.

The door was padlocked, but not for long. Angel disposed of the lock, then raised the door using a brass ring set into the wood. A flight of stairs was revealed disappearing into the darkness below. Angel looked up at me as if I was to blame.

'Why is everything always underground?' he whispered.

'Why are you whispering?' I replied.

'Shit,' said Angel loudly. 'I hate it when I do that.'

Louis and I knelt beside him.

'You smell that?' asked Louis.

I sniffed. The air below smelled a little like the chicken carcass in the kitchen trash, but the stink was very faint, as though something had once rotted down there and had since been removed, leaving only the memory of its decay trapped in the stillness.

I went down first, Angel behind me. Louis remained above, in case anyone approached the house. At first sight, the cellar appeared to be even emptier than the rest of the rooms. There were no tools on the walls, no benches at which to work, no boxes stored, no discarded relics of old lives resting forgotten beneath the main house. Instead, there was only a broom standing against one wall and a hole in the dirt floor before us, perhaps five feet in diameter and six feet deep. Its sides were lined with brick and its base was littered with shards of broken slate.

'Looks like an old well,' said Angel.

'Who builds a house on a well?'

He sniffed the air.

'Smell's coming from down there. Could be something buried beneath the stones.'

I got the broom and handed it to him. He leaned in and poked at the slates below, but it was clear that they were only inches deep. Beneath them was solid concrete.

'Huh,' he said. 'That's weird.'

But I was no longer listening, for I had noticed that the cellar was not as empty as it had first appeared. In a corner behind the stairs, almost invisible in the shadows, was a huge oak closet, the wood so dark and old that it looked almost black. I shined my flashlight on it and saw that it had been ornately carved, filigreed with leaves and creeping vines, less a piece of furniture carved by man than a part of nature itself that had become petrified in its present form. The doorknobs were made from cut glass, and a small brass key gleamed in the keyhole. I shined the light around the basement, trying to figure out how someone had managed to get the closet down here to begin with. The door and stairs were too narrow. At some point in the past, there might have been outer doors to the cellar from the yard, but I couldn't see where they might have been situated. It created the unsettling impression that the cellar had somehow been constructed around this old piece of dark oak for the sole purpose of giving it a quiet, dark place in which to rest.

I reached out and took hold of the key. It seemed to vibrate slightly between my fingers. I touched my hand to the wood. It too was trembling. The sensation appeared to come both from the closet itself and the ground beneath my feet, as though deep below the house some great machinery was grinding and throbbing to an unknown end.

'Do you feel that?' I said, but now Angel was both at once nearby and also a speck in the distance, as though space and time had momentarily warped. I could see him examining the hole in the cellar floor, still testing the slates for some clue as to the source of the smell, but when I spoke he didn't seem to hear, and my voice sounded faint even to myself. I turned the key. It clicked loudly in the lock, too loudly for such a small mechanism. I took a handle in each hand and pulled, the doors opening silently and easily to reveal what lay within.

There was movement inside. I lurched backward in shock, almost tripping over my own feet. I raised my gun, the flashlight held high and away from the weapon, and was blinded momentarily by the reflection of the beam.

I was staring at my own image, distorted and shaded with black. A small gilded mirror hung against the back of the closet. Beneath it were spaces for shoes and underwear, all built into

the body of the closet and all empty, the two sections divided
by a horizontal plane of wood that was almost entirely obscured
by a seemingly random assemblage of objects: a pair of silver
earrings, inset with red stones; a gold wedding ring, a date
engraved upon the interior – 'May 18, 1969'; a battered toy
car, probably dating back to the fifties, its red paint almost
entirely worn away; a faded photograph of a woman set in a
cheap locket; a small bowling trophy unmarked by a date or
its winner's name; a clothbound book of child's verses opened
to its title page, upon which the words 'For Emily, with Love
from Mom and Dad, Christmas 1955' had been written in a
crude, halting script; a tie pin; an old Carl Perkins '45, signed
by the man himself across the label; a gold necklace, the chain
broken as though it had been yanked from the wearer's neck;
and a wallet, empty apart from a photograph of a young woman
wearing the cap and gown of the newly graduated.

But these items were merely distractions, although everything about them suggested that they had been treasured at
some time by their owners. Instead, my attention was drawn
to the mirror. Its reflective surface had been severely damaged,
seemingly by fire or some other great heat, so that the wooden
backing was visible at its heart. The glass had warped, the edges
stained with brown and black, and yet it had not cracked and
the wood behind was not charred. The heat that had been
applied to cause such damage was so intense that the mirror
had simply melted beneath it, yet the backboard had been left
unmarked.

I reached out to touch it, then stopped. I had seen this mirror
before, and suddenly I knew who it was that was manipulating
Frank Merrick. Something twisted in my stomach, and I felt a
surge of nausea. I might even have spoken, but the words would
have made no sense. Images flashed through my mind, memories of a house—

'This is not a house. This is a home.'

Symbols on a wall in a dwelling long abandoned, revealed
only when the paper began to come away and loll in the hallway

like a series of great tongues. A man in a threadbare coat, with stains on his trousers and the sole coming away from the base of one of his shoes, demanding payment of a debt owed by another long believed dead.

'*This is an old and wicked world.*'

And a small, gilded mirror, held in this man's nicotine-stained fingers, an image reflected in it of a howling figure that might have been myself or might have been another.

'*He was damned, and his soul is forfeit . . .*'

Angel appeared beside me, looking blankly at the items in the closet.

'What is it?' he asked.

'It's a collection,' I said.

He moved closer, and seemed on the verge of picking up the toy car. I raised my hand.

'Don't touch it. Don't touch any of it. We need to get out of here. Now.'

And then he saw the mirror. 'What happened to—'

'It's from the Grady house,' I said.

He backed away in disgust, then looked over his shoulder in expectation of seeing the man who had brought the mirror to this place suddenly emerge from his hiding place, like one of the hibernating spiders in the rooms above alerted by the coming of spring's first insects.

'Aw, you got to be fucking kidding,' said Angel. 'Why is nothing ever normal?'

I closed the closet doors, the key still vibrating in the lock as I turned it, sealing away the collection once again. We climbed up from the cellar, slid the bolt across, and restored the padlock. Then we departed from that place. We left no signs of our trespass, and as Angel locked the back door behind us the house seemed just as it did when we had arrived.

But I felt it was to no avail.

He would know we had been there.

The Collector would know, and he would come.

21

The journey back to Scarborough was conducted in near silence. Both Angel and Louis had been in the Grady house. They knew what had taken place there, and they knew how it had ended.

John Grady was a child killer in Maine, and his house had been unoccupied for many years after his death. Thinking about it now, perhaps 'unoccupied' was the wrong word. 'Dormant' might have been more appropriate, for something had remained in the Grady house, some trace of the man who had given to it his name. At least, that is how it seemed to me, although it might just as easily have been shadows and fumes, the miasma of its history, and the remembrance of the lives lost there mingling to create phantasms in my brain.

But I was not the only one who suspected that something had secured itself in the Grady house. The Collector had appeared, a raggedy man with yellow nails, asking only that he be given permission to take a souvenir from the house: a mirror, and nothing more. He did not seem willing, or able, to enter the house himself, and I believed that at least one man, a minor thug named Chris Tierney, had died at the Collector's hands after he had dared to get in this strange, sinister man's way. But the permission that the Collector sought had not been mine to grant, and when he saw that he would not be given what he wanted, he had taken it anyway, leaving me bleeding on the ground.

And the last thing that I saw as I lay there, my skull blazing with pain from the force of the Collector's blow, was the image of John Grady trapped behind the glass of the mirror that the Collector had taken, screaming impotently as justice came for him at last.

Now that same mirror, charred and warped, lay beneath a deserted house, reflecting an assemblage of unrelated objects, tokens of other lives, of justice meted out by that emaciated figure. In the past, he had signed his name at least once as 'Kushiel': a black joke, the name stolen from hell's jailer, but nevertheless a hint as to his nature, or what he believed to be his nature. I felt certain that each of the items in that old closet represented a life taken, a debt paid in some way. I recalled the stink that hung over the pit in the cellar. I should make the call, I thought. I should bring the cops down on him. But what could I say? That I smelled blood, yet there was no blood to be seen? That there was a closet of trinkets in the cellar, but with only a first name here, a date there, to connect them to their original owners?

And what were you doing down in the cellar, sir? You do know that breaking and entering is a crime, don't you?

And there was another matter to be considered. I had encountered individuals in the past who were as dangerous as the Collector. Their natures, only some of which I could begin to explain or understand, had been corrupted, and they were capable of great evil. But the Collector was different. He was motivated by something other than a desire to inflict pain. He appeared to occupy a space beyond conventional morality, engaged in work that had no time for concepts of due process, of law or mercy. In his mind, those he sought had already been judged. He was merely executing the sentence. He was like a surgeon removing cancerous growths from the body, excising them with precision and casting the diseased parts into the fire.

Now he was manipulating Merrick, using him to draw unknown individuals from the shadows so that they might reveal themselves to him. Merrick had been in the house, if only for a time: the discarded pack and the rotting chicken told me as much. The Collector also smoked, but his tastes were a little more exotic than American Spirit. Through Eldritch, he had provided Merrick with a car, probably funds too, and also a place in which to stay, a base from which to operate but almost certainly with an injunction attached stipulating that he was not to enter any locked part of the house. And even if Merrick had disobeyed and made his way down to the cellar, would those items in the closet have meant anything to him? They would merely have appeared to be a random jumble, an eccentric amalgam of disparate items held in an old closet that vibrated to the touch, tucked into a corner of a cellar that reeked faintly of old, rotting things.

It was clear now that the Collector was looking for someone connected to Daniel Clay although, if Eldritch was to be believed, not Clay himself. There could be only one answer: he wanted those who had preyed on Clay's patients, the men who, if I was right, were responsible for whatever had happened to Lucy Merrick. So Eldritch had been engaged to ensure that Frank Merrick was freed and pointed in the right direction, but Merrick was not the kind of man to report his every move back to an ancient lawyer in a paper-filled office. He wanted revenge, and the Collector must have known that, at some point, Merrick would move entirely beyond his control. He would have to be shadowed, his movements revealed, so that any information he gleaned would automatically be shared with the one who had freed him to conduct his search. And when the men he sought at last made their move, then the Collector would be waiting, for there was a debt to be paid.

But who was shadowing Merrick? Again, there seemed to be only one possible answer.

Hollow Men.

Angel seemed to be following some of my thoughts.

'We know where he is,' he said. 'If he's tied in with this, then we can find him if we need to.'

I shook my head.

'It's a storehouse, nothing more. Merrick was probably allowed to use it for a while, but I'll bet he never made it down to the cellar, and I'll lay you another ten he never met anyone connected with the house apart from the lawyer.'

'The lock on the back door was new,' said Angel. 'I could

smell it. It had been changed recently, probably in the last day or two.'

'Merrick's key privileges might have been taken away. I don't think Merrick will care. It didn't look like he'd been there in a while, and he's the suspicious kind anyway. My guess is that he cut himself loose as soon as he could. He wouldn't want the lawyer to be able to keep tabs on him, but he had no idea who was bankrolling his search. If he did, he'd never have gone anywhere near that house.'

'But we're still ahead of this guy, right? We left that place just like we found it. We know he's involved, but he doesn't *know* that we know.'

'The fuck are you?' said Louis. 'Nancy Drew? Let him come. He's a freak. We had our share of freaks before. One more ain't goin' to capsize our boat.'

'This one's not like the rest,' I said.

'Why?'

'Because he doesn't take sides. He doesn't care. He just wants what he wants.'

'Which is?'

'To add to his collection.'

'You think he wants Daniel Clay?' asked Angel.

'I think he wants the men who abused Clay's patients. Either way, Clay is the key. The Collector is using Merrick to try to smoke them out.'

Louis shifted in his seat. 'What are the options on Clay?'

'Same as on everyone else: he's alive, or he's dead. If he's dead, then either he killed himself, like his daughter suspects, in which case the question is, why did he do it, or someone helped him along to the same end. If he was murdered, then it's possible that he had some idea of the identities of the men who were abusing those children, and they killed him to keep him quiet.

'But if he's alive, then he's concealed himself well. He's been disciplined. He hasn't contacted his daughter, or she says that he hasn't, which isn't the same thing at all.'

'You takin' her word for it, though,' said Louis.

'I'm inclined to believe her. There's also the Poole thing. She hired Poole to see if he could find her father, and Poole didn't come back. According to O'Rourke in the Portland P.D., Poole was an amateur, and he may have made some bad friends. His disappearance might not be linked to Clay's, but if it is, then either his questions brought him into contact with the men who killed Clay, and Poole died for his trouble, or he found Clay, and Clay killed him. In the end, there are only two possibilities: Clay is dead, and someone doesn't want questions asked about him, or he's alive and doesn't want to be found. But if he wants to stay hidden badly enough to kill someone in order to protect himself, then what is he protecting himself from?'

'It comes back to the children,' said Louis. 'Dead or alive, he knew more than he was telling about what happened to them.'

We were at the Scarborough exit. I took it and followed Route 1, then headed for the coast through moonlit marshes, toward the dark, waiting sea beyond. I drove past my own house, and Rachel's words came back to me. Perhaps she was right. Perhaps I was haunting myself. It wasn't a very consoling thought, but neither was the alternative: that, as at the Grady house, something had found a way to fill those spaces that remained.

Angel saw the way I looked at my home. 'You want us to come in for a while?'

'No, you've paid for your fancy room at the inn. You'd better enjoy it while you can. They don't do fancy up in Jackman.'

'Where's Jackman?' asked Angel.

'Northwest. Next stop, Canada.'

'And what's *in* Jackman?'

'We are, as of tomorrow, or the next day. Jackman's the closest piece of civilization to Gilead, and Gilead, or somewhere close enough to it, was where Andy Kellog was abused, and near where Clay's car was found. Kellog wasn't abused outdoors either, which means that someone had access to a property in the area. Either Merrick was up there already, and he didn't have any luck so he was forced to keep yanking Rebecca Clay's chain back down in Portland, or he hasn't made the connection yet. If he hasn't, then he soon will, but we can still be one step ahead of him.'

The bulk of the Black Point Inn loomed up before us, lights twinkling in the windows. They asked me if I wanted to join them for dinner, but I wasn't hungry. What I had seen in the cellar of that house had deprived me of my appetite. I watched them ascend the steps into the main lobby and vanish into the bar, then reversed the car and headed for home.

According to a note from Bob, Walter was over with the Johnsons. I decided to leave him there. They liked to go to bed early, even if Shirley, Bob's wife, never slept straight through due to the pain of her arthritis, and could often be seen reading at her window, a little night-light attached to her book so that she wouldn't wake her husband, or simply watching the darkness slowly fade into daylight. Still, I didn't want to risk waking them just so I could have the dubious pleasure of giving my dog a bonus walk on a winter's night. Instead, I locked the doors and put on some music: part of a Bach collection that Rachel had bought for me in an effort to broaden my musical parameters. I made some coffee and sat at my living room window, staring out at the woods and the waters, conscious of the movement of every tree, the swaying of every branch, the shifting of every shadow, and wondered at the ways of the honeycomb world that could have led my path and the path of the Collector to cross again. The mathematical precision of the music contrasted with the uneasy quiet of my home, and as I sat in the darkness I realized that the Collector frightened me. He was a hunter, yet there was something almost bestial about his focus and his ruthlessness. I had thought of him as a man unconcerned with morality, but that was not true: instead, it was more correct to say that he was motivated by some strange morality of his own, but it was rendered debased and unsavory by the assemblage of souvenirs that he had accumulated. I wondered if he liked to touch them in the darkness, remembering the lives that they represented, the existences ended. There was a sensuousness to their appeal for him, I thought, a manifestation of an urge that was almost sexual in nature. He took pleasure in what he did, and yet simply to call him a killer was incorrect. He was more complex than that. These people had done something to bring him upon them. If they were like John Grady, then they had committed some sin that was intolerable.

But intolerable to whom? To the Collector, yes, but I sensed that he believed himself to be merely an agent of another power. He might have been deluded in that belief, but nevertheless it was what gave him his authority and his strength, perceived or otherwise.

It was clear that Eldritch was a key, for it was Eldritch who sourced properties for him, bases from which he could move out into the world and do the work for which he believed he had been appointed. The property at Welchville had been acquired long before the possibility of Merrick's release became apparent. True, in the interim he had intervened in the Grady case and retrieved the mirror that now sat in the cellar closet, reflecting a distorted view of the world that might well have matched the Collector's own, and the other items in his trove suggested that he had been busy elsewhere too, yet none of this explained why the Collector made me so uneasy, or why he caused me to fear for my own safety.

Eventually, I left my chair and went to bed, and it was only when sleep threatened to take me that I understood my fear of the Collector. He was always looking, always searching. How he came by his awareness of the sins of others I did not know, but my fear was that I might be judged as others had been judged. I would be found wanting, and he would visit my punishment upon me.

That night, I dreamed the old dream. I was standing by a lake, and its waters were burning, but otherwise the landscape was flat and empty, the earth hard and blackened. A man stood before me, corpulent and grinning, his neck swollen by a great purple goiter but his skin otherwise pale, as though no blood flowed through the veins beneath, for what need have the dead of blood?

Yet this foul thing was not quite dead, for he had never truly been alive, and when he spoke, the voice I heard did not match the movements of his lips, the words spilling forth in a torrent of old languages long lost from the knowledge of men.

Other figures stood behind him, and I knew their names. I knew them all.

The words poured out of him in those harsh tongues, and somehow I understood them. I looked behind me, and saw myself reflected in the burning waters of the lake. For I was one with them, and they called me 'Brother.'

In a quiet township some miles away, a figure ascended a gravel drive, approaching the modest house from the road beyond even though there had been no sound of a car's engine to signal his arrival. His hair was greasy and slicked back from his head. He wore a threadbare dark overcoat and dark trousers, and in one hand there glowed the ember of a burning cigarette.

When he was steps from his house he paused. He knelt down and ran his fingers across the gravel, tracing some half-seen indentation, then rose and followed the wall of the house to the garden at the rear, the fingers of his left hand gently brushing the woodwork, the cigarette now discarded among the weeds. He reached the back door and examined the lock, then took a set of keys from his pocket and used one of them to enter.

He moved through the house, his fingers always searching, touching, exploring, his head slightly raised as he sniffed the air. He opened the empty refrigerator, fanned the pages of the old Bible, stared silently at the marks in the dust of what was once a dining room, until he came at last to the cellar door. This too he unlocked, descending into the last place, his place, yet giving no sign of anger at the trespass that had occurred. He brushed his fingertips against the handle of the broom, stopping when he found the point at which strange hands had gripped it. Again he leaned down, smelling the traces of sweat, picking out the man's scent so that he might know it again. It was unfamiliar to him, as was the second that he had encountered at the cellar door.

One of them had waited there. One waited, while two descended.

But one of those who had descended . . .

At last, he moved toward the great closet in the corner. He turned the key in the lock and opened the doors. His eyes took in his collection, ensuring that nothing was missing, that no item had been displaced. The collection was safe. He would have to move it now, of course, but it would not be the first time that part of his trove had been uncovered in such a way. It was a minor inconvenience, and nothing more.

The face of the ruined mirror found him, and he stared at his partial reflection for a moment, only his hair and the edges of his temples visible in what remained, his own features replaced by bare wood and fused glass. His fingers lingered on the key, caressing it, feeling the vibrations that coursed through it from deep, deep below. He drew in a final breath, as at last he recognized the third scent.

And the Collector smiled.

22

I awoke. It was dark and the house was silent, but it was not an empty darkness and it was not an easy silence. Something had touched my right hand. I tried to move it, but my wrist shifted only an inch or two before it was brought up short.

I opened my eyes. My right hand was cuffed to the frame of the bed. Frank Merrick was sitting on a straight-backed chair that he had placed by my bedside, his body leaning slightly forward, his gloved hands between his knees. He was wearing a blue polyester shirt that was too tight for him, causing the buttons to strain like the fastenings on an overstuffed couch. A small leather satchel lay between his feet, its straps untied. I had left my drapes open, and the descending moonlight shone upon his eyes, turning them to mirrors in the gloom. Immediately I looked for the gun on my nightstand, but it was gone.

'I got your piece,' he said. He reached behind his back and removed the Smith 10 from his belt, weighing it in his hand as he watched me. 'It's quite a piece of weaponry. A man's got to be serious about killing to carry a gun like this. This ain't no lady's gun, uh-uh.'

He shifted it in his hand, folding his fingers around the grip and raising it so that the muzzle was pointing straight at me.

'Are you a killer, is that what you are? Because if you think so, then I got bad news for you. Your killing days are almost done.'

He stood quickly and pressed the muzzle hard against my forehead. His finger lightly tapped the trigger. Instinctively, I closed my eyes.

'Don't do this,' I said. I tried to keep my voice calm. I did not want to sound as if I was pleading for my life. There were men in Merrick's line of work who lived for that moment: the catch in their victim's voice, the acknowledgment that dying was no longer an abstract future concept, that mortality had been given form and purpose. In that instant, the pressure of the finger on the trigger would increase and the hammer would fall, the blade would begin its linear work, the rope would tighten around the neck, and all things would cease to be. So I tried to keep the fear at bay, even as the words scraped like sand-paper in my throat and my tongue caught against my teeth, one part of me trying desperately to find a way out of a situation that was now far beyond its control while another focused only on the pressure against my forehead, knowing that it presaged a greater pressure to come as the bullet tore through skin and bone and gray matter, and then all pain would be gone in the blink of an eye, and I would be transformed.

The pressure against my forehead eased as Merrick removed the muzzle from my skin. When I opened my eyes again, sweat dripped into them. Somehow, I found enough moisture in my mouth to enable me to speak once more.

'How did you get in here?' I asked.

'Through the front door, same as any normal person.'

'The house is alarmed.'

'Is it?' He sounded surprised. 'Guess you might need to get that looked at, then.'

His left hand reached into the bag by his feet. He took out another set of cuffs and threw them at me. They landed on my chest.

'Slip one of them bracelets around your left wrist, then raise your left hand against the far bedpost. Do it slowly, now. I didn't have time to test the pull on this beauty, not with you waking up so suddenly and all, and I don't rightly know how much of a tap it might take to set her off. Bullet from a gun like this would make a real mess, even if I aimed it right and it killed you straight off. But if you was to panic me, well, there's no telling where it might end up. I knew a man once who got caught by a slug from a .22 in the brainpan, right here.' He tapped the frontal lobe above his right eye. 'I got to admit, I don't know what it did in there. I figure it must have rattled around some. Them little sonsofbitches will do that. Didn't kill him, though. Left him speechless, paralyzed. Hell, he couldn't even blink. They had to pay someone to put drops in his eyes so they wouldn't dry up.'

He stared at me for a moment or two, as though I had already become such a man.

'Eventually,' he continued, 'I went back, and I finished the job. I took pity on him, because it wasn't right to leave him that way. I looked into them unblinking eyes, and I swear that something of what he was had stayed alive in there. It was trapped by what I'd made him, but I released it. I set it free. I guess that would count as a mercy, right? I can't promise that I'd do the same for you, so you be real careful putting them cuffs on.'

I did as he had told me, leaning awkwardly across the bed so that my trapped right hand could close the cuff around my left wrist. Then I placed my left hand against the far bedpost. Merrick walked around the bed, the gun never wavering from me, his finger poised over the trigger. The sheet beneath my back was now drenched with perspiration. Carefully, using only his left hand, he secured the cuff, leaving me lying in a cruciform position. He moved in closer.

'You look scared, mister,' he whispered into my ear. His left hand brushed the hair from my brow. 'You're sweating like meat on a grill.'

I jerked my head away. Gun or no gun, I didn't want him touching me like that. He grinned, then stepped back from me.

'You can breathe easy for now. You answer me right and you may live to see another sunrise. I don't hurt anything, man or beast, that I don't have to hurt.'

'I don't believe that.'

His body tensed, as though, somewhere, an unseen puppeteer

had suddenly given his strings a tweak. Then he pulled the sheets away from my body, leaving me naked before him.

'I think you ought to watch what you say,' he said. 'It doesn't seem to me like it's smart for a man with his dick hanging out to start running off at the mouth in front of someone who could do him harm if he chose.'

It seemed absurd, but without that thin covering of cotton I felt more vulnerable than before. Vulnerable, and humiliated.

'What do you want?'

'To talk.'

'You could have done that in daylight. You didn't have to break into my house to do it.'

'You're an excitable man. I was worried that you might over-react. Then there's the small fact that last time we were due to meet, you screwed me over and I ended up with a cop's knee in my back. You could say that I owe you one for that.'

He moved the gun swiftly to his left hand, then knelt on my legs and punched me hard in the kidney. With my body held rigid there was no way that I could move to absorb the pain. It ran riot through my system, forcing bubbles of nausea into my mouth.

The weight came off my legs. Merrick picked up a glass of water from the bedside table, drank from it, then splashed the remainder on my face.

'That's a lesson I shouldn't ought to have been forced to teach you, but you been schooled again in it anyways. You cross a man, you can expect him to come back at you, uh-huh, yes you can.'

He returned to his chair and sat down. Then, in a gesture that was almost tender, he carefully pulled the sheet back over my body.

'All I wanted was to talk to the woman,' he said. 'Then she called you in, and you started interfering in matters that were no concern of yours.'

I found my voice. It came out slowly, like a startled animal emerging from its burrow to test the air for threats.

'She was frightened. It looks like she had good cause to be.'

'I don't hurt women. I told you that before.'

I let that go. I didn't want to anger him again.

'She didn't know what you were talking about. She believes her father is dead.'

'So she says.'

'You think she's lying?'

'She knows more than she's telling, is what I think. I have unfinished business with Mr Daniel Clay, uh-huh. I won't let it lie still until I see him before me, alive or dead. I want recompense. I'm entitled to it, yessir.'

He nodded once, deeply, as though he had just shared something very profound with me. Even the way he spoke and acted had changed somewhat, the little 'uh-huh's' and 'yessir's' becoming more frequent and pronounced. They were ticks, and I knew then that Merrick was drifting out of the control not only of Eldritch and the Collector, but of himself.

'You're being used,' I said. 'Your grief and anger are being exploited by others.'

'I been used before. It's a matter of understanding that, and of receiving proper payment for it.'

'And what's your payment here? Money?'

'Information.'

He let the barrel of the gun drop until it was pointed at the floor. A wave of tiredness seemed to wash over him, breaking against his face so that his features were altered, confused memories twisting and coiling in the aftermath. He dug his fingers deep into the corners of his eyes, then drew them across his face. For a moment, he looked old and frail.

'Information about your daughter,' I said. 'What did the lawyer give you? Names?'

'Maybe. Nobody else offered me help. Nobody else gave a damn about her. You know what it was like for me, being trapped in that jail knowing that something had happened to my little girl, knowing that there was nothing I could do to find her, to help her? Social worker came to the jail, told me my little girl was missing. Bad as it was before, when I figured out what had been done to her, this was worse. She was gone, and I knew she was in trouble. Have you any idea what that will do to a man? I tell you, it near broke me, but I wouldn't let that happen. I'd be no use to her that way, no sir, so I bided my time, and waited for my opportunity. I kept it together for her, and I didn't break.'

But he was broken. Something had fractured deep within him, and the flaw was progressing through his system. He was no longer as he once had been, but as Aimee Price had said, there was no way of knowing if he had been rendered more lethal, and more dangerous, as a result. They were two different things, though, and had I been pressed at that moment, as I lay incapacitated on my own bed, under my own gun, I would have said that he was more dangerous, but less lethal. His edge had been taken from him, but what had replaced it had rendered him unpredictable. He was now a prisoner of his own anger and sadness, and that had made him vulnerable in ways he could not even suspect.

'My little girl didn't just disappear into thin air,' he said. 'She was taken from me, and I'll find whoever was responsible for it. She may still be out there now, somewhere, waiting for me to come and take her home.'

'You know that's not true. She's gone.'

'You shut your mouth! You don't know that.'

I didn't care now. I was sick of Merrick, sick of them all.

'She was a young girl,' I said. 'They took her. Something went wrong. She's dead, Frank. That's what I believe. She's dead like Daniel Clay.'

'You don't know that. How do you know that about my little girl?'

'Because they stopped,' I said. 'After her, they stopped. They got scared.'

He shook his head forcefully. 'No, I won't believe it until I see her. Until they show me her body, then she's alive to me. You say otherwise again, and I'll kill you where you lie, I swear it. You mark me! Yessir, you mark me well.'

He was standing above me now, the gun poised in his hand, ready to fire. It shook slightly, the rage at the heart of his being transferring its energy to the weapon in his hand.

'I met Andy Kellog,' I said.

The gun stopped shaking, but it did not move from me.

'You saw Andy. Well, I guess you was going to figure out where I'd been sooner or later. How is he?'

'Not good.'

'He shouldn't ought to be in there. Those men tore something in him when they took him. They broke his heart. They're not his fault, the things he does.'

He looked down at the floor again, once more unable to keep the memories at bay.

'Your daughter drew pictures like Andy's, didn't she?' I asked him. 'Pictures of men with the heads of birds?'

Merrick nodded. 'That's right, just like Andy did. That was after she started seeing Clay. She sent them to me at the jail. She was trying to tell me something about what was happening to her, but I didn't understand, not until I met Andy. They were the same men. It's not just about my little girl. That boy was like a son to me. They'll pay for what they did to him as well. The lawyer Eldritch understood that. It wasn't about just one child. He's a good man. He wants those people found, just like I do.'

I heard someone laugh, and realized it was me.

'You think he's doing this out of the goodness of his heart? You ever wonder who is paying Eldritch, who employed him to secure your release, to feed you information? Did you take a look around that house in Welchville? Did you venture down into the cellar?'

Merrick's mouth opened slightly, and his features became clouded with doubt. Perhaps the thought had never struck him that there was someone other than Eldritch involved.

'What are you talking about?'

'Eldritch has a client. The client is manipulating you through him. He owns that house you crashed in. He's shadowing you, waiting to see who responds to your actions. When they emerge, he'll take them, not you. He doesn't care whether you find your daughter or not. All he wants is—'

I paused. I understood that to say what he wanted made no sense. To add to his collection? To dispense another form of justice in the face of the law's inability to act against these men? Those were elements of what he desired, but they were not enough to explain his existence.

'You don't know what he wants, if he even exists, and it don't matter anyway,' said Merrick. 'When the time comes, no man will take justice out of my hands. I want recompense. I told you that. I want the men who took my little girl to pay for what they did, to pay at my hand.'

'Recompense?' I tried to hide the disgust in my voice, but I could not. 'You're talking about your daughter, not some . . . *used car* that gave out on you a mile from the lot. This isn't about her. It's about you. You want to lash out at someone. She's just your excuse.'

The anger flared again, and once more I was reminded of the similarities between Frank Merrick and Andy Kellog, of the rage always bubbling away beneath their exteriors. Merrick was right: he and Kellog were like father and son, in some strange way.

'You shut the fuck up!' said Merrick. 'You got no idea what you're saying.'

The gun shifted hands again, and his right fist was suddenly poised above me, the knuckles ready to smash down upon me. And then he seemed to become aware of something, for he paused and looked over his shoulder, and as he did so I sensed it too.

The room had grown colder, and there was a noise from the hallway outside my door. It was soft, like the footsteps of a child.

'You alone here?' said Merrick.

'Yes,' I replied, and I couldn't tell if I was lying.

He turned around and walked slowly to the open door, then

stepped swiftly into the hallway, the gun held close to him in case someone tried to knock it from his grasp. He disappeared from view, and I could hear doors opening, and closets being searched. His shape passed by the doorway again, then he was downstairs, checking that all of the rooms were quiet and un-occupied. When he returned, he looked troubled, and the bedroom was colder still. He shivered.

'The hell is wrong with this place?'

But I was no longer listening to him, because I smelled her now. Blood and perfume. She was close. I thought Merrick might have smelled her too, because his nose wrinkled slightly. He spoke, but he sounded distant, almost distracted. There was an edge of madness to his voice, and I thought then that he was going to kill me for sure. I tried to move my lips to pray, but I could remember no words, and no prayers would come.

'I don't want you meddling in my affairs no more, you under-stand?' he said. His spittle landed on my face. 'I thought you was a man I could reason with, but I was wrong. You've caused me enough trouble already, and I need to make sure you don't trouble me again.'

He returned to the satchel on the floor and withdrew a roll of duct tape. He laid the gun down, then used the tape to cover my mouth before binding my legs tightly together above the ankles. He took a burlap sack and draped it over my head, securing it with more tape wrapped around my neck. Using a blade, he ripped a hole in the sacking just beneath my nostrils, so that I could breathe more easily.

'You listen to me, now,' he said. 'I got to put some harm your way, just to be sure that you got your days filled without worrying about me. After that, you mind your business, and I'll see that justice is done.'

Then he left me, and with him some of the chill departed from the room, as though something was following him through the house, marking his progress to ensure that he went. But another remained: a smaller presence, less angry than the first, yet more afraid.

And I closed my eyes as I felt her hand brush against the sackcloth.

daddy

Go away.

daddy, i'm here

A moment later there was another in the room. I felt her approach. I couldn't breathe properly. More sweat fell into my eyes. I tried to blink it away. I was panicking, suffocating, yet I could almost see her through the perforations in the sack, darkness against darkness, and smell her as she came.

daddy, it's all right, i'm here

But it wasn't all right, because she was approaching: the other, the first wife, or something like her.

hush

No. Get away from me. Please, please, leave me alone.

hush

No.

And then my daughter went silent, and the voice of the other spoke.

hush, for we *are here*

23

Ricky Demarcian was, from all outward appearances, a loser. He lived in a double-wide trailer that, for the early years of his occupancy, had left him freezing in winter and gently roasted him alive in summer, basting him in his own juices and filling every space with the stench of mold and filth and unwashed clothes. The trailer had been green once, but the elements had combined with Ricky's inept painting skills to take their toll upon it, fading it so that it was now a filthy, washed-out blue, like some dying creature at the bottom of a polluted sea.

The trailer stood at the northern perimeter of a park called Tranquility Pines, which was false advertising right there because there wasn't a pine in sight – no mean feat in the grand old state of Maine – and the place was about as tranquil as a nest of ants drowning in caffeine. It lay in a hollow surrounded by scrub-covered slopes, as though the park itself were slowly sinking into the earth, borne down by the weight of disappointment, frustration, and envy that was the burden carried by its residents.

Tranquility Pines was filled with screwups, many of whom, curiously, were women: vicious, foulmouthed harridans who still looked and dressed the same way they did in the eighties, all stone-washed denim and bubble perms, simultaneously hunters and hunted trawling the bars of South Portland and Old Orchard and Scarborough for ratlike men with money to spend, or muscle-bound freaks in wife-beater shirts whose hatred of women gave their temporary partners a respite of sorts from their own self-loathing. Some had kids, and the males among them were well on their way to becoming like the men who shared their mothers' beds, and whom they themselves loathed without understanding how close they were to following in their footsteps. The girls, meanwhile, tried to escape their family circumstances and their despised mothers by creating families of their own, thereby dooming themselves to become the very women they least desired to emulate.

There were male residents at the Pines too, but they were mostly like Ricky had once been: wasted men regretting wasted lives, some on welfare and some with jobs, although what work they had seemed mostly to involve gutting or cutting, and the smell of rotting fish and chicken skins acted as a kind of universal identifier for the park's residents.

Ricky used to have one of those jobs. His left arm was shriveled and useless, the fingers unable to grip or move, the result of some mishap in the womb, but Ricky had learned how to cope with the damaged limb, mainly by hiding it and forgetting about it for a time, until that moment in each day that life threw a curveball at him and reminded him of how much easier things would be if he had two hands to make the catch. It didn't help Ricky's employment prospects much either, although, even if he had boasted two functioning arms, his lack of, in no particular order, education, ambition, energy, resourcefulness, sociability, honesty, reliability, and general humanity would probably have ruled him out of any labor that didn't involve, well, gutting or cutting. So Ricky started on the bottom rung at a chicken processing plant that supplied meat for fast food joints, using a hose to spray blood, feathers, and chicken crap from the floors, his days filled with the sound of panicked clucking; with the casual cruelty of the men operating the line who took pleasure in tormenting the birds, adding extra agony to their final moments by breaking wings and legs; with the fizz of the current as the chickens, dangling upside down on a conveyor belt, were briefly immersed in electrified water, the action sometimes successfully stunning them but often failing, since the birds were so busy squawking and squirming that their heads frequently missed the water entirely, and they were still conscious when the multibladed slaughtering machines slit their throats, their bodies jerking as superheated water defeathered them, leaving their steaming carcasses ready to be chopped into bite-sized pieces of flesh that, raw or cooked, tasted of next to nothing.

The funny thing was, Ricky still ate chicken, even chicken from the plant in which he had once worked. The whole affair hadn't bothered him unduly: not the cruelty, not the casual attitude to safety, not even the foul stink as, truth be told, Ricky's own personal hygiene was unlikely to win him any prizes, and it was only a matter of getting used to a whole new array of odors. Still, Ricky recognized that being a chicken mopper was somewhat less than the mark of a successful, fulfilled life, and so he went looking for a less ignominious way to make a living. He discovered it in computers, for Ricky had a natural aptitude for the machines, a talent that, had it been recognized and cultivated at an earlier age, might well have made him a very wealthy man indeed, or so he liked to tell himself, disregarding the many personal failings that had led to his current modest status amid the pine-free and untranquil surroundings of his trailer park life. It began with Ricky's acquisition of an old Macintosh, then progressed through night school and computer books stolen from chain stores, until eventually he was downloading technical manuals and devouring them in single sittings, the disorder surrounding him in his daily existence standing in stark contrast to the clean lines and ordered diagrams taking form in his mind.

Unbeknownst to most of his neighbors, Ricky Demarcian was probably the wealthiest resident in the park, to the extent that he could easily have afforded to move to a more pleasant home. Ricky's relative wealth was due in no small part to his facility with promoting the kinds of activities that the Internet seemed ready-made to handle, namely those involving the sale of various sexual services, and, as Tranquility Pines had inadvertently given him his start in the business, gratitude had imbued in him an attachment to the place that prevented him from leaving.

There was a woman, Lila Mae, who entertained men for money in her trailer. She advertised in one of the local free papers, but despite her cunning efforts to throw the vice cops off the scent by not using her real name and not giving out her location until the john had made his way to her general vicinity, she got busted and fined repeatedly. Her name ended up in the newspapers, and it was all kind of embarrassing for her, because in places like Tranquility Pines, perhaps more so than in considerably more exalted surroundings, everyone needed someone else on whom to look down, and a whore in a trailer happily filled the bill for most of Lila Mae's neighbors.

She was a good-looking woman, at least by the standards of the park, and she had no desire to give up her reasonably lucrative profession to join Ricky Demarcian in hosing down a chicken slaughterhouse. So Ricky, who was familiar with Lila Mae's situation, and who enjoyed surfing the Net for sexual material of various stripes, and who had, in addition, an enviable grasp of the mysteries of Web sites and their design, suggested to her over a beer one night that maybe she might like to look at an alternative means of advertising her wares. They went back to Ricky's trailer, where Ricky showed her precisely what he meant, once Lila Mae had opened all of the windows and soaked a handkerchief in perfume so that she could hold it discreetly under her nose. She was so impressed with what she saw that she instantly agreed to allow Ricky to design something similar for her, and promised vaguely that, should he ever decide to take a proper bath, she might see fit to service him at a discount on his next birthday.

So Lila Mae was the first, but pretty soon other women began contacting Ricky through her, and he placed them all on one web site, with details of services offered, cost, and even portfolios of the women in question in the case of those who were agreeable and, more important, who were presentable enough not to frighten away the customers if the mysteries of their female forms were revealed. Unfortunately, Ricky became so successful at this that his endeavors attracted the attention of a number of very unhappy men who discovered that their status as minor pimps was being undermined by Ricky, since women who might otherwise have availed themselves of the protection offered by such individuals were instead operating as free agents.

For a time, it looked like Ricky might begin losing the use of other limbs, but then some gentlemen of Eastern European origin with connections in Boston contacted him and suggested a compromise. These gentlemen were mildly curious about the entrepreneurial nature of Ricky, and the women whose interests he looked after. Two of them traveled to Maine to talk to him, and an agreement was quickly reached that led to a change in Ricky's business practices in exchange for leaving him with the continued use of his single, unwithered arm, and guaranteed protection from those who might otherwise have taken issue with him in a physical way. Subsequently, the gentlemen returned, this time with a request that Ricky design a similar site for the women in their charge, as well as some more, um, 'specialized' options that they were in a position to offer. Suddenly Ricky found himself very busy indeed, and he was dealing with material upon which the law enforcement community was unlikely to look kindly, since some of it clearly involved children.

Finally, Ricky became a go-between, and crossed the line from dealing with pictures of women and, in some cases, children to facilitating those who were interested in a more active engagement with the objects of their fascination. Ricky never saw the women or children involved. He was merely the first point of contact. What happened after that was none of his business. A lesser man might have been worried, might even have suffered qualms of conscience, but Ricky Demarcian only had to think of dying chickens in order to banish any such doubts from his mind.

And so, while Ricky might have seemed a loser, living in a misnamed trailer park whose denizens were frequently on nodding terms with poverty, he was, in fact, quite comfortable in his squalor. He spent his money on constantly upgrading his hardware and software, on DVDs and computer games, on sci-fi novels and comic books, and on the occasional hooker whose details caught his fancy. He kept his trailer the way it was in order not to attract unwanted attention from the owners of the park, the IRS, or the law. He even showered more often, after one of the gentlemen from Boston complained that his new suit had smelled all the way back down I-95 after a visit to Ricky, and if that situation arose again, then Ricky would have to learn to peck at his keyboard using a chopstick attached to his forehead, because the gentleman from Boston would make good on his original threat to break Ricky's other arm and stick it up his ass.

And so it was that Ricky Demarcian, the Not-Such-a-Loser-Now, could be found in his trailer that night, tapping away at his keyboard, the long fingers of his right hand extended across the keys as he entered the information that would take a user with the right password and the right combination of point-and-clicks straight to some very dubious material. The system involved the use of certain trigger words familiar to those whose tastes extended to children, the most common being 'Lolly,' which most pedophiles recognized as an indication that their interest was being piqued. Typically, Ricky would give the name Lolly to an ordinary, unremarkable prostitute who, in fact, did not exist, her details and even her appearance a fiction cobbled together from the histories and bodies of other women. Once a potential customer had expressed an interest in Lolly, a further questionnaire would appear on-screen asking for 'preferred ages,' with options ranging from 'sixty plus' to 'barely legal.' If the latter category was ticked, an apparently innocuous e-mail would be sent back to the customer, this time with another trigger word – Ricky favored 'hobby' at this point, another term familiar to pedophiles – and so on until eventually a customer's credit card details would be requested and the flow of images and information would begin in earnest.

Ricky enjoyed working late at night. Tranquility Pines was

almost, well, tranquil at that time, since even the bickering couples and shouty drunks had usually quietened down some by three in the morning. Seated in the darkness of his home, lit only by the glow of his screen, and with the stars sometimes visible in the night sky through the skylight above his head, he might almost have been floating in space, and that was Ricky's great dream: to glide through the heavens in a huge ship, weightless and unencumbered, drifting through beauty and total silence.

Ricky didn't know how old the kids on the screen before him were – he judged twelve or thirteen at most; he was always bad with ages, except when it came to the really little ones, and even Ricky tried not to spend too much time looking at those pictures, because there were some things that didn't bear thinking about for too long – but it wasn't for him to police another man's tastes. Tap, tap, tap, and image after image found its rightful place in Ricky's great scheme, slotting into position in the virtual universe of sex and desire he had created. He was so lost in the sound and rhythm of what he was doing that the knocking at his trailer door was simply absorbed into the general cacophony, and it was only when the visitor increased the force of the impacts that Ricky started to discern the new noise. He paused in his labors.

'Who's there?' he said.

There was no reply.

He went to the window and pulled the drapes aside at one corner. It was raining slightly, and the glass was streaked, but still he could see that there was no one at the door.

Ricky didn't own a gun. He didn't like guns much. He wasn't a violent person. In fact, Ricky's views tended toward the cautious where guns were concerned. In his opinion, there were a lot of people out there who had no right to be carrying even a sharpened pencil, never mind a loaded weapon. Through a process of flawed logic, Ricky had formed an equation whereby guns equaled criminals, and criminals equaled guns. Ricky did not see himself as a criminal, and therefore he did not possess a gun. Alternatively, he did not possess a gun, and therefore he could not possibly be a criminal.

Ricky stepped away from the window and looked at the locked door. He could open it, he supposed, but there now appeared to be no reason for doing so. Whoever had been at the door was gone. He tugged at his lip, then went back to his computer. He had just commenced checking some of the code when the tapping came again, this time at the window he had recently left. Ricky swore and looked out once again into the night. There was now a shape at his door. It was a man, squat and powerful-looking, with a quiff of black hair that glistened with oil.

'What do you want?' said Ricky.

The man indicated with a nod of his head that Ricky should come to the door.

'Hell,' said Ricky. The man didn't look like any cop Ricky had ever seen. In fact, he looked more like one of the gentlemen from Boston, who had a habit of turning up unexpectedly at odd times. Still, you couldn't be too careful where such things were concerned. Ricky went back to his computer and entered a series of instructions. Instantly, windows began to close, firewalls were erected, images were encrypted, and a baffling series of false trails was put in place so that anyone attempting to access the material on his computer would quickly find himself in a maze of useless code and buffer files. If they persisted, the computer would go into virtual meltdown. Ricky knew too much about computers to believe that the material his machine contained would be inaccessible forever, but he reckoned it would take a team of experts many months before they even started retrieving anything worth further investigation.

He stepped away from his desk and walked to the door. He was not frightened. He was protected by Boston. The word had gone out on that a long time ago. He had nothing to fear.

The man on the step wore dark blue jeans, a blue polyester shirt that strained against his body, and a worn black leather jacket. His head was a little too large for his frame, although it also gave the disturbing impression that it had been compressed at one point, as if it had been placed in a vise from chin to crown. Ricky thought he looked like a thug, which, strangely, made him even more inclined to lower his guard. The only thugs with whom he dealt came from Boston. If the man on his step looked like a thug, then he must be from Boston.

'I like your place,' said the man.

Ricky's face furrowed in confusion.

'You've got to be kidding,' he said.

The man leveled a huge gun at Ricky. He wore gloves. Ricky wasn't to know it, but the gun was a Smith 10 designed for use by the FBI. It was an unusual gun for a private individual to own. While Ricky did not know that, the man holding the gun did. In fact, that was why he had chosen to borrow it earlier that night.

'Who are you?' asked Ricky.

'I'm the finger on the scales,' said the man. 'Back up.'

Ricky did as he was told.

'You don't want to do anything you'll regret,' said Ricky, as the man entered the trailer and pulled the door closed behind him. 'There are men in Boston who won't like it.'

'Boston, huh?' said the man.

'That's right.'

'Well, you think these men in Boston can get to you faster than a bullet?'

Ricky thought about the question.

'I guess not.'

'Well, then,' said the man, 'I reckon they ain't much use to you right now, no sir.' He took in the computer and the array of hardware that surrounded it. 'Very impressive,' he said.

'You know about computers?' asked Ricky.

'Not much,' said the man. 'That kind of thing passed me by. You got pictures on there?'

Ricky swallowed.

'I don't know what you're talking about.'

'Oh, I think you do. You don't want to be lying to me, now. You do that and, well, I'm likely to lose my temper with you, yessir, and seeing as how I have a gun and you don't, I don't think that would be in your best interests. So I'll ask you again: you got pictures on there?'

Ricky, realizing that a man who asked a question like that already knew the answer, decided to be honest.

'Maybe. Depends what kind of pictures you want.'

'Oh, you know the kind. Girlie pictures, like in the magazines.'

Ricky tried to breathe a sigh of relief without actually appearing to do so.

'Sure, I got girlie pictures. You want me to show you?'

The man nodded, and Ricky was relieved to see him tuck the gun into the waistband of his trousers. He sat down at his keyboard and brought the equipment back to life. Just before the screen began to glow he saw the man approach him from behind, his figure reflected in the dark. Then images began to appear: women in various stages of undress, in various positions, performing various acts.

'I got all kinds,' said Ricky, stating the obvious.

'You got ones of children?' said the man.

'No,' Ricky lied. 'I don't do kids.'

The man let out a warm breath of disappointment. It smelled of cinnamon gum, but it couldn't hide the mixed scents that the man exuded: cheap cologne, and a stink that was uncomfortably reminiscent of parts of the chicken factory.

'What's wrong with your arm?' he asked.

'Came out of my mother this way. It don't work.'

'You still got feeling in it?'

'Oh yeah, it just ain't no good for—'

Ricky didn't get to finish the sentence. There was a searing red-hot pain in his upper arm. He opened his mouth to scream, but the man's right hand clamped tightly across his face, smothering the sound while his left hand worked a long, thin blade into Ricky's flesh, twisting as he went. Ricky bucked in the chair, his screams filling his own head but emerging into the night air as only the faintest of moans.

'Don't play me for a fool,' said the man. 'I warned you once. I won't warn you again.'

And then the blade was plucked from Ricky's arm, and the hand released its grip upon his face. Ricky arched back in his chair, his right hand moving instinctively to the wound then immediately distancing itself from it again as the pain intensified at the touch. He was crying, and he felt ashamed for doing so.

'I'll ask you one more time: you got pictures of children on there?'

'Yes,' said Ricky. 'Yes. I'll show you. Just tell me what you want: boys, girls, younger, older. I'll show you anything, but please don't hurt me again.'

The man produced a photograph from a black leather wallet.

'You recognize her?'

The girl was pretty, with dark hair. She was wearing a pink dress, and had a matching ribbon in her hair. She was smiling. There was a tooth missing from her upper jaw.

'No,' said Ricky.

The blade moved toward his arm again, and Ricky almost screamed his denial this time. 'No! I'm telling you I don't know her! She's not on there. I'd remember. I swear to God, I'd remember. I got a good memory for these things.'

'Where do you get these pictures from?'

'From Boston, mostly. They send them to me. Sometimes I have to scan them in, but usually they're already on disk. There are films too. They come on computer disks or DVDs. I just put them on the sites. I've never hurt a child in my life. I don't even like that stuff. All I do is what I'm told to do.'

'You said "mostly."'

'Huh?'

'You said "mostly" you get them from Boston. Where else?'

Ricky tried to find a way to lie, but his brain wasn't working right. The pain in his arm was dulling slightly, but so was his mind. He felt sick, and wondered if he was going to faint.

'Sometimes, other people used to bring me stuff,' he said. 'Not so much anymore.'

'Who?'

'Men. A man, I mean. There was a guy, he brought me some good material. Videos. That was a long time ago. Years.'

Ricky was lying by omission. Strangely, the pain in his arm was helping him to keep his head clear by forcing him to recognize the possibility that more pain might be to come if he did not play this the right way. True, the man had brought him material, clearly home-filmed but of unusually high quality, even if it was a little static in its camera movements, but it was as a goodwill gesture. He was one of the first who had approached Ricky directly in the hope of renting a child for a few hours, referred to him by a mutual acquaintance in that part of the state, a man well known to those with such proclivities. The gentlemen in Boston had told him that it would happen, and they had been right.

'What was his name?'

'He never told me his name, and I didn't ask. I just paid him. It was good stuff.'

More half truths, more lies, but Ricky was confident in his abilities. He was far from stupid, and he knew it.

'You weren't afraid that he was a cop?'

'He wasn't no cop. You only had to take one look at him to know that.'

Snot dribbled from his nose, mingling with his tears.

'Where did he come from?'

'I don't know. Up north, somewhere.'

The man was watching Ricky carefully, and caught the way his eyes shifted again as he lied. Dave 'the Guesser' Glovsky might almost have been proud of him at that moment.

'You ever hear tell of a place called Gilead?'

There was the 'tell' again, the body betraying the difficulty the brain felt in disguising the lie.

'No, I never did, unless it was at Sunday school when I was a kid.'

The man was silent for a time. Ricky wondered if that had been a lie too far.

'You got a list of people who pay for all this?'

Ricky shook his head.

'It's done through credit cards. The men in Boston take care of it. All I have is e-mail addresses.'

'And who are these men in Boston?'

'They're Eastern Europeans, Russians. I only know first names. I have some numbers to call if there's trouble.'

Ricky swore. He thought he had made a mistake by telling his assailant once again that there would be repercussions for hurting him, that of course he would have someone to call if the operation was threatened. Ricky didn't want the man to be reminded that it might be better not to leave him alive. The man seemed to understand Ricky's concerns.

'Don't worry,' he said. 'I know you'll be expected to call them about this. I figured they'd hear about it one way or the other, uh-huh. It don't bother me none. Let 'em come. You can get rid of that stuff on your screen now.'

Ricky swallowed. He closed his eyes briefly in gratitude. He turned back to his computer and began clearing it of the images. His lips parted.

'Thank—'

The bullet blew a big hole in the back of Ricky's head, and tore a bigger one in his face as it exited. It shattered the screen, and something in the monitor exploded with a dull pop and began to burn acridly. Blood hissed and bubbled in the exposed workings. The ejected shell casing had bounced off a filing cabinet and lay close to Ricky's chair. Its position was almost too good, so the visitor tapped it with the side of his foot, sending it sliding over toward the trash basket. There were prints on the linoleum from his boots, so he found a rag in a closet, placed it on the floor, and used his right foot to erase the marks. When he was satisfied that all was clean, he opened the door slightly and listened. The sound of the gunshot had been very loud, but despite that the trailers on either side of Demarcian's were still dark, and elsewhere he could see the glow of TVs, could even hear what they were showing, the volume was turned up so high. He left the trailer, closing the door behind him, then disappeared into the night, pausing only at a gas station along the way to report a shot fired at Tranquility Pines, and a glimpse of what looked like an old Mustang speeding away from the scene.

Frank Merrick didn't like people getting in his way, but he had a certain amount of respect for the private detective. In addition, killing him would create more problems than it would solve, but killing someone else with the detective's gun would create just enough problems to keep him occupied, and only a few for Merrick.

Because Merrick knew that he was now entirely alone. He didn't care. He had tired of the old lawyer and his careful questions some time before, and Eldritch had made it clear when he came up to Portland after Merrick's arrest that their professional relationship was now at an end. The private detective's comments about Eldritch's motives and, more to the point, about whoever had instructed the lawyer to aid Merrick had only exacerbated his own doubts. It was time to finish this thing. There was still some business to be concluded down here, but then he would go northwest. He should have gone there long before now, but he had felt certain that some of the answers that he sought were in this small coastal city. But he was no longer so sure, and Gilead beckoned.

Merrick took the duct tape and stuck the detective's gun to the underside of the driver's seat. He had liked the feel of it in his hands. It had been a long time since he had fired a gun, longer still since he had done so in anger. Now he had the taste for it again. He had been careful not to carry a weapon, just in case the cops came for him. He did not want to be incarcerated again. But the time had come to act, and the detective's gun would be more than suitable for the work he had to do.

'It's all right, honey,' Merrick whispered, as he left the light of the gas station and headed east once more. 'Won't be long now. Daddy's coming.'

24

I lost track of time. Hours became minutes, and minutes became hours. My skin itched constantly from the touch of the sacking, and the sense of impending suffocation was never far away. Occasional whispers emerged from the shadows, sometimes close by, and sometimes farther away. Once or twice I began to doze, but the tape across my mouth hindered my breathing and almost as soon as I fell asleep I would wake again, breathing heavily through my nose like a thoroughbred after a long race, my heart rate increasing, my head straining away from the pillow as I struggled to draw in more oxygen. Twice, I thought that something touched my neck before I awoke, and the contact was so cold that my skin burned. When that happened, I tried to work the burlap off, but Merrick had secured it well. By the time I heard the front door open and close, followed by the heavy, deliberate tread of footsteps upon the stairs, I was completely disoriented, but even with my senses confused I was aware of presences receding, moving away from me as the stranger approached.

Someone entered the bedroom. I felt body heat close to me, and smelled Merrick. His fingers worked at the tape around my neck, and then the sack was removed and at last I was able to see again. Small white suns exploded in my field of vision, so that for a moment Merrick's features were indistinguishable to me. His face was a blank visage upon which I could paste whatever demon I chose, constructing an image of all that I feared. Then the spots before my eyes began to fade, and he was once again clear to see. He looked troubled and uncomfortable, no longer as assured as he had appeared when I had first awoken to find him by my bed, and his gaze drifted to the darker corners of the room. I noticed that he no longer stood with his back to the door. Instead, he seemed to be trying to keep it in sight, as though he were afraid to leave himself vulnerable to an approach from behind.

Merrick stared down at me, but he did not speak. He tugged at his lower lip with his left hand while he thought. There was no sign of my gun. Finally, he said: 'I done something tonight that maybe I ought not to have done. It's what it is, though, for good or ill. I got tired of waiting. Time has come to draw them out. It's going to cause you some trouble, mark me, but you'll get out of it. You'll tell them what happened here, and they'll believe you, in the end. In the meantime, word will spread, and they'll come.'

Then Merrick did something strange. He walked slowly to one of the bedroom closets, my gun now visible where it was tucked into his belt, and rested his left hand against the slatted door, his right drawing the Smith 10. He seemed almost to be peering through the slats, as though convinced that someone was hidden inside. When at last he opened it, he did so warily, slowly easing it open with his left hand and using the barrel of the gun to explore the spaces between the jackets, shirts, and coats hanging within.

'You sure you live here alone?' he asked.

I nodded.

'It don't feel like you're alone,' he said. There was no hint of a threat, no sense that he felt I had lied to him, only a deeper unease at something he did not understand. He closed the closet door softly and walked back to the bed.

'I got nothing against you personally,' he said. 'We're even now. I believe you do what you think is right, but you got in my way, and I couldn't have that. Worse, I think you're a man who lets his conscience bother him, and conscience is just a fly buzzing in your head. It's a nuisance, a distraction. I got no time for it. Never did.'

He slowly raised the gun. The muzzle regarded me blackly, like an empty, unblinking eye.

'I could kill you now. You know that. Wouldn't cost me much more than a drop of sorrow. But I'm going to let you live.'

I breathed out hard, unable to suppress a feeling that bordered on gratitude. I was not going to die, not at this man's hands, not today. Merrick knew the sound for what it was.

'That's right, you'll live, but you remember this, and don't you forget it, now. I had you in a mortal grip and I set you free. I know the kind of man you are, conscience or no conscience. You'll be all fired up about how I came into your house, how I hurt you, humiliated you in your own bed. You'll want to strike back, but I'm warning you that the next time I have you under the gun, I won't waste a breath before I pull the trigger. All of this will be over soon enough, and then I'll be gone. I've left you with enough to be thinking about. You save your anger. You'll have cause enough to use it again.'

He put away the gun and reached, once more, for his little satchel. He removed a small glass bottle and a yellow rag, then unscrewed the cap from the bottle and doused the rag with its contents. I knew the smell. It wasn't bad, and I could almost taste the sweetness of the liquid. I shook my head, my eyes growing wider as Merrick leaned over me, the rag in his right hand, the stink of the chloroform already making my head swim. I tried to buck my body, to lash out at him with my legs, but it was no use. He gripped my hair, holding my head still, and pressed the rag against my nose.

And the last words I heard were: 'It's a mercy, Mr Parker.'

I opened my eyes. Light streamed through the drapes. There were needles piercing my skull. I attempted to sit up, but my head felt too heavy. My hands were free, and the tape was gone from my mouth. I could taste blood upon my lips where its removal had torn the skin. I leaned over and reached for the waterglass on the night table. My vision was blurred, and I almost knocked it to the floor. I waited for the room to stop spinning, and for the twin images before me to come together before I tried again. My hand closed on it and I raised it to my lips. It was full. Merrick must have refilled it, then left it within easy reach. I drank deeply, spilling water on the pillow, then lay there for a time. I closed my eyes and tried to quell the sickness that was rising. Eventually, I felt strong enough to roll across the bed until I fell on the floor. The boards were cool against my face. I crawled to the bathroom and rested my head on the toilet bowl. After a minute or two I vomited, then descended once more into a poisoned sleep on the tiles.

The sound of the doorbell woke me. The texture of the light had changed. It must have been past noon. I stood, supporting myself against the bathroom wall until I was sure that my legs would not buckle beneath me, then staggered to the chair where I had left my clothes the night before. I pulled on jeans and a T-shirt, threw a hooded top on to ward off the cold, then tentatively walked barefoot down the stairs to the door. Through the glass, I could see three figures standing outside, and there were two unfamiliar cars in my drive. One was a Scarborough P.D. cruiser.

I opened the door. Conlough and Frederickson, the two detectives from Scarborough who had interviewed Merrick, were on my doorstep, along with a third man whose name I did not know, but whose face I remembered from Merrick's interrogation. It was the man who had been talking to the FBI man, Pender. Behind them, Ben Ronson, one of the Scarborough cops, leaned against his cruiser. Usually, Ben and I would exchange a few words if we passed each other on the road, but now his face was still and without expression.

'Mr Parker,' said Conlough. 'Mind if we come in? You remember Detective Frederickson? We have a few questions we'd like to ask you.' He indicated the third man. 'This here is Detective Hansen from the state police over in Gray. I guess you could say he's in charge.'

Hansen was a fit-looking man with very black hair and a dark shadow on his cheeks that spoke of too many years spent using a cheap electric razor. His eyes were more green than blue, and his posture, relaxed yet poised, suggested a wildcat about to spring on easy prey. He was wearing a nicely cut dark blue jacket. His shirt was very white, and his dark blue tie was striped with gold.

I stepped back and allowed them to enter. I noticed that none of them turned their backs on me. Outside, Ronson's hand had drifted casually toward his gun.

'Kitchen okay?' I said.

'Sure,' said Conlough. 'After you.'

They followed me to the kitchen. I sat down at the breakfast table. Ordinarily, I would have remained standing so as not to give them any advantage, but I still felt weak and uncertain on my legs.

'You don't look so good,' said Frederickson.

'I had a bad night.'

'Want to tell us about it?'

'You want to tell me why you're here first?'

But I knew. Merrick.

Conlough took a seat across from me while the others stayed standing. 'Look,' he said, 'we can clear all of this up here and now if you'll just be straight with us. Otherwise' – He glanced meaningfully in Hansen's direction – 'it could get awkward.'

I should have asked for a lawyer, but a lawyer would have meant a trip there and then to the Scarborough P.D., or maybe to Gray, or even Augusta. A lawyer would have meant hours in a cell or an interrogation room, and I wasn't sure that I was well enough to face that yet. I was going to need a lawyer eventually, but for now I was in my own home, at my own kitchen table, and I wasn't about to leave unless I absolutely had to.

'Frank Merrick broke into my home last night,' I said. 'He cuffed me to my bed' – I showed them the marks on my wrists – 'then he gagged me, blindfolded me, and took my gun. I don't know how long he left me like that. When he came back, he told me that he'd done something that he shouldn't have, then chloroformed me. When I came to, the cuffs and tape were gone. So was Merrick. I think he still has my gun.'

Hansen leaned back against the kitchen counter. His arms were folded across his body.

'That's quite a story,' he said.

'What gun did he take?' asked Conlough.

'Smith & Wesson, ten millimeter.'

'What load?'

'Cor-Bon. One-eighty grams.'

'Kinda tame for a ten,' said Hansen. 'You worried about the frame cracking?'

I shook my head in disbelief.

'You're kidding, right? The hell does that matter now?'

Hansen shrugged.

'Just asking.'

'It's a myth. You happy?'

He didn't reply.

'You got the ammo box for the Cor-Bons?' asked Conlough.

I knew where this was headed. I suppose I knew from the moment I saw the three detectives on my doorstep and, had I not felt so sick, I might almost have admired the circularity of what I suspected Merrick had done. He had used the gun on someone, but he had kept the weapon. If the bullet could be retrieved, then it could be compared with the box of rounds in my possession. It mirrored exactly the manner in which he had been linked to the killing of Barton Riddick in Virginia. Bullet matching might have been discredited, but as he had promised, he had still managed to do enough to land me in a lot of trouble. It was Merrick's little joke at my expense. I did not know how they had traced it back to me so quickly, but I suspected that was Merrick's doing as well.

'I'm going to have to call a lawyer,' I said. 'I'm not answering any more questions.'

'You got something to hide?' asked Hansen. He tried to smile, but it was an unpleasant thing, like a crack in old marble. 'Why you getting all lawyered up now? Relax. We're just talking here.'

'Really, is that what we're doing? If it's all the same to you, I don't care much for your conversation.'

I looked at Conlough. He shrugged.

'Lawyer it is, then,' he said.

'Am I under arrest?' I asked.

'Not yet,' said Hansen. 'But we can take that road, if you want to. So: arrest, or conversation?'

He gave me a cop stare, filled with false amusement and the certainty that he was in control.

'I don't think we've met before,' I said. 'I'm sure I would have remembered, just to make sure that I didn't have the pleasure again.'

Conlough coughed into his hand, and turned his face to the wall. Hansen's expression didn't change.

'I'm a new arrival,' said Hansen. 'I've been around some, though, done my time in the big cities – just like you, I guess, so your reputation doesn't mean shit to me. Maybe up here, with your war stories and the blood on your hands, you seem like a big shot, but I don't care much for men who take the law into their own hands. They represent a failure in the system, a flaw in the works. In your case, I intend to repair that flaw. This is the first step.'

'It's not polite to disrespect a man in his own home,' I said.

'That's why we're all going to leave now, so that I can continue disrespecting you someplace else.'

He waved his fingers, indicating that I should stand. Everything about his attitude toward me spoke of utter contempt, and there was nothing that I could do but take it, for the present. If I reacted further, I would lose my temper, and I didn't want to give Hansen the satisfaction of putting the cuffs on me.

I shook my head and stood, then put on an old pair of sneakers that I always kept by the kitchen door.

'Let's go, then,' I said.

'You want to lean against the wall there first?' said Hansen.

'You've got to be kidding,' I replied.

'Yeah, I'm a regular joker,' said Hansen. 'You and me both. You know what to do.'

I stood with my legs spread and my hands flat against the wall while Hansen patted me down. When he was happy that I wasn't concealing assorted weaponry, he stepped back and I followed him from the house, Conlough and Frederickson behind me. Outside, Ben Ronson already had the back door of the cruiser open for me. I heard a dog barking. Walter was racing across the field dividing my property from the Johnsons'. Bob Johnson was some ways behind Walter, but I could see the expression of concern on his face. As the dog drew nearer, I felt the cops tense around me. Ronson's hand went to his gun again.

'It's okay,' I said. 'He's friendly.'

Walter sensed that the men in the yard had no love for him. He paused at a gap in the trees overlooking the front yard and barked uncertainly, then slowly walked toward me, his tail wagging gently but his ears flat against his head. I looked at Conlough, and he nodded his okay. I went to Walter and rubbed his head.

'You have to stay with Bob and Shirley for a while, puppy,' I said. He pressed his head against my chest and closed his eyes. Bob was now standing where Walter had been minutes before. He knew better than to ask if everything was okay. I grabbed Walter by the collar and took him over to Bob, Hansen watching me all the way.

'Will you take care of him for a few hours?' I asked.

'It's no trouble,' he replied. He was a small, spry man, his eyes alert behind his spectacles. I looked down at the dog, and while I patted him one more time I quietly asked Bob to call the Black Point Inn. I gave him the number of the room in which Angel and Louis were staying, and told him to inform them that a man named Merrick had paid me a visit.

'Sure. Anything else I can do for you?'

I looked around at the four cops.

'You know, Bob, I really don't think so.'

With that, I got in the back of the black-and-white, and Ronson drove me to the Scarborough P.D.

25

They kept me in the interrogation room at Scarborough P.D. headquarters while we waited for Aimee Price to arrive, and once again I felt myself following in Merrick's footsteps. Hansen had wanted to take me to Gray, but Wallace MacArthur, who had come in when he heard that I was being questioned, lobbied on my behalf. I could hear him through the door vouching for me, urging Hansen to hold off the big dogs for a while. I was inexpressibly grateful to him, not so much for saving me an unpleasant trip to Gray with Hansen, but for being willing to step up to the plate when he must have had his own doubts.

Nothing had changed in the room since Merrick had occupied this seat. Even the childish doodles on the whiteboard were the same. I wasn't cuffed and Conlough had given me a cup of coffee and a stale doughnut. My head still hurt, but I was gradually waking up to the fact that I had probably said too much back in the house. I still didn't know what Merrick had done, but I was pretty certain that someone was dead because of it. In the meantime, I realized that I had effectively admitted my gun had been used in the commission of a crime. If Hansen decided to play hardball and charge me, I could find myself behind bars with little hope of making bail. At the very least, he could hold me for days, leaving Merrick to wreak havoc with the Smith 10.

After an hour alone with my thoughts, the door of the interrogation room opened and Aimee Price was admitted. She was wearing a black skirt and jacket, and a white blouse. Her briefcase was shiny and made of expensive leather. She looked all business. I, by contrast, looked terrible, and she told me so.

'Do you have any idea what's happening?' I asked.

'All I know is that they're investigating a shooting. One fatality. Male. Clearly, they think you may be able to help them with some details.'

'Like how I shot him.'

'Bet you're glad you held on to my card now,' she said.

'I think it brought me bad luck.'

'You want to tell me how much?'

I went through everything with her, from Merrick's arrival at the house to Ronson putting me in the back of the cruiser. I left nothing out, apart from the voices. Aimee didn't need to hear about that.

'How dumb are you?' she said when I was done. 'Children know better than to answer a cop's questions without a lawyer being present.'

'I was tired. My head was hurting.' I realized how pathetic I sounded.

'Dummy. Don't say another word, not unless you get the nod from me.'

She went back to the door and knocked to indicate that the cops could enter. Conlough came in, followed by Hansen. They took seats across from us. I wondered how many people were crowded around the computer monitor outside, listening to the questions and answers being relayed from the room, watching four figures dance around one another without moving.

Aimee held up a hand.

'You need to tell us what this is about first,' she said.

Conlough looked to Hansen.

'A man named Ricky Demarcian died last night. He was shot in the head over at a trailer park named Tranquility Pines. We have a witness who says that a Mustang matching the one owned by your client was seen driving away from the scene. He even gave us the tag number.'

I could imagine what was happening at Tranquility Pines as we spoke. The state CID's crime scene unit would be there, along with the white truck of Scarborough's own evidence technician, its rear doors personalized with blow-ups of his thumbprints. He was regarded as one of the best evidence techs in the state, a painfully meticulous man, and it was unlikely that the state guys would discourage him from working along-side their own people. The red-and-white mobile command center, used in conjunction with the fire department, would also be present. There would be bystanders, rubberneckers, potential witnesses being interviewed, trucks from the various local network affiliates, a whole circus converging on one little trailer in one sorry trailer park. They would take casts at the scene, hoping to match the treads to the tires on my Mustang. They wouldn't find any matches, but it wouldn't matter. They could argue that the car might have been parked on the road, away from the dirt. Absence of a link to my car wouldn't prove my innocence. Meanwhile, Hansen had probably set in motion the processes necessary to secure a warrant to search my home, including my garage, if he didn't already have one. He would want the car, and the gun. In the absence of the latter, he would settle for the box of Cor-Bon ammunition.

'A witness?' said Aimee. 'Really?' She gave the word just enough spin to suggest that she found this about as believable as a rumor that the Tooth Fairy had been nabbed with a bag of teeth. 'Who's the witness?'

Hansen didn't move, but Conlough shifted almost impercep-tibly in his chair. No witness. The tip-off was anonymous, in which case it came from Merrick. It didn't help my situation, though. I knew from their questions about the ammunition that Merrick had used my gun to kill Demarcian, and had probably left evidence at the scene. Was it just a bullet or a shell casing, or had he left the gun as well? If he had, then my prints, not his, would be all over it.

I got to put some trouble your way, just to be sure that you got your days filled without worrying about me.

'We can't say right now,' said Hansen. 'And I hate to sound like a bad movie, but we're supposed to be asking the questions.'

Aimee shrugged. 'Ask away. First of all, though, I'd like you to get a doctor in here. I want the bruises on my client's side photographed. You'll see that they contain marks that look like the impact of a fist. A doctor will be able to say how recent they are. He has also recently lost skin from his lips due to the removal of the tape from his mouth. We'll want those injuries photographed too. I'd also like to get blood and urine samples taken to confirm the presence of above-average levels of trichloromethane in my client's bloodstream.'

She fired these demands out like bullets. Conlough seemed to take the full force of them.

'Trichlo-what?' he asked, looking to Hansen for help.

'Chloroform,' explained Hansen. He didn't appear ruffled. 'You could just have said chloroform,' he added to Aimee.

'I could, but it wouldn't have sounded half as impressive. We'll wait for the doctor to arrive, then you can start asking your questions.'

The two detectives left without saying anything further. After another hour had passed, during which Aimee and I sat in silence, a doctor arrived from the Maine Medical Center in Scarborough. He escorted me to the men's room, and there I gave a urine sample, and he took some blood from my arm. When he was done, he examined the bruising on my side. Aimee entered with a digital camera and took photographs of the bruises and the cuts to my lips. When she was done, we were escorted back to the interrogation room, where Conlough and Hansen were already waiting for us.

We went through most of the earlier questions again. Each time, I waited for Aimee to indicate that it was safe to answer before I opened my mouth. When it got to the subject of the ammunition, though, she raised her pen.

'My client has already told you that Mr Merrick stole his weapon.'

'We want to be certain that the ammunition matches,' said Hansen.

'Really?' asked Aimee, and there it was again, that sweetened skepticism, like a lemon coated in castor sugar. 'Why?'

Hansen didn't answer. Neither did Conlough.

'You don't have the gun, do you, detectives?' said Aimee. 'You don't have a witness either. All you have, at a guess, are a discarded shell casing, and probably the bullet itself. Am I right?'

Hansen tried to stare her down, but eventually gave up. Conlough was staring at his fingernails.

'Am I right?' Aimee said again.

Hansen nodded. He looked like a chastened schoolchild.

As I had guessed, it was a nice touch. Merrick had left the same kind of evidence at the scene that at one point might have been used to convict him. No court would now convict on that basis alone, but Merrick had still succeeded in muddying the waters.

'We can get a warrant,' said Hansen.

'Do that,' said Aimee.

'No.'

Aimee glared at me. Hansen and Conlough both looked up.

'You won't need a warrant.'

'What are you – ,' began Aimee, but I stopped her by placing my hand on her arm.

'I'll hand over the ammunition. Match away. He took my gun and used it to kill Demarcian, then left the casing and made the call so you'd come knocking on my door. It's his idea of a joke. Merrick was facing a murder trial in Virginia on the basis of a bullet match and nothing more, but the case fell apart when the FBI started making panicked noises about the reliability of the tests. Even without that, the case probably wouldn't have held up. Merrick did it to cause me trouble, and that's all.'

'And why would he do that?' asked Conlough.

'You know the answer. You interviewed him in this room. His daughter disappeared while he was in jail. He wants to find out what happened to her. He felt I was getting in his way.'

'Why didn't he just kill you?' asked Hansen. He sounded like he could have forgiven Merrick the impulse.

'It wouldn't have been right, not in his eyes. He has a code, of sorts.'

'Not enough of a code to stop him from putting a bullet through Ricky Demarcian's head, assuming you're telling the truth,' said Hansen.

'Why would I want to kill Demarcian?' I asked. 'I never even heard of him until this morning.'

Again, Conlough and Hansen exchanged glances. After a few seconds, Hansen let out a deep breath and made a 'go ahead' gesture with his right hand. He already seemed on the verge of giving up. His earlier confidence was dissipating. The bruising, the tests to confirm the traces of chloroform, all had rattled him. Secretly, too, I think he knew I was telling the truth. He just didn't want to believe it. It would have given him some pleasure to lock me up. I offended his sense of order. Still, however much he disliked me, he was enough of a by-the-book cop not to want to rig the evidence, only to have the case explode in his face the first time it went before a judge.

'Demarcian's trailer was packed to the gills with computer equipment,' said Conlough. 'We think he had ties to organized crime in Boston. Seems like he took care of some escort Web sites.'

'For the Italians?'

Conlough shook his head. 'Russians.'

'Not good people.'

'Nope. We heard talk that it wasn't just older escorts either.'

'Kids?'

Conlough looked to Hansen again, but Hansen had retreated into a studied silence.

'Like I said, it was talk, but there was no evidence. Without evidence, we couldn't get a warrant. We were working on it, trying to find a way onto Demarcian's list, but it was slow.'

'Looks like your problem is solved,' I said.

'You sure you never heard of Demarcian?' asked Hansen. 'He sounds like the kind of guy you'd have no problem shooting in the head.'

'What do you mean by that?' I asked.

'Wouldn't be the first time that gun of yours made a hole in someone. You might just have felt that Demarcian was a deserving cause.'

I felt Aimee's hand touch my leg gently under the table, warning me not to be drawn out by Hansen.

'You want to charge me with something, go ahead,' I said. 'Otherwise, you're just using up good air.' I turned my attention back to Conlough. 'Was the gunshot the only injury to Demarcian?'

Conlough didn't answer. He couldn't, I supposed, without giving away what little evidence they still had against me. I kept going.

'If Merrick tortured him first, then it could be that Demarcian told him something he could use before he died.'

'What would Demarcian know?' asked Conlough. The tone of the interview had altered. Perhaps Conlough hadn't been convinced of my involvement right from the start, but now we had moved from an interrogation situation to two men thinking aloud. Unfortunately, Hansen didn't care much for the new direction. He muttered something that sounded like 'bullshit.' Even though Hansen was ostensibly in charge, Conlough glanced at him in warning, but the remains of the fire that had been lit in Hansen still glowed, and he wasn't about to extinguish it unless he had no other choice. He gave it one last try.

'It's bullshit,' he repeated. 'It's your gun. It's your car the witness saw leaving the scene. It's your finger—'

'Hey!' Conlough interrupted him. He stood and walked to the door, indicating that Hansen should follow him. Hansen threw back his chair and went. The door closed behind them.

'Not a fan of yours?' said Aimee.

'I've never met him properly before today. State cops don't care much for me as a rule, but he has a terminal beef.'

'I may have to juice up my rates. Nobody seems to like you.'

'Occupational hazard. How are we doing?'

'Okay, I think, apart from your inability to keep your mouth shut. Let's assume Merrick used your gun to kill Demarcian. Let's assume also that he made the call about your car. All they have is ballistic evidence, and no direct connection to you apart from the box of shells. It's not enough to charge you with anything, not until they get a ballistics match, or a print from the casing. Even then, I can't see the AG's office going ahead unless the cops come up with more evidence linking you to the scene. They won't have trouble getting a warrant to search your home for the box of ammunition, so you may be right just to hand it over. If things turn bad, it might help us with a judge if you've cooperated from the start. If they have the gun, though, then we could find ourselves with real difficulties.'

'Why would I leave my gun at the scene?'

'You know they won't think that way. If it's enough to hold you, then they'll use it. We'll wait and see. If they have the gun, they'll spring it on us soon enough. My guess, though, from watching you and Detective Conlough bond over the table, is that the gun went with Merrick.'

She tapped her pen on the table.

'Conlough doesn't seem to like Hansen much either.'

'Conlough's okay, but I don't think he'd put it past me to kill someone like Demarcian either. He just figures I'd do a better job of covering my tracks if I did kill him.'

'And maybe you'd have waited until he had a gun in his hand,' added Aimee. 'Jesus, it's like the Wild West.'

The minutes ticked by. Fifteen. Twenty. Thirty.

Aimee checked her watch. 'What the hell are they doing out there?'

She was about to get up and find out what was going on when I heard a peculiar, yet familiar, sound. It was a dog barking. It sounded a lot like Walter.

'I think that's my dog,' I said.

'They brought your dog in? As what, a witness?'

The door of the interrogation room opened and Conlough entered. He looked almost relieved.

'You're off the hook,' he said. 'We'll need you to sign a statement, but otherwise you're free to go.'

Aimee tried to hide her surprise, but failed. We followed Conlough outside. Bob and Shirley Johnson were in the reception area, Bob standing and holding Walter on the end of a leash, Shirley sitting on a hard plastic chair, her wheeled walker beside her.

'Seems the old lady doesn't sleep so good,' said Conlough. 'She likes to sit at her window when her joints hurt. She saw your guy leave the house at three A.M. and then return at five. She swore a statement to say your car never left its garage, and you didn't leave the house. The three-five window matches Demarcian's time of death.' He smiled grimly. 'Hansen's pretty pissed. He liked you for the shooting.'

Then the smile faded.

'You don't need me to remind you, but I will anyway. Merrick has your gun. He used it to kill Demarcian. I was you, I'd be looking to get it back before he uses it again. In the meantime, you ought to learn to take better care of your property.'

He turned on his heel. I went over to the Johnsons to thank them. Predictably, Walter went nuts. A short time later, my statement duly signed, I was allowed to leave. Aimee Price drove me home. The Johnsons had gone ahead with Walter, mainly because Aimee refused to have him in her car.

'Any word on Andy Kellog's transfer?' I asked.

'I'm trying to get a hearing over the next day or two.'

'You ask him about that tattoo?'

'He said there were no dates, no numbers. It was just an eagle's head.'

I swore silently. It meant that Ronald Straydeer's contact would be of no help. Another line of inquiry had ended in nothing.

'How is Andy?'

'Recovering. His nose is still a mess.'

'And mentally?'

'He's been talking about you, and about Merrick.'

'Anything interesting?'

'He thinks Merrick is going to kill you.'

'Well, he wasn't far off the mark, but Merrick had his chance. He didn't take it.'

'It doesn't mean he won't try again. I don't understand why he wants you out of the way so badly.'

'He's a revenger. He doesn't want anyone to deprive him of his chance of retribution.'

'He thinks his daughter's dead?'

'Yes. He doesn't want to admit it, but he knows it's the truth.'

'Do you think she's dead?'

'Yes.'

'So what are you going to do now?'

'I have another lawyer to visit, then I'm going to head up to Jackman.'

'Two lawyers in one day. You must be mellowing.'

'I've had my shots. I should be okay.'

She snorted, but didn't reply.

'Thanks for coming out here,' I said. 'I appreciate it.'

'I'm billing you. It wasn't charity.'

We pulled up in front of my house. I got out of the car and thanked Aimee again.

'Just remember,' she said. 'I'm a lawyer, not a doctor. You tangle with Merrick again and my services won't be much use to you.'

'I tangle with Merrick again and one of us won't need a doctor or a lawyer. He'll be beyond the help of either.'

She shook her head. 'There you go with the Wild West stuff again. You take care of yourself. I can't see anyone else willing to do it.'

She drove away. I walked over to the Johnsons and had a cup of coffee with them. Walter would have to stay with them for a few more days. They didn't mind. I don't think Walter minded either. They fed him better than I did. They even fed him better than I fed myself. Then I went home, showered to remove the smell and feel of the interrogation room, and put on a jacket and shirt. Conlough was right. I had to find Merrick before he used the Smith 10 again. I knew where to start, too. There was a lawyer down in the Commonwealth with some questions to answer. I had avoided confronting him again until now, but I no longer had a choice. As I dressed, I thought about why I had delayed talking to Eldritch again. It was partly because I believed that he wouldn't be of much help unless the stakes were raised, and Merrick's killing of Demarcian had certainly done that. But I also knew that there was another reason for my reluctance: his client. Against my better judgment, and against all of my strongest instincts, I was being drawn inexorably into the world of the Collector.

IV

Into the dark night
Resignedly I go,
I am not so afraid of the dark night
As the friends I do not know,
I do not fear the night above,
As I fear the friends below.

Stevie Smith, Dirge

26

I made the call while I was slipping a speed loader for the .38 into my jacket pocket. Louis answered on the second ring. He and Angel had hit the Collector's safe house within an hour of Bob Johnson's call to the inn, and had left a message on my cell informing me that they were, to use Angel's words, 'in country.'

'So I figure you got busted from the joint,' said Louis.

'Yeah, it was spectacular. Explosions, gunfire, the whole deal. You ought to have been there.'

'Anywhere be better than here.'

He sounded tetchy. Spending long periods of time with his partner in an enclosed space tended to do that to him. I figured their home life must be something to see.

'You say that now. Before this is over, I'll bet you'll be looking back fondly on your time spent in that car. You find anything?'

'We got nothing 'cause there's nothing to get. House is empty. We check before we start freezing our assess off out here. Nothing's changed since then. We still freezing our asses off. Place still looked the same, except for one small difference: the closet in the basement was empty. Looks like the freak moved his collection.'

The Collector knew that someone had been in his house; he had discovered the trespass in his own way.

'Leave it,' I said. 'If Merrick hasn't returned there by now, he's not going to.'

It had been a long shot to begin with. Merrick knew that the house would be the first place we would look for him. He had gone underground instead. I told Louis to have Angel drop

him in Augusta, then pick up a rental car and drive back to
Scarborough. Angel would head north to Jackman to see what
he could find out there, as well as keeping watch for Merrick,
because I was certain that Merrick would head for Jackman,
and Gilead, eventually.

'How come he get to go to Jackman and I got to stay down
there with you?' asked Louis.

'You know when you drop a lump of coal in snow?' I said.

'Yeah.'

'Well, that's why you're not going to Jackman.'

'You a closet racist, man.'

'You know, sometimes I almost forget you're black.'

'Yeah? Well, I never forget you're white. I seen you dance.'

With that, he hung up.

My next call was to Rebecca Clay to inform her that Merrick
was well and truly off the leash. She didn't take the news well,
but agreed to let Jackie Garner shadow her again, with the
Fulcis in tow. Even if she hadn't agreed, I would have brow-
beaten her into it eventually.

Moments after I finished talking to Rebecca, I received a
call from an unexpected source. Joel Harmon was on the end
of the line: not his secretary, not Todd, the driver who knew
how to hold a gun, but the man himself.

'Someone broke into my house early this morning,' he said.
'I was up in Bangor last night so I wasn't there when it happened.
Todd discovered the damage to the window this morning.'

'Why are you telling me this, Mr Harmon?' I wasn't on Joel
Harmon's dime, and my head still ached from the chloroform.

'My office was ransacked. I'm trying to figure out if anything
was taken. But I thought you might be interested to know that
one of Daniel Clay's paintings was vandalized. Nothing else
was damaged in the same way, and none of the other paintings were touched, but the Gilead landscape was torn apart.'

'Don't you have an alarm system?'

'It's hooked up to the telephone. It was bypassed.'

'And there was nobody in the house?'

'Only my wife.' There was a pause. 'She slept through it all.'

'That's quite a deep sleep, Mr Harmon.'

'Don't be a smart-ass. You've met her. You don't need me to tell you that she's doped up to the eyeballs. She could sleep through the apocalypse.'

'Any indication of who might have been responsible?'

'You talk like a fucking lawyer, you know that?' I could almost hear the spittle landing on the phone. 'Of course I have a fucking idea! He took out the phone, but one of the security cameras on the grounds picked him up. The Scarborough cops came out here and identified him as Frank Merrick. This is the same guy who's been terrorizing Rebecca Clay, right? Now I hear he may have blown some deviant's head off in a trailer park on the same night he busted into the house where my wife was sleeping. The hell does he want from me?'

'You were a friend of Daniel Clay's. He wants to find him. Maybe he figured you'd know where he was.'

'If I knew where he was, I'd have told someone long before now. My question is, how did he know to come looking for me?'

'I found out about you and Clay easily enough. So could Merrick.'

'Yeah? Well how come that the night you came to see me, the car Merrick was driving at the time was seen outside my property? You know what I think, you fucking asshole? I think he followed you. You brought him to my door. You put my family at risk, all for a man who's long dead. You prick!'

I hung up. Harmon was probably right, but I didn't want to hear about it. I had enough baggage to carry already, and too much on my mind to worry about his painting, or his anger at me. At least the damage confirmed my suspicion that Gilead was Merrick's ultimate destination. I felt as if I had spent a week wading through mud, and I regretted the day that Rebecca Clay had called me. I wasn't even sure what I was looking for anymore. Rebecca had hired me to get rid of Merrick, and instead he was roaming wild. Ricky Demarcian was dead, and the use of my gun made me culpable in his killing. According to the police, Demarcian had been involved in child pornography, and possibly even the supply of women and children to clients. Someone had handed him on a plate to Merrick, who might simply have killed him out of rage, finding in Demarcian's shooting a convenient outlet for some of his own anger at whoever was responsible for what had happened to his daughter, or he might have learned something from Demarcian before his death. If he did, then Demarcian was also a piece of the puzzle, linked to Clay and Gilead and abusers with the faces of birds, but the man with the eagle tattoo, the only solid means of identifying those responsible for abusing Andy Kellog and, it seemed, Lucy Merrick, remained elusive. I couldn't talk to any more of the victims because they were protected by bonds of confidentiality, or by the simple fact that nobody was aware of who they were. And I was still no closer to discovering the truth about Daniel Clay's disappearance, or the extent of his involvement in the abuse of his patients, but nobody had asked me to do that anyway. I had never felt more frustrated, more at a loss as to how to proceed.

So I decided to place my head in the lion's mouth. I made a call and told the woman on the other end of the phone that I was on my way to see her boss. She didn't reply, but it didn't matter. The Collector would find out soon enough.

The office of Eldritch and Associates was still knee deep in old paper and short on associates when I arrived. It was also short of Eldritches.

'He ain't here,' said the secretary. Her hair was still big and still black, but this time her blouse was dark blue with a white frilled collar. An overlarge silver crucifix hung from a chain around her neck. She looked like a minister who specialized in cheap lesbian weddings. 'You hadn't hung up so soon, I'd have told you you were wasting your time coming down here.'

'When are you expecting him back?'

'When he comes back. I'm his secretary, not his keeper.'

She fed a sheet of paper into an old electric typewriter and began tapping out a letter. Her cigarette never moved from the corner of her mouth. She had perfected the art of puffing on it without touching it with her hand until it became necessary to do so in order to prevent the dangling column of ash from sending her to meet her maker in an inferno of burning paper, assuming her maker was prepared to own up and claim her.

'Maybe you could call him and let him know that I'm here,' I said, after a couple of minutes had passed in noncompanionable silence.

'He doesn't use a cell phone. He doesn't like 'em. Says they give you cancer.' She squinted at me. 'You use a cell phone?'

'Yes.'

'Good.'

She returned to her typing.

I took in the nicotine-encrusted walls and ceiling. 'A safe workplace is a happy workplace,' I said. 'I can wait for him.'

'Not here you can't. We're closing for lunch.'

'Kind of late for lunch.'

'It's been a busy day.'

She finished typing, then carefully removed the letter from the typewriter. The letter was then added to a pile of similar documents in a wire tray, none of which looked like they were ever likely to be sent. Some of those at the bottom had already yellowed.

'Do you ever get rid of any of this stuff?' I asked, indicating the stacks of paper and dusty files.

'Sometimes people die,' she said. 'Then we move their files to a storage facility.'

'They could die here, and just be buried under paper.'

She stood and retrieved a drab olive overcoat from a battered coatrack.

'You have to go now,' she said. 'You're just too much fun for me.'

'I'll come back after lunch.'

'You do that.'

'Any idea when that might be?'

'Nope. Could be a long one.'

'I'll be waiting when you return.'

'Uh-huh. Be still, my heart.'

She opened the office door and waited for me to leave before locking it with a brass key that she kept in her purse. Then she followed me down the stairs and double-locked the main door before climbing into a rusted brown Caddy parked in Tulley's lot. My own car was down the block. There didn't seem to be much more that I could do other than to get a bite to eat and wait around in the hope that Eldritch might materialize, unless I just gave up and drove home. Even if Eldritch made an appearance, he wasn't my principal reason for being there. It was the man who paid his bills. I couldn't force Eldritch to tell me more about him. Well, I could, but I found it hard to imagine myself grappling with the old lawyer in an effort to make him confess what he knew. At worst, I saw him disintegrate into fragments of dust in my hands, staining my jacket with his remains.

And then a pungent hint of nicotine stung my nostrils, blown toward me by the wind. The smell was peculiarly acrid, heavy with poisons, and I could almost feel cells in my body threatening to metastasize in protest. I turned around. The dive bar at the opposite end of the block from Tulley's was open for business, or at least as open as it could be when its windows were covered with wire mesh, its windowless door scuffed and scarred, and the lower half blackened where an attempt had been made to set it on fire. A sign at eye level advised that anyone who looked under the age of twenty-one would be asked for identification. Someone had altered the '2' to make it look like a '1.'

A man stood outside, his dark hair slicked back, the ends congregating in a mass of untidy, greasy curls just below his collar. His once-white shirt had faded to yellow, the collar unbuttoned to reveal dark stains along the inside that no amount of washing could ever remove. His old black coat was frayed at the ends, the stray threads moving slowly in the breeze like the legs of dying insects. His trousers were too long, the ends touching the ground and almost entirely obscuring the thick-soled shoes that he wore. The fingers that clutched the cigarette were burned a deep yellow at the tips. The nails were long and furrowed, with dirt impacted beneath them.

The Collector took a final drag on the cigarette, then flicked it neatly into the gutter. He held in the smoke, as though draining it of every last iota of nicotine, then released it in wisps from his nostrils and the corners of his mouth so that he appeared to be burning within. He regarded me silently through the fumes, then opened the door to the bar and, with a last glance in my direction, disappeared inside.

After only a moment's pause, I followed.

27

The interior of the bar wasn't nearly as bad as its façade might have led a casual observer to expect. On the other hand, the façade suggested that the interior would be occupied by intoxicated twelve-year-olds and frustrated firebugs, so it didn't have to do much to exceed those expectations. It was dark, lit only by a series of flickering lamps on the walls, as the windows facing the street were masked by thick red drapes on the inside. A bartender in a startlingly white shirt prowled the long bar to the right, three or four of its stools occupied by the usual assortment of daytime rummies blinking indignantly at the unwelcome shaft of sunlight from the open door. The bar was strangely ornate, and behind it, reflecting the rows of liquor bottles, were tarnished mirrors bearing the names of whiskeys and beers that had long since ceased to exist. The floor was made of exposed boards, scuffed by decades of traffic, and burnt here and there by the discarded butts of dead smokers, but clean and, it seemed, freshly varnished. The brasswork on the stools, the footrests at the bar, the coat hooks all gleamed, and every table had been dusted and bore fresh coasters. It was as though the exterior had been deliberately designed to discourage casual custom, while retaining a degree of sophistication within that spoke of a once noble past.

A series of booths took up the wall to the left, with a scattering of round tables and old chairs between the booths and the bar. Three of the booths were occupied by office workers eating what looked like good salads and club sandwiches. There seemed to be an unspoken divide between the bar crew and the others, with the circular tables and chairs in between representing a kind of no-man's-land that might as well have been littered with barbed wire and tank traps.

Ahead of me, the Collector was picking his way carefully toward a booth at the back of the bar. A waitress emerged from the kitchens nearby, a huge tray of food balanced on her left shoulder. She didn't look at the Collector but she gave him a wide berth, moving left in the direction of the bar as he came and effectively traversing two sides of a triangle to reach the booth nearest the door. In fact, at no point did anyone in the room even glance at him as he made his way down its entire length, and although it made no sense to me, had I been asked I would have said that their decision to ignore him was an unconscious one. Some part of them was aware of his presence; after all, he had a drink before him in the booth, and someone must have served it to him. His cash would end up in the register. A faint smell of nicotine would hang around the booth for a time even after he was gone. Yet I suspected that one minute after he left, if asked about him, every person in that bar would have had difficulty remembering him. The part of their brain that had been aware of his presence would also have registered even the memory of him as a threat – no, not a threat, but a kind of pollutant of the soul – and would quickly and efficiently have set about erasing all traces of him from itself.

He was sitting in the booth, waiting for me to draw near, and I had to fight my urge to turn away, to retreat from him into the sunlight. *Foul.* The word forced itself up like bile. I could almost feel it forming on my lips. *Foul thing.*

And as I reached the booth, the Collector spoke that word to me.

'Foul,' he said. He seemed to be testing it, tasting it like an unfamiliar food, uncertain as to whether he found it to his liking or not. In the end, he touched his stained tongue with those yellowed fingers and picked a piece of tobacco from it, as though he had given form to the word and chosen to expel it. There was a mirror behind him, and I could see the bald patch at the back of his head. It was slightly flattened, suggesting that at some point in the distant past he had received a blow heavy enough to impact upon the skull and fracture it. I wondered how long ago it might have occurred; in childhood, perhaps, while the skull was still soft. Then I tried to imagine this creature as a child, and found that I could not.

He gestured to the seat across from him, indicating that I should sit, then raised his left hand and allowed his fingers to pluck gently at the air, like a fisherman testing the lure at the end of his line. It summoned the waitress and she approached the booth slowly and reluctantly, her face already trying to form a smile that the muscles seemed unwilling to support. She did not look at the Collector. Instead, she tried to keep her eyes fixed firmly on me, even turning her back on him slightly so as to exclude him from her peripheral vision.

'What can I get ya?' she asked. Her nostrils twitched. The tips of her fingers were white where they gripped the pen. As she waited for me to answer, her eyes and head shifted slightly to the right. The smile, already struggling to survive, entered its death throes. The Collector stared at the back of her head. He grinned. A frown creased the waitress's forehead. She flicked at her hair distractedly. The Collector's mouth moved, soundlessly forming a word. I read it on his lips.

Whore.

The waitress's lips moved too, echoing the word. *Whore.* Then she shook her head, trying to dislodge the insult like an insect that had crawled into her ear.

'No,' she said. 'That's—'

'Coffee,' I said, a little too loudly. 'Just coffee will be fine.'

It brought her back. For a moment, she seemed about to continue, to protest at what she had heard, or thought she had heard. Instead, she swallowed the words. The effort made her eyes water.

'Coffee,' she repeated. She wrote it on her pad, her hand trembling as the pen moved. She looked to be on the verge of tears. 'Sure, I'll be right back with it.'

But I knew she would not be back. I saw her go to the bar and whisper something to the bartender. She began untying her apron and headed for the kitchen. There was probably a staff bathroom in back. She would stay there, I figured, until the crying and the shaking stopped, until she felt that it was safe to come out. She might try to light a cigarette, but the smell of it would remind her of the man in the booth, the one who was both there and not there, present and absent, a raggedy man trying just too hard to be unremarkable.

And as she reached the kitchen door, she found it within herself to look straight at the man in the booth, and her eyes were dulled by fear and anger and shame before she vanished from sight.

'What did you do to her?' I asked.

'Do?' He sounded genuinely surprised. His voice was surprisingly soft. 'I did nothing. She is what she is. Her morals are lax. I merely reminded her of it.'

'And how do you know that?'

'Ways and means.'

'She'd done you no harm.'

The Collector pursed his lips in disapproval.

'I'm disappointed in you. Perhaps your morals are as lax as hers. Whether she had done me harm or not is irrelevant. The fact remains that she is a whore, and she will be judged as such.'

'By you? I don't think you're fit to judge anyone.'

'I don't pretend to be. Unlike you,' he added, with just a hint of malice. 'I am not the judge, but the application of judgment. I do not sentence, but I carry out the punishment.'

'And keep souvenirs of your victims.'

The Collector spread his hands before me.

'What victims? Show them to me. Display for me the bones.'

Now, although we had spoken before, I noticed for the first time the careful way in which he expressed himself, and the occasional strange locutions that emerged when he did. *Display for me the bones.* There was a trace of something foreign to his accent, but it was impossible to place. It seemed to come from anywhere and nowhere, just like him.

His hands closed into fists. He allowed only his right index finger to remain extended.

'But you . . . I smelled you in my house. I marked the places where you had lingered, you and the others who came with you.'

'We were looking for Merrick.' It sounded like I was trying to justify the trespass. Perhaps I was.

'But you did not find him. From what I hear, he found you. You are fortunate to be alive after crossing such a man.'

'Did you set him on me, like you set him on Daniel Clay and on his daughter? Like you set him on Ricky Demarcian?'

'Did I set him on Daniel Clay?' The Collector touched an index finger to his lower lip, a simulation of thoughtfulness. His lips parted slightly, and I glimpsed his crooked teeth, blackening at the roots. 'Perhaps I have no interest in Daniel Clay, or his daughter. As for Demarcian, well, the loss of a life is always regrettable, but in some cases it is less regrettable than in others. I suspect few will mourn his absence from the world. His employers will find another to take his place, and the deviants will congregate around him like flies on a wound.

'But we were talking about your intrusion upon my privacy. At first, I must confess that I was aggrieved. You forced me to move part of my collection. But when I considered the situation, I was grateful. I knew that we were destined to meet again. You could say that we move in the same circles.'

'I owe you for the last time we met in one of those circles.'

'You would not give me what I wanted – no, what I *needed*. You left me no choice. Nevertheless, I apologize for any hurt I inflicted. It appears to have caused no lasting damage.'

It was strange. I should have taken him there and then. I should have rained blows upon him in retribution. I wanted to break his nose and his teeth. I wanted to force him to the floor and shatter his skull with the heel of my boot. I wanted to see him burn, his ashes scattering to the four winds. I wanted his blood on my hands and my face. I wanted to lick it from my lips with the tip of my tongue. I—

I stopped. The voice in my head was mine, yet it was echoed by another. Silken tones goaded me.

'*You see?*' said the Collector, even though his lips did not move. '*You see how easy it could be? Do you want to try? Do you want to punish me? Come, do it. I am alone.*'

But that was a lie. It was not only the Collector that those in the bar had chosen to ignore, if they were aware of the others at all. There was now movement in the shadows, dark on light. Faces formed at the edges of perception, then were gone, their black eyes unblinking, their ruined mouths gaping, the lines on their skin speaking of decay and absence within. In the mirror, I saw some of the businessmen push their food away half finished. One of the afternoon drunks at the bar brushed at a presence beside his ear, swatting it away like the whine of a mosquito. I saw his lips move, repeating something that only he could hear. His hand trembled as he reached for the shot glass before him, his fingers failing to grasp it, so that it slipped away from him, falling on its side and spilling amber liquid across the wood.

They were here. The Hollow Men were here.

And even if he were alone, which he was not, even if there was no sense that half-glimpsed presences trailed behind him like fragments of himself, only a fool would try to tackle the Collector. He exuded menace. He was a killer, of that I was certain. A killer just like Merrick, except Merrick took lives for money and, now, for revenge, never deluding himself into thinking that what he did was right or justified, while the Collector ended lives because he thought he had been given permission to do so. All that the two men had in common was a shared belief in the utter inconsequentiality of those whom they dispatched.

I took a deep breath. I found that I had moved forward in my seat. I sat back and tried to release some of the tension from my shoulders and arms. The Collector seemed almost disappointed.

'You think that you are a good man?' he said. 'How can one tell the good from the bad when their methods are just the same?'

I didn't answer. 'What do you want?' I asked instead.

'I want what you want: to find the abusers of Andrew Kellog and the others.'

'Did they kill Lucy Merrick?'

'Yes.'

'You know that for certain.'

'Yes.'

'How?'

'The living leave one mark on the world, the dead another. It is a matter of learning to read the signs, like' – he searched for the right comparison, and clicked his fingers as he found it – 'like writing on glass, like fingerprints in dust.'

He waited for me to react, but he was disappointed.

And around us, the shadows moved.

'And you thought you'd use Frank Merrick to flush out the men responsible,' I said, as if he had not spoken those words, as if he did not seem to know things of which he could not possibly be aware.

'I thought he might be useful. Mr Eldritch, needless to say, was not convinced, but like a good attorney he does as his client wishes.'

'Looks like Eldritch was right. Merrick is out of control.'

The Collector conceded the point with a click of his tongue.

'It would appear so. Still, he may yet lead me to them. For the present, though, we are no longer aiding him in his searches. Eldritch has already had some awkward questions from the police. That bothers him. He has been forced to open a new file, and despite his love of paper he has files enough as matters stand. Eldritch likes . . . *old things*.'

He rolled the words around in his mouth, savoring them.

'Are you looking for Daniel Clay?'

The Collector grinned slyly. 'Why would I be looking for Daniel Clay?'

'Because children in his care were abused. Because the information that led to that abuse could have come from him.'

'And you believe that if I am looking for him, then he must be guilty, is that not right? Despite your distaste for me, it seems that perhaps you trust my judgment.'

He was right. The realization troubled me, but there was no denying the truth of what he had said. For some reason, I believed that if Clay was guilty, then the Collector would be seeking him out.

'The question remains: are you looking for him?'

'No,' said the Collector. 'I am not.'

'Because he wasn't involved, or because you already know where he is?'

'That would be telling. Would you have me do all your work for you?'

'So what now?'

'I want you to leave Eldritch be. He knows nothing that would be useful to you, and would not tell you even if he did. I wanted to express my regret at what passed between Merrick and you. It was not my doing. Finally, I wanted to tell you that, in this instance, we are working toward the same end. I want those men identified. I want to know who they are.'

'Why?'

'So they can be dealt with.'

'The courts will take care of them.'

'I answer to a higher court.'

'I won't hand them over to you.'

He shrugged. 'I am patient. I can wait. Their souls are forfeit. That is all that matters.'

'What did you say?'

He traced patterns upon the table. They looked like letters, but of some alphabet that was unknown to me. 'Some sins are so terrible that there can be no forgiveness for them. The soul is lost. It returns to the One who created it, to be disposed of as He sees fit. All that is left behind is an empty shell, consciousness without grace.'

'Hollow,' I said, and I thought that something in the darkness responded to the word, like a dog hearing its name called by a stranger.

'Yes,' said the Collector. 'That is an apt word.'

He looked around, seeming to take in the bar and its denizens, yet he focused not on people and objects but on the spaces between them, finding movement where there should have been only stillness, shapes without true form. When he spoke again, his tone was altered. He sounded thoughtful, almost regretful.

'And who would see such things, if they existed?' he said. 'Sensitive children, perhaps, abandoned by their fathers and fearful for their mothers. Holy fools who are attuned to such things. But you are neither.' His eyes flicked toward me, regarding me slyly. 'Why do you see what others do not? Were I in your shoes, I might be troubled by such matters.'

He licked at his lips, but his tongue was dry and gave them no moisture. They were cracked deeply in places, the partly healed cuts a darker red against the pink. 'Hollow.' He repeated the word, drawing out the final syllable. 'Are you a hollow man, Mr Parker? After all, misery loves company. A place might be found in the ranks for a suitable candidate.' He smiled, and one of the cracks on his lower lip opened. A red pearl of blood rose briefly before flowing back into his mouth. 'But no, you lack . . . *spirit*, and it may be that there are others more adaptable to the role. By their actions shall they be known.'

He stood to leave, depositing $20 on the table to cover his drink. It smelled like Jim Beam, although it had remained untouched throughout.

'A generous tip for our waitress,' he said. 'After all, you seem to feel that she has earned it.'

'Are these men the only ones you're looking for?' I asked. I wanted to know if there were others, and if, perhaps, I was among them.

He crooked his head, like a magpie distracted by an object shining in the sunlight.

'I am always searching,' he said. 'There are so many to be dealt with. So many.'

He began to drift away. 'Perhaps we'll meet again, for better or worse. It is almost time to be moving on, and I find the thought that you might choose to snap at my heels slightly troubling. It will be for the best if we find a way to coexist in this world. I'm sure that an accommodation can be reached, a bargain struck.'

He walked toward the door, and shadows followed him along the walls. I saw them in the mirror, smears of white on black, just as I had seen the face of John Grady in a mirror once, howling against his own damnation. It was only when the door opened, and sunlight briefly invaded once again, that I saw the envelope that the Collector had left on the seat across from me. I reached for it. It was thin and unsealed. I opened the tab and looked inside. It contained a black-and-white photograph. I took it out and laid it on the table as the door closed behind me, so that there was only the flickering lamplight to illuminate the picture of my house, the clouds gathering above it, and the men standing beside the car in my drive, one tall, black, and severe, the other smaller, smiling in his dishevelment.

I stared at the picture for a time, then put it back in the envelope and tucked it into my jacket pocket. From the kitchen door, the waitress emerged. Her eyes were red. She glanced at me, and I felt the sting of her blame. I left the bar, left Eldritch and his secretary and his office filled with old paper and the names of the dead. I left them all, and I did not return.

As I drove north, Merrick was engaged in his own work. He approached Rebecca Clay's home. Later, when everything ended in blood and gunfire, a neighbor would recall his presence, but for now he went unnoticed. It was a gift that he had, the ability to blend in when necessary, to avoid attracting attention. He saw the two big men in their enormous truck, and the car owned by the third man parked at the rear of the house. The car was empty, which meant that the man was probably inside. Merrick was sure that he could take him, but there would be noise, and it would draw the others to him. He might be able to kill them as well, but the risk was too great.

Instead, he retreated. He had acquired a new car, boosted from the garage of a summer home at Higgins Beach, and drove it to a warehouse on a decrepit industrial park near Westbrook, and there he found Jerry Legere working alone. He put my gun in Legere's mouth and informed him that when it was removed, Legere would tell him all that his wife had shared with him about her father, and all that he knew or suspected about the events leading up to Daniel Clay's disappearance, or he would blow the back of his head off. Legere was certain that he was going to die. He told Merrick about his wife, the whore. He peddled fantasies to him: lies and half lies, untruths half believed and truths that were worth less than the lies.

But Merrick learned nothing useful from him, and he did not kill Rebecca Clay's ex-husband, because Legere gave him no cause to do so. Merrick drove away, leaving Legere lying in the dirt, crying with shame and relief.

And the man who was watching from the woods took in everything, and began making his calls.

28

I was heading north on I-95 when the call came through. It was Louis. When he had returned to Scarborough, there was an unknown car waiting in my driveway. A couple of phone calls later, and it was not unknown any longer.

'You got company up here,' he said.

'Anyone we know?'

'Not unless you planning on invading Russia.'

'How many?'

'Two.'

'Where?'

'Sitting slap bang in your yard. Seems like there ain't no Russian word for "subtle."'

'Keep an eye on them. I'll let you know when I'm coming off Route 1.'

I guessed they'd be around asking questions eventually. They couldn't let Demarcian's death pass without mention or investigation. I had just hoped that I'd already be gone when they arrived.

I didn't know much about the Russians, except for the little I'd learned from Louis in the past, and what I'd read in the papers. I knew that they were big in California and New York, and that the main groups in each of those places maintained contact with their peers in Massachusetts, Chicago, Miami, New Jersey, and a dozen or more other states, as well as their peers back in Russia, to form what was, in effect, a huge criminal syndicate. Like the individual mobs themselves, it appeared to be loosely structured with little apparent organization, but it was believed that this was a ruse to throw investigators off the scent and make it difficult for them to infiltrate the syndicate. The soldiers were separated from the bosses by layers of buffers, so that those involved in drugs and prostitution at street level had little idea where the money they earned ultimately went. Demarcian had probably not been able to tell Merrick very much about the men with whom he dealt beyond first names, and those were unlikely to have been real anyway.

The Russians also seemed content to leave large-scale narcotics dealing to others, although they were said to have formed links with the Colombians. Mostly, they preferred insurance scams, identity theft, money laundering, and fuel tax fraud, the kind of complex ripoff operations that were hard for the authorities to track and prosecute. I wondered how many of the clients for Demarcian's porn sites realized the kind of individuals to whom they were revealing their credit card details.

I figured they were here only to ask questions. If they'd come for something more serious, they wouldn't have been dumb enough to park in my driveway and wait for me to arrive. Then again, that presupposed they gave a damn about their car being noticed, or even about potential witnesses. The Russians were bad news. It was said that when the Soviet Union collapsed, the Italians sent a few guys over to Moscow to assess the potential for muscling in on the emerging market. They took one look at what was happening on the streets and went straight back home. Unfortunately, the Russians followed them, joining the Odessa Mafia that had been operating in Brighton Beach since the mid-seventies, and now the Italians sometimes seemed almost quaint by comparison with the new arrivals. It was kind of ironic, I thought, that what ultimately brought the Russians to our door was not communism but a belief in capitalism. Joe McCarthy must have been turning in his grave.

I reached Scarborough forty minutes later, and I called Louis when I was at Oak Hill. He asked me to give him five minutes, then head down at a steady thirty. I saw the car as soon as I rounded the bend. It was a big black Chevy 4X4, the kind of vehicle usually driven by people who would cry if they got real dirt on it. As if to confirm the stereotype, the Chevy was scrupulously clean. I did a U-turn as I passed my house, and pulled up behind the Chevy with the passenger door closest to it, effectively blocking it from leaving the drive. It was bigger than the Mustang, and if they got enough power behind it they might manage to knock my car out of their way, but in the process they'd probably wipe out the back of their vehicle. Apparently, nobody had yet thought of putting bull bars on the rear of 4X4s, although I was sure that it could only be a matter of time. Both front doors of the Chevy opened and two men emerged. They were dressed in standard hood chic: black leather jackets, black jeans, and black sweaters. One of them, a bald man built like a piece of Eastern Bloc architecture, was reaching inside his jacket for his gun when a voice behind him said only a single word: 'Don't.'

The Russian's hand froze. Louis stood in the shadows of my house, his Glock in his gloved hand. They were trapped between us. I stayed where I was, my .38 now drawn and trained on them.

'Take your hand out of your jacket,' I told the bald Russian. 'Slowly. When I see it, fingernails had better be the only thing on the end of it.'

The Russian did as he was told. His partner had already raised his hands. I came out from behind the car and advanced on them.

'Flat on the ground,' said Louis.

They did as they were told. Louis then frisked them both while I kept the gun on them. They were each armed with matching Colt nine-millimeter semiautomatics. Louis ejected the clips from the guns, then checked for any in the chute. When he was sure that they were empty, he tossed the clips into the undergrowth and retreated five feet from the two men.

'Up and kneel,' I told them. 'Keep your hands behind your heads.'

They struggled to a kneeling position, then glared at me.

'Who are you?' I said.

They didn't reply.

'*Shestyorki*,' said Louis. 'Ain't that what you are? Messenger boys.'

'*Niet*,' said the bald one. '*Boyeviki*.'

'*Boyeviki* my ass,' said Louis. 'He says they're soldiers. Guess it's hard to get good staff these days. This one can't even answer a question in English. What happened, you fall off the boat and get left behind?'

'I speak English,' said the Russian. 'I speak English good.'

'No shit?' said Louis. 'What you want, a medal? A gold star?'

'Why are you here?' I asked, although I already knew.

'*Razborka*,' he said. 'We want, uh—' He searched for the English word.

'—clarification,' he finished.

'Well, let me give you clarification,' I said. 'I don't like armed men on my property. If I shot you now, you think that would be clarification enough for your bosses?'

The redheaded one glanced at his partner, then spoke.

'You kill us and this gets worse. We are here to talk about Demarcian.' His English was better than his partner's. He spoke it with only the faintest hint of an accent. It was clear that he was the one in charge, although he had been content to hide the fact until it became obvious that his bald friend was out of his depth in the current negotiations.

'I don't know anything about him, apart from the fact that he's dead.'

'The police questioned you. The rumor is that your gun was used to kill him.'

'The gun was taken from me,' I said. 'I don't know for certain that it was used to kill Demarcian. My guess is that it probably was, but I don't go loaning it out for killings. The man who took it wanted it real bad.'

'It was careless of you to lose your gun,' said the Russian.

'As you can see, I have another. If I lose that, I can always borrow one from my friend behind you. He has *lots* of guns.

Anyway, I didn't have anything to do with Demarcian's death, the weapon apart.'

'So you say,' said the Russian.

'Yeah, but we have guns and you don't, so our word wins.'

The Russian shrugged, as though the whole matter was immaterial to him anyway. 'I believe you, then. We would still like to know about the man who killed Demarcian, this Merrick. Tell us about Merrick.'

'Do your own homework. You want him, you find him.'

'But we think you too are looking for him. You want your gun back. Perhaps we find him, and we get it back for you.'

His bald companion snickered and said something under his breath. It sounded like *'frayeri.'* Louis responded by striking him across the back of the head with the barrel of the Glock. It wasn't enough to knock him out, but it laid him flat on his face. His scalp began to bleed.

'He called us suckers,' explained Louis. 'That's not nice.'

The redheaded man didn't move. He just shook his head in apparent disappointment at his colleague's stupidity. 'I think your friend does not like Russians very much,' he said.

'My friend doesn't like anybody very much, but he does appear to have a particular problem with you two,' I admitted.

'Perhaps he is a racist. Is that what you are?'

He turned his head slightly, trying to see Louis. I had to give him credit: he wasn't easily intimidated.

'I can't be no racist, man,' said Louis. 'I'm black.'

It didn't quite answer the Russian's question, but he seemed content with what he heard. 'We want Frank Merrick,' he continued. 'We could make it worth your while if you tell us what you know.'

'Money?'

'Sure, money.' His face brightened. This was the kind of negotiation that he liked.

'I don't need money,' I said. 'I got too much as it is. What I need is for you to take your friend and get out of here. He's bleeding on my driveway.'

The Russian looked genuinely regretful. 'That is a shame.'

'It's okay, it'll wash off.'

'I meant about the money.'

'I know. Get up.'

He stood. Behind him, Louis was checking the interior of the Chevy. He found a little H&K P7 in the glove compartment, and a Benelli M1 tactical shotgun with a pistol grip stock and click-adjustable military ghost wing sights in a flip compartment under the rear seat. Again, he emptied both, then opened the back of the Chevy, wiped his prints from the weapons, and stuck them under the gray lining in the trunk.

'Go back to Boston,' I said. 'We're all done here.'

'And what do I tell my bosses?' said the Russian. 'Someone must answer for what happened to Demarcian. It has caused many problems for us.'

'I'm sure you'll think of something.'

He sighed deeply. 'Can I put my hands down now?' he asked.

'Slowly,' I said.

He let his hands drop then bent down to help his companion to his feet. The back of the bald man's head was wet with blood. The redhead took in Louis for the first time. They exchanged nods of professional respect. Louis removed a pristine white handkerchief from the pocket of his jacket and handed it to the Russian.

'For your friend's head,' he said.

'Thank you.'

'You know what *blat* means?' said Louis.

'Sure,' said the Russian.

'Well, my friend here has major *blat*. You be sure to tell your bosses that.'

The Russian nodded again. The bald man climbed gingerly into the passenger seat and rested his left cheek against the cool leather, his eyes closed. His colleague turned back to me.

'Good-bye, *volk*,' he said. 'Until we meet again.'

He climbed into the Chevy, then began to reverse it down the drive, Louis keeping pace with him all the way, the Glock never wavering. I went back to my Mustang and moved it out of the way, then watched the Chevy head toward Route 1, Louis beside me.

'Ukrainians,' he said. 'Maybe Georgians. Not Chechens.'

'Is that good?'

He shrugged. It seemed to be contagious. 'They all bad,' he said. 'Chechens just *real* bad.'

'The redhead didn't seem like a foot soldier.'

'Underboss. Means they real pissed about Demarcian.'

'He doesn't seem worth that kind of effort.'

'They lose business. Cops start tracing their clients, ask questions about pictures of children. Can't let it slide.'

But he seemed to be holding something back.

'What else?'

'I don't know. Feels off. I'll ask around, see what I hear.'

'Will they be back?'

'Uh-huh. Might help if we found Merrick first, buy us a little influence.'

'I'm not going to give them Merrick.'

'Might not have a choice.' He started to walk back to the house.

'What does "*blat*" mean?' I asked.

'Connections,' he replied. 'And not the legal kind.'

'And "*volk*"?'

'It's slang, word for a cop or an investigator. Kind of a compliment.' He put his gun back in its shoulder holster. 'It means "wolf."'

29

We drove north to Jackman late that afternoon, through Shawmut and Hinckley and Skowhegan, through Solon and Bingham, Moscow and Caratunk, past places without names and names without places, the road following the bends and curves of the Kennebec, the banks lined with bare trees, the forest floor brilliant with their lost foliage. Gradually, the nature of the forest began to change as the evergreens raised their spires, dark against the dying light as winter winds whispered of the promise of snow. And as the cold began to bite, the woods would grow ever quieter as animals retreated into hibernation and even birds grew torpid to preserve their energy.

We were following the route that Arnold took on his expedition up the Kennebec to Quebec. His force of twelve hundred men marched from Cambridge to Newburyport, then took to the river on transports, navigating the crooked channel of the Kennebec as far as Gardinerstown. From there, they transferred to light bateaux, more than two hundred of them, each capable of holding six or seven men along with their provisions and baggage, perhaps four hundred pounds of weight in all. They were built hastily and from green lumber by Reuben Colburn at Gardinerstown, and they quickly began to leak and fall to pieces, ruining the troops' supplies of powder, bread, and flour. Three companies were sent ahead under Daniel Morgan to the Great Carrying Place between the Kennebec and Dead Rivers, the others following slowly behind, using ox teams borrowed from settlers to move the bateaux around the impassable falls above Fort Western, hoisting them up the steep, icy banks at Skowhegan Falls, most of the men reduced to walking in order to ease the burden on the boats until they came at last to the twelve low, marshy miles of the Carrying Place. The soldiers sank into deep, green moss that looked firm from a distance but proved treacherous underfoot, a kind of calenture on land, so that the madness suffered by sailors too long at sea, who hallucinated dry earth where there was no earth and drowned beneath the waves when they jumped, found its echo in ground that was soft and yielding as water. They stumbled on logs and fell in creeks, and in time they cleared a road in order to travel, so that for many years the path they took could be traced by the difference in the color of the foliage on either side of the route.

I was struck by a sense of landscape layered upon landscape, past upon present. These rivers and forests were inseparable from their history; the distinction between what was now and what had gone before was fragile here. It was a place where the ghosts of dead soldiers passed through forests and over streams that had changed little in the intervening years, a place where family names had remained unaltered, where people still owned the land that their great-grandfathers had bought with gold and silver coin, a place where old sins persisted, for great change had not come to wash away the memory of them.

So this was the land traversed by Arnold's army, the soldiers equipped with rifles, axes, and long knives. Now other bands of armed men moved through this landscape, adding their clamor to the creeping silence of winter, holding it at bay with the roar of their guns and the growl of the trucks and quads that carried them into the wilderness. The woods were alive with orange-clad fools, businessmen from Massachusetts and New York taking a break from the golf course to blast at moose and bear and buck, guided by locals who were grateful for the money the outsiders spent yet remained resentful of the fact that they needed it to survive.

We made but one stop along the way, at a house that was little more than a shack, three or four rooms in all, its windows unwashed and the interior hidden by cheap drapes. The yard was overgrown. A garage door gaped open, revealing rusted tools and stacks of firewood. There was no car, because one of the conditions of Mason Dubus's parole was that he was not permitted to drive a vehicle.

Louis waited outside. I think, perhaps, that he would have found Dubus's company intolerable, for Dubus was a man like those who had abused Louis's beloved Angel, and it was Louis's greatest regret that he had never been given the opportunity to punish those who had scarred his lover's soul. So he leaned against the car, and watched silently as the door was opened slightly, a chain securing it, and a man's face appeared. His skin was yellow and his eyes were rheumy. His one visible hand shook with uncontrollable tremors.

'Yes?' he said.

'Mr Dubus, my name's Charlie Parker. I think someone called to let you know I might want to speak with you.'

The eyes narrowed. 'Maybe. You got some, whatchacallit, ID? A license or something?'

I showed him my PI's license. He took it from me and held it close to his face, examining each and every word upon it, then handed it back to me. He looked beyond me to where Louis was standing.

'Who's the other fella?'

'He's a friend.'

'He's gonna catch cold out there. He's welcome to come in, if he chooses.'

'I think he'd prefer to wait where he is.'

'Well, it's his call. Don't say I didn't offer.'

The door closed for a moment, and I could hear the rattling as the security chain was removed. When it opened again, I got my first proper look at Dubus. He was hunched by age and illness, and by his years in prison, but there was still a vestige of the big, strong man that he had once been. His clothes were clean and carefully ironed. He wore dark trousers, a blue-striped shirt, and a tightly knotted pink tie. He was wearing an old-fashioned eau de cologne that bore hints of sandalwood and incense. The interior of the house gave the lie to any first impressions evoked by the exterior. The floorboards shone, and it smelled of furniture polish and air freshener. There were paperback books on a small shelf in the hallway, on top of which stood an old-fashioned rotary dial telephone. Nailed to the wall above it was a copy of the 'Desiderata,' a kind of twelve-step program for those afflicted by the trials of modern life. The rest of the walls were decorated with prints of paintings in cheap frames – some modern, some much older, and most unfamiliar to me – although the images had clearly been carefully chosen.

I followed Dubus into his living room. Again, everything was clean, even though the furniture had come from thrift stores and was scuffed and worn. A small TV sat on a pine table, tuned to a comedy show. There were more prints on the walls here, as well as a couple of originals, each depicting a landscape. One of them seemed familiar. I walked over to take a closer look at it. From a distance, it appeared to be a painting of a forest, a line of green trees against a red sunset, but then I saw that one of the trees stood taller than the rest, and had a cross at its highest point. Daniel Clay's signature was visible in the bottom right-hand corner. It was Gilead.

'He gave it to me,' said Dubus. He was standing at the opposite side of the room, keeping a distance between us. It was probably a result of his time in jail, where you learned to give every man his space, even in such a confined area, or you faced the consequences.

'Why?'

'For talking to him about Gilead. You mind if we sit down? I get tired. I have to take this medication.' He gestured at some bottles of pills on the mantel above the fireplace, where three logs were hissing and sparking. 'It makes me drowsy.'

I sat down on the couch across from him.

'If you want coffee, I can make some,' he said.

'I'm fine, thank you.'

'Okay.' He tapped his fingers on the arm of the chair, his eyes flicking toward the TV. It appeared that I had disturbed his viewing. Then, apparently resigning himself to the fact that he wasn't going to be left to watch it in peace, he hit a button on the remote and the picture died.

'So what do you want to know?' he asked. 'I get people through here now and again: students, doctors. You can't ask me anything I ain't already been asked a hundred times before.'

'I'd like to know what you discussed with Daniel Clay.'

'I talked about Gilead,' he said. 'That's all I ever talk about. They used to test me, show me pictures and stuff, but they don't do that no more. I guess they think they know all that they need to know about me.'

'And do they?'

His Adam's apple bobbed. I could hear the sound that it made deep in his throat. He regarded me for a time, then seemed to come to some decision.

'No, they don't,' he said. 'They got as much as they're going to get. Don't think you're going to get anything more than they did.'

'What was Clay's interest in Gilead?' I asked. I didn't want to alienate Dubus. He might have been drowsy and medicated, but he was still sharp.

'He wanted to know about what happened. I told him. I didn't leave nothing out. I don't have nothing to hide. I'm not ashamed of what we did together. It was all' – he screwed up his face in distaste – 'misunderstood, misinterpreted. They made it out to be something it wasn't.'

'What we did together,' as though it was a mutual decision reached between the adults and the children, as natural as fishing, or picking berries in summer.

'Children died, Mr Dubus.'

He nodded. 'That was bad. That shouldn't have happened. They was babies, though, and times were hard up there. Might almost have been a blessing, what happened to them.'

'As I understand it, one was stabbed to death with a knitting needle. That's a peculiar definition of a blessing.'

'You judging me, sir?' He squinted at me, the trembling of

his hands giving the impression that he was struggling, yet failing, to control great anger.

'It's not for me to do.'

'That's right. That was why I got on with Dr Clay. He didn't judge me.'

'Did Daniel Clay ever talk about the children in his care?'

'No.' Something unpleasant animated his features for an instant. 'I tried, though. He didn't bite.' Dubus snickered.

'How many times did he come here?'

'Two or three, far as I can remember. He visited me in jail, too, but that was just once.'

'And it was all very businesslike. He interviewed you, and you talked.'

'That's right.'

'And yet he gave you one of his paintings. I hear he was very particular about those to whom he gave his paintings. Very selective.'

Dubus shifted in his chair. That Adam's apple began bobbing again, and I was reminded of Andy Kellog worrying at his loose tooth. Both were indicators of stress.

'Maybe I was helpful to him. Maybe he didn't view me as no monster. I could see it in your friend's face out there, and I could see it in yours when I opened the door. You tried to hide it with politeness and good manners, but I knew what you were thinking. And then you came in here, and you saw the pictures on my wall, and how clean and neat everything was. I wasn't wallowing in my own filth. I wasn't stinking, or dressed in dirty, tattered clothes. You think I want the outside of my place to look the way it does? You don't think I want to paint it, to fix it up some? Well, I can't. I do what I can around here, but there ain't nobody going to help a man like me to keep his house in order. I paid for what they said I done, paid with years of my life, and they're going to make me keep paying until I die, but I won't give them the satisfaction of being ground down. You want monsters, you look elsewhere.'

'Was Daniel Clay a monster?'

The question seemed to shock him into silence. Then, for a second time, I saw the intelligence at work behind the withered façade, that creeping, nasty, corrupted thing that had allowed him to do what he had done, and to justify it to himself. I thought it might even have been what the children of Gilead had glimpsed as he moved upon them, his hand clasped across their mouths to stifle their cries.

'You got your suspicions of him, like the rest,' said Dubus. 'You want me to tell you if they're true, because if we shared something like that, if we both had the same tastes, then maybe I'd have known, or he'd have opened himself up to me. Well, if you think that, you're a fool, Mr Parker. You're a fool, and someday you'll die for your foolishness. I got no time to talk to foolish men. Why don't you head off now? Drive on up the road there, because I know where you're going. Could be you'll find the answer in Gilead. That's where Daniel Clay found the answers to his questions. Oh yes, he found what he was looking for up there, but he didn't come back from that place. You best step carefully, or else you won't come back neither. It gets inside your soul, old Gilead.'

He was smiling broadly now, the keeper of the truth of Gilead.

'Did you ever meet a man called Jim Poole, Mr Dubus?'

He pantomimed deep thought.

'You know, I think I did. He was a fool, just like you.'

'He disappeared.'

'He got lost. Gilead took him.'

'Is that what you think?'

'I know it. Doesn't matter where he is, or if he's alive or dead, he's a prisoner of Gilead. You set foot in Gilead, and you're lost.' His gaze turned inward. His eyes stopped blinking. 'They said that we brought evil to that place, but it was there already,' he said, and there was a touch of wonder to his voice. 'I felt it as soon as I set foot there. Old Lumley picked a bad spot for his city of refuge. The ground was poisoned, and we were poisoned too. When we left, the forest, or something under it, took it back.'

He gave a small, sick laugh. 'Too much time to myself,' he said. 'Too much time to dwell on things.'

'What was the Project, Mr Dubus?'

His laugh faded away. 'The Project. The Hobby. The Game. They all mean the same thing.'

'The abuse of children.'

He shook his head. 'You may call it that, but that's because you don't understand. It's a beautiful thing. That's what I try to explain to those who come here, but they don't listen. They don't want to know.'

'Did Daniel Clay listen?'

'He was different. He understood.'

'Understood how?'

But Dubus did not reply.

'Do you know where Daniel Clay is?' I asked.

Dubus leaned forward. 'Who knows where dead men go?' he said. 'You head north, and maybe you'll find out. It's time for my stories.'

He hit the remote again, adjusting the volume as he did so, and the TV blared into life. He turned in his chair, no longer facing toward me. I let myself out.

And as we drove away, I saw the drapes move at Dubus's window. A hand was raised in farewell, and I felt sure that in his clean, neat house, the old man was laughing at me.

In the days that followed, the police would attempt to piece together the chain of events, to connect body to body, contacts to killings. During the final hours of his life, Dubus made two telephone calls, both to the same number. After his death, the cell phone would be found beside his body. He had hidden it under a loose plank beneath his bed, and to discourage any of those entrusted with monitoring him from discovering it, he kept a half-filled chamberpot above it, its stink enough to ensure that no fastidious parole officer would dare to venture there, although it might have struck a careful searcher that, in his otherwise pristine house, it was the only place where Dubus's orderliness appeared to have lapsed. The phone was prepaid, and had been bought for cash at a big box store one month previously. It was not, the police guessed, the first time that someone had helped Dubus to circumvent the restrictions on his telephone use in this way.

Dubus made the second-to-last call of his life minutes after Louis and I had departed, then presumably returned the phone to its hiding place and went back to watching his TV shows. Tick-tick-tick went the seconds, counting down to the moment when Mason Dubus would at last depart this earth and face the greater justice that waits for every man.

But that was all to come. For now, the daylight was gone. There was no moon. We drove on, speaking rarely. The music was low, the National on the car stereo singing of doves in the brain and hawks in the heart, and I thought of men with the heads of birds.

And in time we came to Jackman, and old Gilead got into our souls.

V

Revenge proves its own executioner.

John Ford, *The Broken Heart*

30

It is often said that there are two Maines. There is the Maine of the summer tourists, the Maine of lobster rolls and ice cream, of yachts and boat clubs, a Maine that occupies a neat strip of coastline about as far north as Bar Harbor, with high hopes and property prices to match, apart from those towns without the good looks or good fortune to attract the tourist dollar, or those that have seen their industries fade and die, marooning them in a lake of prosperity. The rest of Maine derisively refers to the inhabitants of this region as 'flatlanders' or, in even darker moments, dismisses them entirely as residents of 'northern Massachusetts.'

The other Maine is very different. It is a Maine primarily of forests, not ocean, dominated by 'the County,' or Aroostook, which has always seemed a separate entity due to its sheer size, if nothing else. It is northern and inland, rural and conservative, and its heart is the Great North Woods.

But those woods had begun to change. The big paper companies, once the backbone of the economy, were slowly relinquishing their hold on the land, recognizing that there was more money in property than raising and cutting trees. Plum Creek, the nation's largest paper company, which owned nearly five hundred thousand acres around Moosehead Lake, had earmarked thousands of those acres for a massive commercial development of RV parks, houses, rental cabins, and an industrial park. For those in the south, it represented the despoiling of the state's greatest area of natural beauty; but for those in the other Maine, it meant jobs and money and an influx of new blood into dying communities.

The reality was that the forest canopy hid the fastest-growing poverty rate in the nation. Towns were shrinking, schools were getting smaller, and the bright young hopes of the future were leaving for York and Cumberland, for Boston and New York. When the mills shut down, high-paying jobs were replaced by minimum-wage labor. Tax revenues fell. Crime, domestic violence, and substance abuse increased. Long Pond, once bigger than Jackman, had virtually died with the closure of its mill. Up in Washington County, almost within sight of the summer playground of Bar Harbor, one in five people lived in poverty. In Somerset, where Jackman lay, it was one in six, and a steady stream of people made their way to Youth and Family Services in Skowhegan, seeking food and clothing. In some areas, there was a waiting list of years for a Section 8 voucher, at a time when rural rental assistance and funding for Section 8 was steadily falling.

Yet Jackman, oddly, had prospered in recent years, in part because of the events of 9/11. Its population had fallen rapidly during the 1990s, and half of its housing units had been vacant. The town still had its lumber mill, but the changing nature of tourism meant that those who now headed north came in camper vans, or rented cabins and cooked for themselves, leaving little money in the town. Then the planes hit and suddenly Jackman found itself on the front line of the fight to secure the nation's borders. U.S. Customs and Border Protection doubled its manpower, house prices shot up, and all things considered, Jackman was now in a better position than it had been for a long time. But even by Maine standards, Jackman remained remote. The nearest courthouse was in Skowhegan, sixty miles to the south, and the cops had to come up to Jackman from Bingham, almost forty miles away. It was, in its strange way, a lawless place.

Just as we came out of Solon, the Kennebec appeared before us. There was a sign by the side of the road. It read: *Welcome to Moose River Valley. If you don't stop, smile on the way through.*

I looked at Louis.

'You're not smiling,' I said.

'That's 'cause we're stopping.'

I guessed that statement could be taken a number of ways.

We didn't head into Jackman that night. Instead, we pulled off the road a little way outside town. There was an inn on a small hill, with motel-style rooms, a tiny bar beside the reception area, and a restaurant with long benches designed to feed the hunters who gave it a reason to exist in winter. Angel had already checked in, although he was nowhere to be seen. I went to my room, which was simply furnished and had a small kitchen area in one corner. There was underfloor heating. It was stiflingly hot. I turned off the heating, ignoring the warning that it would take twelve hours for the system to warm the room to its maximum again, then went back to the main building.

Angel was at the bar, a beer before him. He was sitting on a stool, reading a newspaper. He didn't acknowledge me, although he saw me enter. There were two men to his left. One of them looked at Angel and whispered to his friend. They laughed unpleasantly, and something told me that this exchange had been going on for a time. I drifted closer. The one who had spoken was muscular and wanted people to know it. He wore a tight green T-shirt crisscrossed by the suspenders attached to his orange hunter's oilskins. His head was closely shaved but the ghost of his widow's peak stood out like an arrow upon his forehead. His friend was smaller and heavier, his T-shirt worn bigger and looser to hide his gut. His beard looked like an unsuccessful attempt to disguise the weakness of his chin. Everything about him spoke of concealment, of his awareness of his failings. Although he was grinning, his eyes flicked uneasily from Angel to his colleague, as though the pleasure he was taking in the casual tormenting of another was tinged by relief that he was not the victim this time, a relief qualified by the knowledge that the muscular man could turn just as easily on him, and if he did so it would probably not be for the first time.

The big man tapped a fingertip on Angel's newspaper.

'You okay, buddy?' he said.

'Yeah, I'm good,' said Angel.

'I'll bet.' The man made an obscene gesture with his hand and tongue. 'I'm sure you're real good.'

He laughed loudly. His friend joined in, a puppy barking with the big dog. Angel kept his eyes on his newspaper.

'Hey, I don't mean nothing by it,' said the man. 'We're just having a little fun, that's all.'

'I can see that,' said Angel. 'I can tell that you're a fun guy.'

The man's smile died as the sarcasm started to burn.

'What's that supposed to mean?' he asked. 'You got a problem?'

Angel sipped his beer, closed his paper, and sighed. His main aggressor moved in closer, his friend muscling in alongside him. Angel spread his hands wide and patted both men gently on the chest. The barman was doing his best to stay out of the affair, but I could see him watching what was taking place in the mirror above the register. He was young, but he had still seen all of this before. Guns, beer, and the smell of blood was a combination guaranteed to bring out the worst in ignorant men.

'Get your fucking hands off me,' said the first man. 'I asked you a question – you got a problem? – because it seems to me like you have a problem. So, do you?'

Angel seemed to consider the question. 'Well,' he said, 'my back aches, I'm stuck in the boonies with a bunch of crackers with guns, and I'm not always sure that I'm with the right man.'

There was momentary confusion.

'What?' said the big man.

Angel mirrored his expression, then his face cleared. 'Oh,' he said. 'You mean, do I have a problem with *you*?' He made a dismissive gesture with his right hand. 'I don't have a problem with you at all,' he said. 'But my friend behind you, on the other hand, I think he may have a *big* problem with you.'

The larger man turned around. His buddy had already backed away, giving Louis space at the bar.

'How you doin'?' said Louis, who had entered the bar shortly after me, and had spotted what was happening just as quickly as I had. I was now standing alongside him, but it was clear that he was the main attraction.

The two men took in Louis and weighed up their options. None of them looked good. At least one of them involved a world of hurt. The alpha male made his choice, opting for the loss of a little dignity over something that might prove terminal.

'I'm doin' good,' he said.

'Then we all happy,' said Louis.

'I guess so.'

'Looks like they about to serve up dinner.'

'Yeah, looks like it.'

'I guess you better be getting along. Wouldn't want to miss your vittles.'

'Uh-huh.'

He tried to slip past Louis, but came up short against his fat friend, who hadn't moved, and was forced to elbow him out of the way. His face was growing purple with humiliation. The friend risked one more look at Louis, then trotted along after the bald man.

'Looks like you picked a good place to stay,' I said to Angel. 'A little heavy on the testosterone, maybe, and you could have some trouble filling your dance card, but it's cute.'

'You took your fucking time getting up here,' said Angel. 'You know, there's not a whole lot to do once night falls, and it gets dark like someone just threw a switch. There isn't even a TV in the room.'

We ordered hamburgers and fries, opting not to join the parties of hunters in the next room, and moved to a table beside the bar.

'You find out anything?' I asked Angel.

'I found out that nobody wants to talk about Gilead, is what I found out. Best I could get was from some old ladies tending the cemetery. According to them, what's left of Gilead is now on private land. A guy named Caswell bought it about fifteen years ago, along with another fifty acres of woodland around it. He lives close by. Always has. Doesn't entertain much. Not a Rotarian. I took a trip up there. There was a sign, and a locked gate. Apparently, he doesn't like hunters, trespassers, or salesmen.'

'Has Merrick been here?'

'If he has, then nobody saw him.'

'Maybe Caswell did.'

'Only one way to find out.'

'Yeah.'

I watched the hunters eating, and picked out the two men who had targeted Angel. They were seated in a corner, ignoring the others around them. The bigger man's face was still red. There were a lot of guns around the place, and a lot of machismo to go with them. It wasn't a good situation.

'Your friends from the bar?' I said.

Angel nodded. 'Phil and Steve. From Hoboken.'

'I think it might be a good idea to send them on their way.'

'It'll be a pleasure,' said Angel.

'By the way, how'd you know their names?'

Angel slipped his hands into his jacket pockets. They emerged holding two wallets. 'Old habits . . .'

The lodge was constructed around a hollow, with the bar and reception building on the higher ground by the road, and the rooms and cabins at the bottom of the slope beyond it. It wasn't difficult to find out where the resident homophobes were staying, as each guest was forced to carry his key on a fob cut from the trunk of a small tree. The key had been lying in front of the two guys as they taunted Angel. They were in cabin number fourteen.

They left the table about fifteen minutes after their meal was over. By that time, Angel and Louis were gone. The two men didn't look at me as they departed, but I could feel their anger simmering. They had drunk seven pints of beer between them during and after their meal, and it was only a matter of time before they decided to seek some form of retribution for being bested at the bar.

The temperature had dropped suddenly with nightfall. In the shaded places, that morning's frost had not yet melted. The two men walked quickly back to their cabin, the bigger man leading, the smaller, bearded man behind. They entered to find that their hunting rifles had been disassembled and now lay in pieces on the floor. Their bags were beside the guns, packed and locked.

To their immediate left stood Louis. Angel was seated at the table beside the stove. Phil and Steve from Hoboken took in the two men. Phil, the larger and more aggressive of the two, seemed about to say something when he saw the guns in the hands of the two visitors. He closed his mouth again.

'You know there isn't a cabin number thirteen?' said Angel.

'What?' said Phil.

'I said, you know that there isn't a cabin number thirteen in this place? The numbers jump from twelve to fourteen, on account of how nobody wants to be in number thirteen. But this is still the thirteenth cabin, so you're really in number thirteen after all, which is how come you're so unlucky.'

'Why are we unlucky?' Phil's natural animosity was returning, beefed up with some of the Dutch courage from the bar. 'All I see is two shitheads wandered into the wrong cabin and started to fuck with the wrong guys. You're the unlucky ones. You have no idea who you're screwing with here.'

Beside him, Steve shifted uneasily on his feet. Appearances to the contrary, he was smart enough, or sober enough, to realize that it wasn't a good idea to rile two men with guns when you had no guns at all, at least none that could be reassembled in time to make them useful.

Angel took the wallets from his pocket and waved them at the two men.

'But we do,' he said. 'We know just who you are. We know where you live, where you work. We know what your wife looks like, Steve, and we know that Phil seems to be separated from the mother of his children. Sad, Phil. Pictures of the kids, but no sign of Mommy. Still, you are kind of a prick so it's hard to blame her for giving you the bullet.

'You, on the other hand, know nothing about us other than the fact that we're here now, and we got good reason to be aggrieved with you on account of your big mouths. So this is what we propose: you put your shit in your car and you start heading south. Your buddy there can do the driving, Phil, 'cause I can tell you've had a few more than he has. When you've driven, oh, maybe a hundred miles, you stop and find yourselves a room. Get a good night's sleep. Tomorrow, you head back to Hoboken, and you'll never see us again. Well, you'll *probably* never see us again. You never know. We might feel the urge to visit someday. Maybe there's a Sinatra tour we can take. Gives us an excuse to drop by and say 'hi' to you and Steve. Unless, of course, you'd like to give us a more pressing reason to follow you down there.'

Phil made one last play. His pigheadedness was almost admirable.

'We got friends in Jersey,' he said meaningfully.

Angel looked genuinely puzzled. His reply, when it came, could only have come from a New Yorker.

'Why would somebody boast about something like that?' he asked. 'Who the fuck wants to visit Jersey anyway?'

'Man means,' said Louis, 'that he got *friends* in Jersey.'

'Oh,' said Angel. '*Oh*, I get it. Hey, we watch *The Sopranos* too. The bad news for you, Phil, is even if that were true, which I know it's not, we are the kind of people that the friends in Jersey call, if you catch my drift. It's easy to tell, if you look hard enough. You see, we have pistols. You have hunting rifles. You came here to hunt deer. We didn't come here to hunt deer. You don't hunt deer with a Glock. You hunt other things with a Glock, but not deer.'

Phil's shoulders slumped. It was time to admit defeat. 'Let's go,' he said to Steve.

Angel tossed him the wallets. He and Louis watched as the two men loaded up their bags and the pieces of the rifles, minus the firing pins, which Angel had thrown into the forest. When they were done, Steve took the driver's seat and Phil stood at the passenger door. Angel and Louis leaned casually on the rail of the cabin, only the guns suggesting that this wasn't merely a quartet of acquaintances exchanging final farewells.

'All of this because we were having a little fun with you at the bar,' said Phil.

'No,' said Àngel. 'All of this because you're assholes.'

Phil got in the car and they drove away. Louis waited until their lights had faded then tapped Angel gently on the back of the hand.

'Hey,' he said, 'we never get calls from Jersey.'

'I know,' said Angel. 'Why would we want to talk to anyone in Jersey?'

And their work done, they retired to bed.

31

The next morning, we headed north into Jackman. We got stuck waiting for a truck to reverse at the Jackman Trading Post, even in November its display of T-shirts hanging outside like laundry drying. To one side of it was an old black-and-white with a mannequin in the driver's seat, which was as close as anyone was going to get to a sighting of a cop this far north.

'They ever have cops up here?' asked Louis.

'I think there used to be a policeman in the sixties or seventies.'

'What happened to him? He die of boredom?'

'I guess it is kinda quiet. There's a constable now, far as I know.'

'Bet the long winter nights just fly by for him.'

'Hey, they had a killing once.'

'Once?' He didn't sound impressed.

'It was a pretty famous story at the time. A guy named Nelson Bartley, used to own the Moose River House, got shot in the head. They found his body jammed under an uprooted tree.'

'Yeah, and when was this?'

'Nineteen nineteen. There was rum-running involved somehow, I seem to recall.'

'You telling me there's been nothing since then?'

'Most people in this part of the world take their time about dying, if they can,' I said. 'You may find that startling.'

'I guess I move in different circles.'

'I guess so. You don't like rural life much, do you?'

'I had my fill of rural life when I was a boy. I didn't care much for it then. Don't figure it's improved much since.'

There were also twin outhouses beside the trading post, one on top of the other. On the door of the upper outhouse was written the word *Conservative*. On the door of the lower one was the word *Liberal*.

'Your people,' I said to Louis.

'Not my people. I'm a liberal Republican.'

'I've never really understood what that means.'

'Means I believe people can do whatever they want, as long as they don't do it anywhere near me.'

'I thought it would be more complex than that.'

'Nope, that's about it. You think I should go in and tell them I'm gay?'

'If I was you, I wouldn't even tell them you're black,' said Angel, from the backseat.

'Don't judge this place by that outhouse back there,' I said. 'That's just to give the tourists something to laugh at. A small town like this doesn't survive, even prosper some, if the people who live here are bigots and idiots. Don't make that mistake about them.'

Incredibly, this silenced both of them.

Beyond the trading post, and to the left, the impressive twin steeples of St Anthony's Church, built from local granite in 1930, loomed against the pale gray sky. The church wouldn't have looked out of place in a big city, but it seemed incongruous here in a town of a thousand souls. Still, it had given Bennet Lumley something to aim for in the creation of Gilead, and he had determined that the spire of his church would exceed even that of St Anthony's.

Jackman, or Holden as it was originally known, was founded by the English and the Irish, and the French came down to join them later. Back where the Trading Post lay used to be part of an area called Little Canada, and from there to the bridge was the Catholic part of town, which was why St Anthony's was on the eastern side of the river. Once you crossed the bridge, that was Protestant territory. There was the Congregational church, and the Episcopalians too, who were the

Protestants it was okay to like if you were a Catholic, or so my grandfather used to say. I didn't know how much the place had changed since then, but I was pretty certain that the old divide still remained, give or take a couple of houses.

The red Jackman station stood by the railway line that cut through the town, but it was now privately owned. The main bridge in town was being repaired, so a detour took us over a temporary structure and into the township of Moose River. On the right was the modest Moose River Congregational Church, which bore the same relationship to St Anthony's as the local Little League team bore to the Red Sox.

Eventually, we came to the sign for Holden Cemetery, across from the Windfall Outdoor Center, its blue school buses, now empty, lined up sleepily outside. A dirt-and-stone road led down to the cemetery but it looked steep and slick with ice, so we left the car at the top of the road and walked the rest of the way. The road led past a frozen pond on one side and a patch of beaver bog on the other, before the gravestones of the cemetery appeared on a hill to the left. It was small, and bordered by a wire fence, with an unlocked gate wide enough for one person to pass through at a time. The graves dated as far back as the nineteenth century, probably to the days when this was still just a settlement.

I looked at the five stones nearest the gate, three large stones, two small. The first read, HATTIE E., WIFE OF JOHN F. CHILDS, and gave the dates of her birth and death: April 11, 1865, and November 26, 1891. Beside her stood the two smaller stones: Clara M. and Vinal F. According to the stone, Clara M. was born on August 16, 1895, and died just over a month later, on September 30, 1895. Vinal F.'s time on this earth was even briefer: born on September 5, 1903, he was dead by September 28. The fourth stone was that of Lillian L., John's second wife and presumably the mother of Clara and Vinal. She was born on July 11, 1873, and died less than a year after her son, on May 16, 1904. The last stone was that of John F. Childs himself, born September 8, 1860, and died, having outlived two wives and two children, March 18 1935. There were no other stones nearby. I wondered if John F. had been the last of his line. Here, in this tiny cemetery, the story of his life was laid bare in the space of five carved pieces of rock.

But the stone we were looking for stood in the farthest southern corner of the cemetery. There were no names upon it, and no dates of birth or death. It read only, THE CHILDREN OF GILEAD, followed by the same word carved three times—

INFANT

INFANT

INFANT

—and a plea to God to have mercy on their souls. As unbaptized children, they would originally have been laid to rest outside the cemetery, but it was clear that at some point in the past the position of the cemetery fence had been discreetly altered in this corner, and the Children of Gilead now lay within its boundaries. It said a lot about the people of the town that quietly, and without fuss, they had embraced these lost infants and allowed them to rest within the precincts of the graveyard.

'What happened to the men who did this?' asked Angel. I looked at him, and saw the grief etched on his face.

'Men and women,' I corrected him. 'The women must have known and colluded in what happened, for whatever reason. Two of those children died of unknown causes, but one was stabbed with a knitting needle shortly after birth. You ever hear of a man stabbing a child with a knitting needle? No, the women covered it up, whether out of fear or shame, or something else. I don't think Dubus was lying about that much. Nobody was ever charged. The authorities examined two girls and confirmed that they'd given birth at some point in the recent past, but there was no evidence to connect those births with the bodies that they found. The community got together and claimed that the children were given up for private adoption. There was no paperwork for the births, which was a crime in itself but one that nobody felt the urge to prosecute. Dubus told the investigators that the kids were sent to somewhere in Utah. A car came along, he said, collected them, then disappeared into the night. That was the story, and it was only years later that he recanted and claimed that the mothers of the girls who had given birth had killed the infants. Anyway, a week or so after the bodies were found, the community had already broken up, and people were going their separate ways.'

'Free to abuse somewhere else,' said Angel.

I didn't reply. What was there to say, particularly to Angel, who had been a victim of such abuse himself, farmed out by his father to men who took their pleasures from the body of a child? That was why he was here now, in this cold cemetery in a remote northern town. That was why they were both here, these hunters among hunters. It was no longer a question of money for them, or their own convenience. That might once have been true, but it was true no longer. They were here now for the same reason that I was: because to ignore what had happened to children in the recent and distant pasts, to turn away and look elsewhere because it was easier to do so, was to be an accomplice to the crimes that were committed. To refuse to delve deeper would be to collude with the offenders.

'Somebody's tended to this grave,' said Angel.

He was right. There were no weeds, and the grass had been cut back so that it would not obscure the marker. Even the words on the stone had been enhanced with black paint so that they would stand out.

'Who takes care of a fifty-year-old grave?' he asked.

'Maybe the man who now owns Gilead,' I replied. 'Let's go ask him.'

About five miles along the 201, beyond Moose River and past the Sandy Bay town line, a sign pointed north to the Bald Mountain Hiking Trail, and I knew that we were nearing Gilead. Without Angel's prior knowledge, the site itself would have been difficult to find. The road we took had no name. It was marked only by a sign reading *Private Property* and, as Angel had said, an additional warning listing those who were particularly unwelcome. About a half mile up the road was a gate. It was locked, and a fence disappeared into the forest on either side.

'Gilead's in there,' said Angel, pointing north into the woods. 'Maybe another half mile or more.'

'And the house?'

'Same distance, but straight up the road. You can see it from farther up that track.' He pointed to a rutted dirt trail that followed the fence southeast.

I pulled the car to the side of the road. We climbed over the gate and immediately cut into the forest.

We had walked for fifteen or twenty minutes when we came to the clearing.

Most of the buildings still remained. In a place where wood was the main building material, Lumley had chosen to use stone for a number of the houses, so confident was he that his ideal community would last. The dwellings varied in size from two-room cottages to larger structures comfortably capable of housing families of six or more. Most had fallen into ruin, and some had clearly been burned, but one appeared to have been restored to some degree. It had a roof, and its four windows were barred. The front door, a solid piece of rough-hewn oak, was locked. All told, the community could not have numbered more than a dozen families at its peak. There were many such places in Maine: forgotten villages, towns that had withered away and died, settlements founded on misplaced faith in a charismatic leader. I thought of the ruins of Sanctuary, out on Casco Bay, and of Faulkner and his slaughtered flock in Aroostook. Gilead was another in a long and ignominious line of failed ventures, doomed by unscrupulous men and base instincts.

And above it all loomed the great steeple of the Savior's Church, Lumley's rival to St Anthony's. The walls had been built, the steeple raised, but the roof had never been placed upon it, and no one had ever worshiped within its walls. It was less a tribute to God than a monument to one man's vanity. Now the forest had claimed it for its own. It was smothered in ivy so that it appeared as though nature itself had built it, creating a temple from leaves and tendrils, with grass and weeds for its floor and a tree for a tabernacle, for a shagbark hickory had grown where the altar might have stood, spreading its bare arms like the skeletal remains of a deranged preacher, stripped of his flesh by the cold wind as he railed against the world, his bones browned by the actions of the sun and the rain.

Everything about Gilead spoke of loss and decay and corruption. Had I not been aware of the crimes that were committed here, the children who had suffered and the infants who had died, it would still have left me feeling uneasy and soiled. True, there was a kind of grandeur to the half-built church, but it was without beauty, and even nature itself seemed to have been corrupted by its contact with this place. Dubus was right. Lumley had chosen badly for the site of his community.

As Angel moved to examine the church more closely, I stopped him with my hand.

'What's the matter?' he said.

'Don't touch any of the plants,' I said.

'Why not?'

'They're all poisonous.'

And it was true: it was as though every foul weed, every noxious flower, had found a home here, some of which I had never seen before this far north, or clustered together in this way. There was mountain laurel, with its shredded, rusty bark, its pink-and-white flowers, dotted with red like the blood of insects and with stamens that responded to the touch like insects or animals, now absent. I saw white snakeroot, some of its flowers still in their final bloom, that could render cow's milk fatal to drink if the animal fed upon the plant. Near a patch of marsh, iced over at its banks, water hemlock, all toothed leaves and streaked stems, beckoned, each part of it potentially lethal. There was jimson weed, which belonged more properly in fields, and celandine, and stinging nettles. Even the ivy was poisonous. No birds would ever come here, I thought, not even in summer. It would always be a silent, desolate place.

We stared up at the massive steeple, its peak higher even than the trees around it. Sections of the alcove windows glared darkly over the forest through layers of ivy, and the empty space intended to house the bell was now almost entirely covered by the plant. There were no doors, merely rectangular gaps at the base of the steeple and at one side of the church itself, and no glass filled the windows. Even to attempt to enter would be to invite cuts and stings from the weeds and nettles that blocked the way, although when I looked closer it did appear that someone had, at some point, cut a way through, for the weeds were taller and thicker at the sides. To the west of the church, I saw the remains of a trail that had been cut through the forest, its path clear from the absence of tall trees. That was how they had transported the building materials into the forest, but half a century later all that was left was a divide conquered by shrubs.

We walked over to the intact house. I nodded to Angel and he began working on the lock.

'Hasn't been opened in a while,' he said. He took a small can of WD-40 from his jacket pocket, sprayed the lock, then went at it again. After several minutes, we heard a click. He applied pressure to the door with his shoulder and it creaked open.

There were two rooms inside, both empty. The floor was concrete, and was clearly not part of the original structure. The sun, which had struggled for so long to shine through the filthy glass, now took the opportunity afforded by the open door to bathe the interior with light, but there was nothing to see and nothing to illuminate. Louis tapped one of the windows lightly with his knuckle.

'It's Plexiglas,' he said. He traced his finger around the edge of the frame. It looked as if someone had once tried to chip away at the cement holding it in place. They hadn't gotten far, but the evidence of the failed attempt still remained.

He leaned in closer to the glass, then knelt, trying to get a clearer look at something that his sharp eyes had picked out.

'See here,' he said.

There were tiny marks scratched upon it in the bottom right-hand corner. I moved my head in an effort to see what they might be, but it was Angel who deciphered them first.

'L. M.,' he said.

'Lucy Merrick,' I said. It had to be. There were no other markings on the walls or the windows. Had the letters been carved by a kid seeking a thrill, there would have been other initials too, other names. But Gilead was not a place to come to alone, not willingly.

And I knew then that this was where they had taken Andy Kellog and, later, Merrick's daughter. Andy Kellog had come back damaged, traumatized, but still alive. Lucy Merrick, though, had never returned. Instantly, the air in the house smelled stale and dead to me, infected by what I knew in my heart had occurred in its rooms.

'Why here?' said Louis, softly. 'Why did they bring them here?'

'Because of what happened before,' said Angel. He touched his finger to the marks made by Lucy on the glass, tracing each one carefully and tenderly in an act of remembrance. I thought of my own actions in the attic of my house, reading a message written in dust. 'It added to the pleasure, knowing they were repeating something that had been done in the past, like they were continuing a tradition.'

His words echoed Christian's talk of 'clusters'. Was that what lay behind Clay's fascination with Gilead? Did he want to re-create the events of half a century before, or did he help others to do so? Then again, perhaps his interest was not prurient or lascivious. Maybe he wasn't to blame in any way for what had happened, and only his professional curiosity drew him to this site deep in the woods, haunting his memory and finding form in the picture that Merrick had torn apart on Joel Harmon's wall, and that Mason Dubus proudly displayed on his. But I was starting to believe that less and less. If men had sought to re-create the original crimes here, then perhaps they would have sought out their instigator, Mason Dubus. I was aware that we were following a path trodden by Clay, tracing the marks that he had left as he moved north. He had given one of his precious artworks to Dubus. It did not seem like a mere act of thanks. It was closer to a gesture of respect, almost of affection.

I walked through the two rooms, looking for any further trace of Lucy Merrick's presence in that house, but there was none. There had probably been mattresses once, blankets, even some books or magazines. There were light switches on the walls, but the sockets were bare of bulbs. I saw marks in the upper corner of the second room, where a metal plate of some kind had been held in place, a neat hole drilled below them. A larger hole in the wall, since filled in but its shape still visible, indicated the spot where a stove had once stood, and the fireplace had long ago been bricked up. Lucy Merrick had disappeared in September. It must already have been cold up here. How did she stay warm, if this was where they had kept her? I could find no answer. Everything had been removed, and it was clear too that these rooms had not been used for many years.

'They killed her here, didn't they?' asked Angel. He was still by the window, his fingers maintaining contact with the carved letters on the glass, as though by doing so he could somehow touch Lucy Merrick herself and comfort her, so that, wherever she was, she might know that someone had found the marks she had left, and was grieving for her. The letters were small, barely there. She did not want the men who had abducted her to see them. Perhaps she believed they would provide proof of her story when she was released, or did she fear, even then, that she might never be freed, and she hoped these letters might serve as a sign in case anyone cared enough about her to try to discover her fate?

'They didn't kill any of the others,' I said. 'That's why they wore masks, so they could let them go without worrying about being identified. They might have taken it a step farther, or something could just have gone wrong. Somehow, she died, and they cleared away any sign that anyone had ever been here, then locked it up and never came back again.'

Angel let his fingers drop.

'Caswell, the guy who owns the land, he must have known what was happening.'

'Yes,' I said softly. 'He must have known.'

I turned to leave. Louis was ahead of me. He stood, framed in the doorway, dark against the morning sunlight. He opened his mouth to speak, then stopped. The sound had carried clearly to each of us. It was a shotgun shell being jacked. A voice spoke. It said: 'Boy, you better not move an inch, or I'll blow your damn head off.'

32

Angel and I stood silently in the house, unwilling to move or speak. Louis remained frozen in the doorway, his arms outstretched from his sides to show the man beyond that they were empty.

'You come out slowly now,' said the voice. 'You can put your hands on your head. Them fellas inside can do the same. You won't see me, but I can see you. I tell you now, just one of you moves and Slick here in his fancy coat will have a hole where his face used to be. You're trespassing on private property. Might be that you have guns too. Not a judge in the state will convict if you make me kill you while you're armed.'

Louis slowly stepped out of the doorway and stood with his hands on the back of his head, facing out into the woods. With no choice, Angel and I followed. I tried to find the source of the voice, but there was only silence as we stepped from the shelter of the house. Then a man emerged from a grove of fetterbush and hoptree. He was dressed in green camouflage pants and a matching jacket, and armed with a Browning twelve-gauge. He was in his early fifties, big but not muscular. His face was pale and his hair was too long, squatting untidily on his head like a filthy mop. He didn't look as if he had slept properly in a long time. His eyes were almost falling out of his head, as though the pressure on his skull was too much for them to bear, and the sockets were so rimmed with red that the skin seemed to be slowly peeling away from the flesh beneath. There were fresh sores on his cheeks, chin, and neck, flecked with red where he had cut them as he tried to shave.

'Who are you?' he said. He held the gun steady, but his voice trembled as though he could only project confidence physically or vocally, but not both at once.

'Hunters,' I replied.

'Yeah?' He sneered at us. 'And what do you hunt without a rifle?'

'Men,' said Louis simply.

Another crack opened in the man's veneer. I had a vision of the skin beneath his clothing crisscrossed with tiny fractures, like a china doll on the verge of shattering into a thousand pieces.

'Are you Caswell?' I asked.

'Who's asking?'

'My name is Charlie Parker. I'm a private investigator. These are my colleagues.'

'My name's Caswell all right, and this is my land. You got no business being here.'

'In a way, our business is exactly why we're here.'

'You got business, you take it to a store.'

'We wanted to ask you some questions.'

Caswell raised the muzzle of the gun slightly and fired off a round. It went some distance over our heads, but I still flinched. He jacked another load and the eye of the gun maintained its unblinking vigil on us once again.

'I don't think you heard me. You're in no position to ask questions.'

'Talk to us, or talk to the police. It's your choice.'

Caswell's hands worked on the grip and stock of the rifle. 'The hell are you talking about? I got no problems with the police.'

'Did you fix up this house?' I indicated the building behind us.

'What if I did? It's my land.'

'Seems like a curious thing to do, fixing up a ruin in a deserted village.'

'There's no law against it.'

'No, I guess not. Might be a law against what was done in it, though.'

I was taking a chance. Caswell might try to shoot us just for goading him, but I didn't think so. He didn't look the type. Despite the shotgun and the camo clothing, there was something soft about him, as though someone had just armed the Pillsbury Doughboy.

'I don't know what you're talking about,' he said, but he retreated a step from us.

'I mean what was done in Gilead,' I lied, 'and those children who were killed.'

A peculiar range of emotions played themselves out in dumb show upon Caswell's face. There was shock first of all, then fear, followed by a slow-dawning realization that I was talking about the distant, not the recent, past. I watched with satisfaction as he tried unsuccessfully to disguise his relief. He knew. He knew what had happened to Lucy Merrick.

'Yeah,' he said. 'I reckon so. That's why I try to keep folks away from here. Never know what kind of people it might attract.'

'Sure,' I said. 'And what kind of people might they be?'

Caswell didn't manage to answer the question. He had talked himself into a corner, and now he planned to bluster his way out.

'People, that's all,' he said.

'Why did you buy this place, Mr Caswell? It seems like an odd thing to have done, given all that happened here.'

'There's no law against a man buying property. I've lived up here all my life. The land came cheap, on account of its history.'

'And its history didn't trouble you?'

'No, it didn't trouble me one bit. Now—'

I didn't let him finish. 'I'm just wondering, because something is clearly troubling you. You don't look well. You look kind of stressed, to tell the truth. In fact, you seem downright frightened.'

I'd hit the bull's-eye. The truth of what I had said manifested itself in Caswell's reaction. The little cracks opened wider and deeper, and the gun tilted slightly toward the ground. I could sense

Louis considering his options, his body tensing as he prepared to draw on Caswell.

'No,' I whispered, and Louis relaxed without question.

Caswell became aware of the impression he was creating. He drew himself up straight and raised the stock of the gun to his shoulder, sighting down the barrel, the slatted rib along the top of the Browning like the raised spine of an animal. I heard Louis give a low hiss, but I was no longer worried about Caswell. He was all front.

'I'm not scared of you,' he said. 'Don't make that mistake.'

'Then who are you scared of?'

Caswell shook his head to free some drops of moisture that clung to the ends of his hair. 'I think you'd better be getting back to your car, you and your "colleagues." Keep your hands on your head too while you do it, and don't come around here again. You got your first and last warning.'

He waited for us to begin walking, then started to retreat into the woods.

'You ever hear of a Lucy Merrick, Mr Caswell?' I called to him. I paused and looked back over my shoulder, still keeping my hands on my head.

'No,' he said. There was a pause before he spoke again, as though he were trying to convince himself that the name had not been spoken aloud. 'I never heard that name before.'

'How about Daniel Clay?'

He shook his head. 'Just walk on out of here. I'm done talking to you.'

'We'll be back, Mr Caswell. I think you know that.'

Caswell didn't answer. He kept retreating, moving deeper and deeper into the forest, no longer caring if we were moving or not, just trying to put as much distance between himself and us as he could. I wondered who Caswell would call, once he was back in the safety of his own house. It didn't matter now. We were close. For whatever reason, Caswell was falling apart, and I had every intention of speeding up the process.

★   ★   ★

That afternoon, I got talking to the young guy behind the bar at the lodge, the one who had witnessed the altercation between Angel and the men from Jersey. His name was Skip, although I didn't hold that against him, and he was twenty-two and taking his master's degree in community planning and development at USM. Skip's father was part owner of the place, and he told me that he worked there during the summer, and whenever he could spare time in hunting season. He planned on finding a job in Somerset County once he had finished his degree. Unlike some of his peers, he didn't want to leave. Instead, he hoped to find a way to make it a better place in which to live, although he was smart enough to realize that the odds were currently stacked against the region.

Skip told me that Caswell's family had lived in these parts for three or four generations, but they'd always been dirt poor. Caswell sometimes worked as a guide during the season, and the rest of the year he picked up jobs as a general handyman, but as the years had gone by he had let the guide work slip, although he was still in demand when repairs needed to be done to local houses. When he had bought the Gilead tract, he'd paid for it without taking out a bank loan. The land hadn't exactly been cheap, despite what Caswell had told us, even if its history hadn't made it the most attractive of propositions, and it was more money than anyone expected Otis Caswell to come up with, but he hadn't bitched about the price or even attempted to bargain with the realtor, who was selling it on behalf of the descendants of the late Bennett Lumley. Since then, he had posted his *No Trespassing* notices and kept himself pretty much to himself. Nobody bothered him up there. Nobody had cause to.

There were two possibilities, neither of which reflected well on Caswell. The first was that someone had given him the money to make the purchase in order to keep their interest in the land secret, after which Caswell turned a blind eye to the uses to which the restored house was being put. The other possibility was that he was an active participant in what occurred there. Either way, he knew enough to make him worth pursuing. I found his number in the local directory and called him from my room. He picked up on the second ring.

'Expecting a call, Mr Caswell?' I asked.

'Who is this?'

'We met earlier. My name is Parker.'

He hung up. I dialed again. This time three or four rings went by before he picked up the phone.

'What do you want?' he said. 'I told you: I got nothing to say to you.'

'I think you know what I want, Mr Caswell. I want you to tell me about what went on in that empty house with the Plexiglas windows and the strong door. I want you to tell me about Andy Kellog and Lucy Merrick. If you do that, then maybe I can save you.'

'Save me? Save me from what? What are you talking about?'

'From Frank Merrick.'

There was silence on the other end of the line.

'Don't call here again,' said Caswell. 'I don't know a Frank Merrick, or any of them other names you said.'

'He's coming, Otis. You'd better believe that. He wants to know what happened to his daughter. And he's not going to be reasonable like my friends and me. I think your buddies are going to cut you loose, Otis, and leave you to him. Or maybe they'll decide that you're the weak link, and do to you what they did to Daniel Clay.'

'We didn't – ,' began Caswell, then caught himself.

'Didn't what, Otis? Didn't do anything to Daniel Clay? Didn't kill him? Why don't you tell me about it.'

'Fuck you,' said Caswell. 'Fuck you to hell and back.'

He hung up. When I called a third time nobody picked up. The phone just rang and rang at the other end, and I pictured Otis Caswell in his white-trash house, his hands over his ears to block out the sound, until at last the ringing changed to a busy signal as he removed the connection from the wall.

★   ★   ★

Night descended. Our encounter with Caswell marked the beginning of the end. Men were heading northwest, Merrick among them, but the sands of his life were slowly trickling away, not through the neck of some old hourglass but from the palm of his own hand, his fingers clasped tightly against his skin as the dry grains slipped through the gap below his little finger. By asking questions about Daniel Clay, he had shortened the span of his existence. He had held open his hands and accepted the sands, knowing that he would be unable to hold them for long, that now they would peter away twice as fast. He had merely hoped that he could stay alive long enough to discover his daughter's final resting place.

And so, as darkness fell, Merrick found himself in the Old Moose Lodge. Its name sounded quaint, evoking images of wooden floors, comfortable chairs, friendly Maine hosts to greet the guests, a roaring log fire in the lobby, rooms that managed to be clean and modern while never losing touch with their rustic roots, and breakfasts of maple syrup, bacon, and pancakes, served by smiling young women at tables overlooking placid lakes and mile upon mile of evergreen forest.

In fact, nobody had ever stayed in the Old Moose Lodge, at least not in a bed. In the past, men might have slept off their drunks in a back room, but they had done so on the floor, so stupefied by alcohol that comfort mattered less than a place in which to lie flat and allow the blankness they had been seeking to overwhelm them. Now even that small concession had been taken away for fear that the lodge's liquor license, annual speculation about the renewal of which provided regular fodder for the local newspaper, and most of the populace, might finally be removed if it was found to be operating as a crash pad for drunks. Still, the impression created by its name was not entirely inapt.

It did have wooden floors.

Merrick sat at a deuce near the back of the bar, facing away from the door but with a mirror on the wall in front of him that allowed him to see all those who entered without anyone immediately being able to spot him. Although the bar was warm, causing him to sweat profusely, he did not take off his heavy tan suede coat. In part, it enabled him to keep the gun in its pocket within easy reach. It also meant that the wound in his side, which had begun to bleed again, would not be visible if it soaked through the bandages and into his shirt.

He had killed the Russians just beyond Bingham, where Stream Road branched off the 201 and followed the path of the Austin Stream toward Mayfield Township. He had known that they would come. The killing of Demarcian alone might have been enough to draw them to him, but there were also grudges outstanding against him relating to a pair of jobs at the beginning of the nineties, one in Little Odessa, the other in Boston. He was surprised that they had not made a move on him in prison, but the Supermax had protected him by isolating him, and his reputation had done the rest. After the killing of Demarcian, word would have spread. Calls would have been made, favors requested, debts wiped out. Perhaps he should not have killed Demarcian, but the little man with the withered arm had repelled him, and he was a link in the chain of events that had taken Merrick's daughter from him. If nothing else, the lawyer Eldritch had been right about that much. If the price to be paid for Demarcian's death was more killing, then Merrick was willing to oblige. They would not stop him from reaching Gilead. There, he felt certain, he would find the answers that he sought.

He wondered how the Russians had found him so quickly. After all, he had changed his car, yet here they were, those two men in their black 4X4. Merrick reflected that perhaps he should not have left Rebecca Clay's ex-husband alive, but Merrick was not a man who killed without some cause, and as far he could tell, Legere knew nothing. Even his ex-wife had not trusted him enough to share anything about her father with him.

But Merrick was also certain that, almost since his quest had begun, his progress was being shadowed and his every move watched. He thought of the old lawyer in his paper-filled office, and his unseen benefactor, the mysterious other who had instructed Eldritch to help him, who had provided funds, a place to hide, and information. The lawyer had never given a satisfactory explanation for his willingness to aid Merrick, and Merrick's distrust of him had quickly grown, leading him to distance himself from the old man as soon as was feasible, the period of his recent brief incarceration apart. Yet even after that, when he was taking care to cover his tracks, there were times when he had felt himself being watched, sometimes when he was in a crowd, trying to lose himself in a mall or a bar, and other times when he was alone. He thought that he had caught a glimpse of a man once, a ragged figure in an old black coat who was examining Merrick thoughtfully through a cloud of cigarette smoke, but when he tried to follow him, the man had vanished, and Merrick had not seen him again.

Then there were the nightmares. They had begun in the safe house, shortly after Merrick had been given the car and the money by Eldritch: visions of pale, wasted creatures, their eye sockets black, their mouths lipless and wrinkled, all dressed in soiled tan coats, old mackintoshes with buttons missing and reddish-brown stains on the collars and the sleeves. Merrick would awaken in the darkness, and in that moment between sleeping and consciousness he thought that he could almost see them receding from him, as though they had been leaning over him while he slept, no breath emerging from their mouths, only a stale smell of something old and noxious lodged deep within themselves. Since he had abandoned the safe house, the dreams had come less often, but there were still nights when he ascended from the depths of sleep to a crawling sensation on his skin and a faint stench that had not been there when he closed his eyes.

Had Eldritch, reckoning Merrick to be a liability, told the Russians where he was, facilitated by the other, the man in the ragged black coat? Were this man and Eldritch's client one and the same? Merrick did not know, and it no longer mattered. It was all nearing an end, and soon there would be peace.

The Russians had been careless. He had seen them coming, watching in the rearview as they hung three or four cars back, occasionally overtaking when it was necessary to keep him in sight. He had pulled over at one point to see if they would pass him, and they had, keeping their eyes fixed straight ahead, scrupulously ignoring him as he spread a map upon the steering wheel and pretended to trace his route with a finger, too many trucks passing for them to be able to take him while he was stopped. He had let them go, then pulled out after a few minutes had gone by. He saw them ahead, hanging back in the slow lane, hoping that he would pass them again, and he obliged. After a couple of miles, he turned onto Stream Road, and from there found a dirt track that would suit his purpose. He followed it for over a mile, past abandoned shacks set back from the road, past a double-wide trailer and cars slouched on tireless rims, until even those humble tokens of human habitation disappeared and the road became rougher yet, bouncing him in his seat and causing his spine to ache. When there was only forest before and behind, to north and south, east and west, he cut the engine. He could hear them approaching. He got out of the car, leaving the driver's door open, and moved into the trees, heading back in the direction in which he had come, until the Russians appeared. They stopped when they came to his abandoned car. He could almost guess the conversation that was taking place within. They would have known that they had followed him into a trap. The only question for them now was how to free themselves from it while ensuring Merrick's death and their own survival. Crouched in the undergrowth, Merrick saw the one in the passenger seat, the man with red hair, look over his shoulder. Their options were limited. They could reverse and leave, hoping to catch him again on the road, whether he tried to escape on foot or by car; or they could get out, one from each side, and try to hunt him on foot. They would be at their most vulnerable when they opened the doors, but their reasoning would be that if he opened fire on them he might hit one of them at most, if he was lucky, and in doing so he would expose his position.

In the end, Merrick did not wait for them to open the doors. As soon as the redheaded man looked away Merrick lunged out of the bushes and began firing through the rear window; once, twice, three times, and as it disintegrated he saw a wash of blood appear on the windshield and the driver collapse sideways. His partner opened the passenger door and dropped to the ground, firing at Merrick as the older man advanced, for there was no retreating now. Merrick felt a tug at his side and a sensation of numbness, followed by a searing, red-hot pain, but still he fired, experiencing a surge of satisfaction as the body of the second Russian jerked on the ground and the shooting stopped.

He advanced slowly on the slumped figure, feeling the blood flowing down his side, soaking his shirt and his pants. He kicked the Russian's gun away and stood over him. The redheaded man was lying on his side against the right rear wheel. There was a wound beneath his neck and another almost dead in the center of his chest. His eyes were half closed, but he was still breathing. Gasping at the pain of his injury, Merrick bent down, picked up the Russian's Colt, then searched the pockets of the man's jacket until he found a wallet and a spare magazine for the pistol. The name on the driver's license was Yevgeny Utarov. It meant nothing to him.

Merrick took the $326 from the wallet and jammed it into his own pocket, then tossed the wallet on the dying man's lap. He spit on the ground and was happy to see that there was no blood in the sputum. Nevertheless, he was angry at himself for being wounded. It was the first time he had been hit in many, many years. It seemed to speak to him of the slow march of time, of his age and his impending mortality. He swayed slightly on his feet. The movement seemed to distract the man named Yevgeny from the fact of his own dying. His eyes opened wider and he tried to say something. Merrick stood over him.

'Give me a name,' he said. 'You got time in you yet. Otherwise,

I'll leave you here to die. It'll be slow, and that pain you're feeling will get worse. You give me a name, and it'll go easier on you.'

Utarov whispered something.

'Speak up, now,' said Merrick. 'I ain't bending down to hear you.'

Utarov tried again. This time, the words sounded like blades being whetted against rough stone deep in his throat.

'Dubus,' he said.

Merrick shot the Russian twice more in the chest, then staggered away, leaving a trail of blood behind him on the road like squashed berries. He leaned against his car and stripped to the waist, exposing the wound. The bullet was lodged deep in the flesh. In the past, there were men whom he could have called upon to help him, but they were all gone now. He tied the shirt around his waist to stem the bleeding, then put his coat and jacket on over his naked torso and got in the car. He slipped the Smith 10, now with only three rounds left, back under the driver's seat, and placed the Colt in the pocket of his coat. Turning the car back toward the main road was agony, and the ride along the trail caused him to grit his teeth so that he would not have to hear himself cry out, but he managed it. He drove for three miles before he found a veterinary practice, and there he made the old man whose name was on the sign outside remove the bullet while Merrick held a gun on him. He did not pass out from the pain, but it was a close thing.

Merrick knew who Dubus was. Somehow, all of this had started with him, had begun the first time Dubus forced himself upon a child. He had brought his appetites with him to Gilead, and from there they had spread. Merrick held a gun to the veterinarian's head and asked him if he knew where Mason Dubus lived, and the old man told him, for Dubus was well-known in the region. Merrick locked the veterinarian in the basement, with two pint bottles of water and some bread and cheese so that he could keep body and soul together. He promised the vet that he would call the cops within twenty-four hours. Until then, he would just have to amuse himself as best he could. He found a bottle of Tylenol in a medicine cabinet, and helped himself to some rolls of clean dressing and a pair of fresh pants from the old man's closet, then left and continued on his journey, but driving was hard. The Tylenol took some of the edge off the pain, though, and at Caratunk he turned off the 201 again, as the vet had told him to do, and came at last to Mason Dubus's house.

Dubus saw him coming. In a way, Dubus had been expecting him. He was still talking on his cell phone when Merrick shot the lock from the front door and entered the house, already dripping spots of blood on the pristine floor. Dubus pressed the red button to end the call, then tossed the phone on a chair beside him.

'I know who you are,' he said.

'That's good,' said Merrick.

'Your little girl is dead.'

'I know that.'

'Soon, you'll be dead too.'

'Maybe, but you'll be dead sooner.'

Dubus pointed a trembling finger at Merrick. 'You think I'm going to plead with you for my life? You think I'm going to help you?'

Merrick raised the Colt. 'No, I don't,' he said, and he shot Dubus twice. As the old man lay spasming on the floor, Merrick picked up the cell phone and redialed. The phone was answered after two rings. There was no voice, but Merrick could hear a man breathing. Then the connection was ended. Merrick put the phone down and left the house, Dubus's final breaths slowly fading from hearing as he left him to die.

Dubus listened to Merrick's footsteps, then the noise of a car driving away. There was a great weight on his chest, studded with pain, as though a bed of nails had been laid upon him. He stared at the ceiling. There was blood in his mouth. He knew that he was only moments away from death. He began to pray, to ask God to forgive his sins. His lips moved soundlessly as he tried to remember the right words, but he was distracted by memories, and by his anger at the fact that he should die this way, the victim of a killer who would shoot an unarmed old man.

He felt cold air, and there came a sound from behind him. Someone approached, and he thought that Merrick had come back to finish him off, but when he moved his head he saw, not Merrick, but the end of a filthy tan coat, and old brown shoes stained with dirt. There was a stench in the air, and even in the time of his dying it made him gag. Then there were more footsteps to his left, and he was aware of presences behind him, of unseen figures watching him. Dubus tilted his head and saw pale features, and black holes gaping in withered skin. He opened his mouth to speak, but there were no more words left to say, and no more breaths left in his body.

And he died with the Hollow Men in his eyes.

Merrick drove for miles, but his vision began to blur, and the pain and the loss of blood had weakened him. He made it as far as the Old Moose Lodge and there, fooled, like so many others in the past, by the name's false promise of a bed, he stopped.

Now he was sitting at the deuce, drinking Four Roses on top of the Tylenol, snoozing a little in the hope that he might recover some of his strength so that he could continue on to Gilead. Nobody bothered him. The Old Moose Lodge actively encouraged its customers to take the occasional short rest, as long as they got back to drinking when they were done. A jukebox played honky-tonk music, and the glass eyes of dead animals stared down at the patrons from the walls, while Merrick drifted, unsure if he was sleeping or waking. At some point, a waitress asked him if he was okay and Merrick nodded, pointing to his glass to order another bourbon, even though he had barely touched the first. He was afraid that they might ask him to move on, and he wasn't ready to do that yet.

Waking. Sleeping. Music, then no music. Voices. Whispers.

daddy

Merrick opened his eyes. There was a little girl sitting across from him. She had dark hair, and her skin was broken where the gas had erupted from within. A bug was crawling across her forehead. He wanted to brush it away, but his hands wouldn't move.

'Hi, honey,' he said. 'Where you been?'

There was dirt on the little girl's hands, and two of her fingernails were broken.

waiting

'Waiting for what, honey?'

for you

Merrick nodded. 'I couldn't come until now. I was – they had me locked up, but I was always thinking about you. I never forgot about you.'

i know. you were too far away. now you're near. now I can come to you.

'What happened to you, darlin'? Why'd you go away?'

i fell asleep. i fell asleep and i couldn't wake up.

There was no emotion in her voice. Her eyes never blinked. Merrick noticed that the left side of her face was cherry red and purple, marked by the colors of lividity.

'Won't be long now, honey,' he said. He found the strength to move his hand. He reached for her, and felt something cold and hard against his fingers. The whiskey glass toppled on the table, distracting him for a moment so that when he looked back the girl was gone. The whiskey flowed around his fingers and dripped onto the floor, and the waitress appeared and said, 'I think maybe you ought to be heading home now,' and Merrick nodded and replied, 'Yeah, I think maybe you're right. It's time to go home.'

He stood, feeling the blood squelch in his shoe. The room began to spin around him, and he gripped the table to give himself some support. The sensation of giddiness went away, and he was aware once again of the pain in his side. He looked down. The side of his trousers was soaked a deep red. The waitress also saw the stain.

'Hey,' she said. 'What—'

And then she looked into Merrick's eyes and thought better of asking the question. Merrick reached into his pocket and found some bills. There was a twenty and a ten among them, and he threw them all on the waitress's tray.

'Thank you, darlin',' he said, and now there was a kindness in his eyes and the waitress was uncertain whether he thought that he was talking to her or to another who had taken her place in his mind. 'I'm ready now.'

He walked from the bar, passing through the ranks of dancing couples and noisy drunks, of lovers and friends, moving from light to darkness, from the life within to the life beyond. When he stepped outside, the cool of the night air made him reel again for a moment, then cleared his head. He took his keys from his jacket pocket and headed for his car, each step forcing more blood from his wound, each step taking him a little closer to the end.

He stopped at the car and used his left hand to support himself against the roof while his right fitted the key into the lock. He opened the door and saw himself reflected in the glass of the side window, then another reflection joined his, hovering behind his shoulder. It was a bird, a monstrous dove with a white face and a dark beak and human eyes buried deep in its sockets. It raised a wing, but the wing was black, not white, with claws at the end that held something long and metal in their grip.

And then the wing began to beat with a soft swishing sound, and he felt a new, sharp pain as his collarbone was broken by a blow. He twisted, trying to get to the gun in his pocket, but another bird appeared, this time a hawk, and this bird was holding a baseball bat, a good old-fashioned Louisville Slugger designed, if held in the right hands, to knock that baby right out of the ballpark, except now the Slugger was aimed at his head. He couldn't duck to avoid the blow, so he raised his left arm instead. The impact shattered his elbow, and the wings were beating and the blows were raining down upon him, and he dropped to his knees as something in his head came apart with a noise like bread breaking and his eyes were filled with red. He opened his mouth to speak, although there were no words for him to form, and his jaw was almost torn from his face as the crowbar swung in a lazy arc, felling him like a tree so that he lay flat on the cold gravel while the blood flowed and the beating went on, his body making strange, soft sounds, bones moving inside where bones had no right to move, the framework within fracturing, the tender organs bursting.

And still he lived.

The blows stopped, but the pain did not. A foot slid under his belly, levering him upward so that he flopped onto his back, resting slightly against the open door, half in, half out of the car, one hand lying useless by his side, the other thrown back into the interior. He saw the whole world through a red prism, dominated by birds like men and men like birds.

'He's gone,' said a voice, and it sounded familiar to Merrick.

'No he ain't,' said another. 'Not yet.'

There was hot breath close to his ear.

'You shouldn't have come here,' said the second voice. 'You should have just forgot about her. She's long dead, but she was good while she lasted.'

He was conscious of movement to his left. The crowbar struck him just above the ear and light shone through the prism, refracting the world in a red-tinged rainbow, turning it to splinters of color in his fading consciousness.

daddy

Almost there, honey, almost there.

And still, still he lived.

The fingers of his right hand clawed at the floor of the car. They found the barrel of the Smith 10, and he tugged it free of the tape and flicked at it until he could reach the grip, pulling it toward him, willing the blackness to lift, if only for a moment.

daddy

In a minute, honey. Daddy's got something he has to do first.

Slowly, he drew the gun to him. He tried to lift it, but his shattered arm would not hold the weight. Instead, he allowed himself to fall on his side, and the pain was almost beyond endurance as broken bone and torn flesh shuddered from the impact. He opened his eyes, or perhaps they had always been open and it was just the new waves of pain provoked by the movement that caused the mist briefly to lift. His cheek was flat against the gravel. His right arm was outstretched before him, the gun lying on the horizontal. There were two figures ahead of him, walking side by side perhaps fifteen feet from where he lay. He shifted his hand slightly, ignoring the feeling of his fractured bones rubbing against one another, until the gun was pointing at the two men.

And somehow, Merrick found the strength within himself to pull the trigger, or perhaps it was the strength of another added to his own, for he thought he felt a pressure on the knuckle of his index finger as though someone were pressing softly upon it.

The man on the right seemed to do a little jog, then stumbled and fell as his ruined ankle gave way. He shouted something that Merrick could not understand, but Merrick's finger was tightening on the trigger for the second shot and he had no time for the utterances of others. He fired again, the target larger now, for the injured man was lying on his side, his friend trying to lift him, but the shot was wild, the gun bucking in his hand and sending the bullet over the recumbent figure.

Merrick had the time and the strength to pull the trigger one last time. He fired as the blackness descended, and the bullet tore through the forehead of the wounded man, exiting in a red cloud. The survivor tried to drag the body away, but the dead man's foot caught in a storm drain. People appeared at the door of the Old Moose Lodge, for even in a place like this the sound of gunfire was bound to attract attention. Voices shouted, and figures began to run toward him. The survivor fled, leaving the dead man behind.

Merrick exhaled a final breath. A woman stood over him,

the waitress from the bar. She spoke, but Merrick did not hear
what she said

   daddy?

   i'm here

for Merrick was gone.

33

While Frank Merrick died with his daughter's name upon his lips, Angel, Louis, and I decided on a course of action to deal with Caswell. We were in the bar, the remains of our meal still scattered around us, but we weren't drinking.

We agreed that Caswell appeared close to some form of breakdown, although whether caused by incipient guilt or something else we could not tell. It was Angel who put it best, as he often did.

'If he's so overcome with guilt, then why? Lucy Merrick has been missing for years. Unless they kept her there for all that time, which doesn't seem too likely, then why is he so conscience-stricken now, all of a sudden?'

'Merrick, perhaps,' I said.

'Which means somebody told him that Merrick has been asking questions.'

'Not necessarily. It's not like Merrick has been keeping a low profile. The cops are aware of him, and thanks to Demarcian's killing, the Russians are too. Demarcian was involved somehow. Merrick didn't just pick his name out of a hat.'

'You think maybe these guys were sharing images of the abuse, and that's the connection to Demarcian?' asked Angel.

'Dr Christian said that he hadn't heard of anything involving men with masks turning up in photos or on video, but that doesn't mean there's nothing like that out there.'

'They would have been taking a chance by selling it,' said Angel. 'Might have risked drawing attention to themselves.'

'Maybe they needed the money,' said Louis.

'Caswell had enough to buy the Gilead land outright,' I replied. 'It doesn't sound like money was an issue.'

'But where did the cash come from?' asked Angel. 'Had to have come from somewhere, so maybe they were selling this stuff.'

'How much does it go for, though?' I said. 'Enough to buy a patch of unwanted land in a forest? The barman said that the land wasn't exactly given away for free, but it didn't cost the earth either. He could have bought it for the equivalent of nickels and dimes.'

Angel shrugged. 'Depends what they were selling. Depends how bad it was. For the kids, I mean.'

None of us said anything more for a time. I tried to create patterns in my mind, to put together a sequence of events that made sense, but I kept losing myself in contradictory statements and false trails. More and more, I was convinced that Clay was involved with what had occurred, but how then to balance that with Christian's view of him as a man who was almost obsessed with finding evidence of abuse, even to the detriment of his own career, or Rebecca Clay's description of a loving father devoted to the children in his charge? Then there were the Russians. Louis had asked some questions, and discovered the identity of the redheaded man who had come to my house. His name was Utarov, and he was one of the most trusted captains in the New England operation. According to Louis, there was paper out on Merrick, a piece of unfinished business relating to some jobs he had undertaken against the Russians sometime in the past, but there were also rumors of unease in New England. Prostitutes, mainly those of Asian, African, and Eastern European origin, had been moved out of Massachusetts and Providence and told to lie low, or they had been forced to do so by the men who controlled them. More specialized services had also been curtailed, particularly those relating to child pornography and child prostitution.

'Trafficking,' Louis had concluded. 'Explains why they took

the Asians and the others off the streets and left the pure American womanhood to take up the slack. They're worried about something, and it's connected to Demarcian.'

Their appetites would have stayed the same, wasn't that what Christian had told me? These men wouldn't have stopped abusing, but they might have found another outlet for their urges: young children acquired through Boston, perhaps, with Demarcian as one of the points of contact? What then? Did they film the abuse and sell it back to Demarcian and others like him, one operation funding another? Was that the nature of their particular 'Project'?

Caswell was part of it, and he was weak and vulnerable. I was certain that he had put in a call as soon as he had encountered us, a plea for help from those whom he had assisted in the past. It increased the pressure on all of them, forcing them to respond, and we would be waiting for them when they came.

Angel and Louis went to their car and drove up to Caswell's place, parking out of sight of the road and his house to take the first watch. I could almost see them there as I went to my room to get some sleep before my turn came, the car dark and quiet, perhaps some music playing low on the radio, Angel dozing, Louis still and intent, part of his attention on the road beyond while some hidden part of him wandered unknown worlds in his mind.

In my dreams, I walked through Gilead, and I heard the voices of children crying. I turned to the church and saw that there were young girls and boys wrapped in stinging ivy, the creepers tightening on their naked bodies as they were absorbed into the green world. I saw blood on the ground, and the remains of an infant wrapped in swaddling clothes, points of red seeping through the cloth.

And a thin man crawled out of a hole in the ground, his face torn and ruined by decay, his teeth visible through the holes in his cheeks.

'Old Gilead,' said Daniel Clay. 'It gets in your soul . . .'

* * *

The call came through on the phone in my room while I was sleeping. It was O'Rourke. Since there was no cell phone coverage in Jackman, it had seemed like a good idea to let someone know where I was in case anything happened back east, so both O'Rourke and Jackie Garner had the number of the lodge. After all, my gun was still out there, and I would bear some responsibility for whatever Merrick did with it.

'Merrick's dead,' he said.

I sat up. I could still taste food in my mouth, but it tasted of dirt, and the memory of my dream was strong. 'How?'

'Killed in the parking lot of the Old Moose Lodge. It sounds like he had an eventful final day. He was busy, right up to the end. Mason Dubus was shot dead yesterday with a ten-millimeter bullet. We're still waiting on a ballistics match, but it's not like people get shot here every day, and not usually with a ten. Couple of hours ago, a Somerset County sheriff's deputy found two bodies on a side road just out of Bingham. Russians, it looks like. Then they got a call from a woman who found her father locked in his basement a couple of miles north of the scene. Seems the old guy was a vet – the animal kind, not the war kind – and a man matching Merrick's description forced him to treat a gunshot wound and give him directions to Dubus's house before locking him up. From what the vet said, the wound was pretty serious, but he sewed it and strapped it as best he could. It looks like Merrick continued northwest, killed Dubus, then had to stop at the lodge. He was bleeding badly by then. According to witnesses, he sat in a corner, drank some whiskey, talked to himself, then headed outside. They were waiting for him there.'

'How many?'

'Two, both wearing bird masks. Ring any bells? They beat him to death, or near enough to it. I guess they thought the job was done when they left him.'

'How long did he survive?'

'Long enough to take your gun from under the driver's seat and shoot one of his attackers. I'm going on what I've been told, but the cops at the scene can't figure out how he managed it. They broke just about every bone in his body. He must have wanted to kill this guy real bad. He got him with one in the left ankle, then one in the head. His pal tried to drag him away, but he got the dead guy's foot caught in a drain so he had to leave him.'

'Did the vic have a name?'

'I'm sure he did, but he wasn't carrying a wallet. That, or his friend removed it before he left to try to cover his tracks. You want, maybe I can make some calls and arrange for you to take a look at him. He's down in Augusta now. ME's due to conduct an autopsy in the morning. How you liking Jackman? I never took you for the hunting kind. Not animals, anyhow.'

He stopped talking, then repeated the name of the town. 'Jackman,' he said, thoughtfully. 'The Old Moose Lodge is kind of on the way to Jackman, I guess.'

'I guess,' I echoed him.

'And Jackman's pretty close to Gilead, and Mason Dubus was the big dog when Gilead was open for business.'

'That's about it,' I said neutrally. I didn't know if O'Rourke was aware of Merrick's act of vandalism at Harmon's house, and I was sure he didn't know about Andy Kellog's pictures. I didn't want the cops up here dancing all over the site, not yet. I wanted to break Caswell for myself. I now felt that I owed it to Frank Merrick.

'If I can work it out, you can bet that soon a lot of other cops will have worked it out too,' said O'Rourke. 'I think you may be having some company up there. You know, I might feel bad if I thought you'd been holding out on me, but you wouldn't do that, would you?'

'I'm figuring it out as I go along, that's all,' I said. 'Wouldn't want to waste your time before I was certain of what I knew.'

'Yeah, I'll bet,' said O'Rourke. 'You give me a call when you go to look at that body.'

'I will.'

'Don't forget, now, otherwise I really might start to take things personally.'

He hung up.

It was time. I called Caswell. It took him four rings to pick up. He sounded groggy. Given the hour, I wasn't surprised.

'Who is this?'

'It's Charlie Parker.'

'I told you, I got nothing—'

'Shut up, Otis. Merrick is dead.' I didn't tell him that Merrick had managed to kill one of his attackers. It was better that he didn't know, not yet. If Merrick had been killed at the Old Moose last night, then anyone who was planning on hitting Jackman afterward would have been here by now, and would have run into Angel and Louis, but we had heard nothing, which meant that Merrick's killing of one of the men had scared them off for the moment. 'They're closing in on you, Otis. Two men attacked Merrick on the 201. I'd say that they were on their way up here when they took him, and this is their next stop. It could be that they'll try and take my friends and me out, but I don't think they're that brave. They took Merrick from behind, with bats and bars. We carry guns. Maybe they do too, but we're better than they are, I guarantee it. It's like I told you, Otis: you're the weak link. They get rid of you, and they can remake the chain stronger than it was before. Right now, I'm your best hope for making it alive to daybreak.'

There was silence on the other end of the line, then what sounded like a sob.

'I know you didn't mean to hurt her, Otis. You don't look like the kind of man who'd hurt a little girl.'

This time the crying was clearer. I pressed on.

'These other men, the ones who killed Frank Merrick, they're different from you. You're not like them, Otis. Don't let them drag you down to their level. You're not a killer, Otis. You don't kill men, and you don't kill little girls. I can't see it in you. I just can't.'

Caswell drew in a ragged breath. 'I wouldn't hurt a child,' he said. 'I love children.'

And there was something in the way he said it that made me feel filthy inside and out. It made me want to bathe in acid, then swallow what was left in the bottle to purge my insides.

'I know,' I said, and I had to force the words from my mouth. 'I bet you take care of those graves out at Moose River too, don't you? I'm right, aren't I?'

'Yes,' he said. 'They shouldn't ought to have done that to little babies. They shouldn't ought to have killed them.'

I tried not to think about why he thought that they should have been spared, why they should have been allowed to grow into young children. It wouldn't help, not now.

'Otis, what happened to Lucy Merrick? She was there, wasn't she, in that house? Then she disappeared. What happened, Otis? Where did she go?'

I heard him sniffing, could see him wiping his nose on his arm.

'It was an accident,' he said. 'They brought her here and—'

He stopped. He had never had to put a name to what he did to children before, not to someone who was not like him. This was not the time to make him.

'There's no need to tell me that, Otis, not yet. Just tell me how it ended.'

He did not reply, and I feared that I had lost him.

'I did bad,' said Caswell, like a child that had soiled itself. 'I did bad, and now they've come.'

'What?' I didn't understand. 'There are men there now?' I cursed the lack of coverage up here. Maybe I should have gone straight to Angel and Louis, but I remembered Caswell's sweaty hands on his shotgun. He might have been on the verge of a breakdown, but there was always the risk that he could be willing to take someone with him when he finally fell apart. According to Angel, his cottage had barred windows and a heavy oak door, like the house in which Lucy Merrick had been held. Breaking in without being shot at would have been anything from difficult to impossible.

'They've been here all along,' Caswell continued, the words slipping from his mouth in near-whispers, 'least for this past week, maybe more. I don't recall properly. It feels like they've always been here, and I don't sleep so good now because of them. I see them at night, mostly, out of the corner of my eye. They don't do nothing. They just stand there, like they're waiting for something.'

'Who are they, Otis?' But I already knew. They were the Hollow Men.

'Faces in shadow. Old dirty coats. I've tried talking to them, asking them what they want, but they don't answer, and when I try to look straight at them, it's like they're not there. I have to make them go away, but I don't know how.'

'My friends and I will come up there, Otis. We'll take you somewhere safe. You just hold on.'

'You know,' said Caswell faintly, 'I don't think they'll let me leave.'

'Are they there because of Lucy, Otis? Is that why they've come?'

'Her. The others.'

'But the others didn't die, Otis. That's right, isn't it?'

'We were always careful. We had to be. They were children.'

Something sour bubbled in my throat. I forced it back down.

'Had Lucy been with you before?'

'Not up here. A couple of times someplace else. I wasn't there. They gave her pot, booze. They liked her. She was different somehow. They made her promise not to tell. They had ways of doing that.'

I thought of Andy Kellog, of how he had sacrificed himself to save another little girl.

They had ways . . .

'What happened to Lucy, Otis. What went wrong?'

'It was a mistake,' he said. He had grown almost calm, as though he were talking about a minor fender bender, or an error on his taxes. 'They left her with me after . . . after.' He coughed, then went on, again letting what was done to Lucy

Merrick, a fourteen-year-old girl who had lost her way, remain unsaid. 'They were going to come back the next day, or could be it was a couple of days. I don't remember. I'm confused now. I just had to look after her. She had a blanket and a mattress. I fed her, and I gave her some soda and some books. But it got real cold all of a sudden, real cold. I was going to bring her up to my place, but I was afraid that she might see something up there, something that would help them to iden- tify me when we let her go. I had a little gasoline generator in the house, so I turned it on for her and she went to sleep.

'I had a mind to check on her every few hours, but I dozed off myself. When I woke up, she was lying on the floor.' He started sobbing again, and it took him almost a minute before he could continue. 'I smelled the fumes when I got to the door. I wrapped a cloth around my face, and I still could hardly breathe. She was lying on the floor, and she was all red and purple. She'd been sick on herself. I don't know how long she'd been dead.

'I swear, the generator had been working fine earlier. Maybe she'd tried to tinker with it. I just don't know. I didn't mean for it to happen. Oh God, I didn't mean for it to happen that way.'

He started to wail. I let him cry for a while, then interrupted him.

'Where did you put her, Otis?'

'I wanted her to rest somewhere nice, near God and the angels. I buried her behind the steeple of the old church. It was the closest I could get to hallowed ground. I couldn't mark the place or nothing, but she's there. I sometimes put flowers on the spot in summer. I talk to her. I tell her I'm sorry for what happened.'

'And the private detective? What about Poole?'

'I had nothing to do with that.' He sounded indignant. 'He wouldn't walk away. He kept asking questions. I had to make a call. I buried him in the church too, but away from Lucy. Her place was special.'

'Who killed him?'

'I'll confess my own sins, but I won't confess another man's. It's not for me to do.'

'Daniel Clay? Was he involved?'

'I never met him,' Otis replied. 'I don't know what happened to him. I just heard the name. You remember, now: I didn't mean for it to happen the way it did. I just wanted her to be warm. I told you: I love children.'

'What was the Project, Otis?'

'The children were the Project,' he replied. 'The little children. The others found them and brought them up here. That's what we called it: the Project. It was our secret.'

'Who were those other men?'

'I can't tell you. I got nothing more to say to you.'

'Okay, Otis, we're going to come up there now. We'll take you somewhere safe.'

But now, as the last minutes of his life slipped slowly by, the barriers that Otis Caswell had erected between himself and the reality of what he had done seemed to fall away.

'Nowhere's safe,' he said. 'I just want it to end.' He drew in a deep breath, stifling another sob. It seemed to give him some strength. 'I gotta go now. I gotta let some men in.'

He put the phone down, and the connection was broken. I was on the road five minutes later, and at the spot where the trail to Caswell's place joined the main road in ten. I flashed my lights where I knew Louis and Angel to be, but there was no sign of them. Farther ahead, the gate was open and the lock busted. I followed the trail to the house. There was a truck parked outside. Louis's Lexus was beside it. The front door to the house was open, a light shining outside.

'It's me,' I called.

'In here,' replied Louis, from somewhere to my right.

I followed his voice into a sparsely furnished bedroom. It had whitewashed walls. Exposed beams ran along the ceiling. Otis Caswell was hanging from one of them. There was an overturned chair on the floor, and drops of urine were still falling from his bare feet.

'I was out taking a leak,' said Angel. 'I saw – ' He struggled to find the words. 'I saw the door was open, and I *thought* I saw men go in, but when we got up here there was nobody but Caswell, and he was already dead.'

I stepped forward and rolled up each sleeve of his shirt in turn. His skin was bare of tattoos. However else he was involved, Otis Caswell was not the man with the eagle on his arm. Angel and Louis looked at me, but said nothing.

'He knew,' I said. 'He knew who they were, but he wouldn't tell.'

Now he was dead, and that knowledge had died with him. Then I remembered the man killed by Frank Merrick. There was still time. First, though, we searched the house, carefully going through drawers and closets, checking the floors and the skirting for any hiding places. It was Angel who found the stash, in the end. There was a hole in the wall behind a half-empty bookcase. It contained bags of photographs, most printed from a computer, and dozens of unmarked videocassettes and DVDs. Angel leafed through a couple of the pictures, then put them down and stepped away. I glanced at them but did not have the stomach to go through them all. There was no need. I knew what they would contain. Only the faces of the children would change.

Louis gestured at the cassettes and DVDs. There was a metal stand in one corner, dominated by a new flat-screen TV. It looked out of place in Caswell's home.

'You want to look at these?'

'No. I have to leave,' I said. 'Clean down anything you've touched, then you get out of here too.'

'You going to call the cops?' asked Angel.

I shook my head. 'Not for a couple of hours.'

'What did he tell you?'

'He said that Merrick's daughter died of carbon monoxide poisoning. He buried her behind the steeple in the forest.'

'You believed him?'

'I don't know.' I looked at Caswell's face, purple with blood.

I could feel no pity for him, and my only regret was that he had died without revealing more.

'You want us to stay close?' asked Louis.

'Go back to Portland, but stay away from Scarborough. I need to look at a body, then I'll call you.'

We went outside. The air was still, the forest quiet. There was an alien scent in the air. Behind me, I heard Louis sniff.

'Someone's been smoking,' he said.

I walked past Caswell's truck, over short grass and a small vegetable patch, until I came to where the forest began. After a few steps I found it: a roll-up, discarded in the dirt. I lifted it carefully and blew on the tip. It glowed red for an instant, then died.

Louis appeared beside me, Angel close behind. They both had guns in their hands. I showed them the cigarette.

'He was here,' I said. 'We led him to Caswell.'

'There's a mark on the little finger of Caswell's right hand,' said Angel. 'Looks like there was a pinkie ring once. No sign of it now.'

I stared into the darkness of the forest, but I had no sense of the presence of another. The Collector was gone.

O'Rourke had done as he had promised. He had left word with the ME's office to say that I might be able to identify the dead man. I was at the office by seven, and was joined soon after by O'Rourke and a pair of state police detectives, one of whom was Hansen. He didn't speak as I was led into the icebox to view the body. In total, there were five bodies set to go under the ME's knife: the unidentified man from the Old Moose Lodge, Mason Dubus, the two Russians, and Merrick. They were so pressed for space that the two Russians were being stored at an undertaker's office nearby.

'Which one is Merrick?' I asked the ME's assistant.

The man, whose name I did not know, pointed at the body nearest the wall. It was covered with a white plastic sheet.

'You feeling sorry for him?' It was Hansen. 'He killed five

men with your gun. You ought to be feeling sorry, but not for him.'

I said nothing. Instead, I stood over the body of Merrick's killer. I think I even managed to keep my face expressionless when the man's face was revealed, the red wound on the right side of his forehead still messy with dirt and congealed matter.

'I don't know him,' I said.

'You sure?' asked O'Rourke.

'Yeah, I'm sure,' I said, as I turned away from the body of Jerry Legere, Rebecca Clay's ex-husband. 'He's nobody I know.'

They would come back to haunt me, of course, all of the lies and half-truths. They would cost me more than I could then have imagined, although perhaps I had been living on borrowed time for so long that I shouldn't have been surprised at the consequences. I could have given the detectives all that I knew. I could have told them about Andy Kellog and Otis Caswell and the bodies that might be buried within the walls of a ruined church, but I did not. I don't know why. I think that maybe it was because I was close to the truth, and I wanted to reveal it for myself.

And even in that I was to be disappointed, for what, in the end, was the truth? Like the lawyer Elwin Stark had said, the only truth was that everybody lied.

Or perhaps it was because of Frank Merrick. I knew what he had done. I knew he had killed, and would have killed again if he had been allowed to live. I was still bruised and sore from where he had punched me, and I was aware of a lingering resentment at the way he had humiliated me in my own home. But in his love for his daughter, and in his single-minded obsession with discovering the truth behind her disappearance, and with punishing those responsible for it, I had seen something of myself reflected.

Now that Lucy Merrick's burial place had been revealed, the rest of the men who had led her to that place remained to be found. Three – Caswell, Legere, and Dubus – were dead.

Andy Kellog had recalled four masks, and I had seen no tattoos on the arms of Caswell, or of Legere when I had viewed his body at the ME's office. The man with the eagle, the one who Andy felt was the leader, the dominant one, was still alive.

I was climbing into my car when a piece fell into place. I thought of the damage to one corner of the cottage in which Lucy Merrick had died, the holes in the wall and the marks where screws had once held something in place, and recalled part of what Caswell had said to me on the phone. It had bothered me at the time, but I was too intent upon squeezing him for more information to notice it. It came back to me now – *'I had a mind to check on her every few hours, but I dozed off myself. When I woke up, she was lying on the floor'* – and I found the connection.

Three were dead, but now I had another name.

34

Raymon Lang lived between Bath and Brunswick, on a small patch of land off Route 1, close by the northern bank of the New Meadows River. I'd taken a cursory look at Lang's home when I got there just before nine. He hadn't done much with his property, apart from plant a tan trailer home on it that looked, at first sight, like a strong sneeze might blow it away. The trailer sat high off the ground. In a cursory nod to aesthetics, a kind of picket fence had been erected between the bottom of the trailer and the earth, masking the dirt and pipes beneath.

I had managed only three or four hours' sleep that night, but I was not tired. The more I thought about what Caswell had told me before he died, the more convinced I was that Raymon Lang was involved in the abduction of Lucy Merrick. Caswell had told me that he had seen Lucy lying on the floor, dying or already dead. The question was: how had Caswell known? How could he have seen her when he had woken up? After all, had he been in the cabin with her, then he too would have died. He hadn't fallen asleep there. He was sleeping back in his own place, which meant that there was a way of watching the cabin from his home. There was a camera. The mark in the corner of the cabin wall indicated where the camera had been. And whom did we know who put cameras in places? Raymon Lang, helped by his old buddy Jerry Legere, regrettably no longer with us. A-Secure, the firm for which Lang worked, had also installed the security system at Daniel Clay's house, which now seemed less like a coincidence than before. I wondered how Rebecca would take the news of her ex-husband's death. I doubted that she would be overcome by grief, but who could be certain? I had seen wives weep themselves into a stupor over the sickbeds of abusive husbands, and children cry hysterically at the funerals of fathers who had torn stripes in their thighs and buttocks with a belt. Sometimes, I didn't think they even understood why they were in tears, but grief was as good a name as any to give to their reason.

I guessed that Lang was also the other man involved in the killing of Frank Merrick. According to eyewitnesses, a silver or gray car had been seen leaving the scene, and from where I sat I could see Lang's silver Sierra shining through the trees. The cops hadn't picked it up on the road to the Old Moose Lodge as they headed north, but that didn't mean anything. In the panic after the shooting, it might have taken the cops a while to get witness statements, by which time Lang could have driven as far as the highway. Even if someone had reported seeing a car during the initial 911 call, Lang would still have had time to get at least as far as Bingham, and there he would have enjoyed the choice of three routes: 16 north, 16 south, or to continue on the 201. He would probably have kept going south, but there were enough side roads after Bingham to enable him to avoid dozens of cops, if he was lucky and kept his cool.

I was parked by the side of a gas station about fifty feet west of Lang's drive, drinking coffee and reading the *Press Herald*. There was a Dunkin' Donuts attached to the gas station, with seating for only a handful of customers, so that it wasn't unusual to see people eating and drinking in their cars. It meant that I wasn't likely to stand out while I was watching Lang's place. After an hour, Lang emerged from the trailer, and the patch of silver started to move as he turned onto the main road and headed in the direction of Bath. Seconds later, Louis and Angel followed him in the Lexus. I had my cell phone close to hand in case it turned out to be just a short trip, even though Lang had his toolbox with him when he was walking to his car. I still gave him a half hour, on the off chance that he decided to head back for some reason, then left my car where it was and cut through the trees to get to the trailer.

Lang didn't seem to keep a dog, which was good news. It's hard to perform a little breaking and entering while a dog is trying to rip your throat out. The trailer door didn't look like much, but I still didn't have Angel's ability to pick a lock. Frankly, it's a lot harder than it looks, and I didn't want to spend half an hour squatting in front of Lang's door trying to open it with a pick and tension tool. I used to own an electric rake, which did the job just as well, but the rake got lost when my old Mustang was shot up a few years back and I'd never bothered to replace it. Anyway, the only reason a private detective might keep a rake in his car would be in order to bust illegally into someone's place, and if my car was searched for any reason by the cops it would look bad and I didn't need to look any worse to cops than I already did.

I didn't need Angel to help me break into Lang's trailer, because I didn't plan on leaving Lang in any doubt that his place had been searched. At the very least, it would rattle him, and I wanted him rattled. Unlike Caswell, Lang didn't look like the kind of guy who was going to reach for a noose when things got tough. Instead, if Merrick's fate was any indication, he was the kind to lash out. The thought that Lang might not be guilty of anything never really crossed my mind.

For the purposes of breaking into Lang's trailer, I had a crowbar under my coat. I forced it between the door and the frame of the trailer, then kept pushing until the lock broke. The first thing that struck me about the interior of Lang's trailer was that it was stiflingly hot inside. The second was that it was tidy, and therefore not what I had expected from a single man's trailer. To the left was a galley-style kitchen with a table beyond it, surrounded by a three-sided couch arrangement that took up the entire lower quarter of the trailer. To the right, just before the sleeping area, was a La-Z-Boy recliner and an expensive Sony wide-screen television, beneath which stood a matching DVD, a DVD recorder, and a twin VCR. There were tapes and DVDs on a shelf beside it: action movies, some comedies, even a couple of Bogart and Cagney classics. Under them was a selection of porn on both DVD and video. I glanced at some of the titles but they seemed like pretty average fare. There was nothing related to children, but then I supposed that most of the stuff involving children was probably packaged to look like something else anyway; that, or it was buried on other tapes or disks so that it would not be found in the event of a casual search. I turned on the TV and picked some of the porn at random, skipping forward in case anything unusual was to be seen, but it was just as advertised. I could have spent an entire day trying to go through all of the movies in the hope that I might find something, but there didn't seem to be much point. It was also kind of depressing.

Next to the TV was a Home Depot computer desk, and a new PC. I tried accessing the computer but it was password protected. I turned it off and went through the books on the shelves, and the magazines stacked beneath a small corner table. Again, there was nothing, not even porn. It was possible that Lang had other material hidden elsewhere, but after searching the entire trailer I couldn't find any trace of it. All that was left was the laundry basket in the spotless bathroom, which seemed to be full of Lang's dirty T-shirts, underwear, and socks. I tipped it onto the floor just in case, but all it left me with was a pile of stained clothing and the smell of stale perspiration. In every other way, Lang appeared to be clean. I was disappointed, and for the first time I started to doubt my actions in relation to him. Maybe I should have called the cops. If there was incriminating material on his computer, then they could have found it. I had also managed to contaminate the trailer, so that even if they found evidence that Lang had been involved in Merrick's killing – a bloodstained baseball bat, or a splattered bar – it wouldn't take much of a lawyer to argue that I could have planted the weapons, assuming I confessed what I knew to the cops. For the moment, it seemed like Lang was a dead end. I would just have to wait and see how he reacted to the break-in.

I looked out of the window to make sure there was nobody

approaching, then opened the door and prepared to head back to my car. It was only when my foot touched the gravel and I glanced at the picket fence that I realized that, while I had searched the inside of the trailer, I hadn't checked underneath. I went around to the rear, out of sight of the road, then knelt and squinted through the fencing.

There was a large metal container, seven or eight feet in length and four feet in height, under the trailer. It seemed to be bolted to the underside. I did a full circuit with the flashlight and could see no sign of a door, which meant that the only way in was through the trailer itself. I went back inside and examined the floor. It was carpeted from wall to wall in a thick brown fabric that looked like wet dog fur. I went over it with my fingers and felt rough patches and gaps. I dug my fingers into one of the gaps and pulled. There was the crackle of Velcro releasing, and the carpet came away. I was looking down at a two-foot-by-two-foot trapdoor, with locks at either side. I took off my coat and went to work with the crowbar, but this time it wasn't as easy as it had been with the door. It was steel, and no matter how hard I tried I couldn't raise it enough to press home the crowbar. I sat back down on the floor and considered my options. I could leave things as they were, replace the carpet, and try to come back another time, which would give Lang ample opportunity to remove anything incriminating once he realized that someone had broken into his place. I could call the cops, in which case I'd have to explain just what I thought I was doing busting into the man's trailer to begin with. Assuming they were even able and willing to get a warrant to search Lang's trailer, the metal box might just be storing the manuscript of his great novel, or his late mother's dresses and jewelry, and I'd be facing jail time on top of everything else.

I called Angel.

'Where is he?'

'Bath Iron Works,' he said. 'I can see him from where we are. Looks like there's some problem with the monitors for their surveillance system. He's checking cables and opening shit. Should be a while.'

'Disable his car,' I said. 'Two tires should be enough. Then come back here.'

A half hour later, they were with me at Lang's place. I pointed Angel to the door in the floor and he went to work. He didn't speak once, not even when, five minutes later, he cracked the first lock and, shortly after, the second. He didn't speak when a flat metal storage shelf was revealed, containing unmarked videocassettes, DVDs, computer disks, and plastic files with transparent pages within, each page containing images of naked children, sometimes with adults and sometimes with other children. He didn't speak when he released the shelf using a pair of clasps at either end, raising it up to uncover a boxlike cell in which was crouched a small girl wrapped in layer upon layer of blankets, her eyes blinking in the light, some old dolls scattered around her alongside chocolate bars, cookies, and a box of breakfast cereal. He didn't speak when he saw the bucket she was forced to use as a toilet, or the circular opening in the wall, covered by a grille, that allowed air into the prison.

He only spoke when he leaned down and reached out a hand to the frightened girl.

'It's okay now,' he said. 'We won't let nobody hurt you again.'

And the child opened her mouth and howled.

I called the cops. Angel and Louis left. There was only me and a ten-year-old girl with sallow skin whose name appeared to be Anya. She wore a cheap necklace around her neck with those four letters picked out in silver upon it. I put her in the front seat of my car and she sat there unmoving, her face turned away from the trailer, her eyes fixed on a spot on the car floor. She couldn't tell me how long she had been held there, and I could only get confirmation of her name and her age out of her in thickly accented English before she went silent again. She said she was ten years old. I doubted that she trusted me, and I didn't blame her.

While she sat in the car, lost in her own thoughts, I went through Raymon Lang's album of photographs. Some of them were very recent: Anya was among the children pictured, men's bodies on either side of her. I looked closely at one of the photographs and thought I saw, on the arm of the man on the right, what might have been the yellow beak of a bird. I flicked back through the rest, the tones and colors changing as the pictures grew older, Polaroids taking the place of computer images before their place was taken in turn by the oldest of the photographs: black-and-white pictures, probably developed by Lang himself in a home darkroom. There were boys and girls, sometimes photographed alone and at other times with men, their identities hidden by bird masks. It was a history of abuse that spanned years, probably decades.

The oldest images in the album were photocopies, their quality poor. They showed a young girl on a bed, two men taking turns with her, the pictures cropped to remove their heads. In one of the photos, I saw a tattoo on the arm of one of the men. It was blurred. I imagined that it could be cleaned up, and that when it did it would reveal an eagle.

But one of the photographs was different from the rest. I looked at it for a long time, then removed it from its plastic sleeve and carefully rearranged the other images to disguise what I had done. I tucked the picture beneath the rubber mat on the floor of my car, then sat on the cold, hard gravel with my head in my hands and waited for the police to come.

They arrived out of uniform and in a pair of unmarked cars. Anya watched them coming and curled up fetally, repeating a single word over and over in a language that I did not recognize. It was only when the doors of the first car opened, and a pair of women emerged, that Anya started to believe she might be safe. The two women approached us. The passenger door of my car was open, and they could see the little girl just as she could see them. I hadn't wanted Anya to feel she had simply been moved from one cell to another.

The first cop squatted before her. She was slim, with long

red hair tied back tightly on her head. She reminded me of Rachel.

'Hi,' she said. 'My name is Jill. You're Anya, is that right?'

Anya nodded, recognizing her name, if nothing else. Her face began to soften. Her lips turned down at the corners, and she started to cry. This wasn't the animal response that had greeted Angel. This was something else.

Jill opened her arms to the little girl and she fell into them, burying her face in the woman's neck, her body jerking with the force of her sobs. Jill looked over Anya's shoulder at me, and nodded. I turned away, and left them to each other.

35

Bath isn't a very beautiful town when seen from the water, but then most places dependent upon one form of heavy industry rarely are, and nobody ever designed a shipyard with aesthetics in mind. Still, there was something majestic about its massive cranes and the great ships that the yards still turned out at a time when most of its rivals had seen shipbuilding either collapse entirely or become a mere shadow of its former grandeur. The shipyard might have been ugly, yet it was an ugliness born not of decay but of growth, with four hundred years of history behind it, four centuries of noise and steam and sparks, of wood replaced by steel, of sons following fathers into trades that had been passed down for generations. The fate of Bath and the fate of the shipyard were forever entwined in a bond that could never be severed.

Like any town where large numbers of people traveled to work for one major employer, parking was an issue, and the huge lot at King Street, right at the intersection with Commercial and nearest to the main north gate to the yard, was packed with cars. The first shift was about to end and buses idled nearby, waiting to transport those who came from out of town and preferred to avoid the hassle of parking either by dispensing with their cars entirely or by leaving them in the suburbs. A sign warned that the Bath Iron Works was a defense contractor and all photography was prohibited. Over the employee entrance was another sign that read: *Through These Gates Pass the Best Shipbuilders in the World.*

The cops had gathered at the Riverside Sports Club. There were a dozen all told, a mix of Bath P.D. and state police, all of them in plain clothes. In addition, two cruisers lurked out of sight. The yard's own security people had been advised that an arrest was imminent, and at their request it had been decided to take Raymon Lang as he emerged into the parking lot. He was being watched continuously, and the yard's head of security was in direct contact with Jill Carrier, the state police detective who had taken Anya into her arms, and who was in charge of apprehending Lang. I was parked in the lot, with a clear view of the gates. I had been allowed to tag along on condition that I stayed out of sight and took no part in what occurred. I had spun the cops quite a story to tell them how I'd come to find the little girl in Lang's trailer, and why I had been at the trailer to begin with, but in the end I had to admit to lying during the viewing of Legere's body. I was in trouble, but Carrier had been kind enough to let me see the Lang thing through to its end, even if one of the conditions she attached was to have a plainclothes officer seated beside me in my car at all times. His name was Weintraub, and he didn't say very much, which was fine with me.

At 3.30 P.M., the gates opened with a rumble and men began to pour out, all dressed near identically in baseball caps and jeans, and lumberjack shirts open over T-shirts, each carrying his flask and his lunch pail. I saw Carrier speaking on her cell phone, and half a dozen of the cops broke away from the main group, Carrier leading, and began to ease their way through the throng of men. Over to the right, I saw Raymon Lang emerge from a turnstile carrying his long metal toolbox. He was dressed just like the shipbuilders and was smoking the end of a cigarette. As he took a final drag and prepared to throw the butt to the ground, he saw Carrier and the others approaching, and he knew instantly who they were and for whom they had come, a predator immediately aware of other, more powerful predators descending upon him. He dropped the toolbox and started to run, heading east away from his pursuers, but a Bath P.D. cruiser appeared and blocked the road out of the lot. Lang altered direction, weaving in and out of cars, even as the second cruiser appeared and uniforms moved in on him. Now Carrier was closing, faster and more lithe than the men she was with. She had her gun in her hand. She ordered Lang to stop. Lang turned, and reached behind his back, his hand searching for something beneath his shirt. I heard Carrier give him a final warning to put his hands up, but he did not. Then I saw the gun buck in Carrier's hand, and heard the shot as Lang spun and fell to the ground.

He died on the way to the hospital. He did not speak as the paramedics struggled to save his life, and nothing was learned from him. They stripped him of his shirt as they placed him on a gurney, and I saw that his arms were bare of tattoos.

Raymon Lang had been unarmed. There seemed to have been no reason for him to reach behind his back, no reason for him to draw Carrier's fire upon himself. I think, though, that in the end he just didn't want to go to jail, perhaps out of cowardice, or perhaps because he couldn't bear to be separated from children for the rest of his life.

VI

And in my best behavior
I am really just like him.
Look beneath the floorboards
For the secrets I have hid.

Sufjan Stevens, *John Wayne Gacy Jr.*

I rang the doorbell of Rebecca Clay's house. I could hear the waves breaking in the darkness. Jackie Garner and the Fulcis were long gone, now that Merrick was dead. I had called ahead and filled her in on what had happened. She told me that the police had called her after I admitted that I had lied about Jerry Legere, and she had made a formal identification of his body earlier that day. They had interviewed her about her ex-husband's death, but there was little that she could add to what they already knew. She and Legere had been completely estranged, and she had neither seen nor heard from him in a long time until I had begun asking questions and he had called her a couple of nights before his death, drunk, and demanding to know what she thought she was doing by setting a private eye on him. She had hung up, and he had not called back.

. She answered the door wearing an old sweater and a pair of loose-fitting jeans. Her feet were bare. I could hear the TV in the living room, and through the open door I saw Jenna seated on the floor, watching an animated movie. She looked up to see who had entered, decided that I wasn't anyone for whom it was worth missing anything, and returned to her viewing.

I followed Rebecca into the kitchen. She offered me coffee or a drink, but I declined both. Legere, she said, would be released for burial the following day. Apparently, he had a half brother down in North Dakota who was flying up to take care of the arrangements. She told me that she would be attending the funeral for the half brother's sake, but that she wouldn't be taking her daughter along. 'It's not something that she needs to see.' She sat at the kitchen table. 'So it's all over,' she said.

'In a way. Frank Merrick is dead. Your ex-husband is dead. Ricky Demarcian and Raymon Lang are dead. Otis Caswell is dead. Mason Dubus is dead. The Somerset County Sheriff's Department and the ME's office are digging for the remains of Lucy Merrick and Jim Poole up at Gilead. That's a lot of dead people, but I suppose you're right: it's over for all of them.'

'You sound sick of it.'

I was. I had wanted answers, and the truth about what had happened to Lucy Merrick and Andy Kellog and the other children who had been abused by men masked as birds. Instead, I was left with the sense that, the girl named Anya apart, and the removal of a little evil from the world, it had all been for nothing. I had few answers, and at least one of the abusers remained at large: the man with the eagle tattoo. I also knew that I had been lied to all along, lied to in particular by the woman who now sat before me, and yet I could not find it in my heart to blame her.

I reached into my pocket and removed the photograph that I had taken from Raymon Lang's album. The little girl's face was almost hidden by the body of the man who knelt above her on the bed, and he himself was visible only from the neck down. His body was almost absurdly thin, the bones visible through the skin of his arms and legs, every muscle and sinew standing out upon his frame. The photo had been taken more than a quarter of a century before, judging by the age of the girl. She couldn't have been more than six or seven. Beside her, jammed between two pillows, was a doll with long red hair and dressed in a blue pinafore. It was the same doll that Rebecca Clay's daughter now carried around with her, a doll passed on to her by her mother, a doll that had given Rebecca comfort during the years of her abuse.

Rebecca looked at the photograph, but she did not touch it. Her eyes grew glassy, then damp with tears, as she stared at the little girl that she once was.

'Where did you find it?' she asked.

'In Raymon Lang's trailer.'

'Were there others?'

'Yes, but none like this one. This was the only one in which the doll was visible.'

She pressed her hand against the picture, blotting out the form of the man who towered above her younger self, covering the naked body of Daniel Clay.

'Rebecca,' I asked, 'where is your father?'

She stood and walked to a door behind the kitchen table. She opened it and flicked a switch. Light shone on a set of wooden steps that led down to the basement. Without looking back at me, she began to descend, and I followed.

The basement was used for storage. There was a bicycle, now too small for her daughter, and assorted boxes and cartons, but there was nothing that looked as if it had been moved or used in a long time. It smelled of dust, and the concrete floor had begun to crack in places, long dark lines extending like veins from a spot in the center. Rebecca Clay extended a bare foot and pointed her painted toes at the floor.

'He's down there,' she said. 'That's where I put him.'

She had been working down in Saco that Friday, and there had been a message on her answering machine when she got back to her apartment. Her babysitter, Ellen, who looked after three or four kids each day, had been taken to the hospital following a heart scare, and Ellen's husband had called to say that, obviously, she would be unable to pick up any of her charges from the school. Rebecca checked her cell and found that the battery had run down while she was in Saco. She had been so busy that she had failed to notice. For a moment, she felt utter panic. Where was Jenna? She called the school, but everyone had gone home. She then called Ellen's husband, but he didn't know who had taken Jenna after school. He suggested that she call the principal, or the school secretary, for both had been informed that Jenna would not be picked up that day. Instead, Rebecca called her best friend, April, whose daughter, Carole, was in Jenna's class. Jenna wasn't with her either, but April knew where she was.

'Your father collected her,' she said. 'Seems the school found his number in the book and called him when they heard about Ellen and couldn't get in touch with you. He came by and took her back to his house. I saw him at the school when he came to collect her. She's fine, Rebecca.'

But Rebecca thought that nothing would ever be fine again. She was so scared that she threw up on her way to the car, and threw up again as she drove to her father's house, coughing up bread and bile into an empty convenience store bag as she waited at the lights. When she got to the house, her father was out in the garden, raking dead leaves, and the front door was open. She rushed past him without speaking and found her daughter in the living room, doing just what she was doing now: watching TV from the floor, and eating ice cream. She couldn't understand why her mommy was so upset, why she was hugging her and crying and scolding her for being with Grandpa. She had been with Grandpa before, after all, although never alone and always with her mommy. It was Grandpa. He had bought her fries and a hot dog and a soda. He had taken her to the beach and they had collected seashells. Then he had given her a big bowl of chocolate ice cream and left her to watch TV. She'd had a nice day, she told her mommy, although it would have been even better if her mommy had been there with her.

And then Daniel Clay was at the living room door, asking her what was wrong, as though he was just a regular grandfather and a regular father and not the man who had taken his daughter to his bed from the age of six until fifteen, always being gentle and kind, trying not to hurt her, and sometimes, when he was sad or when he had been drinking, apologizing for the night that he had let another man touch her. Because he loved her, you see. That was what he always told her: 'I'm your father, and I love you, and I'll never let that happen to you again.'

I could hear the bass notes of the television vibrating above our heads. Then it went silent, and there were footsteps as Jenna headed upstairs.

'It's her bedtime,' said Rebecca. 'I never have to tell her when to go. She just heads up to bed all by herself. She likes her sleep. I'll leave her to clean her teeth and read, then I'll kiss her good night. I always try to kiss her good night, because then I know that she's safe.'

She leaned back against the brick wall of the basement and ran the fingers of her hand through her hair, pushing it back from her forehead and exposing her face.

'He hadn't touched her,' she said. 'He'd done just what she said he'd done, but I understood what was happening. There was a moment, just before I brushed past him and took Jenna home, when I could see it in his eyes, and he knew that I saw it. He was tempted by her. It was starting again. It wasn't his fault. It was an illness. He was sick. It was like a disease that had been in remission, and now it was returning.'

'Why didn't you tell someone?' I asked.

'Because he was my father, and I loved him,' she replied. She didn't look at me as she spoke. 'I suppose that sounds ridiculous to you, after what he did to me.'

'No,' I said. 'Nothing sounds ridiculous to me anymore.'

She worried at the floor with her foot. 'Well, it's the truth, for what it's worth. I loved him. I loved him so much that I went back to the house that night. I left Jenna with April. I told her that I had some work to do at home, and asked if she'd mind letting Jenna sleep over with Carole. They often did that, so it was no big deal. Then I came here. My father answered the door, and I told him that we needed to talk about what had happened that day. He tried to laugh it off. He was doing some work in the basement and I followed him down here. He was going to lay a new floor, and he had already begun breaking up the old concrete. The rumors had started, by that point, and he'd virtually been forced to cancel all of his appointments. He was becoming a total pariah, and he knew it. He tried to hide his unhappiness about it. He said it would give him the time to do all kinds of jobs around the house that he'd been threatening to do for so long.

'So he just kept breaking the floor while I screamed at him. He wouldn't listen. It was as though I was making it all up, all the things that had happened to me, all the things that he'd done and that I believed he wanted to do again, but this time with Jenna. He would only say that whatever he had done, he'd done out of love. "You're my daughter," he said. "I love you. I've always loved you. And I love Jenna too."

'And when he said that, something fell apart inside me. He had a pickax in his hands, and he was trying to lever up a slab of concrete. There was a hammer on the shelf beside me. He had his back to me and I hit him on the crown of the head. He didn't fall down, not at first. He just bent over and put his hand to his scalp, like he'd smacked it against a beam. I hit him again, and he fell over. I think I hit him twice more. He started to bleed into the dirt and I left him there. I went upstairs to the kitchen. Blood had splashed on my face and hands, and I washed it off. I cleaned the hammer too. There was hair caught in it, I remember, and I had to pick at it with my fingers. I heard him moving down in the basement, and I thought he tried to say something. I couldn't go back down, though. I just couldn't. Instead, I locked the door and sat in the kitchen until it got dark and I couldn't hear him moving around any longer. When I unlocked the door, he had crawled to the bottom of the stairs, but he hadn't been able to climb up. I went down to him then, and he was dead.

'I found some plastic sheeting in the garage and I wrapped him in it. There used to be a greenhouse in the back garden. It had a dirt floor. It was dark by then, and I dragged him out there. That was the hardest part: getting him up from the basement. He didn't look like he weighed a lot, but it was all muscle and bone. I dug a hole and put him in, then covered him up again. I suppose I was already planning, already thinking ahead. It never crossed my mind to call the police or to confess to what I'd done. I just knew that I didn't want to be separated from Jenna. She was everything to me.

'When it was all done, I went home. The next night, I waited until dark then drove my father's car up to Jackman and left it there. I reported him missing once the car was taken care of. The police came. Some detectives looked at the basement floor, like I knew they would, but my father had only just started tearing it up, and it was clear that there was nothing underneath it. They knew all about my father, and when they found the car up in Jackman they figured he'd fled.

'After a couple of days, I came back and moved the body. I'd been lucky. It had been wicked cold that month. I guess it kept him, you know, from rotting too much, so there wasn't a smell, not really. I started to dig in the basement. It took me most of the night, but he had taught me what to do. He always said that a girl should know how to take care of a house, how to fix things and keep them in order. I cleared a space of rubble and dug down until there was a hole big enough to take him. I covered him up, then I went upstairs and fell asleep in my old room. You wouldn't think that someone could just fall asleep after doing something like that, but I slept straight through until midday. I slept so peacefully, better than I could ever remember doing before. Then I went back down and kept working. Everything that I needed to use was there, even a little mixer for the cement. Getting the rubble up took some time, and my back ached for weeks after, but once that was done it was all pretty easy. It took me a day or two over the weekend, all told. Jenna stayed with April. Everything just worked out.'

'And then you moved into this house.'

'I couldn't sell it because it wasn't mine to sell, and anyway I would have been afraid to do that even if it had been, just in case someone decided to renovate the basement and found what was there. It seemed better to move in. Then we just stayed here. You know what the strange thing is, though? You see those cracks in the floor? They're new. They only started appearing in the last couple of weeks, ever since Frank Merrick came around causing trouble. It's like he awakened something down there, as if my father heard him asking questions and tried to find a way back into the world. I've started to have nightmares.

I dream that I hear noises from the basement, and when I open the door my father is climbing the steps, hauling himself up from the dirt to make me pay for what I've done, because he loved me and I'd hurt him. In my dream, he ignores me and starts crawling toward Jenna's room, and I keep hitting him, over and over, but he won't stop. He just keeps crawling, like a bug that won't die.'

Her toe had begun to explore one of the cracks in the floor. She withdrew it quickly when she became aware of what she was doing, the description of her nightmares reminding her of what lay below.

'Who helped you with all of this?' I asked.

'Nobody,' she said. 'I did it alone.'

'You drove your father's car up to Jackman. How did you get back down after you'd abandoned it?'

'I hitched a ride.'

'Really?'

'Yes, really.'

But I knew that she was lying. After all that she had done, she wouldn't have taken a chance like that. Someone followed her up to Jackman, then drove her back east again. I thought it might have been the woman April. I remembered the way they had looked at each other that night after Merrick had broken the window. Something had passed between them, a gesture of complicity, an acknowledgment of a shared under-standing. It didn't matter. None of it really mattered.

'Who was the other man, Rebecca, the one who took the photograph?'

'I don't know. It was late. I heard someone drinking with my father, then they came to my room. They both smelled pretty bad. I can still recall it. It's why I've never been able to drink whiskey. They turned on the bedside light. The man had a mask on, an old Halloween mask of a ghost that my father used to wear to frighten the trick-or-treaters. My father told me that the man was a friend of his, and that I should do the same things that I did for him. I didn't want to, but . . .' She stopped for a moment. 'I was seven years old,' she whispered. 'That's all. I was seven. They took pictures. It was like it was a game, a big joke. It was the only time it ever happened. The next day, my father cried and told me he was sorry. He told me again that he loved me, and that he never wanted to share me with anyone else. And he never did.'

'And you've no idea who it might have been?'

She shook her head, but she would not look at me.

'There were more pictures of that night in Raymon Lang's trailer. Your father's drinking buddy was in them, but his head wasn't visible. He had a tattoo of an eagle on his arm. Do you remember it?'

'No. It was dark. If I did see it, I've forgotten it over the years.'

'One of the other children who was abused mentioned the same mark. Someone suggested to me that it might be a military tattoo. Do you know if any of your father's friends served in the army?'

'Elwin Stark, he did,' she said. 'I think Eddie Haver might have been in the army too. They're the only ones, but I don't think either of them had a tattoo like that on his arm. They came on vacation with us sometimes. I saw them on the beach. I would have noticed.'

I let it go. I didn't see what else I could do.

'Your father betrayed those children, didn't he?' I asked.

She nodded. 'I think so. They had those pictures of him with me. I guess that's how they made him do what he did.'

'How did they get them?'

'I suppose the other man from that night passed them on to them. But you know, my father really did care about the kids he treated. He tried to look out for them. Those men made him choose the ones that he gave to them, made him pick children to be abused, but he seemed to work twice as hard for the rest because of it. I know it makes no sense at all, but it was almost like there were two Daniel Clays, the bad one and the good one. There was the one who abused his daughter and betrayed children to save his reputation, and the one who fought tooth and nail to save other kids from abuse. Maybe that was the only way he could survive without going insane: by separating the two parts, and by taking all of the bad stuff and calling it "love."'

'And Jerry Legere? You suspected him after you found him with Jenna, didn't you?'

'I saw something of what I had seen in my father in him,' she said, 'but I didn't know he was involved, not until the police came and told me how he had died. I think I hate him more than anyone. I mean, he must have known about me. He knew what my father had done, and somehow, it made me more attractive to him.' She shuddered. 'It was like, when he was fucking me, he was fucking the child I was as well.'

She sank down on the floor and laid her forehead on her arms. I could barely hear her when she spoke again.

'What happens now?' she asked. 'Will they take Jenna away from me? Will I go to jail?'

'Nothing,' I said. 'Nothing happens.'

She lifted her head. 'You're not going to tell the police?'

'No.'

There was no more to say. I left her in the basement, sitting at the foot of the grave she had dug for her father. I got in my car and I drove away to the susurration of the sea, like an infinite number of voices offering quiet consolation. It was the last time I would ever hear the sea in that place, for I never returned to Willard again.

There was one more link, one more connection that remained to be explored. After Gilead, I knew what connected Legere to Lang, and what in turn connected Lang to Gilead and to Daniel Clay. It wasn't merely a personal link, but a professional one: the security firm, A-Secure.

Joel Harmon was in his garden when I arrived, and it was Todd who answered the door and escorted me through the house to see him.

'You look like you might have spent time in the army, Todd,' I said.

'I ought to bust your ass for that,' he replied good-humoredly. 'Navy. Five years. I was a signalman, a damned good one too.'

'You get all tattooed up in the navy?'

'Damn straight,' he said. He rolled up the right sleeve of his jacket, revealing a twisted mass of anchors and mermaids. 'I'm real traditional,' he said. He let the sleeve fall. 'You got a reason for asking?'

'Just curious. I saw how you handled your gun on the night of the party. It looked like you'd held one before.'

'Yeah, well, Mr Harmon's a wealthy man. He wanted someone who could look out for him.'

'You ever have to look out for him, Todd?' I asked.

He stopped as we reached the garden, and stared at me. 'Not yet,' he said. 'Not like that.'

Harmon's son and daughter were both home that day, and halfway down the lawn Harmon was pointing out changes to them that he hoped to make to the flowers and shrubs come the spring.

'He loves the garden,' said Todd, following the direction of my gaze and seemingly anxious to move the subject away from his gun and his obligations, real or potential, to Harmon. 'Everything out there he planted himself, or helped to plant. The kids lent a hand too. It's their garden as much as his.'

But now I wasn't looking at Harmon, or his children, or his garden. I was looking at the surveillance cameras that kept vigil on the lawn and the entrances to the house.

'It looks like an expensive system,' I said to Todd.

'It is. The cameras themselves switch from color output to black-and-white when the lighting conditions are poor. They've got focus and zoom capabilities, pan and tilt, and we have quad switchers that allow us to view all camera images simultaneously. There are monitors in the kitchen, Mr Harmon's office, the bedroom, and in my quarters. You can't be too careful.'

'No, I guess not. Who installed the system?'

'A company called A-Secure, out of South Portland.'

'Uh-huh. That was the company Raymon Lang worked for, wasn't it?'

Todd jerked like he'd just been hit with a mild electric shock.

'I – I suppose it was.' Lang's shooting, and the discovery of the child beneath his trailer, had been big news. It would have been hard for Todd to have missed it.

'Was he ever out here, possibly to check the system? I'm sure it needs maintenance once or twice a year.'

'I couldn't say,' said Todd. He was already going on the defensive, wondering if he'd said too much. 'A-Secure sends someone out regularly as part of the contract, but it's not always the same guy.'

'Sure. That figures. Maybe Jerry Legere came out here instead. I suppose the company will have to find someone else to take care of it, now that they're both dead.'

Todd didn't reply. He seemed about to walk me down to Harmon, but I told him it wasn't necessary. He opened his mouth to protest, but I raised a hand and he closed it again.

He was smart enough to know that there was something going on that he didn't fully understand, and the best thing to do might be to watch and listen, and intervene only if it became absolutely necessary. I left him on the porch and made my way across the grass. I passed Harmon's kids on the way down as they headed back to the house. They looked at me curiously, and Harmon's son seemed about to say something, but they both relaxed a little when I smiled at them in greeting. They were good-looking kids: tall, healthy, and neatly but casually dressed in various shades of Abercrombie & Fitch.

Harmon didn't hear me approach. He was kneeling by an Alpine garden flower bed dotted with weathered limestone, the rocks sunk firmly into the ground, the grain running inward and the soil around them scattered with stone chips. Low plants poked through the gaps between the rocks, their foliage purple and green, silver and bronze.

My shadow fell across Harmon and he looked up.

'Mr Parker,' he said. 'I wasn't expecting company, and you sneaked up on my bad side. Nevertheless, now that you're here it gives me the chance to apologize for what I said to you on the telephone when last we spoke.'

He struggled a little to stand. I offered him my right hand and he took it. As I helped him up, I gripped his arm with my left hand, forcing the sleeve of his shirt and his sweater up on his forearm. The claws of a bird were briefly revealed upon his skin.

'Thank you,' he said. He saw where my attention was directed, and moved to pull his sleeve back down.

'I never asked you how you damaged your hearing,' I said.

'It's a little embarrassing,' he replied. 'My left ear was always weaker than my right, the hearing just slightly worse. It wasn't too serious, and it didn't interfere any with my life. I wanted to serve in Vietnam. I didn't want to wait for the draft. I was twenty, and full of fire. I was assigned to Fort Campbell for my basic training. I hoped to join the 173rd Airborne. You know, the 173rd was the only unit to make an airborne assault on an enemy position in Vietnam. Operation Junction City in sixty-seven. I might have made it over there too, except a shell exploded too close to my head during basic training. Shattered my eardrum. Left me near deaf in one ear and affected my balance. I was discharged, and that was as close as I ever got to combat. I was one week away from finishing basic.'

'Is that where you got the tattoo?'

Harmon rubbed his shirt against the place on his arm where the tattoo lay, but he did not expose the skin again.

'Yeah, I was overoptimistic. I put the cart before the horse. Never got to add any years of service underneath. I'm just embarrassed by it now. I don't show it much.' He peered carefully at me. 'You seem to have come here armed with a lot of questions.'

'I've got more. Did you know Raymon Lang, Mr Harmon?'

I watched him think for a moment.

'Raymon Lang? Wasn't he the guy who got shot up in Bath, the one who had the child stashed under his trailer? Why would I know him?'

'He worked for A-Secure, the company that installed your surveillance system. He did maintenance for them on cameras and monitors. I wondered if you might have met him in the course of his work.'

Harmon shrugged. 'I might have. Why?'

I turned and looked back toward the house. Todd was talking with Harmon's children. All three were watching me. I recalled a remark of Christian's that a pedophile might prey on the children of others yet never make any approaches to his own children, that his family might remain entirely unaware of his urges, allowing him to preserve the image of a loving father and husband, an image that was, in a sense, simultaneously both the truth and a lie. When I had spoken to Christian, it was Daniel Clay whom I had in mind, but I had been wrong. Rebecca Clay knew exactly what her father was, but there were other children who did not. There might have been many men with tattoos of eagles on their right arms, even men who had abused children, but the links between Lang and Harmon and Clay, however tentative, could not be denied. How did it happen? I wondered. How did Lang and Harmon come to recognize something in each other, a similar weakness, a hunger that they both shared? When did they decide to approach Clay, using his access to target those who were particularly vulnerable, or those who might not be believed if they made allegations of abuse? Did Harmon bring up that drunken night when Clay had allowed him to abuse Rebecca as leverage against the psychiatrist, for Harmon had been the other man in the house on the night that Daniel Clay, for the first and last time, had shared his daughter with another, and had drunkenly allowed pictures to be taken of the encounter. If those were used carefully, Harmon could have destroyed Clay with them while making sure that his hands were clean. Even an anonymous mailing to the cops or the Board of Licensure would have been enough.

Or did Clay even have to be blackmailed? Did they share the evidence of their abuse with him? Was that how he fed his own hunger in those years after he ceased to torment his own daughter, as she grew older, before the reemergence of those old urges that Rebecca saw in his face as her own child began to bloom?

I turned back to Harmon. His expression had changed. It was the face of a man who was calculating the odds, assessing his degree of risk and exposure.

'Mr Parker,' he said, 'I asked you a question.'

I ignored him. 'How did you do it?' I continued. 'What brought you together, you and Lang, and Caswell and Legere? Bad luck? Mutual admiration? What was it? Then, after Clay disappeared, your supply dried up, didn't it? That was when you had to look elsewhere, and that brought you into contact with Demarcian and his friends in Boston, and maybe Mason Dubus too, or had you paid him a visit long before then, you and Clay both? Did you worship at his feet? Did you tell him about your Project: the systematic abuse of the most vulnerable children, the ones who were troubled, or whose stories were less likely to be believed, all targeted through Clay's inside knowledge?'

'You be careful, now,' said Harmon. 'You be real careful.'

'I saw a photograph,' I said. 'It was in Lang's trailer. It was a picture of a man abusing a little girl. I know who that girl was. The photo's not much to go on, but it will be a start. I'll bet the cops have all sorts of ways to compare a picture of a tattoo with an actual mark on skin.'

Harmon smiled. It was an ugly, malicious thing, like the opening of a wound upon his face.

'You ever find out what happened to Daniel Clay, Mr Parker?' he said. 'I always had my suspicions about his disappearance, but I never spoke them aloud out of respect for his daughter. Who knows what might turn up if I started poking around in corners? I might find pictures too, and maybe I might recognize the little girl in them as well. If I looked hard enough, I might even recognize one of her abusers. Her father was a distinctive-looking man, all skin and bone. I discover something like that and I might have to turn it in to the proper authorities. After all, that little girl would be a woman by now, a woman with troubles and torments of her own. She might need help, or counseling. All kinds of things might come out, all kinds. You start digging, Mr Parker, and there's no telling what skeletons could be exposed.'

I heard footsteps behind me, and a young man's voice said: 'Everything okay here, Dad?'

'Everything's fine, son,' said Harmon. 'Mr Parker's about to leave. I'd ask him to stay for lunch, but I know he has things to do. He's a busy man. He has a lot to think about.'

I didn't say anything more. I walked away, leaving Harmon and his son behind. His daughter was gone, but a figure stood at one of the upper windows, staring down at us all. It was Mrs Harmon. She was wearing a green dress and her nails were red against the white of the drape she held back from the glass. Todd followed me through the house to make sure that I left. I was almost at the front door when Mrs Harmon appeared on the landing above my head. She smiled emptily at me, seemingly lost in a pharmaceutical haze, but the smile didn't extend farther than her lips and her eyes were full of unspeakable things.

VII

and what i want to know is
how do you like your blueeyed boy
Mister Death

E E cummings, *Buffalo Bill's defunct*

Epilogue

For a few days, nothing more happened. Life went back to much the way it had been. Angel and Louis returned to New York. I walked Walter, and took calls from people who wanted to hire my services. I turned them down. I was tired, and there was a bad taste in my mouth of which I could not rid myself. Even the house was still and quiet, as though watchful presences were waiting to see what would transpire.

The initial letter was not entirely unexpected. It informed me that my gun was being held as evidence in the commission of a crime, and might possibly be returned to me at a later date. I didn't care. I didn't want it back, not now.

The next two letters arrived almost simultaneously by special delivery. The first, from the office of the chief of the state police, informed me that an application had been made to the District Court for the suspension of my private investigator's license with immediate effect on the grounds of fraud and deceit in connection with my work, and the uttering of false statements. The application had been filed by the state police. The court had granted an interim temporary suspension, and a full hearing would follow in due course, at which I would be given the opportunity to defend myself.

The second letter was also from the office of the chief of the state police, notifying me that my concealed weapons permit was being revoked pending the outcome of the hearing, and that I should return it, along with any other relevant documentation, to his office. After all that had happened, and after all that I had done, things had fallen apart in the aftermath of a case in which I had not even fired a weapon.

I spent the days that followed the receipt of the letters away from my house. I traveled to Vermont with Walter and passed two days with Rachel and Sam, staying at a motel a few miles from the house. The visit passed without incident and without a harsh word spoken between us. It was as if Rachel's words when last we met had cleared the air somewhat. I told her of what had happened, about the loss of my license and my permit. She asked me what I was going to do and I told her that I did not know. Money was not a huge problem, not yet. The mortgage on the house was small, as most of the cost of its purchase had been covered by the cash the U.S. Postal Service had paid for my grandfather's land and the old house upon it. There would be bills to pay, though, and I wanted to continue to help Rachel with Sam. She told me not to worry too much about it, although she understood why it was important to me. When I was about to leave, Rachel held me close and kissed me softly on the mouth, and I tasted her, and she tasted me.

The following evening, there was a dinner at Natasha's for June Fitzpatrick. Joel Harmon wasn't present. There were just some of June's friends, and Phil Isaacson, the *Press Herald*'s art critic, and a couple of other people that I knew by reputation. I hadn't wanted to attend, but June had insisted, and in the end it turned out to be a pretty nice evening. I left them after a couple of hours with bottles of wine to finish and desserts to be ordered.

A harsh wind was blowing in off the sea. It stung my cheeks and made my eyes water as I headed for my car. I had parked on Middle Street, not far from City Hall. There were plenty of empty spaces, and I passed few people on the streets as I walked.

Ahead of me, a man stood outside an apartment block not far from the headquarters of the Portland P.D. He was smoking a cigarette. I could see the end glow in shadows cast by the awning above the doorway. As I drew closer, he stepped into my path.

'I came to say good-bye,' he said. 'For now.'

The Collector was dressed as he was always dressed, in a dark coat that had seen better days, beneath which was a navy jacket and an old-fashioned, wide-collared shirt buttoned up to the neck. He took a long, final drag on his cigarette, then flicked it away. 'I hear things have gotten bad for you.'

I didn't want to talk to this man, whoever he truly was, but it didn't seem like I had much choice. Anyway, I doubted that he was here just to wish me farewell. He didn't seem like the sentimental type.

'You're bad luck for me,' I said. 'You'll forgive me for not shedding a tear when you go.'

'I think you may be bad luck for me too. I've had to move part of my collection, I've lost a secure house, and Mr Eldritch has been subject to some unwelcome publicity. He fears that it will be the death of him.'

'Heartbreaking. He always seemed so full of life.'

The Collector removed his tobacco and papers from his pocket and carefully rolled, then lit, another cigarette while the first still smoldered in the gutter. He appeared unable to think properly without something burning between his fingers or his lips.

'Since you're here, I have a question for you,' I said.

He inhaled deeply, then blew a cloud of smoke into the night air. As he did so, he waved a hand in the air, inviting the question.

'Why those men?' I asked. 'Why the interest in this case?'

'Equally, the same question could be asked of you,' he replied. 'After all, you were not being paid to find them. Perhaps a more apt question might be: why not those men? It has always seemed to me that there are two types of people in this world: those rendered impotent by the sheer weight of evil it contains, and who refuse to act because they see no point, and those who choose their battles and fight them to the end, as they understand that to do nothing is infinitely worse than to do something and fail. Like you, I decided to pursue this investigation, and to follow it through to the end.'

'I hope the outcome was more satisfactory for you than it was for me.'

The Collector laughed. 'You can't be entirely surprised by what has happened to you,' he said. 'You were living on borrowed time, and even your friends couldn't protect you any longer.'

'My friends?'

'My mistake: your unseen friends, your *secret* friends. I don't mean your lethally amusing colleagues from New York. Oh, and don't worry about them. I have other, more worthy objects of my disaffection to pursue. I think I'll leave them be, for now. They are making recompense for past evils, and I wouldn't want to render you entirely bereft. No, I'm talking about those who have followed your progress quietly, the ones who have facilitated all that you have done, who have smoothed over the damage that you have left in your wake, who have leaned gently on those who would rather have seen you resting behind bars.'

'I don't know what you're talking about.'

'No, I don't suppose that you do. You were careless this time: your lies tripped you up. There was momentum building against you, and the consequences have now become apparent. You are a curious, empathic man who has been deprived of a license to do the thing that he does best, a violent individual whose toys have been taken away. Who can say what will happen to you now?'

'Don't tell me that you're one of these "secret friends," otherwise I'm in more trouble than I thought.'

'No, I'm neither your friend nor your enemy, and I answer to a higher power.'

'You're deluded.'

'Am I? Very well, then it is a delusion that we both share. I've just done you a favor of which you don't yet know. Now I'll do you one final service. You have spent years drifting from the light into the shadows and back again, moving between them in your search for answers, but the longer you spend in the darkness, the greater the chance that the presence within it will become aware of you, and will move against you. Soon, it will come.'

'I've met things in the darkness before. They've gone, and I am here.'

'This is not a "thing" in the darkness,' he replied. 'This *is* the darkness. Now, we are done.'

He turned to walk away, sending another dying cigarette after the first. I reached out to stop him. I wanted more. I grabbed his shoulder and my hand brushed his skin—

And I had a vision of figures writhing in torment, of others alone in desolate places, crying for He who had abandoned them. And I saw the Hollow Men, and in that instant I knew truly what they were.

The Collector pirouetted like a dancer. My grip on him was broken with a sweep of his arm, and then I was against the wall, his fingers on my neck, my feet slowly leaving the ground as he forced me up. I tried to kick out at him and he closed the distance between us as the pressure on my neck increased, choking the life from me.

'Don't ever touch me,' he said. 'Nobody touches me.'

He released his hold upon me, and I slid down the wall and collapsed onto my knees, painfully drawing ragged gulps of air through my open mouth. My skin itched and burned where his fingers had gripped me, and I could smell nicotine and decay upon myself.

'Look at you,' he said, and his words dripped with pity and contempt. 'A man tormented by unanswered questions, a man without a father, without a mother, a man who has allowed two families to slip through his fingers.'

'I had a father,' I said. 'I had a mother, and I still have my family.'

'Do you? Not for long.' Something cruel transformed his features, like a small boy who sees the opportunity to continue the torture of a dumb animal. 'And as for a father and a mother, answer this: your blood type is B. See the things I know about you? Now, here's my question.' He leaned in close to me. 'How can a child with B blood have a father who was type A and a mother who was type O? It's quite the mystery.'

'You're lying.'

'Am I? Well, then, so be it.'

He stepped away from me. 'But perhaps you have other things to occupy your time: half seen things, dead things, a child who whispers in the night and a mother who rages in the dark. Stay with them, if you wish. Live with them, in the place where they wait.'

'Where are my wife and child?' The words flayed my damaged throat, and I hated myself for seeking answers from this vile creature. 'You spoke of beings cut off from the Divine. You knew about the writing in the dust. You *know*. Tell me, is that what they are, lost souls? Is that what I am?'

'Do you even have a soul?' he whispered. 'As for where your wife and child dwell, they are where you keep them.'

He squatted before me, bathing me in his stench as he spoke his final words.

'I took him while you were at dinner, so you would have an alibi. That is my last gift to you, Mr Parker, and my last indulgence.'

He rose and walked away, and by the time I got to my feet he was long gone. I went to my car and drove home, and I thought about what he had said.

Joel Harmon disappeared that night. Todd was ill and Harmon had driven himself to a town meeting in Falmouth, where he handed over a check for $25,000 as part of a drive to buy minibuses for a local school. His car was found abandoned at Wildwood Park, and he was never seen again.

Shortly after nine the next morning, I received a telephone call. The caller didn't identify himself, but he told me that a search warrant for my property had just been signed by Judge Hight, authorizing the state police to seek any and all unlicensed firearms. They would be at my house within the hour.

They were led by Hansen when they came, and they went through every room. They managed to open the panel in the wall behind which I used to keep the guns I had retained, despite the suspension of my permit, but I had sealed them in oilcloths and plastic and dropped them in a marsh pond at the back of my property, anchored by a rope to a rock on the bank, so all they found was dust. They even searched the attic, but they did not stay there long, and I could see in the faces of the uniformed men who descended that they were grateful to leave that cold, dark space. Hansen did not speak to me from the time the warrant was served until the moment the search was complete. His final words to me were: 'This isn't over.'

When they were gone, I began to empty the attic. I removed boxes and cases without even looking at their contents, casting them onto the landing before carrying them down to the patch of bare earth and stones at the end of my yard. I opened the attic window and let cold air flood in, and I wiped away the dust from the glass, cleansing it of the words that remained upon it. Then I went through the rest of the house, cleaning every surface, opening cupboards and airing rooms, until all was in order and it was as cold inside the house as it was outside.

They are where you keep them.

I thought that I felt their anger and their rage, or perhaps it was all inside me, and even as I purged it, it fought to survive. As the sun went down, I lit a pyre, and I watched as grief and memories ascended into the sky, forming gray smoke and charred fragments that fell into dust as the wind carried them away.

'I am sorry,' I whispered. 'I am sorry for all of the ways that I failed you. I am sorry that I was not there to save you, or to die alongside you. I am sorry that I have kept you with me for so long, trapped in my heart, bound in sorrow and remorse. I forgive you too. I forgive you for leaving me, and I forgive you for returning. I forgive you your anger, and your grief. Let this be an end to it. Let this be an end to it all.

'You have to go now,' I said aloud to the shadows. 'It's time for you to leave.'

And through the flames, I saw the marshes gleaming, and the moonlight picked out two shapes upon the water, shimmering in the heat of the fire. Then they turned away as others joined them, a host journeying onward, soul upon soul, until they were lost at last in the crashing triumph of dying waves.

That night, as though summoned by the fire, Rachel rang the doorbell of the house that we once shared, driving Walter into a frenzy when he recognized her. She said that she'd been worrying about me. We talked and ate, and drank a little too much wine. When I woke the next morning, she was sleeping beside me. I did not know if it was a beginning or an ending, and I was too afraid to ask. She left before midday, with just a kiss and words unspoken on our lips.

And far away, a car pulled up before a nondescript house on a quiet country road. The trunk was opened, and a man was dragged from within, falling to the ground before he was hauled to his feet, his eyes blindfolded, his mouth gagged, his hands tied behind his back with wire that had bitten into his wrists, causing blood to flow onto his hands, his legs bound in the same way above the ankles. He tried to remain standing, but almost collapsed as the blood began to flow through his weakened, cramped limbs. He felt hands on his legs, then the wire was clipped away from them so he could walk. He began to run then, but his legs were swept from under him and a voice spoke a single nicotine-smelling word into his ear: 'No.'

He was pulled to his feet once more and led into the house. A door was opened, and he was guided down a set of wooden steps. His feet touched a stone floor. He walked for a time, until the same voice told him to stop and he was forced to his knees. He heard something being moved, as though a board were being hefted away from something in front of him. The blindfold was undone, the gag removed, and he saw that he was in a cellar, empty apart from an old closet in one corner, its twin doors standing open to reveal the trinkets lying within, although they were too far away for his eyesight to distinguish them in the gloom.

There was a hole in the ground before him, and he thought that he smelled blood and old meat. The hole was not deep, perhaps only six or seven feet, and scattered with stones and rocks and broken slates at its base. He blinked, and for a moment it appeared that the hole was deeper, as though the base of stones was somehow suspended above a far greater abyss beneath. He felt hands moving upon his wrists, and then his watch, his treasured Patek Philippe, was being removed.

'Thief!' he said. 'You're nothing but a thief.'

'No,' said the voice. 'I am a *collector*.'

'Then take it,' said Harmon. His voice rasped from lack of water, and he felt weak and sick from the long journey in the trunk of the car. 'Just take it and let me go. I have money too. I can arrange to have it wired to anywhere you want. You can hold me until it's in your hands, and I promise you that you'll have as much again when I'm freed. Please, just let me go. Whatever I've done to you, I'm sorry.'

The voice sounded by his good ear once again. He had not yet seen the man himself. He had been struck from behind as he walked to his car, and he had awoken in the trunk. It seemed to him that they had driven for many, many hours, stopping only once for the man to refill the gas tank. Even then, they had not done so at a gas station, for he had not heard the sound of the gas pump, or the noise of other cars. He guessed that his abductor had kept cans on the backseat of the vehicle so that he would not have to refuel in a public place and risk his captive making noise and attracting attention.

Now he was kneeling in a dusty basement, staring into a hole in the ground that was both shallow and deep, and a voice was saying:

'You are damned.'

'No,' said Harmon. 'No, that's not right.'

'You have been found wanting, and your life is forfeit. Your *soul* is forfeit.'

'No,' said Harmon, his voice rising in pitch. 'It's a mistake! You're making a mistake.'

'There is no mistake. I know what you have done. *They* know.'

Harmon looked into the hole, and four figures stared up at him, their eyes dark holes against the thin, papery covering of their skulls, their mouths black and wrinkled and gaping. His hair was gripped in strong fingers and his head was drawn back, exposing his neck. He felt something cold against his skin, then the blade cut into his throat, showering blood onto the floor and into the hole, splattering on the faces of the men below.

And the Hollow Men raised their arms to him, and welcomed him into their number.

Acknowledgments

This book could not have been written without the patience and kindness of a great many people who gave me the benefit of their knowledge and experience without a murmur of complaint. I am particularly grateful to Dr Larry Ricci, M.D., director of the Spurwink Child Abuse Program in Portland, Maine; Vickie Jacobs Fisher of the Maine Committee to Prevent Child Abuse; and Dr Stephen Herman, M.D., forensic psychiatrist and fountain pen aficionado, of New York. Without the assistance of these three most generous of souls, this would be a much poorer book, if indeed it existed at all.

The following individuals also provided valuable information at crucial moments in the writing of the novel, and to them I am very grateful: Matt Mayberry (real estate); Tom Hyland (Vietnam and matters military); Philip Isaacson (matters of law); Vladimir Doudka and Mark Dunne (matters Russian); and Luis Urrea, my fellow, infinitely more gifted author, who kindly corrected my very poor attempts at Spanish. Officer Joe Giacomantonio of the Scarborough Police Department was, once again, decent enough to answer my questions about matters of procedure. Finally, Ms. Jeanette Holden, of the Jackman Moose River Valley Historical Society, provided me with great material and an afternoon of good company. I am also indebted to the Jackman Chamber of Commerce for its assistance, and the help of the staff at the research library of the Maine Historical Society in Portland. As always, the mistakes that undoubtedly crept through are all my own.

A number of books and articles proved particularly useful for research purposes, including *The Yard* by Michael S. Sanders

(Perennial, 1999); *History of the Moose River Valley* (Jackman Moose River Historical Society, 1994); *Arnold's Expedition up the Kennebec to Quebec in 1775* by H. N. Fairbanks (archive of the Maine Historical Society); *South Portland: A Nostalgic Look At Our Neighborhood Stores* by Kathryn Onos Di Phillipo, (Barren Mill Books, 2006); and the *Portland Phoenix's* award-winning reports on the use of the "Chair" in the Maine Supermax facility, particularly 'Torture in Maine's Prisons' by Lance Tapley (Nov 11, 2005).

On a personal note, I remain immensely fortunate in my editors, Sue Fletcher at Hodder & Stoughton and Emily Bestler at Atria Books, who have the patience of saints and the skills of literary surgeons. Thanks also to Jamie Hodder-Williams, Martin Neild, Lucy Hale, Kerry Hood, Swati Gamble, Auriol Bishop, Kelly Edgson-Wright, Toni Lance, Bill Jones and all at Hodder & Stoughton; to Judith Curr, Louise Burke, David Brown, Sarah Branham, Laura Stern, and everyone at Atria; and Kate and KC O'Hearn, without whom the *Into the Dark* CD would not have been possible. My agent, Darley Anderson, remains a rock of common sense and friendship, and to him and to Emma, Lucie, Elizabeth, Julia, Rosi, Ella, Emma, Maddie and Zoe I am indebted for my career. Finally, to Jennie, Cam, and Alistair, thanks for putting up with me.

Finally, a word on Dave 'the Guesser' Glovsky. Dave really did exist, and he did ply his trade at Old Orchard Beach, although it is my fervent hope that he never encountered a man like Frank Merrick. At one point, I had considered including a thinly disguised version of the Guesser in this novel, but that seemed unfair on this most unusual of men, so he appears as himself, and should any of his relatives encounter him in these pages, I hope that they will recognize it as the tribute to him that it is meant to be.

John Connolly
December 2006

John Connolly on the Parker novels:

'Since about the second book I've thought of the Parker novels as a sequence rather than a series, in that each book develops themes, ideas and plots from the preceding books.'

Although each novel is self-contained, and can be enjoyed as a compelling thriller, collectively the Parker novels form a rich and involving epic sequence in which characters reappear and clues laid down in earlier stories are solved in later ones. Below is a précis of key events in each of the Charlie Parker novels.

Former NYPD Charlie Parker first appears in **Every Dead Thing** on a quest for the killer of his wife and daughter. He is a man consumed by violence, guilt and the desire for revenge. When his ex-partner asks him to track down a missing girl, Parker embarks on a grim odyssey through the bowels of organised crime; to cellars of torture and death; and to a unique serial killer, an artist who uses the human body as his canvas: The Travelling Man. By the end of the novel, Parker realises he is at the beginning of another dark journey – to avenge the voiceless victims of crime: the poor, women and children. It is a journey on which his dead wife and child will be constant ghostly companions.

In **Dark Hollow,** Parker returns to the wintry Maine landscape where he grew up and becomes embroiled in another murder hunt. The chief suspect is Billy Purdue, the ex-husband of the dead woman, and Parker is not the only one on his trail. Aided by his friends, hitmen Angel and Louis (first encountered in **Every Dead Thing**), Parker must go back thirty years into his own grandfather's troubled past and into the violent origins of a mythical killer, the monster Caleb Kyle. Parker's personal life seems to take an upward turn in the attractive form of psychologist Rachel Wolfe.

Parker's empathy with the powerless victims of crime is growing ever stronger. It makes him a natural choice to investigate the death of Grace Peltier in **The Killing Kind** – a death that appears to be a suicide. The discovery of a mass grave – the final resting place of a religious community that had disappeared forty years earlier – convinces Parker that there is a link between Grace and these deaths: a shadowy organisation called The Fellowship. His investigation draws him into increasingly violent confrontations with the Fellowship's enforcer, the demonic arachnophile, Mr Pudd. Genial killers Angel and Louis join Parker again as he descends into a honeycomb world populated by dark angels and lost souls.

Parker's relationship with Rachel reaches a new level in **The White Road**, but he is still driven to solve the most challenging of cases. A black youth faces the death penalty for rape and murder; his victim, the daughter of one of the wealthiest men in South Carolina. It is a case with its roots in old evil, and old evil is Charlie Parker's speciality. But this turns out not to be an investigation, but rather a descent into the abyss, a confrontation with dark forces that threaten all Parker holds dear.

Evil men from his past unite to exact a terrible revenge on the private detective. Seemingly unconnected events turn out to be part of a complex and intricate pattern.

The Killing Kind and **The White Road** effectively form two halves of a single, larger narrative and are probably best read in order.

In 'The Reflecting Eye', a long novella featured in the **Nocturnes** collection, Parker becomes involved in a curious investigation into a former killer's abandoned house, and learns that someone, or something, seems be using its empty rooms as a base from which to hunt for victims. This novella introduces us for the first time to the character known as the Collector, an individual who will come to play an important and sinister role in the books that follow, most particularly in **The Unquiet** and **The Lovers**.

The Black Angel is not an object; it is not a myth. The Black Angel lives. And it is a prize sought for centuries by evil men. Not that Charlie Parker's latest case starts this way; it starts with the disappearance of a young woman in New York. Her abductors believe that no one will come looking for her, but they are wrong. For Alice is 'blood' to Parker's sidekick, the assassin Louis, and Louis will tear apart anyone who attempts to stop him finding her.

The hunt turns into an epic quest that will take Parker and his team to an ornate church of bones in Eastern Europe and a cataclysmic battle between good and evil. It marks a dawning realisation in Parker that there is another dimension to his crusade, a dangerous dimension that Rachel finds herself increasingly unable to live with.

The Unquiet begins with a missing man, a once respected psychiatrist who went absent following revelations about harm done to children in his care. His daughter believes him dead, but is not allowed to come to terms with her father's legacy. For someone is asking questions about Daniel Clay: the revenger Merrick, a father and a killer obsessed with discovering the truth about his own daughter's disappearance. Living apart from Rachel and their child, Charlie Parker is hired to make Merrick go away, but finds strange bonds with the revenger, who has drawn from the shadows pale wraiths drifting through the ranks of the unquiet dead. At the end of the novel comes a tantalising reference to Parker's own parentage that will inform events in **The Lovers**.

But first Angel and Louis take centre stage in **The Reapers,** where the elite killers themselves become targets. A wealthy recluse sends them north to a town that no longer exists on a map. A town ruled by a man with very personal reasons for wanting Louis' blood spilt. There they find themselves trapped, isolated and at the mercy of a killer feared above all others: the assassin of assassins, Bliss. Thanks to Parker, help is on its way. But can Angel and Louis stay alive long enough for it to reach them?

The bloody events in **The Unquiet** result in Parker losing his PI licence, so he returns to Maine and takes a job in a Portland bar while the fuss dies down. But **The Lovers** shows Parker engaged on his most personal case yet: an investigation into his own origins and the circumstances surrounding the death of his father. When he was a boy, Parker's father, himself a cop, killed a pair of teenagers then took his own life. His actions were never explained. Parker's quest for that explanation reveals lies, secrets and betrayal. Haunting it – as they have done all his life – are two figures in the shadows, an unidentified man and woman with one purpose: to bring an end to Parker's existence.

In **The Whisperers**, Parker is asked to investigate the apparent suicide of Damian Patchett, a former soldier. But this is not an isolated death; former combatants are dying in epidemic quantities, driven by someone or something to take their own lives.

Parker cannot defeat this evil on his own. To combat it, he is forced into an uneasy alliance with a man he fears more than any other. The Collector first appeared in the novella 'The Reflecting Eye' and remains a sinister presence in Parker's consciousness. It is as though the two men are twin moons orbiting a dark, unknown planet. Now he steps out of the shadows and as their eyes meet, Parker sees for the first time that he himself inspires fear in the Collector.

In **The Burning Soul**, Charlie Parker becomes reluctantly involved in investigating the abduction of a fourteen-year-old girl.

The small Maine town of Pastor's Bay is the home of Randall Haight, a man with a secret. When he was a teenager, he and his friend killed a girl. He did his time and has built a life for himself, not sharing details of his past with anyone. But someone has found out, and is sending anonymous threatening messages. And Anna Kore – the missing girl – lived in Pastor's Bay, not two miles away from Haight.

Randall Haight is not the kind of man Charlie Parker wants to help. But he is already drawn to the case of Anna Kore and cannot turn away from the chance to find her.

In the course of the investigation he comes up against the police, the FBI and a doomed mobster, Tommy Morris.

The Wrath of Angels, the eleventh Parker novel, is a sequel of sorts to **The Black Angel**, and returns to some of the themes and characters in that earlier novel.

Parker hears tales of a plane lost in the Maine woods, the mystery of its vanished pilots, and the possibility that it contained a living cargo. What draws Parker's interest is the possibility that the plane was also carrying a list of those who had struck deals with the Antichrist himself, a record of individuals who had committed acts of evil, or were yet capable of committing them. But the list's existence also draws others, both those interested in protecting it and also individuals who want to secure it for their own ends, among them Parker's nemesis, the serial killer known as the Collector. Yet it soon becomes clear that someone, or something, has survived the crash, and is waiting in the woods. **The Wrath of Angels** brings to an end certain elements in the Parker series, while also containing events that lead directly into the novel that follows it, **The Wolf in Winter**.

JOHN CONNOLLY

BAD MEN

'With BAD MEN, there's no chance of indifference.
This . . . will knock your socks off' *Daily Mirror*

In 1693, the settlers on the small Maine island of Sanctuary were
betrayed to their enemies and slaughtered. Since then, the island
has known three hundred years of peace.

Until now. For men are descending on Sanctuary, their purpose
to hunt down and kill the wife of their leader and retrieve the
money that she stole from him. All that stands in their way are
a young rookie officer, Sharon Macy, and the island's strange,
troubled policeman, the giant known as Melancholy Joe Dupree.
But Joe Dupree is no ordinary policeman. He is the guardian of
the island's secrets, the repository of its memories. He knows that
Sanctuary has been steeped in blood once; it will tolerate the
shedding of innocent blood no longer. Now a band of killers is
set to desecrate Sanctuary and unleash the fury of its ghosts upon
themselves and all who stand by them.

On Sanctuary, evil is about to meet its match . . .

'Five-star chill with enough menace to keep the pages turning well
into the wee small hours.' *Irish Times*

JOHN CONNOLLY

NOCTURNES

'Terrifying and delightful.' *Time Out*

Take his hand and follow him into the darkness.

John Connolly, bestselling author of Charlie Parker thrillers, turns his pen to the short story to give us a volume of chilling tales of the supernatural. In this macabre collection, echoing masters of the genre from M.R. James to Stephen King, Connolly delves into our darkest fears – lost lovers, missing children, subterranean creatures, and predatory demons.

Framing the collection are two substantial novellas: *The Cancer Cowboy Rides* charts the fatal progress of a modern-day grim reaper, while *The Reflecting Eye* is a haunted house tale with a twist and marks the return of private detective Charlie Parker, the troubled hero of Connolly's crime novels.

Nocturnes is a masterly volume to be read with the lights on – menace has never been so seductive . . .

'Twists the classic ghost story in a modern macabre way'
Radio Times

JOHN CONNOLLY

THE BOOK OF LOST THINGS

'A moving fable, brilliantly imagined' *The Times*

'Everything you can imagine is real'

High in his attic bedroom, twelve-year-old David mourns the loss
of his mother. He is angry and he is alone, with only the books
on his shelf for company.

But those books have begun to whisper to him in the darkness
and as he takes refuge in the myths and fairytales, so beloved
by his dead mother, he finds that the real world and the fantasy
world have begun to meld. The Crooked Man has come, with his
mocking smile and his enigmatic words: 'Welcome, you majesty.
All hail the new king.'

And as war rages across Europe, David is violently propelled
into a land that is both a construct of his imagination yet
frighteningly real, a strange reflection of his own world
composed of myths and stories, populated by wolves and
worse-than-wolves, and ruled over by a faded king who

keeps his secrets in a mysterious book . . .

THE BOOK OF LOST THINGS.

'Written in the clear, evocative manner of the best British fairy
tales from JM Barrie to CS Lewis, *The Book of Lost Things* is an
engaging, magical, thoughtful read' *Independent*

BOOKS TO DIE FOR

Edited by
JOHN CONNOLLY
and
DECLAN BURKE

'Indispensable' *Sunday Telegraph*

**Winner of the 2013 Agatha, Anthony and the Macavity
Awards for Best Crime Non-Fiction.**

With so many mystery novels to choose from and so many new
titles appearing each year, where should the reader start? What
are the classics of the genre? Which are the hidden gems?

In the most ambitious anthology of its kind yet attempted, the
world's leading mystery writers have come together to champion
the greatest mystery novels ever written. In a series of personal
essays that often reveal as much about themselves and their
work as they do about the books that they love, more than 120
authors from twenty countries have created a guide that will be
indispensable for generations of readers and writers.

From Christie to Child and Poe to P.D. James, from Sherlock
Holmes to Hannibal Lecter and Philip Marlowe to Peter Wimsey,
Books to Die For brings together the cream of the mystery world
for a feast of reading pleasure, a treasure trove for those new to
the genre and those who believe that there is nothing new left
to discover.

This is the one essential book for every reader who has ever
finished a mystery novel and thought . . . 'I want more!'

'This volume challenges a few myths and is worth reading for
that pleasure alone.' *Sunday Times*

JOHN CONNOLLY

THE WANDERER IN UNKNOWN REALMS

A short story in digital form

Lionel Maulding, a rare-book collector, has gone missing
from his country home in Norfolk. World War I
veteran-turned-detective, Soter investigates into the
matter at Maulding's solicitor's behest.

From the nature of books in Lionel Maulding's impressive library
at Bromdun Hall, it is clear that he was greatly interested in the
occult. But how far did that take him? There is evidence of
the withdrawal of £10,000, an extraordinary sum of money
for the purchase of a single book.

As Soter's investigations take him from the slowly decaying
Bromdun Hall to the sinister bookseller in Chelsea and the
book scout in Whitechapel, he enters a nightmare world where
his horrific experiences in the trenches echo the fearful reality
unleashed by his search.

JOHN CONNOLLY

THE GATES:

A Samuel Johnson Adventure – 1

'Demonic, darkly comic'
Daily Telegraph

A brilliant new departure for bestselling author John Connolly.

Young Samuel Johnson and his dachshund Boswell are trying
to show initiative by trick-or-treating a full three days before
Hallowe'en. Which is how they come to witness strange
goings-on at 666 Crowley Avenue.

The Abernathys don't mean any harm by their flirtation
with Satanism. But it just happens to coincide with a
malfunction in the Large Hadron Collider that creates a gap
in the universe. A gap in which there is a pair of enormous
gates. The gates to Hell. And there are some pretty terrifying
beings just itching to get out . . .

Can Samuel persuade anyone to take this seriously? Can he
harness the power of science to save the world as we know it?

'Destined to be another runaway success appealing to
both young adults and their parent alike.'
Sunday Independent

JOHN CONNOLLY

HELL'S BELLS:

A Samuel Johnson Adventure – 2

'Demonic, darkly comic'
Daily Telegraph

Samuel Johnson is in trouble. The demon Mrs Abernathy is
seeking revenge on him for his part in foiling the invasion of
Earth by the forces of Darkness. She wants Samuel, and when a
scientific experiment goes wrong, she gets her chance: Samuel
and his faithful dachshund, Boswell, are pulled
through a portal into Hell.

But catching Samuel is not going to be easy. Mrs Abernathy
has reckoned without the bravery and cleverness of one boy and
his dog, or the loyalty of Samuel's friend, the hapless demon
Nurd. Most of all, she hasn't planned on the intervention of an
unexpected band of little men, for Samuel and Boswell are not
the only inhabitants of Earth who have found themselves in Hell.

If you thought demons were frightening, just wait until
you meet Mr Merryweather's Elves . . .

'Hilarious, intelligent and fun. I loved it.'
Derek Landy

JOHN CONNOLLY

THE CREEPS:

A Samuel Johnson Adventure – 3

'Funny and a great read for teens'
Sun

Samuel Johnson is not in a happy place. He is dating the wrong
girl, demons are occupying his spare room, and the town in
which he lives appears to be cursed.

But there is some good news on the horizon. After years of
neglect, the grand old building that once housed Wreckit & Sons
is about to reopen as the greatest toyshop that Biddlecombe has
ever seen, and Samuel and his faithful dachshund Boswell are
to be guests of honour at the big event. A splendid time will be
had by all, as long as they can ignore the sinister statue that keeps
moving around the town, the Shadows that are slowly blocking
out the stars, the murderous Christmas elves, and the fact that
somewhere in Biddlecombe a rotten black heart is beating a
rhythm of revenge.

A trap has been set. The Earth is doomed. The last hope for
humanity lies with one young boy and the girl who's secretly in
love with him. Oh, and a dog, two demons, four dwarfs and a
very polite monster.

We Wish You a Merry Christmas and a Happy End of the World.

'Comedy is never far away'
Sunday Express